THE VISIT OF THE
ROYAL PHYSICIAN

Per Olov Enquist, born in 1934 in northern Sweden, is one of his country's most distinguished authors: a novelist, playwright and poet, with works translated into more than 20 languages. *The Visit of the Royal Physician* won the prestigious August Prize.

Tiina Nunnally's translations have won many awards, most recently the PEN/Book-of-the-Month Club Translation Prize for Sigrid Undset's *Kristin Lavransdatter vol. III*.

Per Olov Enquist

THE VISIT OF THE ROYAL PHYSICIAN

TRANSLATED FROM THE SWEDISH BY
Tiina Nunnally

VINTAGE

Published by Vintage 2003

2 4 6 8 10 9 7 5 3 1

Lines on p. 50 translated from the French by
Steven T. Murray

Lines from Voltaire on pp. 216-17 translated
from the French by Cal Kinnear

First published with the title *Livläkarens Besök* in 2000 by
Norstedts Förlag

First published in Great Britain in 2002 by
The Harvill Press

Vintage
Random House, 20 Vauxhall Bridge Road,
London SW1V 2SA

Random House Australia (Pty) Limited
20 Alfred Street, Milsons Point, Sydney
New South Wales 2061, Australia

Random House New Zealand Limited
18 Poland Road, Glenfield,
Auckland 10, New Zealand

Random House (Pty) Limited
Endulini, 5A Jubilee Road, Parktown 2193,
South Africa

The Random House Group Limited Reg. No. 954009
www.randomhouse.co.uk

A CIP catalogue record for this book
is available from the British Library

ISBN 0 099 44705 3

Papers used by Random House are natural, recyclable
products made from wood grown in sustainable forests.
The manufacturing processes conform to the environ-
mental regulations of the country of origin

Printed and bound in Great Britain by
Bookmarque Ltd, Croydon, Surrey

CONTENTS

Enlightenment is the triumph of the human being over his self-imposed immaturity. Immaturity is the lack of ability to make use of one's own intellect without the guidance of someone else. This immaturity is self-imposed when the cause is not a lack of intellect but a lack of courage to make use of that intellect. Enlightenment demands nothing more than freedom – the freedom that consists in making public use, under all circumstances, of one's reason. For it is the birthright of every human being to think for himself.

IMMANUEL KANT (1783)

The King confided in me that there was a woman who was secretly ruling the Universe. And that there existed a circle of men who had been chosen to commit all evil in the world, and among them were seven, of which he was one, who had been specially selected. For him to establish a friendship with anyone depended on whether that person was also a member of this chosen circle.

U. A. HOLSTEIN, *Memoirs*

PART I

THE FOUR

Chapter 1 · The Wine Treader

Johann Friedrich Struensee was appointed Royal Physician to King Christian VII on April 5, 1768, and four years later he was executed.

Ten years after that, on September 21, 1782, by the time "the Struensee era" had become a term in common use, Robert Murray Keith, the British Ambassador to the Danish court sent a report to his government of an incident he had witnessed. He considered the incident puzzling.

That was why he reported it.

He had attended a dramatic performance at the Royal Theatre in Copenhagen. Also in the audience was King Christian VII, along with Ove Høegh-Guldberg, the true holder of power in Denmark and in practice the absolute ruler.

He had assumed the title of Prime Minister.

The report concerned the Ambassador's encounter with the King.

He begins with his impressions of the King's appearance, Christian VII being only 33 years old: "He looks as if he is already an old man, very short and gaunt, with a sunken face, his smouldering eyes testifying to the sickly state of his mind." He writes that before the performance the "mad" King Christian began wandering around among the audience, muttering, his face twitching oddly.

Guldberg kept a watchful eye on him the whole time.

The strange thing was the relationship between them. It might be described as that of an orderly and his patient, or a pair of siblings, or as if Guldberg were the father of an unruly or sick child; but Keith uses the expression "almost loving".

At the same time, he writes that the two seemed to be united in an "almost perverse way".

What was perverse was not that these two, who he knew had played such important rôles during the Danish revolution, then as enemies, were now dependent upon each other in this way. What was perverse was that the King behaved like a frightened but obedient dog and Guldberg his stern yet loving master.

His Majesty acted as if he were cringing ingratiatingly, almost cowering. The members of the court showed no deference towards the monarch, but instead ignored him or retreated with a laugh whenever he approached, as if they wished to avoid his embarrassing presence.

As if he were a difficult child they had tired of long ago.

The only one who took any notice of the King was Guldberg. The King always kept three or four paces behind Guldberg, following him obsequiously, seeming anxious not to be abandoned. Sometimes Guldberg, with a gesture or look, would give the King a small signal. This happened whenever he muttered too loudly, behaved disruptively, or moved too far away from Guldberg.

At the signal, King Christian would hastily and obediently "come scurrying".

Once, when the King's muttering was particularly disruptive and loud, Guldberg went over to him, took him gently by the arm, and whispered something. The King then began bowing mechanically, over and over, with fitful, almost spastic movements, as if the Danish King were a dog seeking to declare his utter submission and devotion to his beloved master. He kept on bowing until Guldberg, with another whispered remark, brought the peculiar gestures of the royal personage to a halt.

Then Guldberg patted the King on the cheek and was in turn rewarded with a smile so full of gratitude and submission that the Ambassador's eyes "filled with tears". He writes that the scene was so charged with despair that it was almost unbearable. He made note of Guldberg's kindness or, as he writes, of "his willingness to take responsibility for the ill little King", also that the contempt and derision expressed by the rest of the audience was not evident in Guldberg. He seemed to be the only one paying any heed to the King.

Yet there was one recurring expression in the report: "like a dog". The sovereign ruler of Denmark was treated like a dog. The difference was that Guldberg seemed to show a loving sense of responsibility for this dog.

"To see them together – and both of them were of remarkably short and stunted stature – was for me a strange and unsettling experience, since in a formal and practical sense all power in the land emanated from those two peculiar dwarfs."

The report dwells most, however, on what happened during and after the theatrical performance.

In the middle of the play, which was *Le Méchant*, a comedy by the French playwright Gresset, King Christian got up suddenly from his seat in the front row, staggered onto the stage, and began behaving as if he were one of the actors. He took up an actor's pose and recited what might be assumed to be lines; the words "tracasserie" and "anthropophagie" were the only ones distinguishable. Keith took particular note of the latter, which he knew meant "cannibalism". It was clear that the King was very much engaged in the play and believed himself to be one of the actors, but Guldberg, in his calmness, went up on stage and kindly took the King by the hand. The monarch fell silent at once and allowed himself to be led back to his seat.

The audience, which consisted of members of the court alone, seemed accustomed to this type of interruption. No-one reacted with consternation. Scattered laughter could be heard.

After the performance, wine was served. Keith then happened to be standing near the King. He turned to Keith, whom he apparently recognized as the British Ambassador, and made a stammering attempt to explain the central theme of the drama. "The King told me that the play was about evil existing to such a high degree among members of the court that they resembled apes or devils. They rejoiced at each other's misfortunes and bewailed their successes; this was what was called in the time of the druids cannibalism, *anthropophagie*. That was why we found ourselves among cannibals."

The King's "outburst", coming as it did from a madman, was very well formulated from a linguistic point of view.

Keith had merely nodded with an expression of interest, as if everything the King said was interesting and sensible. He did note, however, that Christian had not given an entirely incorrect analysis of the satirical content of the play.

The King had spoken in a whisper, as if confiding an important secret to Keith.

Guldberg, from a distance of a few yards, kept a watchful or uneasy eye on their conversation. Slowly he approached them.

Christian noticed this and sought to bring the conversation to an end. Raising his voice, almost as if in provocation, he exclaimed:

"They're lying. Lying! Brandt was a clever but wild man. Struensee was a fine man. I wasn't the one who killed them. Do you understand?"

Keith simply bowed without answering.

Then Christian added:

"He's alive! They think he was executed, but Struensee is alive. Do you know that?"

By this time Guldberg had come so close that he could hear the last words. He took a firm grip on the King's arm and with a stony but soothing smile he said:

"Struensee is dead, Your Majesty. We know that, don't we? Don't we

4

know that? We've agreed on that, haven't we? Haven't we?"

His tone was kindly but reproving. Christian at once began his strange, mechanical bowing again, but then stopped and said:

"But people refer to the Struensee era, don't they? Not the Guldberg era. Struensee's era! How odd!"

For a moment Guldberg regarded the King in silence, as if he had been struck dumb or was lost for an answer. Keith noted that he seemed tense or distressed; then Guldberg pulled himself together and calmly said:

"His Majesty must compose himself. We think His Majesty must soon retire for the night, to sleep. We are quite sure of this."

He then gave a signal with his hand and withdrew. Christian started up his manic bowing again, but then stopped; as if in thought, he turned towards Ambassador Keith and in a voice that was quite calm and collected said:

"I'm in danger. That's why I must seek out my benefactress, who is the Sovereign of the Universe."

A few minutes later he was gone. This was the incident, in its entirety, as the British Ambassador reported it to his government.

2

Today there is not a single monument to Struensee in Denmark.

During his Danish visit a large number of portraits were made of him: engravings, pencil sketches, and oil paintings. Since no portraits were undertaken after his death, most of them are idealized and none are offensive. This is only natural. Before his visit he had no power, so there was no reason to immortalize him; after his death no-one wanted to be reminded of his existence.

Why should any monuments have been erected? An equestrian statue perhaps?

Of all the rulers of Denmark who were so often immortalized on horseback, he was no doubt the most capable horseman and the one who loved horses the most. When Struensee was led to the scaffold at Østre Fælled, General Eichstedt, perhaps as an expression of contempt or subtle cruelty towards the condemned man, had come riding up on Struensee's own horse, a white mare which he had named Margrethe, an unusual name for a horse. But if the intention was to cause the condemned man further pain, it failed. Struensee's eyes lit up, he stopped, raised his hand as if he wanted to pat the horse on the muzzle, and a faint, almost happy smile passed over his face, as if he thought the horse had come to bid him farewell.

He wanted to pat the horse on the muzzle but was unable to reach that far.

But why an equestrian statue? Only victors were honoured this way.

It's possible to imagine an equestrian statue of Struensee in Østre Fælled where he was executed, portrayed astride his Margrethe, whom he loved so much, in the park that is still there today, now used for demonstrations and public events, next to the athletic field. A park for games and festivals that almost resembles the royal parks Struensee once opened for a populace that until then had been shown little favour. The park is still there today, a marvellous open expanse where, on an October evening in 1941, Niels Bohr and Heisenberg took their famous stroll and had that mysterious conversation, as a result of which Hitler never managed to build his atomic bomb. One of history's crossroads. It is still there, although the scaffold is gone, just as is the memory of Struensee. There are no equestrian statues to commemorate a loser.

Guldberg was not awarded an equestrian statue either, and yet he was the victor and the one who crushed the Danish revolution. But equestrian statues are not given to a little upstart whose name was Høegh before he took the name of Guldberg and who was the son of an undertaker from Horsens.

Indeed both of them were upstarts, but few have left as clear a mark on history as they did; for that matter, they both deserved equestrian statues. "No-one refers to the Guldberg era" – that was obviously unfair.

Guldberg could justly take offence. He was the victor, after all. Posterity would indeed speak of "the Guldberg era". It lasted twelve years.

Then it too came to an end.

3

Guldberg had learned to handle the scorn with composure.

He knew his enemies. They spoke of light but spread darkness. His enemies assuredly believed that the Struensee era would last forever. That's what they thought. That was their characteristic infamy, and it had no relation to reality. They *wished* for it to be so. But he had always known how to hold himself in check, as when the British Ambassador was within earshot. That was necessary in a person who was slight in stature.

Guldberg was slight in stature. Yet his rôle in the Danish revolution and the period that followed was not slight. Guldberg had always wished that his biography would begin with the words: "There once was a man named Guldberg." This was the style of the Icelandic sagas, in which a man's greatness was not judged by his outward appearance.

Guldberg was four feet ten inches tall; his face was grey and prematurely aged, criss-crossed with tiny wrinkles that he had acquired as quite a young man. He seemed to have been transformed into an old man prematurely; that was why at first he was scorned and overlooked because of his insignificance, and later feared.

After he came to power, people learned to ignore his physical lack of significance. After he seized power he had himself portrayed with an iron jaw. The best portraits of him were done while he was in power. They express his inner self, which was considerable. The paintings give weight to his brilliance, education, and brutality, laying less emphasis on his outward appearance. And that was only proper. In his opinion, that was the purpose of art.

His eyes were icy grey like a wolf's and he never blinked as he fixed his gaze on the person who was speaking. Before he crushed the Danish revolution, they called him "the Lizard".

Afterwards they no longer did.

There once was a man named Guldberg, of slight physical stature but filled with inner greatness; that was the proper tone.

He himself never used the expression "the Danish revolution".

In the existing portraits from the time everyone has unnaturally big eyes.

Since the eyes are regarded as the mirror of the soul, the eyes were painted larger than life, much too large; they seem to be forcing their way out of the face, they are gleaming and shrewd; the eyes are meaningfully, almost grotesquely insistent. A subject's innermost self is documented in the eyes.

The interpretation of the eyes is then left to the beholder.

Apparently Guldberg himself dismissed with disgust any thought of an equestrian statue. He hated horses and harboured a real fear of them. Not once in his life had he ever sat on a horse.

His books, his writings, what he created before his days as a politician and afterwards, were monument enough. In all the portraits of Guldberg he is depicted as strong and robust, never as prematurely old. He controlled the way he was portrayed by possessing power; he never had to give instructions about the nature of the portraits. The artists invariably complied without being told.

He regarded artists and portraitists as the servants of politics. They were required to shape the facts, which in this case meant the inner truths that were disguised by his external slightness.

And yet for a long time this slightness proved useful. He was the one during the Danish revolution who was protected by his insignificance. Those who were significant fell, destroying each other. Until only Guldberg remained, insignificant and yet the tallest thing in the landscape of fallen trees all around him.

He found the image of the huge but fallen trees insidious. In a letter, he writes about the relative smallness of the great living trees and about their demise. For many hundreds of years the Crown had been cutting down all the great trees in Denmark. This was particularly the case with oak trees. They were felled for shipbuilding. Until what remained was a kingdom with no mature oaks. Guldberg tells of growing up in this devastated landscape, like a shrub rising above the stumps of the fallen and vanquished great trees.

He doesn't put it into writing, but the meaning is clear. This is how greatness springs from insignificance.

He considered himself an artist who had given up his art and chosen the realm of politics. That was why he admired and disdained artists.

His dissertation on Milton's "Paradise Lost", which was published in 1761 during his time as professor at Sorø Academy, is a study that repudiates fictional depictions of heaven; fictional in the sense that the poem takes liberties regarding the objective facts that were established in the Bible. Milton, he writes, was a magnificent poet, but he must be rebuked for being speculative. He takes liberties. The "so-called sacred poetry" takes liberties. In Chapter XVI he presents pointed arguments to repudiate as "fabricators" the "apostles of emancipated thinking". They create ambiguity, causing the dikes to burst and the poem's filth to defile everything.

The poem should not distort the document. The poem is a defiler of the document. Though in his view a painting is not.

It was often the case that artists took liberties. These liberties could lead to unrest, chaos and filth. For this reason the pious poets also had to be rebuked. And yet he admired Milton, albeit reluctantly. He labelled him "magnificent". He is a magnificent poet who takes liberties.

Holberg he despised.

The book about Milton brought him success. It was particularly admired by the pious Dowager Queen who praised its razor-sharp, pious analysis. For that reason she appointed Guldberg as tutor to the Crown Prince, who was King Christian's half-brother and feeble-minded, or, to use the word often employed: moronic.

Thus began his political career: through a study of the relationship between facts, as clearly evidenced in the Bible, and fiction, as represented by Milton's *Paradise Lost*.

4

So, no equestrian statues.

Guldberg's paradise was what he conquered along his path from the undertaking business in Horsens to the palace of Christiansborg. It made him tenacious, and it taught him to hate squalor.

Guldberg's paradise was something he conquered on his own. He did not inherit it. He conquered it.

He was hounded for some years by a nasty rumour. People had maliciously interpreted his unassuming appearance – the same appearance that in the end was corrected and enhanced, with the help of artists, after he seized power in 1772. According to the rumour, when he was four years old and his singing voice filled everyone with amazement and admiration, he was castrated by his loving but impoverished parents who had heard that in Italy there were great opportunities for singers. But to their disappointment and sorrow, he refused to sing after he turned 15 and instead entered the political arena.

None of this was true.

His father was a poor undertaker from Horsens who had never seen an opera and never dreamed of earning money from a castrated child. Guldberg was convinced that this smear had come from the Italian opera divas at the court in Copenhagen, who were all whores. All the blasphemers and men of the Enlightenment, particularly in Altona, which was the vipers' nest of the Enlightenment, made use of the Italian whores. From them came all filth, including the filthy rumour.

The peculiar premature ageing which, however, manifested itself only outwardly, had set in early, at the age of 15, and could not be explained by the doctors. For this reason he despised doctors. Struensee was a doctor.

Regarding the rumour of his "operation": he could not get rid of it until he came to power and no longer appeared insignificant. He knew that the assertion that he had been "cut" affected everyone with a feeling of discomfort. He had learned to live with this.

And yet he seized hold of the rumour's inner meaning, although untrue. The essential truth was that his pious parents had assigned him the rôle of undertaker, and he had rejected it.

He chose for himself the rôle of politician.

The British Ambassador's account of the King and Guldberg from the year 1782 is astonishing and yet contains an inner truth.

The Ambassador seems to express surprise at Guldberg's "love" for the King, whose power he had stolen and whose reputation he had destroyed. But hadn't Guldberg himself always been astonished by the manifestations of love? How could it possibly be described? He had always asked himself this question. Those handsome, imposing, distinguished people, those who had a knowledge of love and yet were so blind! Politics was a mechanism that could be analysed and constructed; in that sense it was a machine. But those strong, prominent people who possessed knowledge of love, how naïvely they allowed the clear-cut political game to be obscured by the hydra of passion!

That ceaseless confusion of emotion and reason on the part of the intellectual men of the Enlightenment! Guldberg knew that this was the soft, vulnerable point in the monster's belly. And he realized how close he had once been to succumbing to the contagion of this sin. It had come from "the little English whore". He had been forced to his knees at his bedside.

He would never forget it.

It is in this connection that he speaks of the mighty oak forest where the trees were felled and only the lowly shrub remained as conqueror. Then he describes what happened in the felled forest and how he, stunted and insignificant, was allowed to grow and prevail from the site where he watched everything happen, among the sprawled trunks in the felled forest.

And he thought he was the only one to see it.

5

Guldberg must be treated with respect. He is still nearly invisible. Soon he will make himself visible.

He saw and understood early on.

In the autumn of 1769 Guldberg writes in a note that the young queen is to him "an ever-growing mystery".

He calls her "the little English whore". He was quite familiar with the impurities at court. He knew its history. Frederik IV was pious and had countless mistresses. Christian VI was a Pietist but lived a lecherous life. At night Frederik V frequented the Copenhagen whorehouses, and spent his time with drinking, gambling, and vulgar, lewd conversations. He drank himself to death. The whores flocked around his bed. It was the same everywhere in Europe. It started in Paris and then spread like a disease to all the courts. Filth everywhere.

Who would defend purity?

As a child he had learned to live with corpses. His father, whose profession it was to tend to the bodies, had allowed Guldberg to assist him in his work. How many rigid, ice-cold limbs had he clutched and buried? The dead were pure. They did not roll in muck. They awaited the great purifying fire that would either deliver them or plague them in eternity.

He had seen filth. But never so squalid as at court.

*

After the little English whore arrived and was married to the King, Fru von Plessen was appointed chief lady-in-waiting. Fru von Plessen was pure. It was her nature. She wished to protect the young girl from life's filth, and for a long time she succeeded.

One occurence in June 1767 had particularly disturbed Guldberg. It was important that before this date, no sexual relations had taken place between the royal couple, despite the fact that they had been married seven months.

On the morning of June 3, 1767, lady-in-waiting Fru von Plessen came to complain to Guldberg. She entered the room he used for his tutoring unannounced, and without mincing words, began castigating the Queen's behaviour. Guldberg is said to have held Fru von Plessen to be a thoroughly repulsive creature but, because of her inner purity, of value to the Queen. Fru von Plessen smelled. It was not the odour of a stall, of sweat, or of any other secretion, but rather the odour of old woman, like mildew.

And yet she was only 41 years old.

The Queen, Caroline Mathilde, was 15 at the time. As usual, Fru von Plessen had gone to the Queen's bedchamber to keep her company or to play chess, and by her presence ease the Queen's loneliness. The Queen was lying on her bed, which was quite large, and staring up at the ceiling. She was fully dressed. Fru von Plessen asked the Queen why she did not speak. The Queen was silent for a long time, not moving either her fully-dressed form or her head, not replying. Finally she said:

"I'm feeling melancholy."

Fru von Plessen then asked the Queen what was weighing so heavily on her heart. The Queen said at last:

"He doesn't come. Why doesn't he come?"

It was chilly in the room. Fru von Plessen stared at her mistress for a moment and then said:

"No doubt the King will see fit to come. Until then Your Majesty should enjoy her freedom from the hydra of passion. She ought not to grieve."

"What do you mean?" the Queen asked.

"The King," Fru von Plessen elucidated with that extraordinary terseness which her voice could summon so well, "the King will undoubtedly overcome his shyness. Until then, the Queen can take pleasure in being free of his passion."

"Why take pleasure?"

"When thus afflicted, it becomes a torment!" Fru von Plessen said with an expression of unexpected fury.

"Leave me," was the Queen's surprising response, after a moment of silence.

The offended Fru von Plessen then left the room.

Guldberg's indignation springs, however, from what happened later the same evening.

He was pretending to read, sitting in the corridor between the Royal Chancellor's antechamber, on the left, and the library of the King's secretary. He doesn't explain why he writes "pretending to". The Queen appeared. He rose to his feet with a bow. She gestured with her hand and they both sat down.

She was wearing the pale rose gown that left her shoulders bare.

"Herr Guldberg," she said in a low voice, "may I ask you a very personal question?"

He nodded, uncomprehending.

"I've been told," she whispered, "that in your youth you were freed from . . . from the torment of passion. Because of that I would like to ask you . . ."

She stopped. He remained silent but could feel a tremendous rage welling up inside him. With the utmost resolve, however, he managed to keep his composure.

"I just wanted to know . . ."

He waited. Finally the silence grew unbearable, and Guldberg said: "Yes, Your Royal Highness?"

"I just wanted to know . . . whether this freedom from passion is . . . a great relief? Or . . . a great emptiness?"

He did not reply.

"Herr Guldberg," she whispered, "is it an emptiness? Or a torment?"

She leaned towards him. The curve of her bosom was near to him. He felt indignation "beyond all reason". He had seen through her at once, and this insight, during the events that later followed, would be of the greatest use to him. Her malice was evident: her naked flesh, the curve of her bosom, the smoothness of her young skin, it was all very close. This was not the first time he understood that throughout the court malicious rumours were being spread about the reason for his physical insignificance. How helpless he was to combat them! How impossible it was to point out that *castrati* resembled fattened cattle, swollen and bloated, and that they completely lacked the grey, sharp, thin, and practically wizened physical clarity possessed by him!

Gossip was circulating about him, and it had reached the Queen's ear. The little whore thought him harmless, someone to be confided in. And with all the intelligence of her young malice, she now leaned very close, and he could see her breasts in almost all their fullness. She seemed to be testing him, trying to see whether there was any life left in him, whether her breasts held any enticement that could summon the remnants of what might be human inside him.

Yes, whether this might entice forth the remnants of a man in him. Of a human being. Or whether he was merely an animal.

Then she looked at him. Like an animal. She exposed herself to him as if she wanted to say: I know. She knew that he was stunted and despicable, no longer human, no longer within the reach of desire. And she did this now with full consciousness, with malicious intent.

On this occasion her face was very close to Guldberg's, and her nearly exposed breasts screamed their insult at him. As he tried to regain his composure he thought: May God punish her, may she suffer the fire of hell for all eternity. May a vengeful stake be driven up into her wanton womb, and may her spiteful intimacy be rewarded with eternal pain and agony.

His agitation was so great that tears welled up in his eyes. And he feared that the young, wanton creature would notice this.

Yet he may have misinterpreted her. Because next he describes how she swiftly, almost like a moth, touched her hand to his cheek and whispered:

"Forgive me. Oh, forgive me, Herr ... Guldberg. I didn't mean to ..."

Guldberg then rose hastily to his feet and left.

As a child he had an exceedingly beautiful singing voice. That much is true. He hated artists. He also hated impurity.

He remembers the rigid bodies as pure. And they never caused chaos.

God's greatness and omnipotence manifested itself in the fact that He chose even those who were small, lowly, stunted, and disdained to be His instruments. That was what was so wondrous. It was God's inexplicable miracle. The King, the young Christian, seemed small, perhaps mentally deficient. But he was chosen.

To him had been given all power. This power, this selection, came from God. It had not been given to the beautiful, strong, or distinguished; they were the ones who were the real upstarts. The lowliest were the chosen. That was God's miracle. Guldberg understood this. In a certain sense the King and Guldberg were part of the same miracle.

This filled him with satisfaction.

He saw Struensee for the first time in Altona in 1766, on the day the young Queen arrived there on her way from London to Copenhagen, shortly before her marriage. Struensee was standing there, hidden by the crowd, surrounded by his enlightened friends.

But Guldberg saw him: imposing, handsome, and lecherous.

Guldberg himself had once emerged from the woodwork.

The person who was once inconsequential emerged from the

woodwork; anyone who does this knows that all woodwork can be an ally. It was simply a matter of organization. Politics involved organization, making the woodwork listen and report.

He had always believed in justice, and he knew that evil would be crushed by a very small, overlooked person whom no-one took seriously. That was his inner driving force. God had chosen him and made him a spidery grey dwarf because God's ways were inscrutable. But God's deeds were full of cunning.

God was the foremost politician.

Quite early on he had learned to hate impurity and evil. Evil meant the dissolute, those who scorned God, the wastrels, the worldly, the whoremongers, the drunkards. All of them were present at court. The court was evil. That was why he had always adopted a tiny, friendly, almost submissive smile whenever he observed evil. Everyone thought that he watched the orgies with envy. Little Guldberg probably wanted to join in, they thought, but he couldn't. He lacks . . . the instrument. Just wants to watch.

Their little, derisive smiles.

But they should have taken note of his eyes.

And someday, he used to think, the time for control will come, when control will conquer all. And then smiles will no longer be necessary. Then the time for cutting will come, the time for purity, then the barren limbs on the tree will be cut away. Then evil will at last be castrated. And then the time for purity will come.

And the time of the wanton women will be over.

What he would do with the wanton women he didn't know. They couldn't be cut, after all. Perhaps the wanton women should sink down and dissolve into decay, like mushrooms in the autumn.

He was very fond of that image. The wanton women would sink down and dissolve, like mushrooms in the autumn.

His dream was purity.

The radicals in Altona were impure. They despised those who were cut and small, and they dreamed the same secret dreams of power which they claimed to be fighting. He had seen through them. They spoke of light. A torch in the dark. But from their torches fell only darkness.

He had been to Altona. It was significant that this Struensee came from Altona. Paris was the vipers' nest of the encyclopedists, but Altona was worse. It was as if they were trying to put a lever under the house of the world: and the world was teetering, and anxiety and nausea and fumes drifted up. But the Almighty God had chosen one of His smallest, the most disdained, Guldberg himself, to confront Evil, to save the King, and to cut away the filth from the one chosen by God. And, as the prophet Isaiah has written:

Who is this that comes from Edom, in crimsoned garments from Bozrah, he that is glorious in his apparel, marching in the greatness of his strength?

"It is I, announcing vindication, mighty to save."

Why is thy apparel red, and thy garments like his that treads in the wine press?

"I have trodden the wine press alone, and from the peoples no-one was with me; I trod them in my anger and trampled them in my wrath; their lifeblood is sprinkled upon my garments, and I have stained all my raiment.

"For the day of vengeance was in my heart, and my year of redemption has come.

"I looked, but there was no-one to help; I was appalled, but there was no-one to uphold; so my own arm brought me victory, and my wrath upheld me.

"I trod down the peoples in my anger, I made them drunk in my wrath, and I poured out their lifeblood on the earth."

"And the outcast shall become the rulers", as it says in the Holy Scriptures.

He was the one who had been called by God. The little Lizard himself. And a great fear would come over the world when the Lowliest and the most Scorned came to hold the reins of vengeance in his hands. And God's wrath would kill them all.

When the evil and the lecherous were cut away, then he would exonerate the King. And even if evil had harmed the King, he would become like a child once again. Guldberg knew that deep inside, Christian had always been a child. He was not insane. And when it was all over and the child chosen by God was saved, the King would once again follow him like a shadow, like a child, meek and pure. He would once again be a pure child, and one of the outcast would once again become one of the rulers.

He would defend the King. Against them. For the King was also one of the most outcast, and the most disdained.

But equestrian statues are not given to wine treaders.

6

Guldberg had been present at the deathbed of Christian's father, King Frederik.

He died in the morning of January 14, 1766.

During his last years King Frederik had become heavier and heavier; he drank steadily, his hands shook, and his flesh had swollen up, becoming doughy and grey; his face resembled that of a drunkard – it looked as if you could pluck pieces of flesh from his face – and hidden deep inside were his eyes, pale and runny with a yellow discharge, as if his body were already beginning to seep.

The King had also been seized with agitation and dread, and he constantly demanded that whores share his bed to assuage his dread. As time passed, more and more of the priests who stood at his side were outraged by this. Those who were commanded at his bedside to say the prayers that would assuage his fear became sickened by this. The King, thanks to his physical flabbiness, was no longer capable of satisfying his fleshly desires; yet he demanded that the whores who were brought to him from the city should share his bed naked. That is when the priests felt that their prayers, in particular the ritual of Holy Communion, became blasphemous. The King would spit out Christ's

Holy Body but drink deeply of His Blood, while the whores, with ill-concealed revulsion, fondled his body.

Even worse was that the rumour of the King's condition had spread among the public, and the priests began to see themselves sullied by common gossip.

The last week before his death, the King was in great fear.

He used this simple word "fear" instead of "dread" or "agitation". His spells of vomiting now occurred more often. On the day he died, he commanded that Crown Prince Christian be called to his sickbed.

The bishop of the city then insisted that all the whores be removed.

For a long time the King stared in silence at those in attendance, which included his valets, the bishop, and two priests. Then in a voice filled with such extraordinary hatred that they almost recoiled, he shouted that the women would one day be with him in heaven; he hoped, on the other hand, that those now flocking around him, especially the Archbishop of Aarhus, would be afflicted by the eternal torments of hell. The King had misunderstood the situation, however: the Archbishop of Aarhus had already returned to his congregation the day before.

Then he vomited and with effort returned to his drinking.

After an hour he again grew intractable and shouted for his son, whom he now wished to bless.

Christian, the Crown Prince, was led in to see him towards nine o'clock. He was accompanied by his Swiss tutor, Reverdil. At the time, Christian was 16 years old. He stared at his father in horror.

The King finally noticed him and motioned him closer, but Christian remained where he was, petrified. Reverdil then took him by the arm to lead him to the King's bedside, but Christian clung to his tutor and uttered a few inaudible words; his lips clearly moved, he was trying to say something, but no sound came out.

"Come . . . here . . . my beloved . . . son," the King then murmured, and with a violent thrust of his arm he flung aside the empty wine tankard.

When Christian refused to obey his command, the King began shouting, wild and plaintive; when one of the priests took pity on him and inquired if there was anything he wanted, the King repeated:

"I want . . . by Satan . . . to bless the little . . . the little . . . wretch!"

After another brief pause Christian, almost without resisting, was led forward to the King's deathbed. The King grabbed Christian by the head and neck and tried to pull him closer.

"How will it all . . . turn out . . . for you . . . you little . . . wretch?"

The King then had difficulty finding words, but in a moment his speech returned.

"You little worm! You have to be hard . . . hard . . . HARD! You little . . . are you hard? Are you hard? You have to make yourself . . . invulnerable! Otherwise . . ."

Christian couldn't say a word since he was being gripped by the neck and pressed against the King's naked flank. The King was now panting loudly, as if he couldn't breathe, but then he seethed:

"Christian! You have to make yourself hard . . . hard . . . hard! Otherwise they'll swallow you up! Otherwise they'll devour . . . crush . . ."

Then he sank back against the pillows. There was utter silence in the room. The only sound to be heard was Christian's vigorous sobbing.

And the King, now dozing and with his head on his pillow, then said in a very low voice, almost without slurring:

"You're not hard enough, you little wretch. I give you my blessing."

Yellow fluid ran out of his mouth. A few minutes later King Frederik V was dead.

Guldberg saw everything and remembered everything. He also saw how the Swiss tutor Reverdil took the boy by the hand, as if the new King were still a little child; he led him by the hand, like a child, something that surprised everyone and was later much discussed. They left the room in this manner, they walked down the corridors, passing the principal guard, who all presented arms, and went out into the palace courtyard. It was now midday, the sun was low in the sky, a light snow had fallen overnight. The boy was still sobbing forlornly and tightly clutching the hand of the Swiss tutor Reverdil.

In the middle of the courtyard they abruptly stopped. Many people were watching them. Why did they stop? Where were they going?

The boy was slender and short. Members of the court, upon learning the news of the King's tragic and unexpected demise, had streamed into the palace courtyard. A hundred people stood there, silent and curious.

Guldberg was among them, still the lowliest of them all. He was still without distinctions. He was present only by right of the title of teacher to the moronic Crown Prince Frederik; with no other rights, with no power, but with the certainty that great trees would fall, that he had time and could wait.

Christian and his tutor stood still, apparently in deep confusion, and waited for nothing. They stood there with the sun low over the palace courtyard, which was covered by a light snow, and waited for nothing as the boy wept on and on.

Reverdil held tight to the young King's hand. How small the new King of Denmark was, like a child. Guldberg felt a boundless sorrow as he looked at them. Someone else had taken the place at the King's side that belonged to him. A great deal of work now remained to conquer that position. His sorrow was still boundless. Then he mustered his courage.

His time would come.

And so it was that Christian was blessed.

The same afternoon Christian VII was proclaimed Denmark's new King.

Chapter 2 · The Invulnerable One

I

The Swiss tutor was gaunt, stooped, and had a dream of the Enlightenment that was like a quiet and very beautiful dawn; at first it was imperceptible, then it was there and the day had begun.

That's how he thought of it. Gentle, quiet, and unresisting. That's how it should always be.

His name was François Reverdil. He was the one in the palace courtyard.

Reverdil took Christian's hand because he had forgotten about protocol and felt only sorrow at the boy's tears.

That was why they stood there, motionless, in the palace courtyard, in the snow, after Christian was blessed.

Christian VII was proclaimed King of Denmark from the palace balcony on the afternoon of the same day. Reverdil stood behind him, to one side. The new King caused displeasure by waving and laughing.

This was regarded as unseemly. No explanation was given for the King's objectionable behaviour.

When the Swiss tutor François Reverdil was hired in 1760 to educate eleven-year-old Crown Prince Christian, he managed to conceal for a long time that he was of Jewish descent. His two other given names – Élie Salomon – were left out of the contract of employment.

Such caution was probably unnecessary. Pogroms had not occurred in Copenhagen for over ten years.

The fact that Reverdil was an enlightened man was also not · reported. In his opinion this was irrelevant information which might cause harm. His political views were a private matter.

Caution was his fundamental principle.

*

His first impression of the boy was quite positive.

Christian was "charming". He was delicate, of slight build, almost girlish, but with a winning appearance and manner. He had a nimble intellect, moved with grace and elegance, and spoke three languages fluently: Danish, German, and French.

But after only a few weeks the picture grew more complicated. The boy soon seemed to develop an attachment to Reverdil, for whom, after one month, the King said he felt "no terror". When Reverdil inquired about the puzzling word "terror", he was given to understand that fear was the boy's natural state.

"Charming" eventually failed to describe all that Christian was.

During the obligatory walks, which were conducted at a brisk pace and with no-one else present, the eleven-year-old expressed feelings and views that Reverdil found more and more alarming. They were also cloaked in a peculiar linguistic garb. Christian's maniacally repeated longing to be "strong" or "hard" by no means expressed a wish to develop a vigorous physical constitution; he meant something else. He wanted to make "progress", but here again it was not possible to interpret this concept in a rational manner. His language seemed to consist of an enormous number of words formulated according to a secret code, and impossible for the uninitiated to break. During conversations that took place in the presence of a third person or within the court, this coded language was quite absent. But in private, with Reverdil, the code words were almost dementedly frequent.

The most peculiar were "flesh", "man-eaters", and "punishment", which were used without any coherent meaning. Several expressions, however, were immediately comprehensible.

When they returned to their studies after these walks, the boy might say that they were now going to an "intense examination" or an "intense interrogation". In Danish legal terms, the expressions meant the same as "torture", which at the time was both permitted and zealously employed within the jurisdiction. Reverdil asked the boy in jest whether he thought himself tormented by fire tongs or pincers.

The boy surprisingly said yes.

It was obvious.

Only after a while did Reverdil realize that this particular expression was not a code word concealing some secretive other meaning, but rather a statement of fact.

They were torturing him. This was normal.

2

The tutor's task was to train a Danish monarch who held absolute power.

Yet he was not alone in this task.

Reverdil assumed his post on the 100th anniversary of the revolution of 1660, which had on the whole crushed the power of the nobles and returned absolute rule to the King. Reverdil also impressed upon the young Prince the importance of his position: that he held in his hands the future of the country. For reasons of discretion, however, he failed to tell the young Prince of the background: that it was the decline of royal power under the previous kings, and their degeneration, which had given complete power to those within the court who now controlled his own upbringing, education, and outlook.

"The boy" (Reverdil uses this term) seems to have known only anxiety, aversion and desperation with regard to his future rôle as King.

The King was the absolute ruler, but the government officials exercised all power. Everyone considered this natural. Pedagogy, for Christian's part, was adjusted accordingly. Power had been conferred by God on the King. He, in turn, did not make use of his power but rather delegated it. The idea that the King should not make use of his power was not assumed. The assumption was that he was insane, seriously alcoholic, or unwilling to work. If he was none of these things, then his will had to be broken. The King's apathy and decline were thus either inherent or could be introduced.

Christian's intelligence indicated to those around him that passivity would have to be instilled in him. Reverdil describes the methods used on "the boy" as "the systematic pedagogy that is used to develop powerlessness and degradation for the purpose of maintaining the influence of the real rulers". He soon realized that the Danish court was also willing to sacrifice the mental health of the young Prince to achieve the results that had been evident in previous kings.

The aim was to create in this child "a new Frederik". As Reverdil later writes in his memoirs, the intent was "through the moral decline of royal power to create a vacuum in which they themselves could exercise power with impunity. What they had not counted on was that one day a royal physician by the name of Struensee would visit this power vacuum."

Reverdil is the one who uses the expression "the royal physician's visit". He does not mean to be ironic. Rather, he witnesses the breaking of the boy with clear eyes – and outrage.

Of Christian's family, it is said that his mother died when he was two, that he knew his father only by his bad reputation, and that the person who planned and guided his upbringing, Count Ditlev Reventlow, was a man of integrity.

Reventlow was a strong personality.

He thought of upbringing as "training that even the most dull-witted peasant could carry out as long as he had a whip in hand". That was why Count Reventlow carried a whip. Great weight was to be placed on "spiritual subjugation", and all "independence should be broken".

He didn't hesitate to bring these principles to bear on little Christian. The methods were hardly unusual in the upbringing of children at the time. What was unique and what made the results so startling, even for those days, was that this was not a child of the nobility or middle classes. The individual who was supposed to be broken through training and spiritual subjugation, with the help of a whip, in order to rob him of all independence, was the absolute monarch of Denmark, chosen by God.

Sufficiently broken, subjugated, and with a shattered will, the monarch was then to be given all power, only to relinquish it to those who had brought him up.

Much later, long after the Danish revolution, Reverdil asks in his memoirs why he did not intervene.

He has no answer to this. He describes himself as an intellectual, and his analysis is clear.

But he gives no answer to this particular question.

Reverdil assumed the post of subordinate language teacher in German and French. Upon his arrival he makes note of the results of the first ten years of pedagogy.

It's true that he was a subordinate. Count Reventlow determined the principles. There were no parents, after all.

"So for five years I left the palace each day in sorrow. I saw how they were all the time trying to break my pupil's spiritual fortitude so that he learned nothing of his rôle as monarch or what came under his authority. He was given no education in the civil laws of his country; he knew nothing about the way the governmental offices divided up their work or the details of how the country was ruled; nor how power emanated from the Crown and was distributed among the individual officials. No-one had ever told him what relationships he might fall into with neighbouring countries; he was ignorant of the kingdom's military and naval forces. His Lord Chancellor, who oversaw his education and each day supervised my lessons, had become finance minister without giving up his position as headmaster, but he didn't teach his pupil anything about the duties of his office. The monies the land contributed to the monarchy, the way in which they were added to the Royal Treasury, and what they were to be used for – these things were completely unknown to the person who

27

would one day rule over all. Several years before, his father the King had given him a country manor; but there the Prince had never appointed a lodgekeeper or personally handed out a single ducat or planted even one tree. The Lord Chancellor and Finance Minister Reventlow ran everything as he saw fit, and he could say with good reason:

"My Melons! My Figs!"

The tutor concludes that the rôle Herr Reventlow – finance minister, country squire, and count – came to play in the King's education was central. It contributed to Reverdil being able to some extent to solve the mystery posed by the boy's code language.

The Prince's physical peculiarities were becoming more and more pronounced. His body seemed to be filled with restlessness: he constantly gestured with his hands, plucked at his stomach, tapped his fingertips against his skin, and muttered that he would soon be "making progress". Then he would achieve the "state of perfection" that would allow him to become "like the Italian actors".

The concepts of "the theatre" and "Passauer Kunst" became intertwined for young Christian. There is no logic to it, other than the logic summoned up in the boy by the "intense interrogations".

Among the many peculiar ideas that flourished in the European courts at the time was the belief that there was a way to make human beings invulnerable. The myth was created during the Thirty Years' War in Germany; it was the dream of invulnerability, and it came to play a particularly important rôle among sovereigns. The belief in this art – which was called "Passauer Kunst" – was embraced by both Christian's father and his grandfather.

For Christian, the belief in "Passauer Kunst" became a secret treasure that he concealed deep within.

He was forever examining his hands and his stomach to see whether he had made progress (*"s'il avançait"*) towards invulnerability. The cannibals surrounding him were enemies that were an ever-present threat. If he became "strong" and his body was "invulnerable", he would be insensitive to mistreatment by his enemies.

Everyone was an enemy, but especially the absolute ruler Reventlow.

The fact that he mentions "the Italian actors" as godlike models has to do with this dream. For young Christian, the actors of the theatre seemed godlike. The gods were hard – and invulnerable.

These gods also played their rôles. Then they were elevated beyond reality.

As a five-year-old he had seen a special performance by an Italian acting troupe. The impressive physical bearing of the actors, their imposing height and magnificently accoutred costumes had made such a strong impression on him that he ended up regarding them as creatures of a higher order. They were godlike. And if he, who was also said to be chosen by God, if he made progress, then surely he should be able to join these gods, become an actor, and in this way be freed from "the monarchy's torments".

He experienced his birthright as a torment.

Over time he also developed the notion that he had been exchanged at birth. He was actually a peasant boy. This became a fixed idea in his mind. To be chosen was a torment. The "intense interrogations" were a torment. If he had been exchanged, shouldn't he then be freed from this torment?

God's chosen was no ordinary human. That was why he searched, ever more feverishly, for proof that he was a human being. A sign! The word "sign" came up again and again. He was searching for a "sign". If he could find proof that he was a human being, not the chosen one, then he would be freed from the rôle of being King, from the torment, the uncertainty, and the intense interrogations. If, on the other hand, he could make himself invulnerable, like the Italian actors, then he might even be able to endure being chosen.

That was how Reverdil perceived Christian's thoughts. Though he wasn't certain. But he *was* certain that he was looking at a ravaged child's image of himself.

That the theatre was illusory and thus the only real life in existence was confirmed more and more for Christian.

His reasoning – and Reverdil tries to follow him here, although with difficulty since the logic was not wholly apparent – his reasoning was that if the theatre alone was real, then everything was comprehensible. The people on stage moved in a godlike fashion, reciting the lines they had memorized; that too was natural. The actors were what was real. He himself had been allotted the rôle of King by the grace of God. This had nothing to do with reality; it was artifice. And for that reason he need not feel any shame.

Shame was otherwise his natural state.

During one of his first lessons, which were conducted in French, Herr Reverdil had discovered that his pupil did not understand the term "*corvée*". In an attempt to relate it to the boy's experience he described the element of theatre in the Prince's own life. "I had to teach him that his travels resembled a military incursion, that advance scouts were dispatched to every district to mobilize the peasants to turn out, some with horses, others merely with small carts; that these peasants then had to wait for hours or even days beside their wagons at assembly places, that they wasted a great deal of time for no good purpose, that those he passed had been summoned forth, and that nothing of what he saw on these occasions was real."

When Lord Chancellor and Finance Minister Reventlow heard about this element in the lessons, he flew into a rage, bellowing that it was useless. Count Ditlev Reventlow often bellowed. His conduct as supervisor of the Prince's education had in no way surprised the Jewish tutor from Switzerland, although for understandable reasons he never dared object to the Finance Minister's principles.

Nothing made any sense. The play was what was natural. The Prince had to learn his lines, not try to understand. He was God's chosen one. He stood above everyone else, and yet he was the most miserable of all. The only constant was the flogging he received on a regular basis.

Herr Reventlow had a reputation for "integrity". Since he considered rote learning to be more important than knowledge, he strongly emphasized that the Prince should memorize theories and assertions, just like in a play. On the other hand, it was not important for the Prince to understand what he was learning. The primary aim of the instruction, using the theatre as a model, was to learn the lines by heart. Despite his integrity and harsh nature, Herr Reventlow procured for this purpose costumes for the heir to the throne, sewn in Paris. Then whenever the boy was displayed and he could speak his lines from memory, the Finance Minister would be pleased; before each recital by the heir to the throne, he would exclaim:

"Look! Now my puppet is about to perform!"

These performances, Reverdil writes, were often a torment for Christian. One day when he was supposed to display his skill in dancing, he was misled by his own ignorance as to what was about to happen. "That was a trying day for the Prince. He was cursed and beaten, and he wept right up until the moment when the ball was about to begin. In his mind what was about to take place became intertwined with his fixed ideas: he imagined that they were leading him off to prison. The military honours that heralded him at the entrance, the drum rolls, and the guards who surrounded his carriage all confirmed his suspicions and aroused in him a great anxiety. All of his perceptions were badly jolted, sleep deserted him for many nights, and he wept continuously."

Herr Reventlow intervened in the lessons – and he did so "constantly" – especially when the nature of the rote learning slipped into what he called "conversation".

"Whenever he noticed that the lessons had 'degenerated' into conversation, that they were taking place quietly, without commotion, and that they interested my pupil, he would shout from his side of the room in his thunderous voice and in German: 'Your Royal Highness, if I don't supervise everything, nothing will get done!' And with that he would come over to us and make the Prince start the lesson all over again, adding his own comments, pinching him hard, squeezing his hands together, and striking him roughly with his fists. The boy would then become confused and fearful and perform worse and worse. The reproaches would increase and the abuse intensify, either because he was saying the lessons verbatim or he was being too free, or because he had omitted some detail or given the correct answer, since it was often the case that his tormentor didn't know what the correct answer should be. The Lord Chancellor would often become more and more enraged, until in the end he would shout through the hall for the cane he used on the child, and would continue to use for a long time. These desperate outbursts were familiar to everyone, since they could be heard out in the palace courtyard where the court had assembled. The crowds that had gathered there to hail the Rising Sun, meaning the screaming child who was now being punished and whom I grew to know as a noble and loveable child, these people listened to it all as the child, his eyes wide and filled with tears, tried to read in his tyrant's face what the man wanted and what the proper words might be. At dinner his Mentor would continue to monopolize his attention, plying the boy with questions and greeting his answers with epithets. In this way the child was exposed to ridicule before his servants and became accustomed to shame.

"Even Sunday was not a day of rest; twice during the day Herr Reventlow would escort his pupil to church, repeating in his booming voice the pastor's most important points in the Prince's ear, pinching and poking him again and again to emphasize certain lines of particular significance. Afterwards the Prince would be forced to repeat what he had heard, and if he forgot or misunderstood anything, he was abused as fiercely as the individual topic warranted."

This was the "intense interrogation". Reverdil notes that Reventlow often mistreated the Crown Prince so severely that "froth would appear on the Count's lips". Later all power, without intermediary, would be transferred to the boy by God, the One who had chosen him.

For this reason he was seeking a "benefactor". He had not yet found one.

Their walks together were the only occasions when Reverdil was able to explain things without supervision. But the boy seemed more and more uncertain and confused.

Nothing seemed to make sense. During these walks, which they sometimes took alone, sometimes accompanied by chamberlains "at a suitable distance of 30 paces", the boy's confusion was more openly expressed.

One might say that his language began to be decoded. Reverdil also began to note that everything which related to "integrity" in the boy's linguistic consciousness was associated with abuse and the fornication at court.

Christian explained, in a stubborn attempt to make sense of things, that he understood the court to be a theatre, that he had to learn his lines, and that he would be punished if he didn't know them by heart.

But was he one person or two?

The Italian actors had a rôle in a play as well as a rôle "outside" when the play was over. But, as the boy said, *his* rôle never ended, did it? When was he ever "outside"? Did he constantly have to strive to be "hard" and to make "progress", and at the same time find himself "inside"? If it was nothing but lines that had to be learned, and Reverdil said that everything was directed, that his life merely had to be memorized and "performed", then could he ever hope to get out of this play?

And yet the actors, the Italian ones he had seen, were two separate beings: one on stage and one outside. What about him?

There was no logic to his reasoning, and yet in some ways it made sense. He had asked Reverdil what a human being was. And was he one? God had sent his only Son to earth, but God had also chosen

33

him, Christian, to be the absolute ruler. Had God also written the lines that he was now learning? Was it God's will that those peasants who were summoned to appear along his travel route should become his fellow actors? Or what was his rôle? Was he God's son? If so, then who was his father Frederik?

Had God also chosen his father and made him almost as much a man of "integrity" as Herr Reventlow? Did a supreme God, a Universal Benefactor, exist who might take mercy on him in moments of dire need?

Herr Reverdil sternly told him that he was not the Lord's anointed, nor was he Christ, that as a matter of fact Reverdil didn't even believe in Christ because he was a Jew; that under no circumstances should he ever hint that he was God's son.

That was blasphemy.

But the Heir to the Throne had then objected that the Dowager Queen, who was a Pietist of the Moravian persuasion, had said true Christians bathed in the blood of the Lamb, that the wounds were grottoes where sinners could hide, and that this was salvation. How did all of this fit together?

Reverdil told him to banish these thoughts from his mind at once.

Christian said he feared that he would be punished since his guilt was so great; *primo* for not knowing his lines, *secundo* for claiming to be God's Chosen when in actual fact he was a changeling peasant boy. And then the spasms would come back, his fingers plucking at his stomach, his legs twitching, and then his hand pointing upwards and a word uttered, repeated, like a cry for help or a prayer.

Yes, perhaps this was how he prayed: the word repeated, like the hand pointing upward at something or someone in the universe that seemed so confusing and terrifying and lacking all sense to the boy.

"A sign! A sign!"

Christian's stubborn monologues continued. He refused to give up. If a person was punished, was he then free of guilt? Did a Benefactor exist? Since he realized that his shame was so great and his faults so numerous, what was then the relationship between guilt and punishment? In what way should he be punished? Were all those around him who whored and drank and were so full of integrity, were they too part of God's play? Jesus was born in a manger, after all. Why was it then so unlikely that he himself might be a changeling who could have lived a much different life with loving parents, among the peasants and beasts?

Jesus was the son of a carpenter. Then who was Christian?

Herr Reverdil was seized by an ever-growing alarm but did his best to answer with sense and calm. And yet he had a feeling that the boy's confusion was increasing, becoming more and more disturbing.

Hadn't Jesus, Christian asked during one of their walks, driven the moneylenders and hawkers from the temple? Those who were whoring and sinning! He had driven those people out, meaning those of integrity, and who was this Jesus?

"A revolutionary," Herr Reverdil replied.

Was it then Christian's mission, he persisted in asking, his mission as God's chosen absolute ruler in this court where people whored and drank and sinned, to smash and crush them all? And to drive out, to smash ... crush ... those of integrity? Reventlow was a man of integrity, wasn't he? Could a Benefactor, who might be the ruler of the whole universe, have pity and take time for this? To crush those of integrity? Would Reverdil perhaps help him to find a Benefactor who could crush them all?

"Why do you want to do this?" Reverdil asked.

With that the boy began to cry.

"To achieve purity," he said at last.

They walked for a long time in silence.

"No," Herr Reverdil said finally, "it is not your mission to crush."

But he knew that he had not given him an answer.

3

Young Christian began talking more often about guilt and punishment.

He was familiar with the little punishment, of course. That was the "rod" that the Lord Chancellor wielded. The little punishment also meant the shame and the laughter of the pages and the "favourites" whenever he made a mistake. The big punishment must be for sinners who were even worse.

The boy's development took an alarming turn with the torture and execution of Sergeant Mörl.

This is what happened.

A sergeant by the name of Mörl, who in a deplorable breach of trust had murdered the benefactor in whose house he resided in order to steal the regiment's payroll, was, in accordance with a royal decree signed by King Frederik, condemned to a gruesome means of execution which made use of certain methods employed only to avenge murder of a particular kind.

Many regarded this as a display of inhuman barbarism. The sentence was a document of a particularly abhorrent type; but Crown Prince Christian was informed of the event, and he showed a peculiar interest in it. This took place during the penultimate year of King Frederik's reign. Christian was then 15 years old. He mentioned to Reverdil that he wished to witness the execution. Reverdil was greatly troubled by this and urged his pupil not to do so.

But the boy – he still calls him the boy – had read the sentence and felt it held an extraordinary attraction. In fact, before his execution, Sergeant Mörl had spent three months in prison, which had given him ample time for religious instruction.

By great fortune he had there fallen into the hands of a pastor who shared the beliefs of Count Zinzendorf, namely the faith commonly known as Moravianism, of which the Dowager Queen was also an adherent. In conversation with Christian – such conversations occurred but were of a purely pious nature – she had discussed the sentence and the imminent means of execution in detail and had informed him that the prisoner had become a Moravian. The prisoner Mörl had come to believe that the gruesome torments before life ended would unite him in a special way with the wounds of Jesus; yes, that even the torture, pain and wounds would allow him to be engulfed in the bosom of Jesus, to be drowned in the wounds of Jesus, and to be warmed by his blood.

The blood and wounds – all of this, in the Dowager Queen's descriptions – had been given a character that Christian found "delightful", and they had filled his dreams at night.

The executioner's cart would be a triumphant conveyance. The glowing tongs that would grip him, the whips, the nails, and finally the wheel – all of these things would be the cross on which he would be united with the blood of Jesus. In prison Mörl had also written hymns that were printed up and distributed for the edification of the public.

During these months the Dowager Queen and the boy became united in what was to Reverdil a repugnant fashion by their interest in this execution. He could not prevent Christian from watching it in secrecy.

Here the expression "in secrecy" has a particular significance in a legal sense. According to custom, if the King or Crown Prince happened to pass the site of the execution, it would mean that the prisoner had to be pardoned.

Christian had witnessed the execution from a closed coach that had been hired. No-one noticed him.

Sergeant Mörl had sung hymns; in a loud voice he declared his burning faith and desire to drown in the wounds of Jesus. But when the lengthy torture on the scaffold began, he could not endure it without breaking out into desperate screams, particularly when the nails punctured "those parts of his body and abdomen that were the centre of the greatest desire and the source of the greatest pain".

His desperation was then so devoid of piety and so wild that the hymns and prayers of the public were silenced; yes, the pious desire to see the martyr's departure from this life had dissolved, and many had left the area at a run.

But Christian had remained seated in his carriage until Sergeant Mörl at last gave up the ghost. He then returned to the palace, sought out Reverdil, fell to his knees before him, clasped his hands, and with anguish and bewilderment but in utter silence, stared at his teacher's face.

Not a word was said on that evening.

Here is what occurred the following night.

Reverdil happened to come by Christian's suite to tell him of a change in the next day's lessons. He stopped in the doorway and witnessed a scene that he says "paralysed" him. Christian was lying on the floor, stretched out on something meant to resemble a torture wheel. Two of his pages were in the process of "crushing his joints" – they were carrying out the execution by using rolled-up paper while the criminal on the wheel begged and moaned and wept.

Reverdil stood petrified but then stepped inside the room and ordered the pages to stop. With that, Christian ran off and afterwards refused to talk about what had happened.

A month later, when Christian mentioned to Reverdil that he could not sleep at night, Reverdil asked him to tell him the reasons for his torment. In tears, Christian then spoke of his belief that he "had become Mörl, who had escaped the hands of Justice, and that by mistake a phantom had been tortured and executed. This game of imitating someone who was put on the wheel and tortured filled his mind with dark ideas and increased his tendency towards melancholy".

4

Reverdil returns again and again to his dream that the light of the Enlightenment would come stealthily: the image of light rising slowly like dawn over the water.

It was the dream of the inevitable. For a long time he seems to have envisioned the development from darkness to light as inevitable, gentle, and free of violence.

Later he abandoned this idea.

With great caution Herr Reverdil tried to plant in the mind of the heir to the throne some of the seeds that he, as an enlightened man, wished to see bear fruit. When the boy, with great curiosity, asked if it would be possible for him to correspond with some of the philosophers who had created the great French encyclopedia, Reverdil replied that a certain Monsieur Voltaire, a Frenchman, might take an interest in the young Danish heir to the throne.

Christian then wrote a letter to Monsieur Voltaire. He received an answer.

In this manner the correspondence, which to posterity would seem so peculiar, began between Voltaire and the deranged King Christian VII of Denmark; the correspondence which is best known by the poem of homage Voltaire wrote in 1771 to Christian, who is heralded as the prince of light and reason in the North. It reached him one evening at Hirschholm, after he was already lost; but it made him happy.

With one of his first letters Monsieur Voltaire enclosed a book that he had himself written. During their afternoon walk Christian who had been urged by Reverdil to keep the correspondence strictly confidential – showed Reverdil this book, which he had read at once, and he recited a passage that had particularly appealed to him.

"But is it not the height of madness to believe that one can convert people and force their minds to submit by slandering them, by persecuting them, by banishing them to the galleys; or attempt to annihilate their ideas by dragging them to the gallows, the wheel, and the stake?"

"That's what Monsieur Voltaire thinks!" Christian triumphantly shouted. "That's what he thinks! He sent me this book! This book! To me!"

Reverdil whispered urgently to his pupil to lower his voice lest he arouse the suspicions of the courtiers who were following them at 30 paces. Christian at once hid the book in his tunic and, whispering, said that Monsieur Voltaire had told him in the letter that he was now being subjected to a legal proceeding that concerned the freedom of ideas; and that Christian, after reading this, had been instantly inspired to send 1,000 riksdaler in support of Monsieur Voltaire's fight for the freedom of expression.

He now asked his teacher whether he shared this view. Whether he ought to send the money. Herr Reverdil, after mustering his courage and suppressing his astonishment, supported the Heir to the Throne in this endeavour.

And later the sum was duly sent off.

On the same occasion Reverdil asked Christian why he wished to join Monsieur Voltaire in this battle, which was not without its risks. And which might be misunderstood, not only in Paris.

"Why?" he asked. "For what reason?"

And then Christian had quite simply and with surprise replied:

"For the sake of purity! Why else? For the purity of the temple!"

Herr Reverdil writes that this reply filled him with a joy that was nevertheless mixed with apprehension.

That same evening his misgivings seemed to be confirmed.

From his room he could hear an unusual commotion going on in the palace courtyard, shouts and the sounds of furniture smashing. Added to that came the sound of breaking glass. When he sprang to his feet he saw that a crowd of people had started to gather outside.

He dashed up to the Prince's apartments and found that Christian, in an apparent fit of confusion, had smashed the furniture in the drawing room next to his bedchamber and tossed the pieces out the window, that broken glass was scattered everywhere, and that two of his "favourites", as certain of the courtiers were called, had tried in vain to calm the Heir to the Throne, and make him stop these "excesses".

But not until Reverdil spoke to him in a forceful and pleading voice did Christian stop throwing furniture out the window.

"My child," Reverdil said, "my dear child, why are you doing this?"

Christian then stared at him in silence, as if he didn't understand how Reverdil could ask such a question. It all seemed quite clear to him.

The Dowager Queen's confidant, a professor at Sorø Academy by the name of Guldberg who served as Crown Prince Frederik's teacher and attendant, a man with peculiar icy-blue eyes but without any other special qualities and insignificant in appearance, had come rushing into the room at that moment. Reverdil was only able to whisper to the Prince:

"My dear child, not like this! Not like this!"

The boy was now calm. In the palace courtyard they began gathering up the splintered pieces.

Afterwards, Guldberg had taken Reverdil by the arm and asked to have a word with him. They stepped out into the corridor.

"Herr Reverdil," Guldberg said, "His Majesty needs a royal physician."

"Why?"

"A royal physician. We must find someone who can win his confidence and prevent his ... outbursts."

"Who?" asked Reverdil.

"We must begin to search," said Guldberg, "search with great care for the right person. Not a Jew."

"But why?" Reverdil asked in surprise.

"Because His Majesty is mad," Guldberg told him.

And Reverdil had not been able to think of a single reply.

5

On January 18, 1765, Councillor Bernstorff informed the young heir to the throne that the government, in its Tuesday cabinet meeting and after nearly two years of negotiation with the English government, had decided to marry him to the 13-year-old Princess Caroline Mathilde, sister to King George III of England.

The wedding would take place in November 1766.

Upon hearing the news of his betrothed's name, Christian had started in with his usual fidgeting, picking at his skin with his fingertips, drumming on his stomach, and moving his feet spastically. After receiving the news he asked:

"Do I need to learn any special words or lines for this purpose?"

Count Bernstorff did not fully comprehend the meaning of this question but replied with a kindly smile:

"Only those of love, Your Royal Highness."

When Frederik died and Christian was blessed, the rigorous upbringing ceased and the young King was ready. He was now prepared to exercise the full powers of an absolute ruler.

He was ready. He could enter into his new rôle. He was 16 years old.

Reverdil had accompanied him to his father's deathbed, witnessed the blessing, and then escorted Christian out. They had stood alone for a long time, hand in hand in the palace courtyard, in the light snow, until the boy stopped crying.

That same afternoon Christian was proclaimed King Christian VII.

Reverdil had stood behind him on the balcony. Christian wanted to hold his hand, but Reverdil had pointed out that this would not be fitting and would be against protocol. But before they stepped outside Christian, who was now shaking from head to toe, had asked Reverdil:

"What feeling should I be expressing right now?"

"Sorrow," Reverdil replied, "and after that joy at the cheers of the people."

But Christian became confused and forgot all about sorrow and despair, the whole time displaying a broad and dazzling smile, waving his arms at the people.

Many took offence at this. The newly crowned King had not shown the proper sorrow. When asked about this later, he was inconsolable; he said that he had forgotten his first line.

Chapter 3 · The English Child

I

Christian's chosen queen was named Caroline Mathilde. She was born on July 22, 1751 in Leicester House in London, and she lacked any talents whatsoever.

That was the perception of her. Yet she came to play a key rôle in what happened – something which no-one could have predicted and which filled everyone with dismay since it was commonly held that she lacked talents.

Afterwards everyone agreed that it was unfortunate that she did indeed have talents. If the proper assessment had been made from the outset, namely that she possessed *some* talents, then the entire catastrophe might have been averted.

But no-one could have predicted this.

Scratched into the windowpane of her bedchamber at Frederiksberg Palace they found, after she left the country, a motto she was presumed to have written on one of her first days in Denmark. It said:

"O, keep me innocent, make others great."

She arrived in Copenhagen on November 8, 1766. She was the youngest sister of King George III of England who, in 1765, 1788, and 1801, suffered severe attacks of madness, but who throughout his life was always faithful to his wife, Charlotte von Mecklenburg-Strelitz; his grandchild would become Queen Victoria.

Caroline Mathilde's father died two months before her birth; she was the youngest of nine siblings, and the only other trace left by her father in history is the appraisal given by King George II of his son: "My dear firstborn son is the greatest ass, the worst liar, the biggest rogue, and the most awful brute in the whole world, and I wish with all my heart that he would disappear from it." Her mother had a stern and closed nature, and for this reason her only lover was the eldest son's tutor, Lord Bute. She was an ardent believer, devoted to her religious duties, and she kept her nine children quite cut off from the world, inside her home which was said to be like "a cloister". Caroline Mathilde was very seldom permitted to set foot outside her home, and then only under strict supervision.

After the betrothal the Danish Ambassador, who was allowed to call on her and was given permission to speak to her for a few minutes, reported that she seemed shy, with a marvellous complexion, long blond hair, lovely blue eyes, full lips, although her lower lip was a bit wide, and in possession of a melodious voice.

He dwells the most, however, on his conversation with the mother, whom he describes as "bitter".

The English court painter Reynolds, who completed Caroline Mathilde's portrait before her departure, is actually the only person who gave any indication of her talents from that period. He describes his work on the portrait as difficult because she wept the entire time.

These are the only negative traits that can be confirmed from the period before her departure. A rather full lower lip, and constant weeping.

Upon hearing the news of her nuptials, Caroline Mathilde was terror-stricken.

In her view, the fact that she was the sister of England's King was the sole justification for her existence, and for this reason she had devised her motto: "O, keep me innocent, make others great."

Otherwise, for the most part, she wept. She was someone, namely a sister, but nothing more than that. She did not exist until her fifteenth year. Later on she refused to reveal any information about that first part of her life – other than to say that the news that she was to enter into a love relationship with the young Danish King came as a shock to her. She had grown up in a cloister. Her mother had decided this was necessary. The normal whoring at court was not for her, since she had been chosen. Whether for something great or small had not been made clear to her.

Yet she did manage to recognize that she was breeding stock. She would supply the peculiar little land of Denmark with a king. For that reason she had to be serviced. At the English court they gathered information about the Danish bull. They then passed this information on to her. She understood that the bull who was to service her was a delicate little boy; she had seen a portrait of him. He looked endearing. Not like a bull. People said the problem was that in all likelihood he was mad.

If he had not been one of God's chosen absolute rulers he would have been locked up.

It was well known that the Danish princes were mad. She had seen David Garrick in the rôle of Hamlet in the Drury Lane Theatre. That this should be her lot doubtless caused her despair.

In the autumn of 1765, chief lady-in-waiting Fru von Plessen arrived to help the Princess prepare. She was, according to her credentials, a person of integrity. Fru von Plessen had frightened the girl out of her wits by stating at once, without being asked, that everything said about the Danish heir to the throne was a slanderous lie. The "excesses" of the monarch-to-be did not exist. He did not smash furniture or windows. His temperament was even and stable. His whims were not the least bit alarming. Since no-one had asked for this refutation and the information was thus unnecessary, the girl was understandably terrified.

Privately she thought herself to be in possession of certain talents.

During the crossing to Denmark she wept the whole time. None of her chambermaids was allowed to accompany her any further than Altona. It was thought that she would better understand the Danish character, as well as the language, if she were confronted with them in a more direct manner.

The name of the Princess, the future Danish queen, meaning the English child who had been selected, was Caroline Mathilde. Her brother, the English King, whom she loved and admired, tolerated her but could not remember her name. He regarded her as charming, shy, docile, and nearly invisible. For this reason it was decided that she should be married to the Danish King, since Denmark, after the "Imperial War" in the 1600s when the country was ruled by the incessantly drunk Christian IV, had lost all its international importance, as well as most of its territories. Of Christian IV it was said at the English court that each time he thought his wife had betrayed him, he would be struck by melancholy. She betrayed him often, and his melancholy deepened. Each time, to counteract his sorrow and restlessness, he would start a war, which he just as regularly lost.

The fact that the country was steadily shrinking was therefore due to his wife's insatiable sexual appetite. This was typical of the Danish kingdom, which therefore had to be labelled insignificant.

She was told all of this. Due to the King's repeated bouts of melancholy, Denmark had become a very small country. The international weakness of the kingdom, which had continued ever since, explained

46

why the selected queen could be someone without talents and of no importance.

She understood this. Gradually she also came to understand that her future would not be bright in this Nordic land, which was described as a madhouse. That was why she was always weeping. Her tears were a talent. They frightened no-one. About her intelligence the opinion was divided. But above all else she was regarded as entirely lacking in will. Perhaps even in character. And so the rôle she later came to play in the events connected with the Danish revolution filled everyone with great astonishment – and dismay.

She became a different person. This was completely unexpected. But now, at the time of her nuptials, she was still weak-willed and without character.

As a young girl she seems to have had a dream of purity. The way she grew up was unexpected. It was only natural for a woman without talents to have dreams, just as she viewed innocence and greatness as opposites but chose the former. What frightened everyone was the fact that later, after she had been defined as weak-willed and without talents, she became a different person.

O, keep me innocent, make others great.

3

She was escorted from England to Denmark; she arrived in Rotterdam after a difficult six-day voyage by sea, and on October 18 she reached Altona, where everyone in her English entourage took leave of her.

In Altona the Danish delegation took custody of the Princess. She was then escorted by carriage through Slesvig and Fyn, "greeted everywhere with wild enthusiasm" by the populace that had been summoned to appear, and on November 3 she reached Roskilde, where she was to meet King Christian VII of Denmark.

For this purpose a glass pavilion with two doors had been erected in the marketplace. The two young lovers were supposed to enter through separate doors and walk forward, meeting at the centre, where they would see each other for the first time. In a merchant's house next to the "glass palace" (as it inappropriately came to be called during the weeks it existed), preparations for the queen-to-be were finalized; they involved reassuring the Princess. Chief lady-in-waiting Flu von Plessen, who was in charge of the escort delegation, had taken pains to quell the little English girl's tears (the expression "the little English girl" was now being used throughout the Danish court) and had urged her not to show her terror before the public.

She had replied that the terror she felt had nothing to do with the Danish Court or the King but rather with love. Upon further questioning it turned out that she could make no clear distinction between these three concepts, but that the Court, the King, and Love, these three things had merged together in her worldview and were associated with "terror".

Fru von Plessen was finally forced to rehearse all the ceremonial moves of the Princess, as if merely remembering the details of the ceremony would reassure the girl.

She spoke soothingly to the 15-year-old, who was dissolved in tears. Take small, slow steps towards His Majesty, she advised. Keep your eyes lowered, count out 15 steps, raise your eyes, look at him, display a modest but happy little smile, take another three steps forward, stop. I will be ten paces behind you.

The girl had nodded as she wept and, sobbing, repeated in French: "Fifteen steps. Smile happily."

Upon succeeding to the throne at the beginning of the year, King Christian VII had received a dog as a gift from his tutor Reverdil; it was a schnauzer, to which over time he became deeply attached. For the meeting with the little English girl in Roskilde he was supposed to arrive by carriage with a great entourage, directly from Copenhagen.

Seated in the King's calash, together with Christian, was a former professor at Sorø Academy by the name of Guldberg, along with the

King's teacher Reverdil and a courtier by the name of Brandt, who played an important rôle in the events that would later take place. Guldberg, who under normal circumstances should not have been seated in the King's carriage since his position at court was still much too insignificant, came along for reasons that will become apparent.

Also in the carriage was the dog, which sat the whole time on Christian's knee.

Before the meeting, Guldberg, who was well versed in classical literature, had especially composed for the meeting a declaration of love that was based on sections of a play by Racine, and in the carriage he was giving what Reverdil in his memoirs calls "the last reassuring directions before the love meeting".

Begin forcefully, Guldberg said to His Majesty, who seemed quite distracted and was desperately hugging the little dog in his arms. The Princess must understand His Majesty's strong passion well before the first meeting. Tempo! "I bow to the god of love . . . I BOW to the god of love . . ." Tempo! Tempo!

The mood in the carriage was strained, and the King's tics and twitchings were at times wilder than ever. Upon arrival Guldberg hinted that the dog should not be present at the love meeting of the royal couple but should be left behind in the carriage. Christian at first refused to let go of the dog but was finally forced to do so.

The dog whimpered and then could be seen barking fiercely in the window of the calash. Reverdil writes that this was "one of the most agonizing moments of the boy's life. Finally, however, he seemed as apathetic as if he were walking in a dream."

The word "terror" recurs frequently. But in the end Princess Caroline Mathilde and her betrothed, Christian VII, did everything nearly perfectly.

A chamber orchestra was positioned next to the glass pavilion. The twilight was very beautiful. The square surrounding the pavilion was filled with thousands of people, who were held back by soldiers standing guard in double rows.

At the same moment, and accompanied by music, the two young royal personages stepped through the doors. They approached one another just as the ceremony prescribed. When they stood three paces from each other the music fell silent. The Princess had gazed steadily at Christian but with an expression that seemed lifeless, or as if she – she too – were walking in a dream.

Christian held the poem in his hand, printed out on a sheet of paper. When they at last stood motionless, facing each other, he said:

"I will now declare my love, dear Princess."

He then waited for a word from her, but she merely looked at him in utter silence. His hands were shaking but at last he mustered his courage and read Guldberg's declaration of love which, like the play it was based on, was in French:

> I bow to the God of Love where'er I go
> Helpless beneath thy power I am brought low
> Before thy beauty astonishment holds sway
> Thy lovely image enchants me when thou art away
> Deep in the woods thy image doth me delight
> In light of day or e'en in darkest night
> My love for thee, a light that shall never fail
> See, that is the reason thou art my Holy Grail

She then gestured with her hand, perhaps by mistake; but he perceived this as a sign for him to stop. He therefore stopped reading and gave her an inquiring glance. After a moment she said:

"Thank you."

"Perhaps that's enough," he whispered.

"Yes, it's enough."

"With these words I wish to profess my ardour for you," he said.

"I feel the same ardour for you, Your Majesty," she whispered, her lips moving almost imperceptibly. Her face was quite pale, her tears had been powdered over, and her face seemed almost whitewashed.

"Thank you."

"Shall we end the ceremony now?" she asked.

He bowed. At a sign from the master of ceremonies, the music started up once more, and the betrothed couple, terrified but in perfect unison, proceeded towards the greater ceremonies, which included the cheering crowds, the arrival in Copenhagen, the wedding, their brief marriage, and the Danish revolution.

On November 8 at 7:30 the young couple entered the cathedral in Copenhagen, where the formal blessing of the marriage would take place. The festivities continued for six days. "Immeasurable hopes rest with the captivating English Queen", writes the British Ambassador in his report to London.

Her conduct was viewed as irreproachable.

No protests against Christian. No outbursts, no *faux pas*. Furthermore, the dog was excluded from the wedding ceremony.

4

In his growing confusion, Christian considered court life to be like the theatre; the performance in which he and the little English girl were now participating was also a depiction of morals. The play dealt with immorality, or "integrity" as Christian called it; but was it piety that prompted lechery or was it *ennui*?

What voluptuousness can be found in contemporary descriptions of the lechery and *ennui* at court! That insular world of courtiers, mistresses, whores, and masked balls, those intrigues alluding to titles and *apanage* but not to work, that endlessly drawn-out dance of absurd intrigues which were linked to one another and which, for posterity's sake, are reflected only in the official texts: which are respectable and learned, perfectly composed correspondence, in French of course, and collected in those exquisite volumes. They provide a description of the way in which the actors in the madhouse carried out their absurdities, which were both tedious and lecherous.

How natural it seemed, in the eyes of posterity, for the outbursts and bizarre actions of the mad King Christian to fit in with the stage sets of the madhouse.

How inextricably linked were piety, lechery, and those who had been ravaged.

There was a great deal of concern about Christian's sex life.

One contemporary explanation in particular is often given for Christian's melancholy, his peculiar fits of rage, his inexplicable spells of despair, and finally his periods of daylong apathy. At the early age of 13 he was introduced to a vice by a favourite named Sperling, who thenceforth disappears from history, which paralysed his will and prompted his dementia and increasing physical weakness. This vice shows up in all the testimonies of the time. The vice is seldom described in direct terms, although several testimonies do venture the leap; the vice is masturbation.

Christian's manic way of quelling his melancholy by means of this vice gradually weakened his spine, assaulted his heart, and contributed to the tragedy that was to come. Madly, for hours, he would try to masturbate forth some form of coherence or try to masturbate away his confusion. But it never seemed to be enough. The arrival of the little English girl had only made everything worse.

Something had collapsed. He seemed at his wits' end.

Reverdil's notes express sorrow, but more than that: "At long last I discovered that what I called 'upbringing' consisted, in his worldview, of those 'hardening' experiences which would help him to make 'progress'. They essentially consisted of rebelling against everything that belonged to his childhood and adolescence, perhaps even against the very court in which he lived. To this end there was no behaviour so aberrant, excessive, or violent that he wouldn't employ it. He grouped all of them under the expression 'becoming healthy', which meant free of scruples, dignity, and pedantry. I then told him that his task was to set the kingdom on its feet again. The kingdom he had inherited was in greater debt and weighed down by more taxes after 85 years of peace than it would have been after a war. I told him that he should try to resolve the nation's debts and ease the people's burdens, a goal he could achieve by abolishing all the unnecessary expenses of the royal household, by reducing the army, by emancipating the peasantry in Denmark, and through sensible legislation that would foster Norway's fishing, mining and forestry."

His response was to go into his room and masturbate.

He refused to visit the Queen. Towards her he felt only terror.

Christian had many faces. One is suffused with terror, confusion, and hatred. Another is bent forward, calm, leaning over the letter he is writing to Monsieur Voltaire, who was the one, by his own testimony, who had taught him to think.

Enevold Brandt was seated in the royal calash on the way to Roskilde.

He belonged to the Altona circle of enlightened men who gathered around Count Rantzau and the young German doctor Struensee in the early 1760s.

He was now in Copenhagen. He was now a climber.

He was driven by an irrepressible desire to please the ladies while at the same time establishing his career at court, and for this reason he sought the title that would best satisfy both of his ambitions. In one of his later letters to Voltaire, Reverdil writes that the Danish court, more than any other, was ruled by those who were title-hungry. "There's a proverb that in France people ask: Is he an educated man? In Germany: Does he come from a good family? In Holland: How large is his fortune? But in Denmark: What is his title? Here life is largely marked by this title hierarchy. Moving from one room to another is done by rank, sitting down at the table likewise, the servants present the dishes in accordance with rank, and if you meet an intelligent and clever man who is the last through the door, meaning he has no title, and you ask who he is, the answer will be: He's nobody. Consequently, those who *are* somebody possess great prestige, rank high in *apanage*, and accomplish nothing, but are merely parasites guarding their rank."

Enevold Brandt, however, saw himself as an artist; he had a lively personality, played the flute, and succeeded in capturing the title of theatre director, later *maître de plaisir*, that is, cultural minister, and grand master of the robes, with the right to be addressed as Excellency.

Unlike other rôles, the rôle of cultural minister included practical duties, which meant power. Among them were summoning the French theatre troupes as well as organizing entertainment and masked balls for the court. He also had influence over and access to the ladies of the theatre troupes, which for many became an imperative reason for promoting the art of the theatre.

Maître de plaisir was therefore the title that was most sought after.

Brandt was also concerned about the King's sex life. One reason was that five months after the marriage of King Christian VII to Caroline Mathilde, no sexual intercourse had yet occurred between the royal personages.

That was horrifying.

At this time Brandt had organized a riding tournament in the palace courtyard. For the event a wooden grandstand had been constructed in which members of the court were invited to take their places according to rank. Armour-clad knights on horseback jousted against each other, and contests of various kinds were arranged.

One of these contests consisted of the jousters racing towards hanging rings to spear them with the lance. The rings hung from ropes that swung back and forth, making the task of the contestants all the more difficult.

One of the contestants missed his first two attempts but succeeded in spearing the third ring. Triumphantly he turned his horse around, made it rear up, and held his lance pointed upward at an angle.

The Queen was seated at King Christian's side. Behind her, off to the side, sat Enevold Brandt. Behind the King was the tutor Guldberg; during recent months, in an odd way, he seemed to have drawn closer to the centre, although he was still quite insignificant.

The royal couple had watched the tournament with expressionless faces. Christian, who under other circumstances certainly would have enjoyed the festivities, seemed paralysed with shame and distaste because of the Queen's intimate presence; she was seated only five inches away. Brandt leaned forward and whispered in the Queen's ear:

"I am already rejoicing at the occasion when the royal lance will be equally victorious."

The Queen then rose indignantly and departed.

Afterwards Guldberg asked Brandt what he had said. Brandt responded with the truth. Guldberg did not admonish him but said merely:

"In his great anguish and confusion, His Majesty needs help and support."

Brandt took this to be a pronouncement that might be considered a form of advice. Yet Guldberg was an insignificant man. How could this be construed as a form of advice, coming from someone so insignificant?

Perhaps Brandt had seen his eyes.

The next day the Queen was sitting on a chair in the palace courtyard.

Christian approached, walking slowly.

As he passed her without saying a word, giving only a small bow, she said in a low voice:

"Christian?"

He pretended not to hear.

She then repeated in a louder voice, almost shouting:

"Christian!"

He merely hastened his steps.

*

It was horrifying. But that wasn't all.

During her visit to England, Fru von Plessen had had a long conversation with Caroline Mathilde's mother. They found that they held common views on many things. The court was a pestilence. Immorality flourished. Purity had to be protected.

As the months passed, Fru von Plessen was seized by a strong, almost burning devotion to the young girl. They developed a bond that was strengthened by the King's aloofness. Fru von Plessen did not grieve over the King's coldness. On the contrary, she saw how it increased the Queen's attachment to her, her dependence, and perhaps with time also her love.

As for the Queen, Fru von Plessen had developed a strategy for "propagating" the King's love and for breaking through the inexplicable wall of ice that now seemed to have arisen between the spouses. The Queen was to appear unapproachable and thereby summon forth his love. A decisive event occurred five months after the Queen's arrival in Denmark.

One evening at around ten o'clock, to everyone's surprise, Christian came to the Queen's suite and announced that he wished to meet with the Queen before she retired for the night.

His intention was all too clear.

Fru von Plessen then explained that the Queen had planned to play a game of chess with her, and Christian would have to wait.

They started their chess game.

Christian wandered around the room with an expression of growing annoyance, which greatly amused the two women. At midnight the game was over, upon the whispered advice of Fru von Plessen. As the two conspirators exchanged secretive laughs, the Queen said that she wanted a rematch.

Fru von Plessen informed the King of this "with a triumphant smile", whereupon he left the room in a fury, slamming the door behind him.

For the next two weeks the King refused to speak to the Queen. He looked away whenever they met; he didn't say a word. The Queen was then seized with despair, but also with rancour towards Fru von Plessen.

It was after this that the event reported by Guldberg occurred. The Queen was lying apathetically on her bed. She asked why Christian didn't come. She told Fru von Plessen to leave. And the Queen then had the unfortunate conversation with Guldberg in which she asked him about release from passion, composure and emptiness; and then she leaned so provocatively towards him that her almost exposed bosom had shouted an affront to him, making him aware of the little English whore's wantonness, of how dangerous she would come to be, and that here was the source of the contagion of sin.

He saw it. That was the source.

That was how it happened.

5

The person who finally convinced Christian to conquer his terror was Reverdil.

He implored Christian to overcome his distaste and make himself hard. Just once, to silence the gossip and to show that he was a man. Later the same day Reverdil saw Christian sitting on the floor with his dog in front of him, muttering to the animal, as if explaining some important problem; and the dog was attentively regarding his master's face.

That very night Christian paid a visit to the Queen's bedchamber.

He didn't say a word, but she understood.

He performed the intercourse with his eyes shut tight in fury.

The young Queen tried in vain to caress his thin white back, but he performed the servicing in spite of it. Nine months later she gave birth to a son, Frederik.

That was the only time he ever came to visit her.

Chapter 4 · The Sovereign of the Universe

I

The portraits of them that exist from this period are in a certain sense misleading. The paintings seem to show adult individuals. Yet that was not the case.

When the conflict between the royal couple intensified in the spring of 1767, Christian was 18 years old, Caroline Mathilde was 15.

It's easy to forget that they were still adolescents. If the portraits were truthful and correct, they would depict dread, terror, but also uncertainty and an air of expectation.

Nothing yet firmly established. As if anything were still possible.

Fru von Plessen was a problem.

There was something about her exaggerated solicitude that had made the Queen, either out of rage or bewilderment, tell her to leave. But Fru von Plessen was the only one who cared. What alternative did she have? Other than silence or the court's rhetoric, which held that the Queen was merely an object. Fru von Plessen was the one who talked to her, advised her, worried about her, listened to her.

Fru von Plessen was a problem, but she was still the only real human being around. So after that one chance quarrel, they renewed their close companionship.

An apparently insignificant event, an incident that occurred three weeks after the King's sexual intercourse with the Queen, ended up causing a crisis.

This is what happened.

One morning Christian came to see the Queen as she was dressing. The Queen, with Fru von Plessen's assistance, was in the midst of tying a silk scarf around her neck. The King then brushed it aside "with his face" and pressed his lips to her throat. Fru von Plessen turned away, looking as if this were a demonstration of the utmost indecency, and made a sign to the Queen; then she too displayed an angry face and observed that it was unseemly, and the silk scarf would be wrinkled.

Christian felt humiliated. The situation seemed childish and comical, hardly befitting a monarch. He had been chastised like a child. He hadn't planned the gesture, but perhaps this loving act seemed far too premeditated to appear natural.

He had made himself ridiculous and was chastised like a child. He had tried to kiss her throat. It looked ridiculous. He was embarrassed. Fru von Plessen had triumphed. It was clear that the two women were acting in collusion.

Christian was enraged by what he perceived as an insult; he grabbed, or rather tore, the scarf away from the Queen, ripped it to shreds, and furiously took his leave.

That was the decisive incident. Once again: They were 18 and 15.

The next day the King issued an edict proclaiming that chief lady-in-waiting Fru von Plessen had fallen out of favour; she was banished from the court and ordered to leave Copenhagen at once. She was given no opportunity to say farewell to the Queen.

She would end up taking residence in Celle.

The Queen learned of the banishment the day after her rash behaviour.

She was then seized by a great rage, rushed in to the King, and showered her consort with furious abuse. Christian was once again seized by that nervousness which manifested itself in twitching gestures and tics. Stammering, he explained to her that he suspected Fru von Plessen of being an evil and perverse woman who harboured an unnatural love for the Queen. She screamed in reply that it was a lie, that as a matter of fact she didn't care what was natural, unnatural, or perverse about her friend, especially considering the perverse state of the court, but that Fru von Plessen was the only one she could talk to. The only one who listened to her, and the only one who spoke to her as if she were a real human being.

It was a formidable performance. In a rage, the Queen walked out, having heaped abuse on Christian to the end. During the following weeks she greeted him only with contempt and revulsion.

She wept a great deal at this time. She refused to eat, merely wept. She said that she was particularly distressed at not being allowed to say farewell to her friend.

Yet they would meet again, much later, in Celle.

2

Following this came the episode with Bottine Caterine. It began on May 4, 1767, late in the evening.

Her name was Anna Catharine Beuthaken; her stepfather was a shoemaker, hence her nickname, Bottine, the French word for "ankle boot". She had once been an actress but "from this profession had slid onto the path of vice".

She was a prostitute.

She was of above average height, well built, and with very feminine curves. When Christian VII made her acquaintance she was 24 years old and "the most notorious person in all of Copenhagen".

In paintings we see a beautiful face with a hint of Negroid features; her mother supposedly had Creole blood. She was strong-willed and, if crossed, was known to knock down and assault with astonishing force men whom no other woman had the courage to confront.

By this time the crisis between the royal couple was a common topic of conversation at court. The King seemed unnaturally eager to seek out solitude; he sank more and more into melancholy, sitting on a chair alone, staring at the wall and mumbling. He was seized with inexplicable fits of rage, he issued orders that were capricious, and he was gripped with suspicion even towards those closest to him.

He seemed more and more preoccupied with conversing with his dog, to whom he muttered about "guilt" and "punishment". But no-one could have predicted the peculiar punishment he would mete out for his guilt.

It fell upon the one he loved most: Reverdil.

One day after Fru von Plessen had been banished and the chill between the two young spouses had grown unbearable, Christian came over to his former Swiss teacher Reverdil at the theatre, embraced him, and assured him with tears in his eyes that he loved and respected him, that Reverdil stood closest to his heart. Then Christian handed him a letter which he asked him to read later that evening.

The letter said that Reverdil no longer had the King's favour, that he must immediately leave the court and the King's service, and that he would not be allowed to stay in Denmark.

It was incomprehensible. Reverdil returned to Switzerland at once.

The following day Christian paid a visit to Caroline Mathilde in her room and told her about it. He sat on a chair by the door, pressing his hands between his knees as if to conceal his twitches and spasms, and told her that he had banished Reverdil. Then he fell silent and waited. The Queen did not understand. She merely asked him what the reason might be.

Why had he done this to Reverdil?

He replied that this was the punishment. "Punishment for what?" she asked him.

He simply repeated that this was the punishment, and that the punishment was necessary.

She stared at him and said that he was mad.

They sat there for quite a while, in silence, on separate chairs in the Queen's sitting room, and stared at each other. Then, after quite a long time, Christian stood up and left.

It was quite incomprehensible. Nothing changed between them. What the word "punishment" meant, she never understood. But the punishment changed nothing.

3

Her name was Anna Catharine Beuthaken, she was called Bottine Caterine, and she was a prostitute. The instability and melancholy of the King was a fact. Enevold Brandt and a courtier by the name of Holck, known for his interest in the theatre and Italian actresses, then decided that Bottine Caterine might be a solution to the King's melancholy.

They resolved to introduce her as a surprise, without mentioning her to the King beforehand. So one evening Brandt escorted Bottine Caterine to the King's suite.

She was dressed in man's attire, her hair was long and henna-red, and the first thing Christian noticed was that she was a head taller than the two courtiers.

He thought she was very beautiful, but he fell into terrified muttering.

He knew at once what was about to take place.

His idea of the word "innocence" was not clear. He seems to have used it interchangeably with "purity" and with "invulnerability".

In his view, apart from the experience he had acquired during the servicing of the Queen, he was at that time still innocent. At court there was a great deal of talk about this, about the "boy's" inexperience – and the news had spread. At the masked balls the ladies, many of whom were either mistresses or coquettes expressly invited for the occasion, often spoke with the King and did not hesitate to let him know that they were at his disposal.

The general impression was that he appeared friendly, shy, but also terrified at the thought of carrying out in practice what they had suggested. There was a great deal of talk about his vice diminishing his strength, and many grieved over this.

Now Bottine Caterine was escorted to his chambers. Now it was serious.

Brandt had brought along goblets of wine, and with jests he tried to lighten the mood, which was very strained. No-one knew how the King would react to the suggestions that would now be put before him.

Caterine went over to the bed, calmly inspected it, and said kindly to the King:

"Come on, Your Majesty."

She then walked slowly over to Christian and began to undress. She started with her jacket and let it fall to the floor, taking off garment after garment until at last she stood naked before His Majesty. She was a true redhead, with ample buttocks and large breasts; she had undressed slowly and matter-of-factly, and was now waiting for Christian, who merely stared at her.

"Christian?" she said in a friendly voice. "Don't you want to, dear?"

The unexpected intimacy in the way she addressed him — using the word "dear" — shocked everyone, but no-one said a word. Christian simply turned on his heel and at first headed for the door, but perhaps remembering the guards stationed outside, he turned again and walked to the window, which was hidden behind drapes; his wandering around the room was completely aimless. His hands now started their restless plucking movements that were so characteristic of him. He drummed his fingers against his stomach but said nothing.

The silence lasted a long time. Christian stared stubbornly at the window drapes.

Holck then said to Brandt:

"Show him."

Brandt, who was seized with uncertainty, began reciting in an affected voice something that he had prepared but that now seemed inappropriate in Caterine's presence.

"Your Majesty, since the Queen, due to her young age, may perhaps be reluctant with regard to the holy sacrament offered by the royal member, there are several historical episodes worth recalling. Even the great Paracelsus writes in his . . ."

"Doesn't he want to?" Caterine asked matter-of-factly.

Brandt went over to Caterine, embraced her, and with an almost shrill laugh began to caress her.

"What the hell are you doing?" she asked.

She had been looking the whole time at Christian standing at the window. Christian turned around and looked at Caterine with an expression that none of them could decipher.

"I will now demonstrate on this object what the Queen should do . . . if she is seized with terror at the royal member . . ."

"Terror?" Christian automatically repeated, as if he didn't understand a word.

"Bend over," Brandt said to Caterine. "I'm going to show him."

But Caterine was all of a sudden and quite inexplicably seized with rage; she pulled away and almost spat at Brandt:

"Can't you see that he's scared? Leave him alone!"

"Shut up," roared Brandt.

Despite being a head shorter than she, he then tried to force her down onto the bed and began to take off his clothes; but in a fury Caterine turned over, violently raised her knee, and struck Brandt so skilfully between his legs that he sank to the floor with a howl.

"You're not going to demonstrate anything on any damned object," Caterine told him savagely.

Brandt lay curled in a ball on the floor with hatred in his eyes, groping for support to pull himself up; and then they all heard Christian start to laugh, as if he were happy. After only a brief moment of surprised hesitation, Caterine joined in.

The two of them were the only ones laughing.

"Out!" Christian then ordered both of the favourites. "Be gone!"

In silence they left the room.

Bottine Caterine hesitated, but after a moment she started to get dressed. When her upper body was once again covered but she was still naked below, where her red hair was the most visible, she stood still, without speaking, and merely looked at Christian. At last she said to the King, in a voice that all of a sudden sounded quite shy and

64

bore no resemblance to the voice she had just used towards Brandt:

"Damn it all," she said. "You mustn't be scared of me."

With a hint of amazement in his voice, Christian then said:

"You . . . knocked him . . . to the ground."

"Yes, I did."

"Cleansed . . . cleansed . . . the temple."

She gave him an inquisitive glance, then went over to him, stood quite close to him, and touched his cheek.

"The temple?" she asked.

He said nothing, explained nothing. He just looked at her, and his body was still trembling. Then she said to him in a hushed voice:

"Dear, you shouldn't put up with this shit, Your Majesty."

He was not upset by her addressing him both as "dear" and "Your Majesty". He just stared at her, but he was calmer now. The trembling in his hands subsided bit by bit, and he no longer seemed filled with terror.

"You mustn't be scared of me," she said. "You should be scared of those swine. They are swine. It's good you told those damned swine to go. And forcefully."

"Forcefully?"

She took his hand and led him to the bed, where they both sat down.

"You're so delicate," she said. "Like a little flower."

He stared at her, as if with inexpressible amazement.

"A . . . flower?"

He began sobbing, cautiously, as if he were ashamed; but paying no mind, she slowly began to undress him.

He didn't try to stop her.

She took off one garment after another. He didn't stop her. His figure seemed so small, fragile and thin next to her body, but he let it happen.

They lay down on the bed. She held his body in her arms for a long, long time, caressing it, and at last he stopped sobbing. She covered both of them with an eiderdown coverlet. He fell asleep.

Towards morning they made love without a sound, and when she left he was sleeping like a happy child.

4

Two days later he went looking for Caterine, and he found her.

He put on a grey cloak, convinced he would not be recognized; he ignored the fact that two soldiers followed him at a distance, even now.

He found her in Christianshavn.

He had woken in the afternoon after his first night with Caterine, and he lay quietly in bed for a long time.

He could not recall what had happened. It seemed impossible to remember. This rôle was new to him.

Perhaps it wasn't a rôle.

He felt as if he were floating in warm water, as if he were a foetus floating in the womb, and knew that this lingering feeling came from her. The servicing of the Queen had left him with the feeling that he was unclean, since his terror had been so great. Now he was no longer "innocent", but to his surprise this was not something that filled him with pride; no, it wasn't pride. Because he knew that innocence was something that everyone lost. But who was able to regain his innocence? That night he had regained his innocence. Now he was a foetus. Therefore he could be reborn, perhaps as a bird, perhaps as a horse, perhaps as a human being, and in that case as a peasant wandering through a field. He could be born free of guilt. He could rise up again from this womb. That was the beginning.

With Caterine he had regained the innocence he had lost with the Queen.

The moments when he imagined that the court was the whole world and nothing existed outside of it, those were the moments when he was filled with dread.

That's when the dreams about Sergeant Mörl recurred.

Before he had the dog, any regular sleep had been impossible; when they gave him the dog, it was better. The dog slept in his bed, and he could practise his lines with the animal.

The dog would sleep while he repeated his lines until the terror disappeared.

It was worse outside the world of the court. He had always been afraid of Denmark. Denmark was what existed outside of his lines. Outside there were no lines to practise and what was outside didn't fit together with what was inside.

Outside it was so inconceivably filthy and bewildering, everybody seemed to be working and preoccupied, and rituals were not observed; he felt a strong admiration for what was outside and dreamed of fleeing there. In his letters and writings Monsieur Voltaire had told him about how things ought to be outside. Outside there was also something called goodness.

Outside existed the greatest goodness and the greatest evil, such as the execution of Sergeant Mörl. But no matter what it was like, it was impossible to learn by heart.

It was the breach of ritual that both enticed and frightened him.

Caterine was a paragon of goodness. A paragon because there was nothing like her and because her goodness included him and excluded everything else.

That was why he went looking for her. And that was why he found her.

5

When he arrived she served him milk and rolls. It was inexplicable.

He drank the milk and ate a roll.

It was like a Holy Communion, he thought.

*

No, the court was not the whole world, but he thought that he had found paradise; it resided in a tiny room behind the bordello at Studiestræde 12.

That was where he found her.

There were no tapestries like at court. There was, however, a bed; and for a few rather painful moments, it occurred to him what went on in that bed and who made use of it; this flickered past him like the drawings that Holck had once shown him, which he borrowed and later used whenever he practised his vice; the vice in which he touched his own member while he looked at the pictures. Why had Almighty God given him this vice? Was it a sign that he belonged to The Seven? And how could someone who was one of God's chosen have a vice that was a worse sin than the fornication at court? The pictures flashed past him when he saw her bed, but he made himself invulnerable and they were gone.

He only practised his vice whenever he grew restless and thought about guilt. The vice made him calm. He regarded the vice as a means given to him by Almighty God to calm him. Now the pictures flickered past and he brushed them aside.

Caterine was not part of these images that signified vice and guilt.

He caught sight of her bed, the pictures came, then he made himself hard, and the pictures disappeared. Caterine had given him the sign. The milk and rolls were a sign. When he looked at her he was back in the warm womb again, with no pictures. She asked no questions. They undressed.

No lines to forget.

They made love. He crept over her like a slender white flower stalk above her dark body. He remembered the incomprehensible thing she had said to him, that he was like a flower. Only Caterine could say such a thing without making him laugh. For her, everything was pure. From him, and from herself! From herself she had driven out the hawkers of impurity.

It meant that she was a temple.

Afterwards, when he lay on top of her, sweaty and empty, he began to whisper and ask questions. Was I strong? He asked. Caterine, you must tell me, was I strong, strong? Idiot, she said at first, but in such a way that it made him happy. Then he asked her again. Yes, dearest, she told him. Hush now, you must learn not to ask questions, not to talk, do you ask those kinds of questions at the palace? Hush, sleep now. Do you know who I am? He asked, but she merely laughed. I am! I am! A peasant boy born 18 years ago in Hirtshals of poor parents, and I'm somebody else, somebody other than you think. Yes, yes, she whispered. Don't you think I'm like a peasant boy, you who know so many?

There was utter silence for a long time.

"Yes," she said at last. "You seem like a little peasant boy I once knew."

"Before . . . ?"

"Before I came here."

"Before?"

"Before I came here."

"Caterine, before . . ."

The sweat had dried, but he was still lying on top of her, and then he heard her whisper:

"I never should have left him. Never. Never."

He began to mutter, at first without making much sense, but little by little more clearly and furiously; not addressed to her but regarding the idea of leaving, or was it about being left? How difficult it was being a changeling. He muttered on. That he had been exchanged, that he couldn't sleep at night. And about his vice and that he had seen her coming towards him one night in the dark, hand in hand with Sergeant Mörl, who demanded that the big punishment be exacted from Christian.

Since he was a stray.

"Do you know," he said, just before sleep overwhelmed him, "do you know whether there exists a sovereign of the universe who stands above the God of wrath? Do you know whether such a benefactor exists?"

"Yes," she told him.

"Who is it?" he asked from the depths of sleep.

"It's me," she said.

"And you will be my benefactor? And you have time?"

"I have time," she whispered. "I have all the time in the universe."

And he understood. She was the Sovereign of the Universe. She had time. She had time.

It was after midnight when they heard a pounding on the door. The royal guards had grown uneasy.

He rolled off her body. The pounding continued. She got up, wrapping a shawl around herself.

Then she said to him:

"They're looking for you. Make yourself hard, Christian."

They both dressed quickly. He stopped at the door, as if terror had taken hold of him and he felt overwhelmed. Then she stroked his cheek. And with caution he opened the door.

The two livery-clad servants regarded the ill-matched pair with undisguised curiosity and greeted the monarch deferentially, but all of a sudden one of them started to laugh.

Bottine Caterine slipped her hand almost imperceptibly into her pocket, a very thin knife became visible in her grasp, and with a swiftness that caught all of them by surprise, she brushed the knife, as gently as if it were a bird's wing, across the cheek of the man who thought the situation worthy of laughter.

The livery-clad man lurched backward and fell. The cut was bright red and the blood ran fast and steady; he howled with astonishment and rage and reached for the hilt of his rapier. But King Christian VII – for at that moment they all thought of him as such, as the absolute ruler chosen by God – began to laugh.

And thus the rapier could not be drawn; not when the King chose to laugh in that manner.

70

"And now, Christian," said Bottine Caterine calmly, "now we're going to paint the town red."

Afterwards a great deal was said about what went on. The King's will was everyone's command, and Caterine was the Queen of the Night.

She accompanied him all the way home. He had stumbled, was covered with mud, and dead drunk. One of his hands was bloody.

She was still beautifully dressed. At the gate the guards discovered that it was the King who approached; thus she could leave him in good hands and be gone. Where she went was not their concern, but when he realized that she was gone, Christian seemed quite inconsolable.

The guards thought they heard him say "beloved ... beloved", although later they could not attest to this.

They carried him inside.

6

Their relationship lasted almost six months. He was convinced it would never end.

Yet it was bound to end.

The turning point occurred at a performance in the Royal Theatre of Cerill's comedy *The Wondrous Garden*. The King had often accompanied Bottine Caterine to masked balls at court; she would sit in his box at the theatre, they would play a game of cards called "Farao", in full view of everyone, and afterwards they would stroll among the members of the court. This time she took off her mask. The King had his arm around Caterine's waist, and they laughed and conversed with great familiarity.

The court was in shock.

Not because of the existence of a coquette among them. It was because of the growing suspicion that this woman, if accepted as the royal mistress, was not going to be content with her influence over His Majesty in bed; she had greater and more dangerous ambitions.

She had laughed in their faces.

Such hatred, and it frightened them so! What manner of revenge was she brooding over? What sort of wrongs were concealed in her silence and smiles? What had she endured to motivate such hatred? It frightened everyone. What was it that shone in her eyes as she walked among them, with the arm of the little kinglike boy around her waist?

What promise did her eyes hold?

Since the Dowager Queen Juliane Marie – who was Christian's stepmother but who wanted her own son Frederik to inherit the throne – had seen what those eyes promised, she summoned Ove Høegh-Guldberg to discuss, as she wrote in her message, a matter which demanded the utmost haste.

She arranged to meet him in the palace chapel. The choice of meeting place surprised Guldberg. But, as he writes, "perhaps Her Majesty wished for the utmost secrecy, and that could only be achieved under the watchful eyes of God". When Guldberg arrived, he found the chapel deserted except for a solitary figure sitting in the front pew.

He walked forward. It was the Dowager Queen. She invited him to be seated.

The problem turned out to be Bottine Caterine.

The Dowager Queen quickly explained the problem with a crude bluntness that surprised him, and in a language he would hardly have expected, especially in a church.

"My informants are quite certain. He goes to her almost every night. It has become common knowledge in Copenhagen. The King and the entire royal family, yes, even the court, have become a laughingstock in the eyes of everyone."

Guldberg sat very still, staring at the crucifix with the suffering Saviour.

"I too have heard about this," he replied. "Your Grace, I'm afraid that your informants happen to be correct."

"I beseech you to intervene. The young consort has no share of the royal seed."

He could hardly believe his ears, but that's what she said, and then she continued:

"The situation is serious. He's pouring his royal seed into Bottine Caterine's filthy womb. Nothing unusual about that. But he must also be forced to service the Queen. They say it happened once, but that's not enough. The succession to the throne is in danger. The succession to the throne!"

He now turned to face her and said:

"But your *own* son . . . in that case, he might succeed to . . ."

She didn't say a word.

They both knew how impossible that was. Or did she? Was she trying to ignore what she knew? Her only son, the Crown Prince, the King's half-brother, was physically deformed, his head pointed and twisted sideways; he was regarded as easily led by those who were kind, as hopelessly moronic by others. The British Ambassador, in a letter to George III, described his appearance: "His head was deformed, he drooled all the time, and whenever he spoke he uttered odd little grunts and kept on smiling with an idiotic expression on his face." It was cruel but true. Both of them knew it. Guldberg had been his tutor for six years.

He also knew how great her love was for this misshapen son.

He had seen her love excuse everything, but had also often observed her tears. Surely even the loving mother didn't truly believe that this poor, misshapen "monster", as he was sometimes called at court, could ever become Denmark's king.

Yet he couldn't be certain.

But the other things she said! Everything she said was, in truth, so extraordinary that he hardly dared reply. Her indignation over the squandered royal seed seemed peculiar: Dowager Queen Juliane Marie had spent her life married to a King who emptied his royal seed into almost all the whores in Copenhagen. She was not ignorant of this

73

fact. She had tolerated it. Her King had also been forced to service her, and she had forced herself to submit. This too she had tolerated. And she had given birth to one son, who was moronic; a poor, drooling child whom she loved.

She didn't merely "tolerate" her son's deformity. She loved him.

"My son," she said at last in her metallic, clear voice, "would no doubt make a better monarch than this . . . confused and lecherous . . . my son would . . . my beloved son would . . ."

Suddenly she had nothing more to say. She fell silent. Both of them sat in silence for a long time. Then she drew herself up and said:

"Guldberg. If you will lend me your support. And support for . . . my son. I will richly reward you. Richly. I see in your sharp intelligence a means of safeguarding the realm. You are, like my son, an outwardly . . . insignificant . . . figure. But inside . . ."

She did not continue. Guldberg was silent.

"For six years you have been the Crown Prince's teacher," she finally whispered. "God gave him a lowly appearance. For that reason many people despise him. But I beseech you – would it be possible for you to love him as much as I do?"

The question was unexpected and seemed much too sentimental. After a moment, when he didn't reply, she repeated:

"For you henceforth to love my son as deeply as I do? Then not only will the almighty and beneficent Father reward you. But I will too."

And after a moment of silence she added:

"The three of us will save this poor kingdom."

Guldberg replied:

"Your Grace. Let it be so, for as long as I live."

She then took his hand and pressed it. He writes that this was a great moment in his life, which was changed forever after. "From that moment I embraced the unfortunate Crown Prince Frederik with such unconditional love that not only he, but also his mother the Dowager Queen, came to have a consummate trust in me."

Afterwards she spoke once again of Bottine Caterine. And finally, the Dowager Queen said, almost snarling, but in a voice loud enough that the echo could be heard for a long time in the palace chapel:

"Get rid of her! PERMANENTLY!"

On the eve of Epiphany, January 5, 1768, Caterine was seized in her home in Christianshavn by four police officers. It was late at night, and a cold rain was falling.

They arrived at around ten o'clock and dragged her outside, where they then threw her into a closed coach. Soldiers saw to it that any curious spectators were kept away.

At first she cried, then furiously cursed the police; not until she was sitting in the coach did she become aware of Guldberg, who was himself overseeing her arrest.

"I knew it!" she screamed. "You wicked little rat, I knew it!"

Guldberg stepped forward and tossed a pouch of gold coins onto the floor of the coach.

"You'll get to see Hamburg," he said in a low voice. "And not every whore is so well paid."

Then the door was slammed shut, the horses started moving, and Bottine Caterine set off on her journey abroad.

7

For the first few days Christian refused to believe that she was gone. Then he began to understand. And he grew nervous.

To the surprise of the court, and without prior invitation, he called on Count Bernstorff and there, without offering any explanation, he ate his dinner. During dinner he talked in great confusion about cannibals. This was interpreted as a manifestation of his nervousness. After all, the King had a reputation for melancholy, nervousness and violence; and all without any explanation. The following days he wandered without rest through the streets of Copenhagen at night, and it was understood that he was looking for Caterine.

After two weeks, when the general concern for the King's well-being had become enormous, the King was advised in a letter that Caterine had undertaken a journey abroad without indicating her destination, but she sent her greetings.

For three days the King kept to his room. Then one morning he disappeared.

The dog was gone too.

A search was begun at once. After only a few hours word came that the King had been found; he was observed wandering along the beach of Køge Bay, and soldiers were keeping watch over him from a distance. The Dowager Queen then sent Guldberg to explain the contents of the letter and to persuade the King to return to the palace.

He was sitting on the beach.

It was a pathetic sight. He had his dog close beside him, and the dog growled at Guldberg.

Guldberg spoke to the King as he would to a friend.

He told Christian that he must regain his royal composure, for the sake of the country. That there was no reason for despair or depression. That the court and the Dowager Queen – yes, everybody! – thought that the King's benevolence towards Caterine had become a source of unease. That this benevolence might well make the King's unquestionably tender feelings for the young Queen fade, and thereby threaten the future of the throne. Yes, perhaps Frøken Beuthaken had even thought of this herself! Perhaps that was the explanation. Perhaps her unexpected departure was due to a desire to serve her country, the Danish kingdom, and she thought she stood in the way of the entire realm's wish to have an heir who would secure the line of succession. He said he was almost certain this was the case.

"Where is she?" Christian asked.

Perhaps she'll come back, Guldberg told him, if the country's succession to the throne is secure. Yes, he said, he was practically convinced that her unselfish concern for Denmark, her surprising flight, that all this unease would then be calmed. And that she would return and could then resume her deep friendship with the King, which . . .

"Where is she?" the King shrieked. "Do you know how they laugh at you? Such a little, insignificant . . . such a . . . Do you know they call you Gold-Lizard?"

He then fell silent, as if he were frightened, and then he asked Guldberg:

"Will I have to be punished now?"

At that moment, writes Guldberg, he was seized with great sorrow and great sympathy.

He sat down next to Christian. And it was true what the King had said: that in appearance he — like the King! Like the King! — was insignificant, despised, that the King was ostensibly the foremost of men, but in reality he was one of the most wretched. If he had not wished to comply with the royal requirements for deference, had not obeyed the rules of ceremony, he would have liked to tell this young boy that he too was one of the most wretched. That he hated impurity; that the impure had to be cut away, just as a member that leads a person astray should be cut off, yes, that the time of cutting would come when the lecherous court, with all those parasites, would be cut away from God's great work; when the squanderers, atheists, drunkards, and whoremongers at the court of Christian VII would be given their just punishment. The security of the Crown would be guaranteed, the power of the monarch would be strengthened, the purifying fire would rage through the stinking realm. And then those on the bottom would become those on the top.

And that he, along with the one chosen by God, would then rejoice at the great purifying work the two of them had carried out.

But he merely said:

"Yes, Your Majesty, I am a small and completely unimportant person. But a human being, nevertheless."

The King looked at him with an expression of surprise on his face. Then he asked again:

"Where is she?"

"Perhaps Altona ... Hamburg ... Paris ... London ... She is a great and affluent personage, worn out with worry about Your Majesty's destiny ... and about her duties to Denmark ... but perhaps she will return if she hears the news that the succession to the throne has been secured. Has been saved."

"Europe?" the King whispered in despair. "The Continent?"

"Paris ... London ..."

The King asked:

"Will I have to search for her in ... Europe?"

The dog whimpered. Fog hovered over the waters of Øresund; the Swedish coast was invisible. Waving his hand, Guldberg summoned the waiting soldiers. Denmark's King was saved from the uttermost distress and delusion.

8

There was no change in the King's mood. But at a special session of the Council called unexpectedly, the King announced his desire to undertake a grand European journey.

He placed a map of Europe on the table in the Council chambers. Three councillors of state were present in the room, along with Guldberg and a certain Count Rantzau; the King, in a decisive and focused manner untypical of him, described his travel route. It was quite clear that what he described was a grand cultural tour. The only one who seemed oddly pensive was Guldberg, but he didn't say a word. The others agreed that the sovereigns of Europe would of course welcome the young Danish monarch as an equal.

After winning their approval the King ran his finger over the map and muttered:

"Altona . . . Hamburg . . . Paris . . . Europe . . ."

After the King left the room, Guldberg and Count Rantzau stayed behind. Rantzau asked Guldberg why he seemed so pensive.

"We cannot allow the King to travel without taking precautionary measures," Guldberg replied after a momentary pause. "The risks are much too great. His nervousness . . . his sudden outbursts of rage . . . they would attract attention of an undesirable nature."

"A royal physician should be procured," Count Rantzau then said. "Who could keep watch. And soothe him."

"But who?"

"I know a very capable doctor," said Rantzau. "Refined, practising in Altona. A specialist in cupping. A German. His parents are devout Pietists, his father a theologian. His name is Struensee. Very capable. Very capable."

"A friend?" asked Guldberg, his face expressionless. "One of your protégés?"

"Precisely."

"And he has been influenced by your . . . enlightened ideas?"

"Completely apolitical," Rantzau told him. "Completely apolitical. Specialist in cupping and the health of the limbs. Wrote his dissertation on the latter."

"Not a Jew, like Reverdil?"

"No."

"A handsome lad . . . I presume?"

Rantzau was suddenly on his guard; as he was uncertain of the intent of this question he gave a rather evasive reply, but with a coldness that indicated he would not tolerate any insinuations:

"Specialist in cupping."

"Can you vouch for him?"

"On my word of honour!"

"Word of honour doesn't usually weigh too heavily for men of the Enlightenment."

An icy silence descended over the room. At last Guldberg broke it, and with one of his rare smiles he said:

"A jest, of course. Was his name . . . Struensee?"

That was how it all began.

PART II

THE ROYAL PHYSICIAN

Chapter 5 · The Silent One from Altona

I

His friends called him "The Silent One". He wasn't someone who talked much, not without cause. But he listened with great attention.

Importance might be given to the fact that he was silent. Or to the fact that he could listen.

His name was Johann Friedrich Struensee.

In Holsten, about 30 miles outside Hamburg and the nearby smaller town of Altona, there was an estate called Ascheberg. The estate had gardens that were famous in many parts of Europe; they were owned by the Rantzau family.

The gardens were laid out in the 1730s and consisted of canals, lanes, and rectangular plantings of shrubbery designed according to a rectilinear system typical of the early baroque period.

"The Ascheberg Gardens" were a magnificent example of landscape architecture.

But it was the way in which the extraordinary natural formations of the terrain had been used that gave the park its reputation. The natural was incorporated with the artificial. The baroque grounds, with their deep, central perspective of lanes and canals, were spread out along the lakeshore. But behind them stood a ridge that was called the "Mountain"; it was a ridge with deep folds interspersed with strange valleys, like lobes, in the mountainside. Beyond the quite unpretentious main building rose this steep terrain, with a natural wildness that was unusual in the gentle Danish landscape.

The "Mountain" was covered with woods; it was a natural slope, tamed and yet at the same time in its natural state.

Gentle, ravine-like valleys. Terraces. Woods. Perfect nature, at once controlled and shaped by human beings, and an expression of freedom and wildness. From the top of the Mountain there was a panoramic view. And it was also possible to see what could be accomplished by human beings: a natural reproduction of wild nature.

The Mountain had an offshoot in the garden. The wild within the tamed. It was a civilized dream of domination, and freedom.

In one of the Mountain's "folds", in a hollowed valley, two very old huts had been discovered. They might have been the homes of peasants or – as people preferred to imagine – shepherds.

One of these huts had been restored, and for a very specific purpose.

In 1762 Rousseau began his exile after the Assembly in Paris ordered the executioner to burn his *Émile*.

He sought refuge in various places throughout Europe, and the owner of Ascheberg, a Count Rantzau who was quite old but who had a lifelong passion for radical ideas, invited the persecuted man to settle at Ascheberg. He would be given the hut on the Mountain; that was where he could live. No doubt it was presumed that the great philosopher, in these primitive conditions and close to nature, which he extolled and to which he wished to return, might here continue his great writing endeavours, and in this way his vital needs and his ideas would enjoy a happy union.

To this end, a "cabbage patch" was also laid out next to the hut.

Here he would cultivate his cabbage, cultivate his garden. It is not known whether the digging of the cabbage patch was a reference to the well-known expression about the person "who in peace and quiet cultivates his cabbage and pays no mind to politics". Nevertheless, the cabbage patch was prepared. And the Count doubtless knew his *Nouvelle Héloïse* and the passage that reads: "Nature flees frequented places; it is on the mountain tops, in the deepest forests, on the remote islands that it shows its true enchantment. Those who love nature and cannot visit it far away are compelled to force themselves upon it, to make it come to them; and none of this can be done without a measure of illusion."

The Ascheberg Gardens represented an illusion of a natural state.

Rousseau never did come to Ascheberg, but his name became mythically associated with the Ascheberg Gardens, lending them a European reputation among those who were zealots of nature and freedom. The Ascheberg Gardens took their place among famous "sentimental sites" in Europe. The "peasant's hut" that was intended for Rousseau became a place of refuge; the hut in the hollowed valley and the cabbage patch, which over time grew more and more neglected, were sites worth visiting. There was no longer any question about it being a shepherd's hut; rather, it was a cult destination for intellectuals on their way from an infatuation with nature to enlightenment. The pathways, doors, and windowsills were painted with elegant French and German quotations from poetry, and verses from contemporary poets and Juvenal.

Even Christian's father, Frederik V, made the climb up to Rousseau's hut. The Mountain was henceforth called "Königsberg".

At this time the hut became something of a holy shrine for Danish and German men of the Enlightenment. They gathered at the Ascheberg estate, and they hiked up to Rousseau's hut, where they discussed the great ideas of the day. Their names were Ahlefeld and Berckentin; their names were Schack Carl Rantzau, von Falkenskjold, Claude Louis de Saint-Germain, Ulrich Adolph Holstein, and Enevold Brandt. They regarded themselves as enlightened men.

One of them was also named Struensee.

Here, in this hut, much later on, he would read a passage from Holberg's *Moral Thoughts* to Caroline Mathilde, the Queen of Denmark.

He had met her in Altona. That much is known.

Struensee saw Caroline Mathilde when she arrived in Altona on her way to her wedding, and he noted that her face was tear-stained.

She, however, did not notice Struensee. He was one of many. They stood in the same room, but she did not see him. Almost no-one seems to have seen him at that time; certainly few have described him. He was kindly and reticent. He was of above average height, blond, with a well-shaped mouth and good teeth. His contemporaries noted that he was one of the first to use toothpaste.

Otherwise there is almost nothing. Reverdil, who had met him early on, in the summer of 1767 in Holsten, merely remarks that Struensee, the young German doctor, had a discreet and reserved manner.

Once again: young, reticent and attentive.

2

Three weeks after Christian VII had decided on his European tour, Count Rantzau, at the request of the Danish government, paid a visit to the German doctor Johann Friedrich Struensee in Altona in order to make him an offer to become royal physician to the Danish King.

They knew each other well. They had spent many weeks together at Ascheberg. They had made the climb up to Rousseau's hut. They belonged to the Circle.

Rantzau was much older, however. Struensee was still young.

At the time Struensee was living in a small apartment at the corner of Papagoyenstrasse and Reichstrasse, but on the day the offer was made, he was as usual out attending to the sick. With some effort, Rantzau found him in a hovel in Altona's slums, where he was in the process of cupping the children of the neighbourhood.

Without equivocating, Rantzau stated the purpose of his visit, and Struensee without hesitation declined.

He regarded the assignment as uninteresting.

He happened to be finishing up cupping a widow and her three children. He seemed in good humour but uninterested. No, he said, that doesn't interest me. He then gathered up his instruments and, with a smile, patted the little children on the head. He accepted the words of gratitude from their mother, as well as her invitation, along with his esteemed guest, to partake of a glass of white wine out in the kitchen.

The kitchen had an earthen floor, and the children were shooed outside.

Count Rantzau waited patiently.

"You're being sentimental, my friend," he said. "Saint Francis among Altona's poor. But remember that you're a man of the Enlightenment. You must take the long view. Right now you see only the people in front of you, but lift your eyes. Look beyond them. You're one of the most brilliant minds I've ever met; you have a great mission in life. You can't say no to this offer. Sickness can be found anywhere. All of Copenhagen is sick."

Struensee did not reply to this; he just smiled.

"You ought to give yourself greater challenges. A king's royal physician can have influence. You could put your theories into practice . . . in real life. In real life."

No answer.

"Why else have I taught you so much?" Rantzau continued, his voice now sounding annoyed. "Those discussions! Those studies! Why just theories? Why not do something in practice? Something . . . substantial."

That elicited a reaction from Struensee, and after a moment's silence he began, in a very low but distinct voice, to talk about his life.

Evidently he felt piqued by the phrase "something substantial".

He spoke in a friendly manner, but with a slightly ironic undertone. "My friend and esteemed teacher," he said, "I was under the impression that I *am* 'doing' something. I have my practice. But in addition – in addition! – I 'do' various other things. Something substantial. I keep statistics on all the medical problems in Altona. I inspect the three dispensaries that exist in this city of 18,000 people. I help the wounded and those who fall victim to accidents. I supervise the treatment of the insane. I observe and assist with the autopsies at the Theatro Anatomico. I crawl into slum dwellings, squalid hovels where people lie in stinking filth, and I seek out those who are powerless. I listen to the needs of the powerless and the ill. I attend to the sick in the women's prison, the general hospital, and the jail; I treat the sick prisoners who are under guard and in the executioner's house. Even the condemned can be sick; I help the condemned to survive in a tolerable fashion until the executioner's axe takes their lives, like a deliverance. Every day I treat eight to ten of the poor who can't pay but who are under the care of the poor relief fund. I treat poor travellers not covered by the poor relief fund. I treat farmhands passing through Altona. I treat patients with contagious diseases. I give lectures on anatomy. I think you can say," he concluded his response, "that I'm familiar with certain not entirely enlightened sectors of reality in this city. Not entirely enlightened! Apropos the Enlightenment."

"Are you quite finished?" Rantzau asked with a smile.

"Yes, I'm finished."

"I'm impressed," Rantzau then said.

This was the longest speech he had ever heard "The Silent One" give. Nevertheless, he continued to try to persuade him. "Look farther," he said. "You who are a doctor should also be able to heal Denmark. Denmark is a madhouse. The court is a madhouse. The King is intelligent but perhaps . . . mad. A clever, enlightened man at his side could clean up the shithouse that is Denmark."

A little smile flickered over Struensee's lips, but he merely shook his head in silence.

"Right now," said Rantzau, "you can do good in a small way. And you do. I'm impressed. But you could also change the larger world. Not simply dream of doing so. You could have power. You can't say no."

They sat quietly for a long time.

"My silent friend," Rantzau said at last in a kind voice. "My silent friend. What will become of you? You who have so many noble dreams, yet harbour this fear of realizing them. But you're an intellectual, as I am, and I understand you. We don't want to sully our ideas with reality."

Struensee then glanced up at Rantzau with an expression of wariness, rather like someone who has felt the whip.

"The intellectuals," he murmured. "The intellectuals, yes. But I don't consider myself an intellectual. I'm simply a doctor."

Later that same evening Struensee accepted.

A brief passage from Struensee's prison confessions throws a peculiar light on this episode.

He says that it was "by chance" that he came to be the royal physician; it was not something he actually wanted. He had quite different plans. He had been thinking of leaving Altona and travelling abroad, "to Málaga or the East Indies".

No explanation. Just the desire for flight *to* something.

3

No, he didn't consider himself an intellectual. There were others in the Altona Circle who deserved the label more than he did.

One of them was his friend and teacher Count Rantzau. He was an intellectual.

He owned the Ascheberg estate, which he had inherited from his father. The estate was 33 miles from Altona, a city that was Danish at the time. The economic basis of the estate was serfdom, peasant slavery, or "ascription"; but as on many other estates in Holsten, there was less brutality and the principles were more humane.

Count Rantzau considered himself an intellectual and an enlightened man.

The reason for this was as follows.

At the age of 35, married and the father of one child, he was appointed regimental commander of the Danish army because of his previous military experience in the French army under Field Marshal Loevendahl. This experience was alleged but difficult to verify. Compared to these experiences, however, the Danish army was a much calmer refuge. As regimental commander there was no need to fear war. He enjoyed the decorum of such a position. Despite this, he fell in love with an Italian singer, and it ruined his reputation; not just because he made her his mistress, but because he also accompanied her travelling operetta company throughout the southern parts of Europe. The company went on tour from town to town, but he was unable to come to his senses and rein himself in. To remain incognito he constantly changed his disguise; one time dressing in an "imposing" fashion, another time dressing as a priest; all of this was necessary since everywhere he went he incurred considerable debts.

In two towns in Sicily he was accused of swindling, though in vain, since by that time he had already returned to the Continent, to Napoli. In Genoa he forged a letter of credit which read "my father, the governor of Norway", but he could not be tried before a court because by then he was in Pisa, where he was indicted, and on his way to Arles. Later the police found it impossible to track him down.

After a jealous squabble, he left the Italian singer in Arles, whereupon he returned briefly to his estate to replenish his funds, which was possible thanks to an additional royal *apanage*. After visiting Ascheberg, where he renewed his acquaintance with his wife and daughter, he set off for Russia. There he visited the Russian Tsarina Elisabeth, who was on her deathbed. According to his analysis, her successor would need him as an expert on Danish and European matters. A further reason for this Russian journey was the rumour that war would break out between Russia and Denmark under the Tsarina's successor, and he could then offer this successor certain services since his knowledge of the Danish and French armies was so great.

In spite of this proposal, which would be quite beneficial for Russia, many regarded the Danish nobleman with animosity. His numerous female relationships and the fact that war had not broken out put him at a disadvantage, and many harboured suspicions about "the Danish spy". After a conflict with the Russian court arising from a dispute over the favours of a highly respected lady, he was forced to flee and ended up in Danzig, where his travel funds gave out.

There he met a manufacturer.

This man wished to settle in Denmark for the purposes of investment and to place himself under the protection of a government that was favourably disposed towards foreign commercial investments. Count Rantzau assured the manufacturer that he, through his contacts at the court, could obtain the desired protection. After using up a certain portion of the manufacturer's capital without, however, obtaining the protection of the Danish government, Count Rantzau managed to return to Denmark, the kingdom he no longer wished to betray to the Russian Tsarina. The court then granted him a yearly *apanage* because of his name and prestige. He explained that he had gone to Russia only as a Danish spy, and that he now possessed secrets that would prove valuable to Denmark.

During all this time his wife and daughter had remained at his Ascheberg estate. Which was where he now gathered around him a group of intellectual, enlightened men.

One of them was a young doctor by the name of Struensee.

It was by virtue of this path in life and his extensive international contacts, as well as the influence he still exerted at the Danish court, that Count Rantzau considered himself to be an intellectual.

He was soon to play a central rôle in the events surrounding the

Danish revolution, a rôle which, in its versatility, can only be understood in light of the aforementioned biography.

The rôle he plays is that of an intellectual.

The first contribution he made to the Denmark state was to recommend that the German doctor J. F. Struensee should become the royal physician to King Christian VII.

4

What a strange city Altona was.

It stood near the mouth of the Elbe River; it was a trading centre with a population of 18,000, and by the mid-1600s it had achieved city charter status. Altona developed into the first free port in the North, but it also became a free port because of various beliefs that were held there.

A liberal outlook was essential for trade.

The intellectual climate seemed to attract both ideas and money, and Altona became Denmark's port to Europe, the city second in importance after Copenhagen. It was not far from the great German free port of Hamburg, and among conservatives it had the reputation of being a vipers' nest of radical thinking.

That was the general opinion. A vipers' nest. But since radicalism had proved to be financially lucrative, Altona was allowed to keep its intellectual freedom.

Struensee was a doctor. He was born in 1737. At the age of 15 he enrolled as a medical student at the University of Halle. His father was the theologian Adam Struensee, who early on was imprisoned for pietism and later became professor of theology at the University of Halle. He was a man of integrity; devout, educated, and sombre, with a tendency towards melancholy, while Struensee's mother is described as having a lighter temperament. Their pietism was of the Francke school, with an emphasis on the importance of public welfare, and it was influenced by the cultivation of reason, which at that time characterized the University of Halle. Struensee's home was authoritarian; virtue and morality were its guiding stars.

Yet the young Struensee rebelled. He became a liberal and an atheist. In his view, if human beings were allowed to choose freely, they would, with the help of reason, choose good. He writes that early on he embraced the idea of the human being "as a machine", an expression that was typical of the dream of rationalism at the time — he actually uses this expression — and that it was solely the human organism that creates spirit, emotions, good and evil.

By this he seems to have meant that acuity and spirituality were not bestowed on human beings by some higher being but were shaped by our experiences in life. It was our obligation to others that gave meaning to everything, that created inner satisfaction, that gave life its purpose and ought to determine a person's actions.

Hence the misleading expression "machine", which must doubtless be regarded as a poetic image.

His doctoral dissertation was entitled "On the risks of aberrant motions of the limbs".

His analysis was formalistic but exemplary. The handwritten dissertation did have one odd feature, however; in the margins Struensee has drawn people's faces in different-coloured ink. Here he presents an ambiguous and confused picture of his inner self. He allows the great intellectual clarity of the dissertation to be obscured by the people's faces.

The main argument of the dissertation is, by the way, that preventive medical treatment is important, that physical exercise is necessary, but that when illness or injury occurs, great caution is essential

He is a skilled artist, judging by the dissertation. The human faces are interesting.

The text is of lesser interest.

*

As a 20-year-old, Struensee moves to Altona and there begins his medical practice. He will always, even later on, be regarded as a doctor.

Not an artist, not a politician, not an intellectual. A doctor.

Yet the other side of his personality is the publicist.

If the Enlightenment has a rational and hard face, which is the belief in reason and empiricism within medicine, mathematics, physics, and astronomy, it also has a soft face, which is the Enlightenment as freedom of thought, tolerance, and liberty.

It could be said that in Altona he moves from the hard side of the Enlightenment, the development of the sciences towards rationalism and empiricism, to the soft side, the necessity of freedom.

The first journal he starts (the *Monthly Journal of Benefit and Pleasure*) contains in the first issue a long analysis of the risks inherent in the population flight from country to city. It is a socio-medical analysis.

Here too he places the doctor in the rôle of politician.

Urbanization, he writes, is a medical threat with political ramifications. Taxation, the risks of military service, wretched medical treatment, alcoholism, all of these things create an urban proletariat which could be prevented with better developed medical treatment among the peasants. He presents a chilling but in actuality formidable sociological picture of Denmark in decay; declining population figures, continuous smallpox epidemics. He notes that "beggars among the peasantry now number more than 60,000".

Other articles bear titles such as "On Transmigration", "On Mosquitoes", and "On Sunstroke".

But a crudely satirical text with the title "Encomium to the Heavenly Effect of Dogs and Dog Shit" is to be his downfall. The text is regarded, and rightly so, as a personal attack on a well-known doctor in Altona who had earned vast sums from a dubious remedy for constipation, extracted from dog shit.

The journal is confiscated.

The following year, however, he starts another journal. He makes an effort to refrain from libellous remarks and from statements that could be viewed as critical of the state or of religion, but he fails in an article about foot-and-mouth disease, which is rightly said to exude religious criticism.

This journal is also confiscated.

In his last writings, composed in prison and finished on the day before his execution, Struensee touches on what might be called the journalistic period of his life. "My moralistic ideas during that time were developed while studying the writings of Voltaire, Rousseau, Helvétius, and Boulanger. I became a freethinker, believing that a higher principle had certainly created the world and human beings, but that there was no life after this one, and that actions only possessed moral power if they influenced society in the proper way. I found unreasonable the belief in punishment in a life after this one. Human beings were punished enough in this life. The virtuous person was one who did something useful. Christianity's concepts were much too strict – and the truths it conveyed could be found expressed equally well in the writings of the philosophers. The offences of sensuality I regarded as highly excusable weaknesses, as long as they had no damaging consequences for oneself or for others."

His adversaries, in a much-too-brief summary of his ideas, remarked: "Struensee considered human beings to be merely machines."

Yet of the greatest importance to him was Ludvig Holberg's *Moral Thoughts*. A well-thumbed and underlined copy, in German, was found after his death.

One of the chapters in this book would change his life.

5

On May 6, 1768, King Christian VII set off on his grand tour of Europe.

His entourage numbered a total of 55 people, and the tour was meant to be a cultural expedition, a sentimental journey in the style of

Laurence Sterne (it was later claimed that Christian had been greatly impressed by *Tristram Shandy*, Book VII). But its purpose was also to give the outside world, by means of the splendour displayed by the royal entourage, a lasting impression of Denmark's wealth and power.

Initially the retinue was meant to include more participants, but it was gradually reduced; one of those sent home was a courier by the name of Andreas Hjort. He was sent back to the capital, and from there he was exiled to the island of Bornholm because one night, "loose-lipped and drunk", he revealed to listening ears that the King had given him the assignment during the journey to search for Bottine Caterine.

In Altona, Struensee joined them.

Their first encounter was extremely odd.

The King was staying at the mayor's residence. One evening, when he asked for the courier Andreas Hjort, he was informed that the man had been called home. No explanation was supplied. The courier's action was described as inexplicable but might have been prompted by illness in his family.

Christian suffered a recurrence of his peculiar spasms and then began furiously to demolish the room, throwing chairs and breaking windows. With a piece of coal taken from the embers in the fireplace he wrote Guldberg's name on the exceedingly beautiful silk tapestries, although he deliberately misspelled it. During the tumult the King's hand was injured and started to bleed, so Struensee's first task on the journey was to bandage the monarch's hand.

The new royal physician had been called in.

His first memory of Christian was this: the quite slender boy was sitting on a chair, his hand was bleeding, and he was staring blankly, straight ahead.

After a very long silence, Struensee asked with a kind voice:

"Your Majesty, can you explain this sudden ... anger? You don't have to, but ..."

"No, I don't have to."

After a moment he added:

"They tricked me. She's not anywhere. Even if she *is* somewhere, that's not where we're going. And if we do, they'll take her away. Perhaps she's dead. It's my fault. I must be punished."

Struensee writes that at the time he didn't understand (though later he did) and that he quietly began to bandage the King's hand.

"Were you born in Altona?" Christian then asked.

Struensee replied:

"In Halle. But I came to Altona at an early age."

"They say," Christian continued, "that in Altona there are nothing but freethinkers and men of the Enlightenment who want to smash society into rubble and ashes."

Struensee nodded calmly.

"Smash! The existing society!"

"Yes, Your Majesty," replied Struensee. "That's what they say. Others say it's the European centre of the Enlightenment."

"And what do you say, Doctor Struensee?"

The bandaging was now done. Struensee was on his knees in front of Christian.

"I'm a man of the Enlightenment," he said, "but first and foremost I am a doctor. If Your Majesty so desires, I will leave my post at once and return to my normal medical practice."

Christian then regarded Struensee with a newly sparked interest, not in the least annoyed or disturbed by the man's almost insolent bluntness.

"Haven't you ever, Doctor Struensee, wanted to cleanse the temple of the fornicators?" he asked in a very low voice.

No reply was given. But the King continued:

"To drive the hawkers out of the temple? To crush everything? So that it can all rise up from the ashes again . . . a Phoenix?"

"Your Majesty certainly knows his Bible," was Struensee's deferential reply.

"Don't you think it's impossible to make progress? PROGRESS! If you don't make yourself hard and . . . smash . . . everything so that the temple . . ."

Suddenly he began to walk around the room, which was littered with chairs and broken glass. The impression he made on Struensee was poignant because his boyish figure was so slender and insignificant that it was hard to believe he could have caused such destruction.

Then he came over, stood quite close to Struensee, and whispered:

"I received a letter. From Monsieur Voltaire. An esteemed philosopher. To whom I gave money for a court proceeding. And he hailed me in his letter. As . . . as . . ."

Struensee waited. Then it came, spoken softly, the first secretive message that was to bind them together. Yes, later on Struensee would remember that moment, which he describes in his prison notes; a moment of absolute intimacy, when the mad young boy, this King by the Grace of God, confided in him a secret that was unprecedented and precious and that would unite them forever.

" . . . he hailed me . . . as an enlightened man."

There was not a sound in the room. And the King continued, in the same whispered tone:

"In Paris I have decided to meet with Monsieur Voltaire. Whom I know. Through our correspondence. Can I take you with me?"

Struensee, with a little smile, replied:

"It would be my pleasure, Your Majesty."

"Can I trust you?"

And Struensee said, simply and quietly:

"Yes, Your Majesty. More than you know."

Chapter 6 · The Travelling Companion

I

The journey was to be a long one.

The tour would last eight months, the 55 people would travel somewhat more than 2,500 miles with horses and coaches, the roads would be miserable, it would be summer and then autumn and finally winter; the coaches were unheated and they proved to be draughty, and what the purpose of this journey might be, no-one knew – only that it had to be undertaken and that therefore the public and the peasants – a distinction was made between the public and the peasants – had to stand gaping and cheering or begging with hostility along the travel route.

The journey was to go on and on, and no doubt there was some objective.

The objective was to carry the little absolute ruler forward through the pelting rain, the increasingly apathetic little King who hated his rôle and hid in his coach, tending to his spasms and dreaming of something else, no-one knew what. He was to be carried by this enormous cortège through Europe, chasing after something that perhaps was once a secret dream of rediscovering the Sovereign of the Universe, she who would make everything seem coherent, an internal dream that was now faded, erased, merely chafing like a rage that he could not put into words.

They made their way like a caterpillar through the European rain, heading towards nothing. The journey took them from Copenhagen to Kolding, Gottorp, Altona, Celle, Hanau, Frankfurt, Darmstadt, Strasbourg, Nancy, Metz, Verdun, Paris, Cambrai, Lille, Calais, Dover, London, Oxford, Newmarket, York, Leeds, Manchester, Derby, Rotterdam, Amsterdam, Antwerp, Ghent, Nijmegen – no, all of it seemed a blur after a while; didn't Nijmegen come before Mannheim, Amsterdam before Metz?

Yes, that's the way it was.

But what was the purpose of this astonishing campaign through the pelting European rain?

Yes, that's right: Amsterdam did come after Nijmegen. That was at the beginning of the journey. Struensee remembered it quite well. It was at the beginning of the inexplicable journey, and it was somewhere before Amsterdam. The King, in his coach, on the approach to Amsterdam and in deepest confidence, had told Struensee that "he now intended to break out of the imprisonment of royal rank, protocol, and morality. He would now realize the idea of flight which he had once discussed with his tutor Reverdil."

And Struensee notes: "He suggested, in all seriousness, that I should flee with him. He would then become a soldier, so as not to continue to be under obligation to anyone but himself."

This was on the approach to Amsterdam. Struensee listened patiently. Then he persuaded Christian to wait a few weeks, or at least until after his meeting with Voltaire and the encyclopedists.

Christian listened, as if to a faint, enticing cry from something that had once been of enormous importance but now seemed infinitely remote.

Voltaire?

In silence they drove into Amsterdam. Listless, the King peered out the window of the coach at the innumerable faces.

"They're staring," he remarked to Struensee. "I'm staring back at them. But no Caterine."

The King never again brought up his plans to flee.

This particular incident was not reported back to the court in Copenhagen.

Almost everything else was. There were countless dispatches, and they were read with great care.

Three times a week it was the custom for the three queens to play cards. They played tarot. The images were suggestive, particularly that of the Hanged Man. The players were: Queen Sophie Magdalene, widow of Christian VI, who had survived His Majesty by 24 years; Juliane Marie, the widow of Frederik V; and Caroline Mathilde.

That three queens, from three generations, could be found at court was considered natural since it was normal in the royal house for the kings to drink themselves to death before they became widowers. Or if the queen should die, for example in childbirth, for a remarriage to occur, which happened on a regular basis, leaving in the end a dowager queen, like a discarded seashell in the sand.

Posterity always spoke of the pietism and great devoutness of the dowager queens. This did not, however, detract from their speech. Juliane Marie, in particular, developed an unusual verbal severity which often manifested itself in vulgarity.

Perhaps it could be said that religion's stern demands for truth and her own appalling experiences had given her language an extraordinary frankness that shocked many people.

During the tarot evenings she had numerous opportunities to offer the young Queen Caroline Mathilde tutelage and advice. She still considered the young Queen to be without talents and lacking in will.

Later she would change her opinion.

"We have received," she announced one evening, "many unsettling dispatches from the travellers. The royal physician who was hired in Altona has won His Majesty's confidence. They are forever sitting together in the King's coach. This Struensee is said to be a man of the Enlightenment. Should that be true, it's a national catastrophe. The fact that Reverdil was banished, which was unexpected good fortune, is of no help. A viper still exists."

Caroline Mathilde, who thought she understood the reason for Reverdil's inexplicable expulsion, said nothing in reply.

"Struensee?" Caroline Mathilde asked. "Is he German?"

"I'm uneasy," said the Dowager Queen. "He is described as intelligent, a charming ladies' man, immoral, and he comes from Altona, which has always been a vipers' nest. Nothing good can ever come from Altona."

"The dispatches also mention," said the elder Dowager Queen, attempting to voice an objection, "that the King is calm and does not seek out whores."

"Be happy," Juliane Marie then told the Queen, "be happy that he stays away for a year. My husband, the late King, had to empty his seed sac every day to have peace in his soul. I told him: Empty it in whores, but not in me! I'm not a gutter! Nor a sink! Learn from this, my young friend. Morality and innocence are things you create yourself. Innocence can be recaptured through resistance."

"If he's a man of the Enlightenment," the elder Dowager Queen then asked, "does that mean we've made a mistake?"

"We didn't," replied the Dowager Queen. "Someone else did."

"Guldberg?"

"He doesn't make mistakes."

But the young Queen simply said, as if questioning a name which she later claimed to have heard for the first time at that tarot table: "What a peculiar name. Struensee?"

2

It was appalling.

Europe was appalling. People stared at Christian. He grew weary. He felt ashamed. He feared something but didn't know what – a punishment? At the same time he longed to be punished so that he would be freed from the shame.

He had set out with an objective for his journey. Later he realized that the objective did not exist. He had then mustered his courage. To muster one's courage was a means of making oneself hard, and invulnerable. He looked for other purposes for his travels. A European tour might well involve excesses or meetings with various people. But that was not the case; his excesses were not those of other people. Meetings frightened him.

All that remained was the torture.

He didn't know what to say to those who stared. Reverdil had taught him many fine lines to show off his brilliance. There were little aphorisms that could almost always be used. Now he was starting to forget his lines. Reverdil was gone.

It was so appalling to be part of a performance and not know any of his lines.

The young Countess van Zuylan writes in a letter that she met King Christian VII of Denmark on his European tour during a stop at the Castle Termeer.

He was small and childish, "like a 15-year-old". He was slight, thin, and his face had a sickly pallor, almost as if powdered white. He seemed paralysed and was unable to carry on a conversation. He fired off a few remarks to the courtiers that sounded memorized, but after the applause faded he simply stared at the tips of his shoes.

To rescue him from this embarrassment, she had escorted him out to the park for a brief stroll.

It was raining lightly, which made her shoes wet, and this was his salvation. "During the entire time we were together in the park His Majesty stared down at my shoes, worried they might get wet, and he talked of nothing else in the time we spent together, which was about half an hour."

She then led him back to the waiting courtiers.

In the end he was practically certain that he was a prisoner who was being escorted, in a gigantic procession, to his punishment.

This no longer frightened him. But an infinite weariness encompassed him; he felt himself slowly sinking into sorrow, and all that could bring him out of it were the regular outbursts of rage, when he would slam chairs against the floor until they shattered.

The reports and dispatches were telling. "There were few hotels along the travel route where a certain amount of destruction could not be found, and in London the furniture in the King's room was almost always smashed."

That was the summary.

It was only with Struensee that he felt calm. He didn't understand why. Once Christian mentions that since he was "an orphan" (his mother died when he was two years old and he had had little contact with his father) and thus didn't know how parents should behave, Struensee, through his composure and his silence, gave him an impression of what a father ("a father in heaven", he writes, strangely enough!) should be.

By chance he happened to ask Struensee if he was "his benefactor". With a smile, Struensee asked him what constituted such a person, and Christian then replied:

"A benefactor has time."

"The Silent One" was what everyone in the travelling party now called Struensee.

Every evening he would read the King to sleep. During the first half of the journey he chose to read from Voltaire's *Histoire de Charles XII*.

"The King," Struensee later wrote, "is one of the most sensitive, gifted, and acute people I have ever met. But while we were travelling he seemed to slowly sink into silence and sorrow, and this was broken only by his inexplicable outbursts of rage. This, however, he directed only at himself and innocent furniture, which was subjected to his inexplicable fury."

When Struensee read from *Histoire de Charles XII* he had to sit on the King's bed, his left hand clasped in the King's hand, his right hand turning the pages. When the King fell asleep Struensee would cautiously withdraw his hand and leave him alone with his dreams.

Gradually Struensee began to understand.

3

Christian VII's host in London was King George III of England, who in that year, 1768, had recovered from his first attack of insanity, although he was still melancholy. He would rule the British Empire for 60 years, until 1820; during his reign he was frequently mad, from 1805 he was blind, and after 1811 he was deranged.

He was considered unintelligent, melancholy, pigheaded, and he was faithful to his wife, on whom he bestowed nine children.

He gave his sister's consort a royal welcome. Christian's stay in England ended up lasting two months.

Eventually things started to go amok.

Uneasiness began to spread through the whole entourage. Nothing seemed to make sense as far as His Majesty was concerned, or what was happening. The splendour, the hysteria, and the fear that Christian's illness would strike in earnest and destroy the great royal campaign – that fear began to grow.

Illness or normal behaviour: no-one knew from one day to the next which would have the upper hand.

It was during their time in London that Struensee began to understand that it wasn't *possible* for anything to make sense. For long hours in the morning the King could sit as if paralysed, staring straight ahead, muttering incomprehensible strings of words, and at times, as if in distress, clinging to Struensee's legs. But then he would change completely, as he did on the evening at the Italian Opera House, where Christian gave a masked ball for 3,000 guests. They were fêted as though he intended to make himself so popular that he might become King of England.

What a festive mood there was! That incomprehensible, generous little Danish King! Who gave a confused speech in Danish (and it was astounding how he suddenly seemed to crawl out of his timid state) and then tossed gold coins from the balcony to the riffraff in the street.

The masked ball cost 20,000 riksdaler, and if Struensee had known this he would have observed that his own generous annual salary as the King's royal physician was 500 riksdaler.

It was said that on the night following the Italian masked orgy, Struensee sat alone in the dark for a long time after the King had fallen asleep, thinking over the situation.

Something was fundamentally wrong. Christian was sick, and he was getting sicker. It was true that His Majesty had, in a strange way, been able to preserve his outward demeanour; but those who had witnessed his weak moments also had sharp tongues. There was a note of derision in their comments which frightened Struensee. Horace Walpole had said that "the King is so small, as if he had come out of a fairy's nutshell"; people spoke of him strutting around like a little marionette. They had noticed the memorized lines; what worried Struensee was that they hadn't noticed the other part, what was underneath.

People took note of his spasms but not the sudden flashes of brilliance. But on the whole, everyone was perplexed. Samuel Johnson requested an audience with Christian, listened for half an hour, and then left.

At the door he simply shook his head.

Only on the streets was Christian VII a success. This might have been because every chorus of cheers that rose up from below the royal hotel's royal balcony was answered with a handful of gold coins. It seemed that all economic bounds would soon be shattered.

The turning point occurred towards the end of October.

4

One of the actors was named David Garrick, and he was also head of the Drury Lane Theatre. He was a magnificent interpreter of Shakespeare, and his productions had rejuvenated the Shakespearean tradition in England. He was considered unsurpassed in both comedic and tragic rôles, but it was particularly his production of *Hamlet*, in which he played the lead, that had attracted tremendous attention.

Because Christian VII had expressed interest in the theatre, a series of matinées and evening performances were staged for his benefit. The high point was to be a production of *Hamlet* with Garrick as the Prince of Denmark.

Struensee was told three days before the planned performance, and he immediately paid a call on Garrick.

It was not an easy conversation.

Struensee indicated that he was quite familiar with the plot of the drama. Hamlet was a Danish crown prince whose father had been murdered. The old saga from Saxo Grammaticus was well known; Shakespeare had reshaped it in a manner that exhibited great brilliance but created a problem. The main question of the play was whether or not Hamlet was mad.

Struensee then asked Garrick whether they were in agreement about this fundamental interpretation of the drama. Garrick asked Struensee what point he was trying to make.

The problem, Struensee told him, was that there was a risk that the visiting Danish retinue, as well as the rest of the audience, might wonder whether the choice of play was a commentary on the royal guest.

Or to put it quite bluntly: Many people considered Denmark's King Christian VII to be mad. Was it then appropriate to perform the play?

What would the reaction of the audience be? And what would King Christian VII's reaction be?

"Does he know about his illness?" asked Garrick.

"He doesn't know about his illness, but he knows how he is, and it confuses him," Struensee said. "He has extremely intense sensibilities. He perceives reality as a dramatic play."

"How interesting," said Garrick.

"No doubt," replied Struensee. "But it's impossible to know how he will react. Perhaps he will see himself as Hamlet."

A long silence ensued.

"Christian Amleth," Garrick said at last, with a smile.

But he agreed at once to a different play in the repertoire.

On October 20, 1768, they performed instead *Richard III* for the Danish King and his retinue.

Christian VII would never see a production of *Hamlet*. But Struensee would always remember Garrick's reply: "Christian Amleth".

On the night of the performance Christian refused to go to sleep.

He didn't want to listen to *Histoire de Charles XII* read aloud. He wanted to talk about something that had evidently distressed him. He asked Struensee why the planned performance of *Hamlet* had been replaced with a different play.

He was familiar with the play *Hamlet*. And in tears, he begged Struensee to be honest. Did people think him mad? He swore that he didn't consider himself to be mad, that was his firm conviction and hope, and he prayed to his Benefactor every night to make it true.

But was there gossip? Were people talking about him? Didn't they understand?

He made no attempt to control himself. He wasn't furious, nor did he behave in a regal manner; he lacked all regal dignity during this outburst. He often lacked dignity. But now, for the first time, he touched on the suspicion and inkling of his own illness, and that made a deep impression on Struensee.

"Your Majesty," Struensee said, "Your Majesty is not always easy to understand."

Then the King gave him a blank look and began to talk about the play he had seen, *Richard III*. Such cruelty, he said. A King by the Grace of God, and what unprecedented cruelty he had displayed. It was unbearable.

"Yes," Struensee said, "it's unbearable."

"But when I witnessed that cruelty," Christian then told him, "I experienced something . . . ghastly. In my heart."

Christian was lying curled up in bed, and he covered his face with the sheet, as if wanting to hide.

"Your Majesty," said Struensee in an extremely calm and kindly voice, "what was so ghastly?"

Finally the King replied:

"Desire," he said. "I felt desire. Am I sick, Doctor Struensee? Tell me that I'm not sick."

What was he to say?

That night for the first time Doctor Struensee began to weep in the presence of the King. And then Christian comforted him.

"We'll leave," said Christian. "We'll leave, my friend. Tomorrow I will order our departure for Paris. We must see the light of reason. Voltaire. We must get away from this English madhouse. Or we'll all go mad."

"Yes," Struensee said. "We must leave. This is unbearable."

5

The abrupt end to their stay in England surprised everyone; they left quickly, as if in flight.

It is not known what Christian may have imagined about Paris. But the ceremonies overwhelmed him.

On the tenth day of their stay the King was said to be "indisposed due to a cold". The truth was that he spent the day in his room in utter apathy, fully dressed, and categorically refused to speak to anyone. Struensee, who was now the person thought to have at least some small measure of influence over the King, was asked whether any medicine could be found to ease the King's melancholy. When he answered in the negative, plans were set in motion for an immediate departure for home. The next day, when the King's inexplicable black mood failed to recede, Struensee went in to see him.

An hour later he came out and reported that His Majesty had decided to receive on the following day the French philosophers who had created the great encyclopedia.

Otherwise, an immediate departure for home would be necessary.

Since this meeting had not been planned, it caused a great stir and many people were filled with dark foreboding, as the French men of the Enlightenment were not favourably regarded at the French court. With the exception of Diderot, that is, who had formerly come under the protection of Louis XV's lover, Madame de Pompadour, whose affections he had shared with the monarch.

The meeting was arranged in all haste. The King's indisposition abruptly ceased, he seemed in good humour, and none of the furniture had been touched.

The meeting took place on November 20, 1768, at the residence of the Danish Ambassador to Paris, Baron Carl Heinrich Gleichen.

All the editors of the great encyclopedia – 18 men – were in attendance. Foremost among them were Matran, d'Alembert, Marmontel, La Condamine, Diderot, Helvétius, and Condillac. But the guest most sought after by the King, Monsieur Voltaire, was not present; he never ventured away from Ferney.

It was a strange gathering.

The little, perhaps mad, Danish adolescent – he was 19 – sat there surrounded by the circle of philosophers of the Enlightenment who were to change the history of Europe for several centuries.

At first he was terrified. Then, as if by a miracle, he grew calm, his terror evaporated, and a feeling of confident trust came over him. When Diderot made a deep bow to greet His Majesty, the King said, almost in a whisper:

"I wish you to tell my friend, the great Voltaire, that he is the one who taught me to think."

His voice shook with strong emotion. But it was not fear. Diderot stared at him in surprise and amazement.

Afterwards Christian was happy.

He had been so clever. He had talked to all of the French philosophers, one by one, and had been able to discuss their work; he had spoken his excellent French, and he had felt warmth flow towards him.

It was perhaps the greatest moment of his life.

The brief speech that Diderot had made to him in conclusion also filled the King with joy. "I believe," Diderot said, "that the fire of the Enlightenment can be ignited in the little land of Denmark. Denmark, under this enlightened monarch, will serve as a model. All the radical reforms — those that build on freedom of thought, tolerance, and humanism — will be instituted under the guidance of the Danish King. Christian VII of Denmark will thus, forever after, be able to assign his name to a chapter in the history of the Enlightenment."

Christian was deeply moved by this and incapable of replying. Monsieur d'Alembert had then added softly:

"And we know that a spark can ignite a prairie fire."

Struensee had escorted the guests out to their carriages as the King waved farewell to them from a window up above. Diderot then pulled Struensee aside for a brief conversation.

"And the King will be travelling back to Copenhagen soon?" he asked, although he didn't seem much interested in the answer, as if he was thinking of something else.

"No plans have been made," said Struensee. "It depends to a certain degree on the King. On the King's health."

"And you are the King's royal *medicus*? And from Altona?"

Struensee, with a little smile, said:

"From Altona. You are well informed."

"And you are, I've heard, well informed about the ideas of the French Enlightenment?"

"Indeed I am, but also about the ideas of Holberg, the great philosopher of the Danish Enlightenment," Struensee replied with a smile that was impossible for the French guest to decipher.

"They say," Diderot continued, "that the King is . . . ill?"

Struensee didn't answer.

"Unstable?"

"A most gifted but sensitive young man."

"Yes. I am very well informed. A peculiar situation. But you seem to have his full confidence."

"I am His Majesty's physician."

"Yes," replied Monsieur Diderot. "I have received many letters from London telling me that you are His Majesty's physician."

It was a moment of extraordinary tension. The horses strained impatiently at their harnesses, a light rain was falling. Monsieur Diderot seemed to want to say something but he was hesitant to do so.

At last he spoke.

"The situation is unique," Monsieur Diderot said in a low voice. "Power is formally in the hands of a gifted, very gifted, but mentally unstable King. Some people claim – I hesitate to say it – that he is mad. You have his trust. That gives you a great responsibility. Very seldom does the opportunity exist, as it does here, for an enlightened monarch to break through the reactionary darkness. We have Catherine in Russia, but Russia is a sea of darkness in the East. In Denmark the opportunity exists. Not through the revolt of the mob or the masses from below. But through the power that has been vested in him by the Almighty."

Struensee then began to laugh and gave him an inquiring look.

"The Almighty? I didn't think you would embrace the belief in the Almighty so warmly."

"King Christian VII of Denmark has been given the power, Doctor

Struensee. He has been given it. No matter who gave it to him, it is his. Is that not true?"

"He's not mad," said Struensee after a brief silence.

"That may well be. That may well be. I don't know. You don't know. But if he is . . . then his illness leaves a void at the centre of power. Whoever enters there has a wonderful opportunity."

They both stood in silence.

"And who," asked Struensee at last, "would be likely to enter?"

"The usual. The government officials. The nobles. Those who usually enter."

"Yes, of course."

"Or someone else," Monsieur Diderot then said.

He shook Struensee's hand, climbed into the carriage, then leaned out and said:

"My friend Voltaire is in the habit of saying that sometimes, by chance, history opens up a unique . . . aperture to the future."

"Is that so?"

"And then one should step through."

6

That was on November 20, 1768.

It was Christian's greatest moment, and afterwards the tributes and receptions continued, and little by little he sank back into the greyness that exists just before the dark.

Everything seemed to revert back. Paris was in actuality much more ghastly than London. But now his fits of rage seemed less violent. He appeared to be quite interested in the theatre, and on each evening not dedicated to receptions, special dramatic performances were staged.

Often he fell asleep.

He was supposed to have travelled much farther, to Prague, Vienna and St. Petersburg, but in the end the situation became untenable. To prevent a greater catastrophe, it was decided to cut short the tour.

On January 6, 1769, King Christian VII once again set foot on Danish soil.

During the last days of the journey he would allow only Struensee to sit with him in the royal coach.

It was understood that something had happened. The young German doctor with the blond hair, the quick but wary smile and the kindly eyes, had become somebody. Since he had no title and could not be placed within a precise hierarchy, this caused uneasiness.

Attempts were made to decipher him. He was not easy to decipher. He was friendly, discreet, and refused to make use of his power, or at least what was considered to be power.

People didn't understand him.

The journey home was dreadful.

A week-long snowstorm, the entire route bitterly cold. The coaches were ice-cold. Everyone wrapped themselves up in blankets. It was like an army in retreat from a campaign through the Russian wilderness. There was nothing splendid or dazzling about the Danish court in retreat. No further thought was given to how much the expedition had cost; it was much too appalling, but taxes could always be levied.

There would have to be taxes. That was a matter for the future. Right now it was time to return.

Struensee sat alone with the sleeping, imploring or whimpering boy who was said to be a king, and he had plenty of time to think.

Since he didn't believe in an afterlife, he had always harboured the greatest fear of wasting the only life he had. Medicine had given his life a mission. He had convinced himself that the medical calling was a form of worship, that it was the only possible sacrament of life. Human life, after all, was the only thing sacred; sanctity distinguished humans from animals, otherwise there was no difference. And those who said that he believed the human being was a machine had not understood.

The sanctity of life was his secular belief. He had taught anatomy in Altona: the bodies of suicides and the executed were the subjects of his teaching. The executed were easy to recognize; they often lacked their right hand or their head. The suicides, however, looked no different from those who died in good faith, those who were buried in hallowed ground; in this sense they were alike. The human machine, which lay there beneath his knife, was now truly a machine. That which was sacred, life, had fled. What then was meant by the *sacred*?

It was what a person did while the sacred was present.

The sacred was what the one who was sacred did. That was the conclusion he had reached. There was some discussion of this in Holberg, but in his 101st epigram in *Moral Thoughts*, Holberg was quite vague; it was the animals who were the machines, according to Holberg, and it was the sanctity of human beings that made them different from animals.

Struensee had read this as a possible guide. At times it seemed to him that everything he thought was an echo of what had been thought by others. Then it was a matter of culling so that he didn't just become an echo chamber, and occasionally he seemed to have an idea that was all his own. Then he would feel dizzy, as if standing on a precipice, and he might think: This is the sacred.

This idea is perhaps all my own, no-one else's, and that is what is sacred, what sets me apart from an animal.

He used to try testing himself against Holberg. Nearly everything could be found in Holberg, and so Holberg had to be tested, since it was the birthright of every individual to think for himself. Holberg was almost always right; but then, occasionally, an idea would arise that was all his own, that did not exist in Holberg, that was his alone.

And then he would feel dizzy, and he would think: This is what is sacred.

I am not a machine.

From Holberg it was also possible to choose what you wanted: to use one part while excluding others. Thus he had excluded Holberg's somewhat confused metaphysical submissiveness and retained what was essential.

In the end it seemed to him very simple and obvious.

The sacred is what the one who is sacred does. And that is a great responsibility.

The responsibility was indeed tremendous.

He was supposed to leave the royal entourage on the return route, at Altona. He had already been paid 1,000 riksdaler, on which he could live for a long time. Yet he stayed on. Perhaps it was . . . the responsibility. He had grown fond of the mad, intelligent, confused boy who was chosen by God, and who was now about to be delivered back to the wolves at court, by whom in all certainty he would be driven even farther into illness.

Perhaps it was inevitable. Perhaps delicate little Christian, the boy with the big, terrified eyes, perhaps he was irretrievably lost. Perhaps he ought to be locked up, become a normal royal cadaver to be exploited by the wolves.

But Struensee was fond of him. In reality it was more than that; he couldn't find the right word for it. But it was a feeling he could not escape.

He had no children of his own.

He had always imagined eternal life to be like having a child. That was how the eternal was achieved: by living on through a child. But the only child he now had was this trembling, mentally-deranged boy who could have been so splendid – if only the wolves hadn't almost torn him to bits.

He hated the wolves.

Rantzau had persuaded him that time, nine months ago; it seemed like an eternity. There was sickness in Copenhagen too, he had said. And no doubt that was true. But it was not as simple as that. He was not naïve. If he now continued on to Copenhagen, it was not to be a doctor to the poor of the Nørrebro district, or to cup impoverished

Danes. Nor the children of the court. He realized what it would mean.

The fact that he did not leave the expedition in Altona. Did not flee to the East Indies. It was a form of responsibility. And he was almost certain that he had made the wrong decision.

If indeed it was a decision.

Or was it that he did not decide to stop the coach in Altona, did not decide to get out, and thus did not decide to remain in his old life: but continued on instead, into a new life. Simply continued, never actually decided, but simply continued.

They stepped ashore in Korsør and continued through the winter storm to Copenhagen.

The King and Struensee were alone in the coach.

Christian was asleep. He had put his head on Struensee's knee, not wearing his wig, but with a blanket over him; and as they slowly drove north-east through the Danish snowstorm, Struensee sat motionless, thinking that the sacred is what the one who is sacred does, all the while stroking Christian's hair with his hand. The European tour would soon be over, and something entirely different would start, something he knew nothing about, nor did he want to.

Christian was asleep. He whimpered, but the sound was impossible to decipher. He seemed to be dreaming about something delightful or ghastly; impossible to tell. Perhaps it was about the reunion of the lovers.

PART III

THE LOVERS

Chapter 7 · The Riding Master

I

On January 14, 1769, the royal entourage finally reached Copenhagen.

Two miles outside the city gates, the worn and muddy coaches were brought to a halt and exchanged; new coaches stood ready, with silk travelling rugs in place of blankets, and the Queen took her place in the coach beside her consort Christian VII.

The two of them were alone. They studied each other closely, as if to discover changes they had hoped for, or feared.

Before the procession started off, darkness had fallen; it was bitterly cold, and the incursion of coaches made its entry through Vesterport. Hundreds of soldiers were posted, with torches in hand. The guardsmen paraded, though without music.

The 16 coaches drove towards the palace gates. Inside the courtyard the court was assembled. Everyone had been waiting in the dark and cold, and spirits were low.

Upon arrival, no-one remembered to introduce Struensee and the Queen to each other.

Under the glow of the torches, in the icy sleet, a welcoming ceremony was held for the King. As soon as the coaches had stopped, he summoned Struensee, who now walked behind and slightly to one side of the royal couple. At the end of the line of those who were waiting – the whole cheering reception committee – stood Guldberg. He fixed an unwavering gaze on the King and his royal physician.

There were many who stared and scrutinized.

As they climbed the stairs, Struensee asked the King:

"Who was that little man who gave you such an evil look?"

"Guldberg."

"Who is he?"

The King waited to give his reply, walking on ahead; then he turned around, and with a quite unexpected expression of hatred, he snarled:

"He knows! KNOWS! Where Caterine is!"

Struensee didn't understand.

"Evil!" the King went on in the same rancorous tone. "Evil and insignificant!"

"His eyes, at least," Struensee then said, "were not insignificant."

2

Alone in the coach with the King, the little English girl hadn't said a word.

She didn't know whether she hated the thought of this reunion, or longed for it. Perhaps it wasn't Christian that she longed for but something else. A change.

She had begun to realize that she had a body.

Before, her body was something which the ladies-in-waiting, their eyes tactfully lowered, helped her to cover, and which she then carried around in its armour under the gaze of the court – like a small warship. At first she thought she consisted only of armour. It was the armour of the Queen that defined her character. Clothed in this rôle she was the little armoured warship, watched by these astonishing Danes who spoke her language so miserably, and whose personal hygiene was so repugnant. All of them were dusty and foul smelling from cheap perfume and old powder.

Then she discovered her body.

After the birth of the child, when her ladies-in-waiting withdrew for the night, she became accustomed to removing her night-gown and lying shamelessly naked under the ice-cold sheets. Then she would touch her body; not to be lewd, no, it was not lewdness, she thought, it was so she could slowly identify and explore this body which now lay freed from its court gowns and powder.

Just her skin.

She had begun to like her body. It felt more and more as if it were hers. After the child was born and her breasts had shrunk back to their normal size, she had begun to like her body. She liked her skin. She liked her stomach, her thighs; she could lie there for hours, thinking: This is, in fact, my body.

It's lovely to touch.

During the King's European travels she had grown plumper, and at the same time she seemed to grow into her body. She could feel that people regarded her not just as the Queen, but as something else besides. She wasn't naïve, after all. She knew that something existed in connection with her naked body under the armour and her title, something that created around her an invisible radiance of sex, desire and death.

The Queen was, of course, forbidden fruit – and a woman. That's how she instinctively knew that men looked right through her clothing and saw her body, which she now liked. She was certain that they wanted to penetrate her, and that it was the death in this that enticed them.

The forbidden fruit was there. It radiated right through the armour. She was the most forbidden of all women, and she knew that the sexual aura surrounding her was utterly irresistible to them.

It was the ultimate interdiction: a naked woman, and the Queen, and for that reason it was also death. To desire the Queen was to touch death. She was forbidden, and desired, and anyone who touched the most forbidden of all would have to die. It excited them; she knew that. She saw it in their eyes. And once she was aware of it, all the others seemed to become ensnared, ever more strongly, in an intense and silent radiance.

She thought about this a great deal. It filled her with a curious exaltation: she was the Holy Grail, and if this Holy Grail were conquered, it would bring them the utmost pleasure – and death.

She could see it in them. Her sex was forever present in their consciousness. It felt like an itch to them. It plagued them. She imagined how they would think about her all the time as they fornicated with their mistresses and whores, how they would shut their eyes and fantasize that it was not their whore or wife but the Queen's exceedingly forbidden body into which they were thrusting; and it filled her with a tremendous sense of power.

She was present in their bodies as a realization that this body meant death. And the Grail.

She was like an itch on the phallus of the court. And they couldn't reach her. Sex and death and an itch. And they couldn't win release from this obsession, no matter how much they tried to fornicate their way out of it, no matter how much they tried to empty their itch into their women. She alone was utterly inaccessible, and alone in uniting passion and death.

It was a form of . . . power.

But sometimes she would think: I like my body. And I know that I'm like an itch on the phallus of the court. But couldn't I also use my body freely, and feel the absolute nearness of death to my sex, and take pleasure from it myself? And sometimes at night, as she lay naked, she would touch herself, touch her sex, and the pleasure would rise like a hot wave through her body, which she now liked even more.

And surprisingly enough, she felt no shame, but that she was a live human being.

3

Christian, that delicate husband who never spoke to her, who was he? Didn't he feel the itch?

He was the one who was outside. And she tried to understand who he was.

In April, the Queen attended a performance at the Royal Theatre of the play *Zaïre* by the Frenchman Voltaire.

Monsieur Voltaire had sent this play to the King with a personal greeting, and the King wanted to play one of the rôles himself. He also rehearsed the rôle.

In the accompanying letter Monsieur Voltaire had intimated that the play contained a secret message, a key to the actions which the Most Estimable King of Denmark, the Light of the North and the saviour of the oppressed, would soon undertake.

After reading the play many times, the King declared his desire to play the rôle of the Sultan.

And he was not at all a bad actor.

He spoke his lines slowly, with peculiar emphasis, which created a surprising tension in the verses. His perplexing pauses created a tension, as if he had suddenly realized some hidden meaning and was stopping himself, as if in mid-stride. And when she saw him on stage, Caroline Mathilde felt a strange and reluctant attraction for her spouse.

On stage he was a different person. His lines seemed more genuine than his conversation. As if he were emerging for the first time.

> *What do I know now, what else have I learned*
> *If not that lies and truth are as alike*
> *As if they were two drops of water.*
> *Doubt! Doubt! Yes, all is doubt.*
> *And nothing but doubt is true.*

In one sense he looked comical in his costume. That Oriental guise! That turban! And the curved sword that seemed much too big for his small, delicate body! And yet he spoke his long monologues with remarkable conviction, as if at that moment, on that stage, and before the entire court, he was creating his lines. It was at that very moment that they were born. Yes, it was as if this mad little boy, who so far had lived his life by saying the court's lines in the court's theatre, was now, for the first time, speaking without a script. For the first time the words came from within.

As if he were creating the lines right there, on the stage.

> *A crime have I committed*
> *Against my ruler's sceptre*
> *And power have I squandered when I tried*
> *To bear it.*

He played his rôle quietly, but with passion, and the other actors seemed stunned by his performance; sometimes they would forget their own lines and freeze in position, staring at the King. Where did His Majesty's controlled rage come from? And that sense of conviction, which could not have come from the theatre?

> *I wish to be alone – in this hell!*
> *My shame in blood, in blood! Shall I*
> *Wipe away myself.*
> *Here is my altar, an altar of revenge*
> *And I – the head priest!*

Afterwards the applause lasted for a long time, but seemed almost fearful. Caroline Mathilde noted that the German royal physician, Doctor Struensee, stopped applauding after only a brief moment, perhaps not for lack of appreciation, she imagined, but for some other reason.

He was regarding Christian with an odd expression of curiosity, leaning forward, as if about to stand up and approach the King, as if with a question on his lips.

She was almost certain that this new favourite, this Doctor Struensee, was her most dangerous enemy. And that it was necessary to crush him.

4

The silence surrounding the Queen gradually seemed to become magnetized after the arrival of the new enemy.

She was quite certain. Something dangerous was going to take place, something would happen, something would change. Before, the world had been insufferably boring; an *ennui* in which life at court and in Copenhagen and in Denmark seemed like one of those winter days when the fog from Øresund was thick and still over the water, and she would ask to be driven down to the shore and she would stand on the rocks and look at the birds resting in the black, motionless, quicksilver-like water; and when a bird rose up, beating the tips of its wings against the surface of the water and disappeared into the mist, she would think: *This water is the vast sea, and on the other side is England, and if I were a bird with wings* . . . but then the cold and *ennui* would force her back.

Back then life stood still and smelled of death and seaweed. Now life stood still, but it smelled of death or life; the difference was that the silence seemed more dangerous, and it filled her with an odd excitement.

What was it? Was it the new enemy?

Doctor Struensee was not like the others, and he was her enemy. He wanted to destroy her, of that she was certain. He was always near the King, and he had power over him. Everyone had taken note of Doctor Struensee's power. But what puzzled everyone, and puzzled her too, was that he didn't seem inclined to make use of his power.

He exerted power more and more, that much was evident. But with a sort of quiet reluctance.

What was it he wanted?

He was considered a handsome man. He was still young. He was a head taller than all the courtiers, he was exceedingly friendly and reticent, and at court he was called "The Silent One".

But what was it he was keeping to himself?

One day she was sitting with her crochet work in the Rose Lane just beyond the inner courtyard of the palace; all at once she was overwhelmed by such great sorrow that she could not control herself. The crochet work fell to her lap, she bent her head and buried her face in her hands, feeling at her wits' end.

This was not the first time she had wept in Copenhagen. Sometimes she felt as if her time in Denmark was nothing but a long period of weeping. But this was the first time she had wept outside her rooms.

As she sat there alone, her face buried, she didn't see Struensee approach. Suddenly he was there. He came up to her calmly and without a sound, pulled out a lace-trimmed handkerchief, and offered it to her.

In this way he indicated that he had seen her tears. What shamelessness, what a breach of discretion.

Yet she took the handkerchief and dried her tears. Then he began to bow and took a step backwards, as if to leave. She felt it necessary to rebuke him.

"Doctor Struensee," she said. "Everyone wants to flock around the King. But soon you'll be the only one. What is it you want so ardently? What is it that you're flocking around?"

He merely smiled, a swift little humorous smile, shook his head, bowed, and left without a word.

Without a word!

What enraged her most was his friendly inaccessibility.

He didn't even seem to look through her clothing the way the others did, at her forbidden body. If she was the most forbidden of women, the Holy Grail, an itch on the phallus of the court, why did he seem so silent, friendly, and uninterested?

Sometimes she thought: Isn't he even enticed by the lure of the black, quicksilver-like sea of death?

5

In April, summer arrived.

It came early, the greenery quickly exploded, and the promenades in Bernstorff Park were magnificent. The Queen wanted to walk alone, ten paces ahead of her attendants. The ladies-in-waiting, with the child in a baby carriage, followed behind.

After Fru von Plessen was taken from her, she had refused to choose any other confidante. It was a decision based on principle.

It was on May 12 that she met Struensee in the park.

He stopped, he was walking alone, and he bowed courteously, with that little, friendly, perhaps ironic smile on his lips that annoyed and bewildered her so much.

Why did she stop, too? Because she had a purpose. That was the reason. She had a legitimate and natural purpose, and that was why she stopped and addressed him.

That was why it was quite natural for her to stop.

"Doctor . . . Struensee," she said. "It is . . . Struensee? Isn't it?"

He pretended not to notice the slight sarcasm, but instead replied: "Yes, Your Majesty?"

"It's about the cupping of the Crown Prince. Smallpox is spreading through Copenhagen; they tell me you're a specialist, but I'm afraid, and I don't know whether we should dare . . ."

He gave her a sombre look.

"There's nothing wrong with being afraid."

"No?"

The ladies-in-waiting with the child in the baby carriage had stopped a respectful distance away and were waiting.

Then he said, "I could, if Your Royal Highness so wishes, perform a cupping. I believe that I have a great deal of experience. I have worked with cuppings in Altona for many years."

"And you are . . . a man of science . . . and know everything about cupping?"

"I did not write my dissertation on cupping," he replied with a little smile. "It has been a matter of practical experience. Several thousand children. My dissertation was not concerned with that topic."

"What was it concerned with, then?"

"'On the risks of aberrant motions of the limbs.'"

He fell silent.

"And which . . . limbs run the greatest risk?"

He didn't reply. What a strange tension there was in the air; she sensed that he grew hesitant, and it filled her with a kind of triumph; now she could continue.

"The King speaks well of you," she said.

He gave a small bow.

"On those occasions when the King speaks to me, he speaks well of you," she clarified and immediately regretted doing so; why had she said that? On those occasions when he speaks to me. No doubt he understood what she meant, but it was no concern of his.

There was no reply.

"But I don't know you," she added in a cool tone.

"No. No-one does. Not in Copenhagen."

"No-one?"

"Not here."

"Do you have other interests aside from . . . the King's health?"

He now seemed curious, as if his inaccessibility had been broken, and for the first time he gave her an intense look, as if waking up and seeing her.

"Philosophy," he told her.

"Aha. Anything else?"

"Horseback riding."

"Oh . . ." she said, "I can't ride."

"It's possible to . . . learn . . . to ride."

"Difficult?"

"Well, yes," he said, "but wonderful."

Now, she thought, now this brief conversation has grown much too intimate. She knew that he had noticed what was forbidden, of that she was certain. Suddenly she was furious with herself, that she was the one who had been forced to bring it to light. He should have noticed on his own. Without help. Like the others.

She began walking. Then she stopped, turned around, and said:

"You are a stranger at court."

It was not a question. It was a statement. Meant to put him in his place.

And it was then that he gave a reply, quite naturally and as if it were self-evident, that was absolutely perfect:

"Yes. As are you, Your Majesty."

Then she couldn't help herself.

"In that case," she said quickly and without expression, "you will teach me to ride."

6

Count Rantzau, who had once, only a year earlier, proposed to Guldberg the idea of the German Doctor Struensee as a beneficial royal *medicus* for the King, could no longer tell what the situation was.

In a strange way he felt as if things were out of control.

Either everything had gone very well, or else he had misjudged his friend and protégé Struensee, who was always with the King but seemed oddly passive. So close to His Majesty, but with such silence surrounding the two of them. It was said that Struensee now opened the King's mail, culled what was important, and wrote the drafts for the King's decrees.

What could this be, if not an indication of power? And more than an indication.

It was for this reason that he had invited Struensee to take a walk through the city to investigate the situation as to the "cupping urgency".

That was how he had expressed it. The cupping urgency was what he believed would be the proper starting-point for renewing the old intimacy with his friend.

The silent man from Altona.

They walked through Copenhagen. Struensee seemed unperturbed by the decay and filth, as if he were all too familiar with such things, but Rantzau was horrified.

"A smallpox epidemic could reach the court," Rantzau said. "It could seep in . . . and leave us defenceless . . ."

"In spite of the Danish national defence," replied Struensee. "In spite of the great appropriations for the army."

"The Crown Prince must be protected," Rantzau retorted coldly, since he didn't find it a suitable topic for jest.

"I know," Struensee replied swiftly. "The Queen has already asked me. I will do it."

Rantzau was almost struck dumb, but he pulled himself together and gave the proper response in the right tone of voice.

"The Queen? Already? How splendid."

"Yes, the Queen."

"The King will idolize you for the rest of your life if the cupping is successful. He already idolizes you. It's amazing. He trusts you."

Struensee did not reply.

"What is the King's . . . situation? In fact?"

"It's complicated," said Struensee.

He said no more than that. And it was precisely what he thought. During the months that had passed since their return from Europe, he felt he had come to understand that the King's situation was just that: complicated.

Christian's conversation with the French encyclopedists in Paris had been an unprecedented moment. And for several weeks he had believed that Christian could be healed; that this little boy might indeed have suffered from frostbite of the soul, but that it was not by any means too late. During those weeks, Christian seemed to awaken from his lethargy; he talked about having a mission to create a kingdom of reason, that the court was a madhouse but that he steadfastly and completely trusted Struensee.

He trusted him steadfastly and completely. Steadfastly and completely. He repeated that often.

But it was the reason behind his devotion that was so puzzling, so ominous. Struensee was to be his "rod", he said; as if he were once again a child, had captured the cane of the dreaded headmaster, and had now placed it in the hands of a new vassal.

Struensee told him that he did not wish to be a "rod", not even a sword, nor an avenger. The kingdom of reason could not be built on revenge. And together, over and over like a liturgy, they had read the letter that Voltaire had written to the King, and about him.

Light. Reason. But at the same time Struensee knew that this light and reason was in the hands of a boy who bore the darkness inside him like a mighty black torch.

How could light be born from that?

Yet there was something about the image of the "rod" that attracted Struensee, in spite of himself. Was the "rod" necessary for the change? Voltaire had said something that he could not forget; about the necessity (or did he say duty?) of stepping through the aperture that might suddenly be created in history. And he had always dreamed that changes might be possible, but thought that he himself, an insignificant German doctor from Altona, was no more than one of life's small workmen whose task it was to scrape away with his knife the filth of life from all those people. He did not think "scalpel"; that was too sharp and ominous. It was linked to the autopsies when he cut open the suicides or those who had been executed. No, he had pictured it as the simple knife of a workman. To cut in order to expose life's pure wood. Like a workman.

To scrape, with the knife of a workman. To scrape away the filth of life. So that the surface of the wood became pure, veined, and alive.

But Diderot's greeting from Voltaire contained something else.

He hadn't used the word "duty". But that's what he meant. And Struensee would wake up at night in his room in that ghastly, ice-cold palace and lie still, staring up at the ceiling and think all of a sudden: Perhaps I am the one, and *this is the moment that will never come again, but if power seizes hold of me, I will be lost and doomed to destruction and I don't want that*; it made him breathe faster, almost in agony, and he began to think that this was a responsibility, that it was a tremendous responsibility, and that this moment would never come again. This moment that was Copenhagen.

That HE was the one!

It was as if he saw the aperture of history open, and he knew that it was the aperture of life, and he was the only one who could step through this opening. Perhaps, just perhaps, it was his duty.

And he was tremendously frightened.

He had not wanted to describe the King's situation to Rantzau. It had at that moment felt sticky. Rantzau was a sticky man. He hadn't seen this before, not at the Ascheberg Gardens, not during those marvellous summer evenings in Rousseau's hut, but now he could clearly feel how sticky it was.

He wanted to keep him out of it.

"Complicated?" Rantzau asked.

"He dreams of creating light," Struensee told him. "And the kingdom of reason. And I fear that I may be able to help him."

"Fear?" said Rantzau.

"Yes, I am afraid."

"Excellent," Rantzau said in an odd tone of voice. "The kingdom of reason. Reason. And the Queen?"

"A strange woman."

"Just as long as reason doesn't kill the hydra of passion," Rantzau said lightly.

Linked to this was an event that took place three days earlier.

Afterwards, Struensee feared that he had misinterpreted it. But it was precisely the . . . complicated . . . nature of the situation that had preoccupied him for several days.

It was perhaps because of this event that he used the word "complicated" with Rantzau.

This is what happened.

Christian and Struensee were alone in the King's study. The dog, as usual, was sitting on the King's knee; Christian was signing with one hand a series of documents that Struensee, at the King's request, had reworked from a purely linguistic point of view.

This was the agreement they had reached. Struensee wrote everything. He insisted, however, that this was nothing more than a linguistic reworking. Christian signed his name slowly and with ceremony, now and then muttering to himself.

"What *outrage* this will provoke. Bernstorff. Guldberg. *Guldberg* will know his place. He will now have to know his place! I will destroy. The cabinet. Everything."

Struensee observed him with caution but said nothing, since he had become quite familiar with the King's deranged litanies about destruction, the Phoenix, and the cleansing of the temple.

"Smash! Everything to bits! Isn't that right, Struensee? I have the right idea, don't I!"

Struensee then said in a calm and quiet voice:

"Yes, Your Majesty. Something must be done with this rotting kingdom."

"A light! From the North!"

He kissed the dog, something that often revolted Struensee, and continued:

"The temple must be cleansed! Total destruction! You're with me, aren't you?"

Everything until that point was very familiar. But Struensee, who felt a momentary weariness at the King's outburst, muttered more or less to himself:

"Your Majesty, it's not always easy to understand you."

He thought this remark would slip past the King unnoticed. But Christian put down his pen and regarded Struensee with an expression of intense sorrow, or terror, or as if he wanted to make Struensee understand.

"Yes," he said, "I have many faces."

Struensee gave him a thoughtful look since he had noted a tone of voice that was new to him.

The King then went on:

"But, Doctor Struensee, in the kingdom of reason that we will create, perhaps there is only room for those who have been cast all of one piece?"

And after a moment he added:

"But if so, would there be room for me?"

7

They seemed to be waiting.

After her encounter with Struensee in the park, the Queen felt a peculiar rage; she had clearly identified it as rage.

She did not feel calm. It was rage.

At night she once again took off her night-gown and stroked her private parts. Three times desire came in a great wave, yet now nothing brought her any peace, but left only rage behind.

I'm about to lose control, she thought. I must regain control.

I must regain control.

Christian, Caroline Mathilde, Struensee. Those three.

They seemed to be observing each other with curiosity and suspicion. The court observed them too. As they observed the court. Everyone seemed to be waiting.

Sometimes they were also observed from the outside. Later that autumn a letter was written which, in a certain way, was a portent of what would come. A sharp-eyed observer, Crown Prince Gustav of Sweden, later to be King Gustav III – he inherits the throne later that same year – travelled to Paris that year and stopped for a short time in Copenhagen. He saw something. Perhaps not something that had occurred but something that might take place.

He reports in several letters to his mother about the situation at the Danish court.

He is disappointed in the Danish court, finding the palace tasteless. Gold, gold, everything is gold, gilded with more gold. No style. The parades are pitiful. The soldiers do not march in step; they turn slowly, without precision. Lechery and depravity at court, "even worse than at our own". Denmark can hardly be considered a military threat to Sweden, in his judgement.

Bad taste and slow turns.

Yet it is the royal couple and Struensee who provoke his greatest interest.

"But the strangest of all is the lord of the palace and everything about him. A fine-looking figure, but he is so small and slender that it would be easy to mistake him for a child of 13 or a girl dressed up as a man. Madame du Londelle in men's clothing would look a good deal like him, and I don't think the King is much bigger than she is.

"What makes it quite impossible to believe that he could be the King is that he wears no medals; not only has he renounced wearing the Order of the Seraphim, but he wears no Order of the Star. He bears a strong resemblance to our Crown Princess, and he talks like her, although he talks more. He seems shy, and whenever he says anything he corrects himself just as she does and seems to fear that he may have said something wrong. His gait is quite extraordinary; as if his legs were about to give way under him.

"The Queen is an entirely different story. She gives the impression of being daring, strong and robust. Her manner is quite unrestrained and without inhibition. Her speech is lively and witty but also very quick. She is neither pretty nor homely; in height she is about the same as most people, but she is stocky without being fat, always clad in a riding habit, with boots, and all the women in her retinue have to dress as she does; this means that in the theatre, in fact anywhere at all, the women in her entourage can be easily distinguished from the others."

Crown Prince Gustav also studied Struensee closely. At the dinner table Struensee was seated directly across from the Queen. He "ogled" the Queen in a manner which displeased the Swedish Crown Prince. "But the strangest thing of all is that Struensee has become lord of the palace; he even rules over the King. There is tremendous disapproval over this, and it seems to be growing daily. If there was as much force in this country right now as there is disapproval, things might take a serious turn."

This was in the autumn. The Swedish Crown Prince seems to have seen something.

And something *had* taken place.

Chapter 8 · *A Live Human Being*

I

Guldberg often seemed to see history as a river inexorably swelling as it moved towards the sea, merging there with the vast waters which he envisioned as the embodiment of the Eternal.

The movement of the waters was God's will. Guldberg was the insignificant observer on the shore.

This appeared to leave little place for him in the great course of history. But at the same time he imagined that this lowly observer, Guldberg, he with his clear, ice-blue eyes, had been given a rôle, thanks to his insignificance, his tenacity, and his sharp and unblinking eyes. He was not only the observer of God's inexorable power, but also an interpreter of the maelstroms in the water. The river was by nature inscrutable. But to some it had been given to see the undercurrents of the maelstroms, to master the logic of the inscrutable, and to understand the secrets of God's will.

That was also why, for safety's sake, he had acquired informants. After his meeting with the Dowager Queen in the palace chapel, he understood what his task was to be. It was not only that of interpreter. His interpretation had to be given a direction. His task was to love her little son, the little misshapen boy; and through his love for this most inconsiderable of all persons, God's will would finally be realized in Denmark.

But it was God's will, first and foremost, to burn away all filth and to consume the ideas of the Enlightenment in God's great fire.

The meeting in the palace chapel was of enormous importance. But he had not become a hired henchman. This task, this calling, was not the result of a desire for reward. He could not be bought. He wanted to say this to the Dowager Queen during their meeting in the chapel, but he had not been able to do so. He had taken offence at the word "reward". She didn't understand that he could not be bought. He didn't want titles, rewards, power; he wanted to remain someone of little consequence, whose task it was to interpret the great, inscrutable waters of God.

He felt most uneasy about the way things were developing. This had to do with his belief that Struensee could not be bought either. If he could, in fact, be bought, Guldberg still had no idea what with. Perhaps he could not be bought. Perhaps this great tree could be felled by something else; but if so, he would have to see through Struensee, and understand where his weak point might be.

Struensee was an upstart; in that sense he was like Guldberg. They were both small shrubs among the great, arrogant trees. He loved these images. Shrubs, trees, felled forests. And finally: triumph. Sometimes he hated Struensee with love, almost with empathy, even tenderness. But he knew that his task was to see through him.

He feared that Struensee was no ordinary intellectual. But he had an inkling of what his weak point might be. Guldberg alone, from the bank of the river, had understood. That Struensee's weakness, paradoxically, was that he had no desire for power. That his hypocritical idealism was genuine. Perhaps it was because Struensee didn't wish to be entrapped or corrupted by power. Perhaps he had renounced the great game. Perhaps he was an entirely pure human being in the service of evil. Perhaps he harboured a naïve dream that purity was possible. Perhaps he didn't want to be sullied by power. Perhaps he might succeed at this, be able to withstand the filth of power, not kill, not annihilate, not play the great power game. Be able to remain pure.

And that was precisely why Struensee was doomed to fall.

2

Guldberg had followed the grand European tour from a distance, almost day by day, through his informants. Without expression he had read the letters about the insane extravagance. Yet he did not grow uneasy until the first letters from Paris began to arrive.

That was when he realized that a new danger was looming.

Who could have known? Rantzau might have known. He had recommended Struensee, and he must have known. The report of the King's meeting with the encyclopedists was the last straw. That was why, in June, he had a long talk with Count Rantzau.

It was carried out in a businesslike tone. Guldberg reviewed part of Rantzau's curriculum vitae, including his alleged espionage for the

Russian Tsarina and how important it was to forget this minor incident, considering the unreasonably harsh punishment for treason. He briefly outlined the conditions for the game. They agreed on certain matters: that Struensee was an interloper and highly dangerous.

Rantzau, for his part, was either silent or seemed nervous.

For Guldberg, this confirmed everything. Rantzau was a spineless individual.

In addition, he had enormous debts.

During their talk Guldberg was forced to exert the utmost restraint, so as not to reveal his contempt. The great, noble trees could be bought, and would be felled.

But the small shrubs: no.

In May the situation became confused, and thus dangerous. In July he was forced to make a special report to the Dowager Queen.

They had agreed to meet at the Royal Theatre, since a conversation in the Dowager Queen's royal box before a performance would hardly be suspected as conspiratorial, and the high degree of public scrutiny was advantageous to a secret conversation.

And besides, the orchestra was tuning up.

He presented a quick, detailed summary. In May the cupping of the little Crown Prince was carried out and proved successful. That had strengthened the position of "The Silent One". The situation of the intrigue was that Holck was out of favour, while Rantzau was in, but a spineless and harmless individual. Bernstorff was to be dismissed in the autumn. Struensee was no longer Rantzau's protégé, and Struensee would soon be all-powerful. That was why Rantzau hated him, although he considered himself to be Struensee's only close friend. Brandt was in favour. The King, beyond anyone's control, had signed the decree without hesitation. The following week Struensee was to be named Royal Counsellor with an annual salary of 1,500 riksdaler. The document regarding a prohibition or "suspension" of the awarding of medals and rewards, which the King had signed the week before, was written by "The Silent One". A flood of reforms was in prospect.

"How do you know?" asked the Dowager Queen. "Surely Struensee hasn't told you of this."

"But he may have told Rantzau," was Guldberg's reply.

"Isn't he Struensee's only friend?"

"Struensee has refused to recommend that his debts should be cancelled," Guldberg explained curtly.

"An intellectual with debts in conflict with an enlightened man with principles," the Dowager Queen said as if to herself, deep in thought. "A tragedy for both of them."

Guldberg then went on with his analysis. What Struensee had recently called "linguistic reworking" of the King's decrees had now become a clear manipulation of power. The King signed everything that Struensee put before him. Reforms were surging forth like a flood. The plans which would soon be realized also included unrestricted freedom of the press, religious freedom, the transfer of Øresund tariffs to the state instead of to the royal household, resolution of the peasant question and the abolition of serfdom, the cessation of subsidies to unprofitable industries owned by the nobility, reformation of the health services, as well as a long list of detailed plans such as the seizure of church facilities on Amaliegade, which would be transformed into an orphanage.

"An orphanage for the spawn of whores," the Dowager Queen bitterly interjected.

"And, of course, a ban on the use of torture during interrogations."

"That point, at any rate," the Dowager Queen retorted, "will be repealed when we capture this rat and disarm him."

The musicians had now finished tuning their instruments, and the Dowager Queen whispered her final question:

"And the Queen's view of Struensee?"

"As to her," Guldberg replied, also in a whisper, "no-one knows a thing. But as soon as anyone does, I'll be the first to hear of it."

3

She ordered her coachman to drive her down to the shore more and more often. She would get out and stand waiting at the very edge of the water. The smell was the same, sea and seaweed, and yet not the same. At first it was boredom. Then it became the fusion of desire and death. Then it became something else.

Perhaps it had something to do with Struensee. She wanted to know what it was.

She had made inquiries and learned of his whereabouts; that was why she had switched her afternoon walk to the Royal Stables, since every Tuesday and Friday Doctor Struensee was accustomed to go out riding.

And true enough, he was there. That was why she went there, without the escort of her ladies-in-waiting. She went there to find out what was causing her such rage, and to put him in his place.

He was at the time saddling his horse, and since she was furious and had decided to put him in his place, she got straight to the point.

"Doctor Struensee," she said, "Oh, I see that you're preoccupied with your riding, I don't wish to disturb you when you're so busy."

Perplexed, he simply bowed and continued to saddle his horse without a word. That was unprecedented. Even the slightest knowledge of royal protocol dictated that he had to answer, and in a prescribed, courtly manner; but he was only a commoner.

"You have insulted the Queen of Denmark," she then told him. "I speak to you, but you do not answer. How shameless."

"That was not my intention," he said.

He did not seem at all fearful.

"Always preoccupied," she went on. "What exactly is it that you do?"

"I'm working," he replied.

"On what?"

"I am at the King's disposal. To prepare documents. To discuss matters. Occasionally to offer advice, if the King so wishes."

"You promised to give me riding lessons; I allowed you to promise that, and you haven't had time ever since! No time! But beware, you can fall into disfavour! DISFAVOUR!"

He then stopped saddling his horse, turned around, and looked at her with surprise, perhaps annoyance.

"May I ask," she added with her voice so out of control that for a moment she heard it herself and was filled with shame, "may I ask whether this WORK is so necessary, may I ask you that? And I will! What is it that . . ."

"Shall I answer?" he asked.

"Do that, Doctor Struensee."

It happened all of a sudden. She hadn't expected it. He answered with a burst of fury that surprised them both.

"Your Majesty, with all due respect, I truly am working," he said, his voice low with rage, "but not as much as I should be. What I should be working on requires time, which I don't have; I also have to sleep. I may be inadequate, but no-one can say that I'm not trying. Unfortunately, I know quite well what I'm not doing, Your Majesty, unfortunately. I ought to work to make this cursed Denmark respectable, work on the rights of the peasants, which I'm not doing; work on cutting the royal household at least by half! At least! But I'm not doing that either. Work on changing the laws so that mothers of illegitimate children are no longer punished, ARE NO LONGER PUNISHED! I'm not doing that. Work on abolishing the hypocritical penalties for adultery; I'm not doing that either, My Highly Esteemed Queen. There is such an inconceivable number of things that I'm not working on, that I ought to do, but cannot. I could go on and on with other examples of what I'm NOT working on, I could . . ."

Abruptly he broke off. He knew that he had lost his temper. A long silence ensued, and then he said:

"I beg your forgiveness. I beg you . . . to forgive me. For this . . ."

"Yes?"

"For this unpardonable indiscretion."

Suddenly she felt quite calm. Her rage vanished, not because she had put him in his place, nor because she had been put in her place; no, it was simply gone.

"What a beautiful horse," she said.

Yes, the horses were beautiful. How wonderful it must be to work with these handsome creatures, their skin, their nostrils, their eyes which regarded her in silence and tranquillity.

She stepped up to the horse, stroked its hindquarters.

"Such a beautiful animal. Do you think horses like their bodies?"

He didn't reply. She kept on stroking: its neck, mane and head. The horse stood quite still, waiting. She did not turn to face Struensee as she said in a low voice:

"Do you despise me?"

"I don't understand," he said.

"Do you think: pretty little girl, 17 years old, stupid, has seen nothing of the world, understands nothing. A beautiful creature. Is that what you think?"

He shook his head.

"No."

"Then what am I?"

He had begun to slowly groom the horse; then he stopped.

"Alive."

"What do you mean?"

"A live human being."

"So you've noticed that?"

"Yes. I've noticed."

"How nice," she said very quietly. "How . . . nice. There aren't many live human beings in Copenhagen."

He looked at her.

"That's not something Your Majesty can know. There is another world outside the court."

She thought: It's true, but imagine that he dares to say so. Perhaps he has seen something other than the armoured warship, or my body. He sees something else, and he is bold. But is he saying this because he sees me as a little girl, or is he saying it because it's true?

"I understand," she said. "You think, she hasn't seen much of the world. Is that it? Is that what you think? Seventeen years old, never lived outside the court? Never seen anything?"

"It's not a question of age," he replied. "Some people can reach 100 and still have seen nothing."

She looked him in the eye and for the first time felt that she was not afraid, or enraged, but instead calm and curious.

"It doesn't matter that you were angry," she said. "It was splendid to see someone . . . on fire. Someone alive. I've never seen that before. It was splendid. Now we can start riding, Doctor Struensee."

4

The cabinet was assembled, for once in its entirety, when the King made the announcement that Doctor J. L. Struensee had been appointed Royal Lecturer with the title of Royal Counsellor.

It was expected. No-one showed any reaction.

He furthermore announced that there was no need for any additional cabinet meetings until the end of September, and that if he happened to sign any royal decrees, they did not need to be confirmed by the cabinet.

An ice-cold, paralysing silence followed. This was not expected. What did this mean in practice?

"At the same time I would like to most graciously announce," concluded the King, "that today I am pleased to appoint my dog, Vitrius, as Imperial Counsellor, and henceforth he shall be treated with the respect befitting this title."

It was very quiet for a very long time.

Then the King rose without a word; everyone followed his example, and the hall emptied out.

In the corridor outside, small groups gathered for several minutes but soon dispersed. During this brief time, however, Guldberg managed to exchange a few words with the Royal Marshal, Count Holck, and the Foreign Minister, Count Bernstorff.

"The country is now facing its greatest crisis ever," he said. "Meet me tonight in the chambers of the Dowager Queen at ten o'clock."

It was an extraordinary situation. Guldberg seemed to be over-stepping both the authority and protocol of his position. But neither of the other two men seemed shocked. And he then added "quite unnecessarily", as he later thought:

"Absolute secrecy."

The next day at the morning meeting only three were in attendance.

King Christian VII; his dog, the schnauzer Vitrius, who was the newly appointed counsellor and who had laid himself over the King's feet and fallen asleep; and Struensee.

Struensee handed one document after another to the King, who after a while indicated with a wave of his hand that he wanted to take a break in their work.

The King stubbornly stared down at his desk; he did not drum his fingers, he did not have spasms, his face seemed marked only by a sorrow so great that for a moment Struensee grew frightened.

Or perhaps it was an unprecedented loneliness?

Without lifting his gaze, and in a voice that was calm and earnestly intent, the King then said:

"The Queen is suffering from melancholy. She's lonely, she's a stranger in this country. I have found it impossible to assuage her melancholy. You must lift this burden from my shoulders. You *must* attend to her."

After a moment's silence Struensee said:

"My only wish is that the present strained relationship between the royal couple might be eased."

The King then repeated:

"You must lift this burden from my shoulders."

Struensee stared at the papers lying in front of him. Christian did not raise his eyes. The dog slept heavily on his feet.

5

He could not figure her out.

Struensee had seen her in Altona during her stay there before going on to Copenhagen, but he had not *really* seen her. It was obvious that she was only a child, and terrified.

He was indignant. People should not be treated like that. But he hadn't truly seen her.

Later on he did see her. All at once he understood that she portended a great danger. Everyone had spoken of her as "enchanting" or "charming", but that was what people were forced to say about queens. It meant nothing. It was assumed that she was weak-willed and charming and that her life would be a hell, although on a higher plane than housewives of the middle class, and on a much different plane than commoners. But something about her made him believe that the little English girl had been underestimated.

Her complexion was magnificent. She had very beautiful hands. Once he found himself imagining her hand wrapped around his member.

Her wish to learn to ride was astonishing.

She almost always astonished him, the few times that they met. He seemed to be watching her grow, but he had no idea where it would end.

The arrangements regarding the first riding lesson were made without any problem. But when the time came, she arrived wearing men's clothing; no woman of the royal house had ever ridden like a man, meaning with her legs apart and on either side of the horse.

It was considered obscene. Yet she appeared dressed in a man's riding outfit.

He made no comment.

He took her gently by the hand and led her over to the horse for the first lesson.

"The first rule," he said, "is caution."

"And the second?"

"Courage."

"I like the second one better," she said.

The horse had been selected with care; it was very calm. They rode in Bernstorff Park for an hour.

The horse walked quietly. Everything went very well.

She rode for the first time in her life.

Open fields. Groves of trees.

Struensee rode at her side. They talked about animals.

About the way animals moved, about whether animals could dream, whether they had a concept of their own lives. Whether their love was reserved for anyone special.

Whether they could experience their own bodies, what their perception of human beings was, and what horses dreamed of.

The Queen said that she imagined horses to be different from other animals. That they were born insignificant, with legs that were much too long, but that very soon they became conscious of their lives, their bodies, and started to dream, that they could feel fear or love, that they possessed secrets that could be read in their eyes, if you simply looked into them. It was necessary to look into their eyes, then you would understand that horses dreamed when they slept, standing, wrapped in their secrets.

He said: I realize that never once in my life have I dared to look at a horse's dreams.

And then the Queen laughed for the first time in the almost three years that she had been in Copenhagen.

The following day, the rumours began to spread.

As Struensee was passing through the arcade of the palace he met the Dowager Queen; she stopped him.

Her face was like stone. If the truth be told, her face was always like stone; but now there was an underlying rage that made her almost terrifying.

"Doctor Struensee," she said, "I have been informed that the Queen went riding dressed in men's attire, sitting astride the horse. Is this true?"

"Yes, it's true," he replied.

"That is a breach of protocol, and a disgrace."

"In Paris," he said, "the women always ride in that manner. On the continent no-one regards it as disgraceful. In Paris it is . . ."

"In Paris," she was quick to reply, "there is much indecency. We don't need to import it to Denmark."

He bowed but said nothing.

"One more question, Doctor Struensee, about these continental . . . ideas."

He gave a small bow.

"What is the ultimate goal of those . . . men of the Enlightenment? I've just been . . . wondering."

He chose his words with care.

"To create a heaven on earth," he then said with a fleeting smile.

"And what then becomes of the . . . real . . . heaven? And by that I mean God's heaven."

With an equally gentle smile he said:

"It becomes . . . according to their opinion . . . less necessary."

The Dowager Queen said in the same calm voice:

"I see. That is also why these blasphemers must be destroyed."

Whereupon she turned on her heel and left.

Struensee stood motionless for a long time, staring after her. He was thinking: To be truthful, I'm not a very brave person, since I can feel an ice-cold flash of terror when an old woman addresses me. If you see an aperture in history and know that you ought to step through – is it right for a man who is frightened by an old woman to take on such a mission?

Later he thought: The opposition is starting to show itself. Not just an old woman. The nobles. Guldberg. There are many. The opposition will very soon become clear.

Those opposed are the ones I will no doubt be able to distinguish. But who are the supporters?

Chapter 9 · Rousseau's Hut

I

It becomes more difficult to understand what is happening.

The spotlight seems to be shrinking around a few actors on stage. Yet they are still standing with their faces turned away from each other.

Ready to speak their lines very soon. Still with averted faces, and silent.

One evening, as Christian was telling Struensee once again about his nightmares of Sergeant Mörl's agonizing death and began getting lost in the details, Struensee started wandering around the room and with some anger told the King to stop.

Christian was astonished. He had been allowed to talk about this while Reverdil was still there, before he was banished as a punishment. Now Struensee seemed to have lost his composure. Christian asked him why. Struensee merely said:

"Your Majesty doesn't understand. And has never made any effort to understand. Despite the fact that we have known each other for a long time. But I'm not a brave person. I'm terrified of pain. I don't want to think about pain. I'm easily frightened. That's how it is, and Your Majesty should have known, if Your Majesty was interested."

Christian stared at Struensee during the doctor's outburst, and then he said:

"I too am afraid of death."

"I'm not afraid of death!" Struensee replied with impatience. "Only of pain. Only of pain!"

From the late summer of 1770 there is a sketch done by Christian of a Negro boy.

He very rarely made any drawings, but those that exist were accomplished with great skill. The sketch depicts Moranti, the Negro page given to the King in order to dispel his melancholy, "so he would have someone to play with".

No-one should speak in that fashion. Melancholy was the correct word, not playmate. But Brandt, who came up with the idea, expresses it in precisely that way: a playmate for His Majesty. A mood of stifled resignation had spread around the King. It was difficult to find playmates among the courtiers. The King seemed to focus all his energy for the day on the hour he spent signing the documents and communiqués that Struensee placed before him; but after they parted, he would be overcome by apathy and sink into his muttering. Brandt had grown weary of the King's company and bought a Negro page as a plaything for him. When he sought permission to do so, Struensee shook his head in resignation, but gave his consent.

Struensee's position at court was now so entrenched that his consent was also required for the purchase of Negro slaves.

It was quite natural that he should grow weary, Brandt had explained, since a playful relationship with His Majesty could not be considered one of his tasks as theatre director. In actual fact, Brandt was exhausted and furious. His relationship with His Majesty had grown more and more monotonous, since the King would often sit in his chair for days on end, waving his hands and muttering to himself or staring blankly at the wall. The King was also in the habit of placing his chair close to the wall and turned towards it, to avoid looking at his surroundings.

What was Brandt to do? Conversation was difficult. He couldn't very well position himself between the chair and the wall, he explained to Struensee.

"Do as you like," Struensee told him. "This place is still a madhouse."

The Negro page was christened Moranti.

Moranti would end up playing a certain rôle in what followed, even in the diplomatic reports.

Later that same autumn, as the situation reached a critical stage and the troubling reports about Struensee's power also reached foreign rulers, the French Ambassador requested an audience with the King. But when the Ambassador arrived, Struensee was the only one present in the room, and he explained that King Christian VII was indisposed that day, but he wished to express his respect and devotion to the Ambassador of the French government.

"Doctor Struensee . . ." the French Ambassador began but was immediately corrected by Struensee.

"Counsellor to the King."

The atmosphere was charged and hostile, but courteous.

" . . . a rumour has reached us regarding the Danish monarch's almost . . . revolutionary plans. Interesting. Interesting. We are, of course, well acquainted with such ideas in Paris. And critical of them. As no doubt you know. We would like, with all due respect, to be assured that no dark . . . revolutionary . . . forces might by mistake! By mistake! Slip out. In your country. Or in Europe. So that the contagion of enlightenment will not . . . yes, that is how I would express it, the contagion! Will not catch hold around us. And since we know that the young monarch has your ear, we would like . . ."

Struensee, against protocol, had not invited the French Ambassador to sit down; they now stood facing each other at a distance of about five paces.

"Are people afraid in Paris?" Struensee asked in a somewhat ironic tone of voice. "Afraid of the little, insignificant country of Denmark? Is that what you want to say?"

"Perhaps we wish to know what is going on."

"What is going on is of Danish concern."

"Which does not concern . . . ?"

"Precisely."

The Ambassador gave Struensee an icy stare and then exclaimed in a fierce voice, as if for a moment he had lost his self-control:

"A man of the Enlightenment such as yourself, Doctor Struensee, ought not be so insolent!"

"We are merely matter-of-fact."

"But if the royal power is in jeopardy . . ."

"It is not in jeopardy."

"We have heard otherwise."

"Then stop listening."

Suddenly wild shouts could be heard from the palace courtyard. Struensee flinched and went over to the window. What he saw was King Christian VII playing with his page. Christian was pretending to be a horse, and the little Negro boy was on his back, shouting wildly as he swung his riding crop and His Majesty crawled around on all fours.

Struensee turned around, but it was too late. The French Ambassador had followed him to the window and looked out. Struensee then drew the drapes, his expression resolute.

But the situation was quite clear.

"Herr Struensee," the French Ambassador said with a tone of derision and fury, "I am not an idiot. Neither is my king, nor are the other regents of Europe. I say this with the frankness you claim to value so highly. You are playing with fire. We will not permit the great consuming revolutionary fire to start in this filthy little country."

And then: the precise bow, as required.

The situation down in the palace courtyard was clear and genuine. There was no escaping it.

Was this the absolute ruler with the torch of reason in his hand? Or a madman? What was Struensee going to do with him?

No, he had no idea what he was going to do with Christian.

The problem was growing all the time. In the end it was a problem that seemed to put Struensee himself in question. Was he the right person? Or was the black torch also inside him?

The week before the little Negro page arrived at court, Struensee was gripped by desperation. Perhaps the voice of reason should speak. Perhaps it would be wisest to leave Christian to his illness, allow him to be swallowed up by the dark.

Could light come from the darkness of the black torch? Reason was supposed to be the lever that would be placed under the house of the world. But without any fixed point? What if reason could find no fulcrum?

But he was fond of the child. He refused to abandon Christian, who was perhaps one of those who was unneeded, someone who had no place in the grand plan. But weren't the unneeded also part of the grand plan?

Wasn't it for the sake of the unneeded that the plan was to be created?

He brooded a great deal over his own uncertainty. Christian was damaged, he had frostbite of the soul, but at the same time his power was necessary. What was it he himself coveted, or at least was now making use of? Christian's illness created a vacuum at the centre of power. This was where he had come to visit. There ought to be some possibility of saving both the boy and the dream of a changed society.

This is what he told himself. Although he wasn't sure whether he was primarily defending Christian or himself.

The image of the black torch that emanated darkness refused to leave him. A black torch burned inside the young monarch, he knew that now, and its glow seemed to extinguish reason. Why wouldn't this image leave him in peace? Perhaps there was a black torch inside him as well. No, probably not.

But what was it that existed inside him?

Light, a prairie fire. Such beautiful words.

But Christian was both light and opportunity, and a black torch shining its darkness over the world.

Was that what a human being was? Both opportunity and a black torch?

Christian had once, in a lucid moment, spoken of people cast in one piece; he himself was not cast in one piece, he said. He had many faces. Then Christian had asked: Is there a place for someone like me in the kingdom of reason?

Such a simple, childish question. And all of a sudden it made Struensee feel so anguished.

There ought to be a place for Christian as well. Wasn't that what this was all about? Wasn't that why the aperture in history would open before Struensee? Wasn't that also a part of his task?

What was his task, after all? He could picture himself in the eyes of posterity as the German doctor who came to visit the madhouse.

And the one who was given a mission?

"Visit" was a better word, better than calling or task. Yes, that's what he had begun to think. It had grown inside him. A visit, a task to be completed, a task that was assigned, an aperture that would open in history; and then he would step inside and disappear.

Holding Christian by the hand. Perhaps this was the important thing. Not to leave Christian behind. He who had many faces and was not cast in one piece, and inside of whom a black torch burned ever stronger, hurling its darkness over everything.

The two of us, Struensee sometimes thought. A splendid pair. The boy with his black torch emanating darkness, and I with my clear gaze and terrible fear, which I conceal so cleverly.

And these two would put a lever under the house of the world.

2

He knew that he should not have permitted the gift.

The little Negro boy was a plaything. A plaything was not what the King needed; it would lead him in the wrong direction, like a poorly aimed jab at a billiard ball.

The reason that he "gave in" – as he later thought – was an incident that occurred during the first week of June 1770.

Christian had started following him around like a dog: babbling devotedly, or imploring him in silence. Something had to be done to jolt the King out of his lethargy. Struensee therefore decided that an excursion would be taken, a brief one, not to the European courts but to reality. Reality would jolt the King out of his melancholy. The journey would take them to the Danish countryside and give the King a picture of the situation of the Danish serfs; but a real, true picture, without court trappings, without the serfs being aware of the King's presence among them, observing their lives.

For that reason the journey had to be made incognito.

The day before the journey, which had been approved by the King without objection since he was neither informed of its true purpose nor would have shown the slightest interest in it, rumours of the plan had leaked out. This led to a fierce confrontation with Rantzau, who at that time seemed to have regained his position at court, was once more in the King's favour, and was considered to be one of Struensee's closest friends.

On that morning Struensee went to the stables to go for an early ride; it was just before dawn. He saddled his horse and rode out through the stable gate, but there Rantzau caught up with him, and took hold of the horse's bridle. Struensee, with a trace of irritation, asked him what he wanted.

"From what I understand," Rantzau said with ill-concealed anger, "you're the one who wants so much. But what's all this about? What *is* all this about? The King is going to be dragged around among the peasants? Not seeking out the decision-makers or others that we need for our reforms. But peasants. To see . . . what?"

"Reality."

"You have his trust. But you're about to make a mistake."

For a moment Struensee was close to losing his temper, but he controlled himself. He explained that the King's lethargy and melancholy had to be cured. The King had spent so much time in this madhouse that he was losing his wits. The King knew nothing about Denmark.

"What does the Queen say?" asked Rantzau.

"I haven't asked her," replied Struensee. "Let go of my horse."

"You're making a mistake," Rantzau then shrieked in such a loud voice that he could be heard by everyone around. "You're being naïve; soon you'll have everything in your hands, but you don't understand the game. Let the fool be, you can't . . ."

"Let go," said Struensee. "And I won't allow you to call him a fool."

But Rantzau refused to let go and continued to talk in a loud voice.

Then Struensee spurred his horse, Rantzau stumbled backward and fell, and Struensee rode off without looking back.

The next morning the King and Struensee set off on their journey of observation among the Danish peasants.

The first two days were most successful. On the third day disaster struck.

It was late in the afternoon, near Hillerød. From the coach they could see in the distance a group of peasants gathered around . . .

something. As if at an innocent meeting. Then the coach drew closer, and the situation became clear.

A group of people was clustered around an object. As the coach neared, a tumult erupted, the group dispersed, and some set off running towards the main building of the nearby manor.

The coach stopped. From inside, the King and Struensee could see someone sitting on a wooden framework. The King commanded the coach to drive closer, and then it was possible to see the figure more clearly.

Seated on a wooden horse made of two trestles with a rough-hewn beam in between, was a young peasant boy, naked, with his hands tied behind his back, and his feet bound together beneath the beam. He was perhaps 16. His back was bloody; it was clear he had been whipped, and the blood had clotted.

He was shaking violently and seemed close to losing consciousness.

"I presume," said Struensee, "that he tried to run away. That's when they put them on wooden horses. The ones who survive never run away again. The ones who die escape from serfdom. That's the way things are in your kingdom, Your Majesty."

Christian, with his mouth agape and overcome with horror, stared at the tortured boy. The small group of people had gradually retreated.

"An entire peasant class is sitting there on that wooden horse," Struensee said. "That is reality. Liberate them. Liberate them."

When ascription was instituted in 1733, it was a means for the nobility to control, or rather to prevent, movement among the work force. A person who was a peasant on an estate was not allowed to leave the estate until the age of 40. The conditions, wages, terms of work, and housing were all determined by the owner of the estate. After 40 years the person was allowed to move. The reality was that by that time most peasants had become so passive, alcoholic, weighed down by debt, or physically debilitated that no moving usually occurred.

It was a Danish form of slavery. It functioned very well as an economic basis for the nobles; conditions were worse in the north than in the south of Jutland, but it was slavery.

Sometimes slaves would escape. Struensee was right about that. And that was why they had to be punished.

But Christian didn't seem to understand; it was as if the scene only reminded him of something else that he had experienced earlier. He didn't seem to follow Struensee's explanations but began to chew wildly, grinding his jaw as if the words refused to come out; and after only a few seconds he began screaming an incoherent string of words, which finally gave way to a muttering.

"But this peasant boy – is perhaps a changeling – like me! Why are they punishing me? Like this! Struensee! What have I done, is it a just punishment, Struensee, am I being punished now . . . ?"

Christian's muttering grew louder.

"He ran away, the punishment is the wooden horse," Struensee tried to explain, but the King only continued with his meaningless paroxysms, which grew more and more confused.

"You must calm yourself," Struensee urged him. "Be calm. Calm." But no.

Dusk had fallen, the back of the bound boy was black with clotted blood; he must have been sitting on the wooden horse for a long time. Struensee, who finally had to give up trying to calm the King, watched as the tortured boy slowly slumped forward, slid under the wooden beam, and hung there with his head down.

Christian gave a sudden shriek, wild and without words. The boy on the wooden horse was silent. Everything was now out of control.

It was impossible to calm the King. People came running from the main building. The King screamed and screamed, shrill and piercing, and refused to be hushed.

The boy on the wooden horse hung there, with his face only a foot above the ground.

Struensee shouted to the coachman to turn the coach around. The King is indisposed, we must return to Copenhagen. But just as the coach was turning in great haste, Struensee happened to think about the boy hanging from the wooden horse. They couldn't leave him like that. He would without doubt die. Struensee jumped out of the coach to try to negotiate a possible pardon; but the coach started off at once, and Christian's desperate screams grew louder.

The boy was hanging motionless. The approaching crowd seemed hostile. Struensee was frightened. It was beyond his control. He was out in the Danish wilderness. Reason, rules, titles, or power had no authority in this wilderness. Here the people were animals. They would tear him limb from limb.

He felt an enormous sense of terror overcome him.

That was why Struensee gave up the idea of rescuing the boy on the wooden horse.

The coach and horses, with the King still screaming as he hung out of the window, was about to vanish in the dusk. It had rained. The road was muddy. Struensee ran, shouting to the coachman to stop; stumbling in the mud, he ran after the coach.

That was the end of the journey to the Danish slaves.

3

The King spent more and more time playing with Moranti, the Negro page.

No-one was surprised. The King was calm whenever he was playing.

In early August, Moranti was struck by a sudden fever and for three weeks lay in bed, making a slow recovery; the King was very upset and reverted to his melancholy. During the two days when Moranti's illness seemed life-threatening, the King's mood was anything but stable. Chief Secretary B. W. Luxdorph, who witnessed the incident from the window of the chancellery building, writes briefly in his diary that: "between 11 and 12 o'clock porcelain dolls, books, bookcases, sheet music, etc. were thrown from the palace balcony. More than 400 people gathered under the balcony. Everyone ran off with whatever they could grab."

After Moranti's recovery, the King became calmer, but the scene was repeated once again, although with a difference that was not insignificant: he was no longer alone on the balcony. The incident was reported by a diplomat, phrased with discretion: "The King, who is young and has a playful temperament, took it into his head on Friday morning to go out on the balcony, accompanied by his little Negro page, and amuse himself by tossing everything he could find over the side. A bottle struck the secretary of the Russian legation in the leg and injured him badly."

There was no mention of whether Moranti also took part in throwing things.

The outburst was characterized as inexplicable.

They were circling around each other, with the circles becoming smaller and smaller. They were moving towards each other.

The relationship between Queen Caroline Mathilde and the royal physician Struensee was growing more intense.

They often went walking in the woods.

In the woods they could converse, in the woods the attendants following them might lag behind; the Queen found it amusing to walk in the woods with Struensee.

It was a beech forest.

Struensee talked about the importance of strengthening the limbs of the little Crown Prince through physical exercises; the boy was now two years old. The Queen talked about horses. Struensee stressed the importance of the little boy learning to play like ordinary children. She spoke of the sea and the swans on the water's surface that was like quicksilver. He thought the little boy should learn all the details of statesmanship; the Queen asked him again whether trees could think.

He answered: Only in situations of utmost danger. She replied: Only when the tree was at its happiest could it think.

When they walked through the woods where there was thick shrubbery, the attendants often could not keep up. She liked walking in the woods. She believed that beech trees could love. She found quite natural the idea that trees could dream. All one had to do was observe a forest at dusk to be convinced.

He asked her whether a tree could also feel fear.

Suddenly she was able to tell him almost everything. No, not quite everything. She could ask him why everyone was upset about her going riding in men's clothing, and he would answer. But she could not ask him why she had been chosen to become this royal cow that had to be serviced. Why am I the first and most exalted of women, when I am only breeding stock, the lowest of the low?

She walked quickly. Sometimes she would get ahead of him; she would get ahead of him on purpose. It was easier to ask certain questions if he couldn't see her face. She would not turn around but ask with her back to him:

"How can you have such patience with that mad fool? I can't understand it."

"The King?"

"He's ill."

"No, no," he told her. "I refuse to allow you to speak of your husband in that way. You love him, after all."

She stopped abruptly.

It was a dense forest. He could see that her back had begun to shake. She was weeping without a sound. Far behind he heard the ladies-in-waiting, their voices as they cautiously worked their way through the thickets.

He went up to her. She sobbed in despair, leaning on his shoulder. They stood motionless for a few moments. The sounds came closer.

"Your Majesty," he said in a low voice. "You must be careful so that . . ."

She looked up at him, now seeming calm.

"Why?"

"People might . . . misinterpret . . ."

The sounds were now quite near, she was still standing close to him, pressing against his shoulder; and she looked up and said almost without expression:

"Then let them. I'm not afraid. Not of anything. Not of anything."

And then he saw the first prying faces among the branches of the trees and bushes; coming nearer, much too near. But for another few moments the Queen was afraid of nothing at all; she too saw the faces through the branches of the forest, but she was not afraid.

He knew that she was not afraid, and this filled him with a sudden terror.

"You're not afraid of anything," he said in a low voice.

Then they continued on their way through the woods.

4

The evening card games, which in the past had taken place on a regular basis for the three queens, now stopped; the Dowager Queen was given no explanation for this. Caroline Mathilde was no longer interested. No explanation why. The tarot evenings had simply ceased.

But the Dowager Queen knew the reason for this. She no longer found herself at the centre of things.

Nevertheless, to extract an explanation, or to settle the matter once and for all, the Dowager Queen went to see Caroline Mathilde in her chamber.

The Dowager Queen did not wish to sit down. She stood in the middle of the room.

"You've changed since you came to Denmark," said the Dowager Queen in an icy voice. "You're no longer charming. In no respect are you as enchanting as you were before. That is not just my opinion, it is everyone's opinion. You keep your distance. You have no idea how to behave."

Caroline Mathilde's expression did not change; but she said:

"That's true."

"I beg you – most urgently – not to go riding in men's clothing. Never before has a woman of royal blood worn men's clothing. It's shocking."

"It doesn't shock me."

"And this Doctor Struensee . . ."

"It doesn't shock him either."

"I beg you."

"I'll do as I please," Caroline Mathilde replied. "I'll dress as I like. I'll ride as I like. I'll talk to whomever I like. I am the Queen. Therefore I make all the rules. The way I behave is also good manners. Aren't you jealous?"

The Dowager Queen did not reply but merely gave her a mute look, rigid with anger.

"Yes, isn't that what it is?" Caroline Mathilde added. "You're jealous of me."

"Mind your tongue," said the Dowager Queen.

"That," said the Queen with a smile, "I shall most certainly do. But only when it pleases me."

"You're shameless."

"Soon," said Caroline Mathilde, "I'll be riding bareback. They say it's so interesting. Aren't you jealous? Because I know what the world looks like? I think you're jealous of me."

"Mind your tongue. You're a child. You know nothing."

"But some people can reach 100 and still have seen nothing. Know nothing. And there is a world outside the court."

And with that, the Dowager Queen left, infuriated.

The Queen remained sitting where she was. She thought: He was right, after all. Some people can reach 100 without seeing a thing. There is a world outside the court; and when I say this, the membrane splits, terror and fury flare up, and I am free.

5

On September 26 the royal couple, accompanied by Struensee and a small entourage, set off on a short holiday trip to Holsten. They were to visit Ascheberg, and Struensee was going to show Rousseau's famous hut to the Queen.

It was such a lovely autumn. A few days of cool weather had coloured the leaves golden and a faint crimson. As they drove towards Ascheberg in the afternoon, the Mountain glittered with all the autumn colours, and the air was mild and marvellous.

It was Indian summer in 1770. By the following day they began taking their walks.

During the summer he had started reading aloud to her. For this journey she had requested that he select a book that particularly engaged him. He was to choose a book that would amuse her, that would capture her interest by offering new information, that would teach her something about Struensee himself, and that was appropriate to the place they were going to visit.

An easy choice, he told her, but refused to say more. He would surprise her, he said, when they had taken their seats in Rousseau's hut.

Then she would understand.

On the second day they walked up to the hut alone. It had been meticulously preserved and furnished with great reverence; it had two small rooms, one room where the philosopher was supposed to work, one where he would sleep. They had forgotten to set up a kitchen; it was assumed that the primitive conditions would be mitigated by having servants bring meals up from the Ascheberg estate.

With great interest she read the poetical quotations that covered the walls and ceiling, and Struensee told her about Rousseau.

She felt very happy.

Then he took out the book. They sat down on the beautiful baroque sofa that stood in the study; the elder Rantzau had purchased it in Paris in 1755 and later had it placed in the hut in anticipation of Rousseau's visit. The book he was going to read to her was Ludvig Holberg's *Moral Thoughts*.

Why had he chosen that particular book?

At first she thought that this book, this choice, was much too gloomy; he then asked her to forget for a moment the name of the book, which was perhaps not that exciting, and allow him to read the titles of the epigrams, which, he intimated, would present a quite different impression.

"Something forbidden?" she asked.

"To the highest degree," he replied.

The titles did indeed catch her interest. "Do not waste time on empty activities. Only the mad are happy. I refuse to marry. Abandon an opinion if it is refuted. All crimes and sins are not equally serious. Only the ignorant believe they know everything. You are happy if you imagine yourself happy. Some people sin and beg by turns. Time and place determine what is moral. Virtue and vice change with the times. Abolish rhyme in the art of poetry. The poet lives in honour and poverty. Reforms easily slip out of control. Weigh with care the consequences of a reform. Doctors should answer questions rather than lecture. Agreement deadens, conflict stimulates. Bad taste has great benefits. We have a great desire for what is forbidden."

There, at the last title, she stopped him.

"That's true," she said. "That's very true. And I want to know what Ludvig Holberg says about it."

"As you wish," he said.

But he started off with a different epigram.

She suggested that he should make his own choice among the epigrams, so that the reading would end with the text about the forbidden. She wanted to have the context first, and Holberg's reflections. He started with Number 84, entitled "Time and place determine

162

what is moral". He began reading the text on the second afternoon they spent at Rousseau's hut, during that late September week at Ascheberg, the estate he knew so well, which was part of his former life, the life he had almost forgotten but was now trying to reclaim.

He was trying to find a sense of continuity in his life. He knew that it had continuity, but he was not yet in control of it.

On the third afternoon he read the epigram that began with the sentence: "Morality is whatever conforms to the accepted fashion of the day, and immorality is what conflicts with it". Then he read epigram Number 20 in Book IV, the one that begins with the sentence, "The most peculiar of human attributes is that people have the greatest desire for what is the most forbidden".

She thought his voice was so lovely.

She liked Ludvig Holberg too. It was as if the voices of Struensee and Holberg merged into one. It was a dark, warm voice that spoke to her of a world she had never known before; the voice embraced her, she felt as if she were floating in warm water, which shut out the court and Denmark and the King and everything else; like water, as if she were floating in the warm sea of life and was not afraid.

She thought his voice was so lovely. She told him so.

"You have such a lovely voice, Doctor Struensee."

He kept on reading.

She was wearing an evening gown made of a light fabric since it was late summer and warm, a very light fabric that she had chosen because of the mild summer night. She felt freer in it. The gown was low-cut. Her skin was very young, and occasionally, when he looked up from the book, his eyes would rest on her skin; then they would pause on her hands, and he all of a sudden remembered his thought about that hand wrapped around his member, a thought he had once had, and then he went back to reading.

"Doctor Struensee," she said, "you must touch my arm while you read."

"Why?" he asked, after only a brief hesitation.

"Because otherwise the words are so dry. You must touch my skin and then I can better understand what the words mean."

And so he touched her arm. It was uncovered and very soft. He could tell at once that it was very soft.

"Touch my hand," she said. "Slowly."

"Your Majesty," he said, "I'm afraid that . . ."

"Touch it," she said.

He went on reading, his hand sliding softly over her bare arm. Then she said:

"I think that Holberg is saying that the most forbidden is a boundary."

"A boundary?"

"A boundary. And wherever the boundary exists, there is life, and death, and thus the greatest desire."

His hand moved, and then she took his hand in her own, and pressed it to her throat.

"The greatest desire," she whispered, "exists at the boundary. It's true. It's true what Holberg writes."

"Where is the boundary?" he whispered.

"Find it," she said.

And then the book fell out of his hand.

It was she, not he, who locked the door.

She was not afraid, she didn't fumble as they took off their clothes; she continued to feel as if she were in the warm water of life and nothing was dangerous and death was quite close and thus everything was exciting. Everything seemed very soft and slow and warm.

They lay down next to each other, naked, in the bed that stood in the inner alcove of the hut, where once the French philosopher Rousseau was supposed to have slept, though he never did. That was where they now lay. It filled her with excitement, it was a sacred place and they were about to cross the boundary, it was the utmost forbidden, the very utmost. The place was forbidden, she was forbidden, it was nearly perfect.

They touched each other. She caressed his member with her hand. She liked it; it was hard but she waited because their nearness to the boundary was so exciting and she wanted to hold onto the moment.

"Wait," she said. "Not yet."

He lay beside her and caressed her, they breathed each other in, quite calmly and filled with desire, and she understood all at once that he was like her. That he could breathe as she did. In the same breath. That he was in her lungs and that they were breathing the same air.

He wanted to come inside her, a little way, he was now very close, she caressed his neck and whispered:

"Not all the way. Not yet."

She felt his member touch her, slip inside a little way, go away, come back.

"Not all the way," she said. "Wait."

He waited, almost inside her, but waiting.

"There," she whispered. "Not yet. My beloved. You must move in and out at the boundary."

"The boundary?" he asked.

"Yes, there. Can you feel the boundary?"

"Don't move," he said. "Don't move."

He understood. They would wait, sniff at each other like horses touching each other's muzzles, everything would happen without a sound, he understood.

And she was seized by a wave of happiness, he understood, he would wait, soon she would give the signal, soon; he understood.

"The boundary," she whispered again and again as desire slowly, slowly rose through her body. "Can you feel it, the greatest desire, more, there's the boundary."

Outside dusk was falling. He lay on top of her, practically motionless, sliding almost imperceptibly in and out.

"There," she whispered. "Very soon. Cross the boundary now. Come in. Oh, go across now."

And at last, very quietly, he slid the tip inside her and passed over the most forbidden of boundaries, and it was as it should be.

Now, she thought, this is like paradise.

When it was over she lay with her eyes closed, and smiled. Silently he dressed and stood by the window for a moment, looking out.

It was dusk and he looked out across the vast park, down at the long valley, the lake, the canal, the trees, the tamed and the wild.

They were on the Mountain. And it had happened.

"We must go down to them," he said in a low voice.

Here nature was perfect. Here was the wild, and the tamed. He thought of what they had left behind, the court, Copenhagen. How it looked when a light mist hovered over Øresund. That was the other world. There the water was no doubt quite black tonight, the swans were curled up and asleep; he thought about what she had told him, about the water being like quicksilver and the birds sleeping wrapped in their dreams. And how all at once a bird would rise up, the tips of its wings beating the surface of the water, how it became free and disappeared into the mist.

Mist, water and birds that slept wrapped in their dreams.

And then the palace, like a menacing, horror-filled ancient castle, biding its time.

PART IV

THE PERFECT SUMMER

Chapter 10 · In the Labyrinth

I

The take-over of power occurred with some speed, almost artlessly. A communiqué was delivered. All it did was confirm something that was already fact.

The formal confirmation of the Danish revolution was a decree. No-one knew who had written or dictated the document that would so dramatically change the history of Denmark. A royal proclamation was issued regarding certain changes in the internal lines of command; they might have been called convulsions close to the dark and inscrutable heart of power.

J. F. Struensee was appointed "Confidential Cabinet Minister", and the royal proclamation was worded as follows: "All commands which I give to him verbally he may then carry out in accordance with my intentions and present for my signature after he has paraphrased them, or execute them in my name under the seal of the Cabinet." It went on to say, as if to elucidate, that the King would, of course, be presented once a week with an "abstract" of the decrees thus issued by Struensee, but it emphasized and clarified, should anyone have misunderstood the fundamental significance of the opening sentence, that a decree with

Struensee's signature "had the same authority as those inscribed with the King's".

The title "Confidential Cabinet Minister", which was new and exclusive, since the newly appointed Struensee was the only one left of the many who were excluded, perhaps did not mean much. It was the right to implement *laws* without the King's signature that was so significant. "Or execute them in my name under the seal of the Cabinet", as it was formulated.

In practice this meant that the absolute ruler, King Christian VII, turned over all power to a German doctor, J. F. Struensee. Denmark was in German hands.

Or in those of the Enlightenment. Within the court it was impossible to determine which was worse.

The take-over of power was a fact. Afterwards no-one could understand how it happened.

Perhaps they both found it practical. There was no talk of a revolution.

A practical reform. The practical part was that Struensee would exercise all power.

After the decision was made, Christian seemed relieved; his tics diminished, his aggressive outbursts ceased altogether for a time, and for brief periods he seemed happy. His dog and the Negro page Moranti took up more and more of his time. He could now devote himself to them. Struensee could devote himself to his work.

Yes, it was practical.

There came a time, after the decree, when practical matters were functioning splendidly, and they drew closer to one another. They drew closer in terms of both the practical and the insane, Struensee often thought. He had the feeling that Christian, he himself, the Negro page Moranti, and the dog were all welded together – like conspiratorial participants in a secret expedition bound for the dark heart of reason. Everything was clarity and reason, but illuminated by the King's insanity, the strange dark torch that burst forth and disappeared, capricious and ruthless, letting its flickering darkness wrap around them in a entirely natural manner. Slowly they drew together, as if in a safe mountain cavern, decelerating, returning to a form of family life that looked quite normal, were it not for the circumstances.

Were it not for the circumstances.

Struensee would sit in his cabinet room, with the door locked and guards outside, with the stacks of documents on the table and the writing materials laid out, while the boys and the dog played around him. The boys were excellent company. He could concentrate so well while the boys were playing. Those were long afternoons of absolute calm and almost joyful solitude; alone in the room except for the boys, as he was in the habit of calling them whenever he thought of them, meaning the King and the Negro page.

The boys played quietly under the table. The dog, a schnauzer, was always with them.

As Struensee wrote and worked, he would hear their movements around the room, their whispering voices; nothing more. He thought: They see me as a father who must not be disturbed. They play at my feet and they hear the scratching of my pen, and they whisper.

They whisper out of consideration. How splendid. And sometimes he would feel a huge tranquil wave of warmth rise up inside him; the room was so quiet, the autumn outside so beautiful, the sounds of the city so distant, the children so endearing, the dog so lively, everything was so splendid. They showed consideration. They played under the gigantic oak table that was no longer surrounded by the mighty of the realm, but only by one Mighty man. But they didn't regard him as the Mighty man, but as the kind, silent man, the one who existed only as a father figure, present through the scratching sound of his pen.

The Silent One. *Vati. Lieber Vati, ich mag Dich, wir spielen, lieber lieber Vati.* Pappa. Dear Pappa, I love you, we're playing, dear dear Pappa.

Perhaps the only children I'll ever have.

Is this how my life will be? He sometimes thought. Quiet work, a pen that scratches, unprecedented reforms that painlessly slip out into real life, my boys playing with the dog under the table.

If so, how splendid.

There were also moments at that writing table that contained an element of fear.

Christian popped up from his quiet games under the table. He sat down on the edge and regarded Struensee thoughtfully, shy but curious. His wig had been tossed into a corner, his clothing was dishevelled; yet, or perhaps for that very reason, he looked endearing.

He simply sat there and watched; then he asked with some timidity what Struensee was writing and what he was about to sign.

"Your Majesty has just reduced the army," Struensee said with a smile. "We have no external enemies. This pointless army will now be smaller, and cheaper; a saving of 16,000 riksdaler per year."

"Is that true?" asked Christian. "That we don't have any external enemies?"

"It's true. Not Russia, not Sweden. And we're not thinking of attacking Turkey. Aren't we in agreement about this?"

"And what do the generals say?"

"They will become our enemies. But we can handle them."

"But what about the enemies we'll have at court?"

"Against them," said Struensee with a smile, "it would be difficult to use this vast army."

"That's true," said Christian with great solemnity. "So we want to cut back the army?"

"Yes, we do."

"Then I agree," said Christian with the same solemnity.

"Not everyone is going to approve," Struensee added.

"But do you approve, Doctor Struensee?"

"Yes. And we're going to do much, much more."

That was when Christian said it. Struensee would never forget it; only a month after the moment when the book fell out of his hand

and he crossed the boundary to the most forbidden. Christian was sitting on the table close to him, the pale October sun was shining in, making great rectangles on the floor, and that's when he said it.

"Doctor Struensee," said Christian in a low voice and with such a solemn tone, as if he had never been the demented boy playing under the cabinet table with his Negro page and his dog. "Doctor Struensee, I beseech you most urgently. The Queen is lonely. Attend to her."

Struensee went rigid.

He put down his pen, and after a moment he said:

"What does His Majesty mean? I don't understand."

"You understand everything. Attend to her. This burden I cannot bear."

"How am I to understand this?"

"You understand everything. I love you."

To that, Struensee made no reply.

He understood, and yet he did not. Did the King know? But Christian touched his arm with a light caress, looked at him with a smile that was so painfully uncertain but at the same time so beautiful that Struensee would never forget it, and then, with an almost imperceptible movement, he slid off the edge of the table and returned to the little Negro page and the dog, down there underneath the table where pain was not visible and the black torch did not burn, and only the little dog and the Negro page existed.

And where everything was quiet happiness and affection with the only family that King Christian VII would ever know.

2

When the Life Guards were demobilized, Guldberg was present, and to his surprise he saw that Count Rantzau had also come to observe this new cost-saving measure.

Collection of weapons and uniforms. Home leaves.

Guldberg went over to Rantzau and greeted him. Together and in silence they watched the ceremonies.

"A transformation of Denmark," Rantzau said with expectation.

"Yes," replied Guldberg, "So many transformations are taking place. All at a rapid pace, as you know. I understand that this pleases you. Your friend, 'The Silent One', works fast. Only this morning I read the decree about 'Freedom of thought and freedom of expression'. So imprudent of you. To abolish censorship. Very imprudent."

"What do you mean?"

"The German doctor doesn't understand that freedom can also be used against him. If you give freedom to the people, pamphlets will be written. Perhaps also against him. Against you, I mean. If you are his friend."

"And what will these pamphlets say?" Rantzau then asked. "What do you think? Or do you know?"

"The people are so unpredictable. Perhaps free pamphlets will be written that tell the truth, and incite the ignorant masses."

Rantzau did not reply.

"Against you," Guldberg repeated.

"I don't understand."

"The masses, unfortunately, don't understand the blessings of the Enlightenment. Unfortunately. For you. The masses are only interested in filth. In rumours."

"What rumours?" asked Rantzau, now very cold and on his guard.

"You know very well what rumours."

Guldberg looked at him with his calm wolf eyes, and for a moment felt something like triumph. Only the most insignificant and scorned, such as himself, were fearless. He knew that this frightened Rantzau. This Rantzau, with his contempt for honours, customs, and for upstarts. How he despised, in his heart, his friend Struensee! The upstart Struensee! It was quite obvious.

He despised upstarts. Including Guldberg himself. The son of an undertaker from Horsens. Although the difference was that Guldberg

172

felt no fear. That was why they could stand there, an upstart from Horsens and a count and an Enlightenment fool, like two enemies who hated each other, and Guldberg could say everything in a calm voice, as if there were no danger. As if Struensee's power were merely an amusing or alarming parenthesis in history; and he knew that Rantzau knew what fear was.

"What rumours?" Rantzau repeated.

"The rumours about Struensee," replied Guldberg in his dry voice, "saying that the young, wanton Queen has now opened her legs to him. All we need is proof. But we shall get it."

Rantzau stared at Guldberg, dumbstruck, as if he couldn't comprehend that anyone would utter such an absurd accusation.

"How dare you!" he said at last.

"That's the difference, Count Rantzau. That's the difference between you and me. I dare. And I assume," said Guldberg in a neutral tone of voice and before he turned around to leave, "that very soon you will be forced to choose sides."

3

He lay quite still inside her and waited for the beat of her pulse.

He had begun to understand that the most intense pleasure was found when he waited for the beat of her pulse deep inside her, when their membranes breathed and moved in time, soft, pulsating. That was the most wonderful thing. He had enjoyed learning to wait for her. She had never needed to say anything, he had learned it almost at once. He could lie quite still, for a long time, with his member deep inside her, and listen to the membranes of her sex as though their bodies had vanished and only their sex remained. He almost didn't move at all, lay still, their bodies gone as well as their thoughts, they were both focused on listening to their pulse and the rhythm. Nothing existed but her moist, soft membranes, she moved her pelvis almost imperceptibly, slow beyond measure, he probed with his member inside of her as if it was the sensitive tip of a tongue that was searching for something, and he would lie still and wait; it was for the beat of her pulse, as if inside her he was searching for her pulsating surfaces that would throb in time with his own member, then he would move cautiously; he waited, there would be a moment when he could feel how she contracted and then relaxed, contracted and relaxed, his member lay waiting inside her narrow sheath, and then he could feel a sort of rhythm, a sort of pulse. If he waited, her pulse would come, and when he found it, everything would happen to the same rhythm as the inner beat of her pulse. She lay with her eyes closed beneath him, and he could feel her waiting for the beat of her pulse, they were both waiting, he deep inside her, but their bodies no longer seemed to exist and instead everything existed inside of her, membrane against membrane, membranes that gently swelled and sank back and searched for the beat of her pulse, that adjusted to each other and moved in unison, very slowly, and when he felt how her membranes and his member shared the same breath, he would gradually begin to move in the rhythm, which sometimes would vanish, and then he would have to lie still again until he found the beat of her pulse, and then his member could breathe in the same tempo as her membranes again, slowly; it was this slow waiting for the pulse of the secret membranes that she had taught him, he didn't understand how she could know, but when the rhythm came and the membranes breathed in unison, they could start to move and this unbelievable pleasure would come, and they would vanish into the same slow, drawn-out breathing.

Very quiet. Awaiting the inner beat of her pulse, the rhythm, and then their bodies would disappear and everything existed inside of her alone, and he breathed with his member in the same slow beat as her membranes, and he had never experienced anything like it before.

He had slept with many women, and she was not the most beautiful. But none of them had taught him to wait for the rhythm of the membranes and the inner pulse of the body.

*

They arranged the placement of their rooms to make sneaking back and forth easier, and during the winter their caution diminished when they made love. They also went riding together more often, in the cold, in snow that fell lightly, across the frozen fields. They began riding along the shore.

She rode along the water's edge, making the ice on the shore crackle, with her hair flowing and without a care in the world.

She weighed a fraction of an ounce, and only the weight of the horse prevented her from flying. Why should she protect her face from the driving snow when she was a bird? She could see farther ahead than ever before, past the dunes of Sjælland and past the coast of Norway and on towards Iceland and even all the way to the towering glaciers of the North Pole.

She would remember that winter; and Struensee on his horse followed close, very close behind her, along the shore, silent, but close to her every thought.

On February 6, 1771, she informed Struensee that she was with child.

They had made love. Then she told him, afterwards.

"I am with child," she said. "And we know that it's yours."

She discovered that she wanted to make love every day.

Her desire would grow each morning, and by twelve o'clock it was enormous; at that moment it was urgent and at its peak, and she wanted him to interrupt his work and join her in a short conference during which she would be briefed on the work he had accomplished that morning.

And so it came to be quite natural. Before that, nothing was natural; now it had become natural.

He adapted accordingly. At first with surprise, then with great joy since he found that his body shared her joy and that her desire aroused his desire. That's how it was. He would never have imagined that her

175

desire could arouse his own in that way. He thought that desire was only the forbidden. There was that too. But the fact that desire and the forbidden, which for her became natural and grew each day so that by noon her desire was burning and uncontrollable, that this natural desire could be relieved each day – that surprised him.

It was much later that he began to feel the fear.

They made love in her bedchamber and afterwards she would lie in his arms with her eyes closed, smiling like a little girl who had conceived his desire and given birth to it and now lay with his desire in her arms, as if it were her child, which she now possessed wholly. It was much later that he began to feel the fear. And yet he said:

"We must be careful. I know that people are talking. And they'll talk about the child too. We must be careful."

"No," she said.

"No?"

"Because I'm no longer afraid of anything."

What could he say to that?

"I knew it," she said. "I knew all along, without a doubt, that you were the one. From the first moment I saw you and felt frightened by you and thought that you were an enemy who had to be destroyed. But that was a sign. A sign in your body that was burned into me, like a branding iron on an animal. I knew it."

"You're not an animal," he said. "But we must be careful."

"You'll come tomorrow?" she said without listening. "You'll come tomorrow at the same time?"

"And if I don't come, because it's too dangerous?"

She closed her eyes. She didn't want to open them.

"It *is* dangerous. You know that. Oh, just imagine if I said that you had violated me. Oh, what if I started to shout for them? And to sob and say that you had violated me. And they took you and executed you and broke you on the wheel, and me, too. No, not me. They would banish me. But I won't shout, my beloved. Because you're mine, and I have you, and we'll make love every day."

He didn't want to reply. She turned towards him with her eyes closed, caressing his arms and chest, at last sliding her hand down towards his member. He had seen this once in his secret dreams, how her hand closed around his member, and now it was true, and he knew that this hand possessed a terrible seduction and power that he never could have imagined, and that it was not only his member around which her hand was wrapped, but also around himself, that she seemed stronger than he ever would have suspected, and this filled him with desire but also with something that did not yet, but perhaps soon might, resemble fear.

"My beloved," he murmured, "I would never have suspected that your body had . . . such a . . ."

"Such a . . . ?"

". . . such a great talent for love."

She opened her eyes and smiled at him. She knew this was true. It had gone inconceivably quickly.

"Thank you," she said.

He could feel his desire rising. He didn't know whether he wanted to. He knew only that she had him in her power, and that his desire rose and that something frightened him, but he didn't yet know what it was.

"My beloved," he whispered, "what shall we do?"

"This," she said. "Always."

He didn't reply. Soon he would once again cross the utterly forbidden boundary; it was different now, but he didn't know in what way.

"And you will never be free of me," she whispered, her voice so low that he almost didn't hear her. "Because you are burned into me. Like a branding iron on an animal."

But he did hear her. And perhaps it was at that moment – just as she let him slip inside her again and they once more began to listen for the secret pulse which would ultimately draw them together in their tremendous rhythm – that he felt the first glimmer of fear.

*

Once she lay naked beside him for a long time, letting her fingers glide through his blond hair, and then with a little smile she said:

"You will be my right hand."

"What do you mean?" he asked.

And playfully, but with confidence, she whispered:

"A hand. A hand does what the head wishes, isn't that true? And I have so many ideas."

Why had he felt fear?

Sometimes he would think: I should have climbed out of Christian's coach in Altona. And gone back to my own life.

Very early one morning, as Struensee was on his way to work, the King, in his dressing gown with his hair dishevelled and wearing no socks or shoes, came running to catch up with him in the Marble Corridor, grabbed hold of his arm, and insisted that he listen.

They sat down in a deserted drawing room. After a while the King grew calmer, his ragged breathing became normal, and he confided to Struensee what he called "a secret that revealed itself last night as I was being ridden by the torments".

What the King told him was as follows.

There was a secret circle of seven men. They had been chosen by God to foment evil in the world. They were the seven apostles of evil. He himself was one of them. The horrible thing was that he could only feel love for someone who also belonged to this circle. If he felt love, it meant that this person also belonged to the seven angels of evil. Last night he had clearly understood, and he felt great dread, and since he felt love for Struensee he now wanted to ask whether this was true, and whether Struensee actually belonged to this secret circle of evil.

Struensee tried to calm the King, asking him to tell more about his "dream". Christian then began muttering in his usual way, becoming incoherent, but all of a sudden he said that the dream had also confirmed that there was a woman who in some secret way ruled the universe.

Struensee asked him what he meant by this.

The King could not answer the question, but repeated that a woman ruled the universe, that a circle of seven evil men was responsible for all evil deeds, that he was one of them, and perhaps he could be saved by the woman who ruled the whole universe; she would then become his benefactress.

He stared at Struensee for a long time, and asked:

"But aren't you one of The Seven?"

Struensee shook his head. At that, the King asked, with despair in his voice:

"Then why do I love you?"

It was early in April 1771.

King Christian VII, his consort Queen Caroline Mathilde and the royal physician J. F. Struensee were having tea at Fredensborg Castle on the little balcony that faced the palace park.

Struensee was talking about the park's ideology. He praised its fabulous design, with pathways forming a labyrinth, and the way the hedges concealed the symmetry of the layout. He pointed out that the labyrinth had been designed so that there was only one point from which the logic of the park's plan was visible. Down there everything was confusion, lanes and corridors that led to dead ends, cul-de-sacs, and chaos. But from a single point everything became clear, logical, and sensible. It was from the balcony where they now sat. It was the Ruler's balcony. It was the only point from which any coherence was apparent. This viewpoint, which was that of reason and coherence, was accessible only to the Ruler.

The Queen asked with a smile what this meant. He elucidated further.

"The Ruler's viewpoint. Which is that of power."

"Does it seem . . . enticing?"

He answered her by smiling. After a brief pause she leaned towards him and whispered close to his ear, so that the King couldn't hear:

"You're forgetting one thing. That you are in *my* power."

4

He would remember that conversation, and the threat.

The Ruler's balcony was a vantagepoint, and it gave coherence to the symmetry of the labyrinth, but that was all. The other connections remained chaotic.

Early summer arrived, and the decision was made to spend the summer at Hirschholm Castle. The packing had begun. Struensee and the Queen had agreed on this. The King was not consulted, but would comply.

He found it natural not to be consulted but to be allowed to go along, and he agreed.

The following was what happened on the day before their departure.

From the balcony, where he now sat alone, Christian watched the two young lovers disappear on their horses, going off on their daily ride, and he suddenly felt very lonely. He called for Moranti, but he was nowhere to be found.

He went inside.

There was the dog, the schnauzer. He was sleeping on the floor in a corner of the room. Christian lay down on the floor with his head on the dog's body; but after a few minutes the dog got up, went to another corner of the room, and lay down there.

Christian followed and once more lay down with the dog's body as his pillow; the dog got up again and moved to another corner.

Christian stayed where he was, staring up at the ceiling. This time he didn't go after the dog. He smiled tentatively at the ceiling; there were cherubs up there, adorning the transition between wall and ceiling. He tried hard to ensure that his smile would be calm and friendly, not contorted; the cherubs gave him an inquisitive look. From the other corner of the room he heard the dog's voice, which muttered to him not to annoy the cherubs. He stopped smiling.

He decided to go out; he was determined to find the centre of the labyrinth, because a message was waiting for him there.

He was convinced that it was there in the centre of the labyrinth. For a long time he had not received any word from The Seven; he had asked Struensee, but the doctor refused to answer his question. But if Struensee also belonged to The Seven, then the two of them were co-conspirators, and he had someone to confide in. He was sure that Struensee was one of them. He loved him, after all; that was the sign.

Perhaps Moranti also belonged to The Seven, and the dog too; then there were four of them. He had now identified four of them.

Three remained. Caterine? But she was the Sovereign of the Universe; no, three remained, but he couldn't find three more. Not three that he loved. Where were they? And the dog was not a sure thing; he loved the dog, and whenever the dog talked to him, he was almost convinced, but the dog seemed to express only love, submission, and indifference. He wasn't sure about the dog. But the dog did talk to him; that made him unique. Otherwise dogs couldn't talk. It was absurd to imagine animals talking, an impossibility. But since the dog did talk, it was a sign. It was a sign that was almost clear, but only almost.

He wasn't sure about the dog.

The Seven would cleanse the temple of impurity. And then he himself would rise up like the Phoenix. This was the smouldering fire of the Enlightenment. Hence The Seven. Evil was necessary to create purity.

It was not quite clear how all of this fitted together. But he believed it was true. The Seven were fallen angels from heaven. He had to find out what he was supposed to do. A sign. A message. It was without doubt in the centre of the labyrinth, a message from The Seven, or from the Sovereign of the Universe.

He dashed, staggering and lurching, into the labyrinth of pruned hedges, trying to remember the picture he had of the corridors, the picture from up on the balcony where chaos was reason.

After a while he began to walk slower. He was breathing hard, and he knew that he had to calm down. He veered to the left, to the right, his picture of the labyrinth's design was quite clear, he was sure that it was quite clear. After a few minutes he came to a cul-de-sac. The hedge stood like a wall before him; he turned around, took a right, then another right. Now the picture in his mind was less clear, but he tried to muster his courage, and then started running again. Once more he was gasping for breath. When he began to sweat, he tore off his wig and kept running; it was easier that way.

The picture in his mind had now vanished.

There was no longer any sense of clarity. The walls around him were green and thorny. He stopped. He had to be very close to the centre. In the centre there was clarity. He stood quite still, listening. No birds, not a sound; he glanced down at his hand, his hand was bleeding, he didn't know how it had happened. He knew that he was very close to the centre. In the centre he would find the message, or Caterine.

Absolute silence. Why wasn't a single bird singing?

Suddenly he heard a voice whispering. He stood motionless. He recognized the voice; it came from the other side of the wall of hedges, from a place that had to be the centre.

"Here it is," said the voice. "Come here."

It was beyond all doubt Caterine's voice.

He tried to see through the hedge, but it was impossible. All was quiet now, but there was no longer any doubt, it was Caterine's voice, and she was on the other side. He caught his breath, he had to be very calm, but he had to get through. He took a step inside the hedge, trying to bend the branches aside. They were thorny, and he immediately understood that this was going to hurt badly, but he was calm now, this had to be done, he had to be strong, hard. He had to be invulnerable. There was no other way. The first few inches were easy, then the hedge wall was very thick. He leaned forward, as if he wanted to fall through. And he did fall forward, but the resistance was strong. The thorns cut like small swords across his face, they stung; he tried to raise his arms to free himself, but then he just fell forward even more. Now the hedge was extremely dense, and he must be very close to the middle of the labyrinth, but he still couldn't see through. He kicked his legs in desperation, his body was shoved a little bit farther, but there the branches were even thicker, it was impossible to bend them aside, they were no longer branches but trunks. He tried to stand up but made it only halfway. His hands were burning, his face was burning. Mechanically he fought with the branches, but there were thorns everywhere, the tiny knives kept on stinging his skin, he screamed for a moment but controlled himself and tried once more to stand up. But he couldn't.

He hung there, imprisoned. Blood ran down his face. He started to sob. It was utterly silent. Caterine's voice could no longer be heard. He was very close to the centre, he knew that, but he was imprisoned.

The courtiers who saw him enter the labyrinth had grown uneasy, and after an hour a search was launched. They found him lying inside the hedge; only one foot was sticking out. Help was summoned. The King was freed, but he refused to stand up.

He seemed wholly apathetic. In a weak voice, however, he commanded that Guldberg be called.

Guldberg arrived.

The blood had dried on the King's face, arms, and hands, but he lay motionless on the ground, staring straight up. Guldberg ordered a stretcher to be brought and told the attendants to withdraw so that he could speak with the King.

Guldberg sat down near the King, covered his chest with his own cloak, and tried to hide his agitation by speaking to Christian in a whisper.

At first, because of his agitation, which made his lips tremble violently, he whispered in such soft tones that Christian couldn't hear him. Gradually he became audible. "Your Majesty," he whispered, "don't be afraid, I will save you from this degradation, I love you, all these immoral," (and here his whispering grew stronger) "all these immoral people degrade us, but revenge will destroy them. They despise us, they look down on those of us who are insignificant, but we will cut away these limbs of sin from the body of Denmark. The wine treader's time will come. They laugh at us and scoff at us, but they have scoffed at us for the last time; God's vengeance will destroy them, and we, Your Majesty, I will be your ... we will ..."

Suddenly Christian was jolted out of his apathy; he stared at Guldberg like a madman and sat up.

"We?" he shouted. "US? Who are you talking about? Are you crazy, crazy? I am God's chosen one, and you dare to ... you dare to ..."

Guldberg cringed, as if from a whip, and bowed his head in silence.

Then, with some difficulty, the King got to his feet, and Guldberg would never forget that sight: the boy with his head and face covered with black, congealed blood, his hair straggly and matted, his clothes torn to shreds. Yes, in appearance he looked the very image of a madman covered in blood and filth; and yet, and yet, he now seemed to possess a composure and authority as if he were not mad but rather God's chosen one.

Perhaps he was a human being after all.

Christian signalled for Guldberg to rise. He gave Guldberg his cloak. And he said in a very calm and firm voice:

"You are the only one who knows where she is."

He didn't wait for a reply but continued:

"I want you today to draw up a certificate of pardon. And I will sign it. Myself. Not Struensee. I myself."

"Who is to be pardoned, Your Majesty?" Guldberg asked.

"Bottine Caterine."

And to that voice no objections could be raised, and no questions could be asked. Then the courtiers arrived with the stretcher. But it wasn't needed; Christian walked on his own, unassisted, out of the labyrinth.

Chapter 11 · The Child of the Revolution

They bathed and bandaged Christian's wounds, they postponed the departure for Hirschholm for three days, they made up an explanation for the King's unfortunate fall into a rose bush; everything gradually returned to normal. The packing was resumed along with the other preparations, and by ten in the morning the expedition was ready to leave for Hirschholm.

The whole court would not be going. Only a small group was included, yet it was large enough. An enormous amount of baggage filled 24 coaches in all; the number of attendants was considered small, a total of 18; in addition, there was a handful of soldiers (several of whom were sent home after the first week), as well as the kitchen staff. At the centre was the royal couple, Struensee, and the little Crown Prince, who was now three. That was the extent of the very small group.

Except for Enevold Brandt. He was the King's "nursemaid", as malicious rumour had it. In addition, several mistresses of the lower officials. And two carpenters.

At the time of departure, it was quite evident from the Queen's figure that she was pregnant. The court talked of nothing else. No-one had any doubts who the father was.

On that morning four coaches stood waiting in the palace courtyard when Rantzau sought out Struensee to have "an urgent conversation", as he put it.

First he asked whether it was intended that he should accompany them. Struensee replied, with a friendly bow: If you wish. "Do you want me to come with you?" was the immediate response from

Rantzau, who seemed tense and restrained. They regarded each other with suspicion.

No answer.

Rantzau thought he had correctly interpreted the silence. He asked, "quite bluntly", whether it would be wise at this time to spend the summer and perhaps even the autumn at Hirschholm with such a small retinue. Struensee asked what he meant by this question. Rantzau replied that there was unrest in the country. That the flood of decrees and reforms which now flowed from Struensee's hand (and he deliberately used that expression, "from Struensee's hand", because he was quite familiar with the King's state of mind and besides, he was no idiot) – these reforms were no doubt beneficial for the country. They were often wise, well-intentioned, and at times in keeping with the very best principles of reason. No doubt about it. In short, very well formulated. But, also in short, numerous! Almost too many to count!

The country was not prepared for this, or at least the administration wasn't! Ergo, it was most dangerous both for Struensee and for all of his friends. But, Rantzau continued without giving Struensee even a second to interrupt or reply, why such breakneck imprudence? Wasn't this flood of reforms, this in truth revolutionary wave that was now rising up over the kingdom of Denmark, wasn't this sudden revolution a good reason, or at any rate a good reason in tactical terms, for Struensee and the King, but above all Struensee, to stay somewhat closer to the enemy's camp?

In order to observe their enemies to some extent. Or rather: the thoughts and deeds of the enemy troops.

It was an astonishing outpouring.

"In brief, is it wise to leave?" he concluded.

"That was far from brief," Struensee replied. "And I can't tell whether the person speaking is friend or foe."

"I'm the one speaking," said Rantzau. "A friend. Perhaps your only friend."

"My only friend," said Struensee. "My only friend? That sounds ominous."

That was the tone. Formal, and fundamentally hostile. A long silence followed.

"Do you remember Altona?" Struensee said at last in a low voice.

"Yes, I remember. That was a very long time ago, it seems to me."

"Three years? Is that so long ago?"

"You've changed," was Rantzau's chilly reply.

"I haven't changed," said Struensee. "Not I. In Altona we agreed about almost everything. In fact, I admired you. You had read everything. And you taught me a great deal. For that I am grateful. I was so young back then."

"But now you're old and wise. And no longer feel any admiration."

"Now I'm transforming reality."

"Transforming reality?"

"Yes. In practice. Not just in theory."

"I seem to hear a note of contempt," said Rantzau. "'Not just in theory.'"

"If I knew where you stood, I would answer."

"Something 'real'. No theories. No desk speculations. And what is the latest . . . real thing?"

It was an unpleasant conversation. And the coaches were waiting. Struensee slowly stretched out his hand for the documents stacked on the table, and picked them up, as if to show them to Rantzau. But he didn't. He just looked, silent and joyless, at the communiqués in his hand, and for a moment he felt as if a great sorrow, or an overwhelming weariness, had seized hold of him.

"I was working last night," he said.

"Yes, they say you work hard at night."

Struensee pretended not to hear the insinuation.

He couldn't be candid with Rantzau. He couldn't mention anything about the stickiness. But something in what Rantzau had said made him ill at ease. It was the old feeling cropping up, the feeling of inferiority compared to his brilliant colleagues at Ascheberg Gardens.

The silent doctor from Altona among his brilliant friends. Perhaps they hadn't understood the real reason for his silence.

Perhaps now they did. He was the unlawful practitioner who had been elevated in a manner that couldn't be explained! That was what Rantzau was hinting at. You're not good enough. You were silent because you had nothing to say. You should have stayed in Altona.

And it was true: sometimes he saw his life as a series of points lined up on a piece of paper, a long list of numbered tasks, *that someone else had tallied up, someone else!* His life enumerated in order of priority, with numbers one to twelve like on a clock face, as the most important; then 13 to 24, like the 24 hours in a day; followed by 25 to 100, in a long cyclical curve with all the lesser but important tasks. And next to every single number, after completing the work, he was supposed to put a double checkmark: the patient has been treated. And when his life was over the final accounts would be drawn up, and clarity established. And he could go home.

The changes checked off, the tasks completed, the patients treated, then statistics and a report summarizing his experiences.

But where were the patients here? They were out there, but he had never met them. He had to rely on theories that someone else had devised: the brilliant men, those who were better read, the remarkable philosophers; theories that his friends in Rousseau's hut had mastered so splendidly.

The patients in Danish society, which he was now about to revolutionize, he would have to imagine – like the small heads he once sketched when he was writing his dissertation about aberrant motions of the body. They were the people inside the machine. Because it had to be possible, he always thought as he lay awake at night and sensed the Monstrous Danish Royal Palace like a lead weight on his chest, possible! Possible both to penetrate and to master the mechanism, and to see the people.

The human being was not a machine; rather, it was inside the machine. That was the trick. To master the machine. Then the faces he had drawn would smile kindly at him in all their gratefulness. But the difficult thing, the truly difficult thing, was that they didn't seem to be grateful. Those small, wicked heads between the points, the ones that were checked off! Finished! Solved! Those peering faces were spiteful and malicious and ungrateful.

Above all, they were not his friends. Society was a machine, and the faces were malicious. No, there was no longer any clarity.

He was now looking at his friend Rantzau, whom he knew might be an enemy. Or, what was worse, a traitor. Yes, Altona was definitely far away.

"This week the 'real' thing," he began slowly, "is the abolition of the law against adultery, as well as reductions in the redundant pensions to public officials, and the prohibition of torture. I am preparing the transfer of Øresund tariffs from the Royal Treasury to the state, the establishment of a welfare fund for illegitimate children, who will be christened in accordance with church ceremonies, and . . ."

"And what about ascription? Or are you going to settle for legislating morality?"

There was the face between the paragraphs again; suspicious, laughing maliciously. Ascription was a big issue! The biggest of them all! It belonged among the 24 points; no, among the twelve! The twelve that made up the numbers of the clock. He left the boy on the wooden horse to a merciless death and ran after the coach in the dusk; he was afraid. In some ways he had run away from the greatest of all challenges: serfdom. Inside the coach he stubbornly told himself that the important thing was for him to survive.

And be able to act with resolve. Issue decrees. Yes. And act. With resolve.

What he was now doing was just the small part: morals. He was legislating for improved morals; he was legislating to make the good

189

human being emerge; no, that was wrong, it was just the opposite. It was impossible to legislate away the evil person. "Morals cannot be improved with police laws", was what he had in fact written.

Yet, and he knew this was his weak point, he was spending a great deal of time on morals, customs, prohibitions, and spiritual freedom.

Was it because the other part was so difficult?

"Ascription?" Rantzau repeated, ruthlessly.

"Soon," he replied.

"How?"

"Reverdil," he began with some hesitation, "who was the King's tutor; he made a plan before he was banished. I've written to him, asking him to return."

"The little Jew," said Rantzau in a sober but hostile tone of voice, "the despicable little Jew. So he's the one who will free the Danish peasants. Do you know how many enemies that will make you?"

Struensee put the documents back on the table. It was pointless to continue this conversation. Rantzau bowed without a word, turned, and walked towards the door. But before he pulled it shut behind him, the last of the malicious faces appeared: from Rantzau, who called himself Struensee's last friend, and perhaps in some sense he was, the great teacher of theory, who now looked at him so critically, his friend, or former friend if indeed he ever had been.

"You no longer have many friends. And to spend the summer at Hirschholm is madness. But you have another problem."

"And what is that?" asked Struensee.

"You lack the ability to choose the proper enemies."

2

They were not fleeing, they would later think, but then why such frantic haste, such swift movements, such laughter, slamming doors?

They were not fleeing, but departing for the wonderful summer at Hirschholm.

The coaches were loaded. On the first day only four coaches were to leave. The next day the rest of the enormous amount of baggage would follow. Living a simple country life required extensive organization.

In the first coach rode the Queen, Struensee, King Christian VII, the Negro page Moranti, and the King's dog.

They travelled in silence.

Christian was quite calm. He regarded his fellow passengers with a secretive smile which they could not interpret. He was sure of that. He was thinking that if Caroline Mathilde were not sitting with them right now, listening, then four of The Seven would have been all alone in the coach. And then he could have safely asked advice from Struensee, Moranti, or the dog, the three he loved, about the time of overwhelming difficulty and hardship that was ahead.

Of this he was certain. Also that advice and instructions from his Benefactor, the Sovereign of the Universe, would not be forthcoming for some time.

Once upon a time a castle stood here. That's how it has to be said: Here it stood, and here it was swallowed up by the Danish revolution. And nothing is left of it.

Hirschholm Castle was situated on an island. The castle was surrounded by water. It stood in the middle of a lake, and at night the water was covered with the sleeping birds she loved so much, especially when they slept wrapped in their dreams. It took half a century to build the castle, and it wasn't completed until 1746. It was magnificent and beautiful, a Nordic Versailles, but the same thing happened to the castle as happens to very brief dreams: it lasted only one summer, the summer of 1771. After that the dream was over, and the castle stood alone and deserted and over time sank into decay.

It didn't burn. It wasn't pillaged. It simply died of grief, and then it was no more. It was as if that long and happy summer had infected the castle with the plague; the castle belonged to Caroline Mathilde and to Struensee, and when catastrophe struck, no-one wanted to set foot on that soil again, filled as it was with the contagion of sin.

By 1774, all work at the castle had ceased; by the turn of the century, its decline was complete. And when the palace of Christiansborg burned, it was decided to tear down Hirschholm and use the materials to rebuild Christiansborg. Everything was removed. The "sumptuous and tastefully furnished state halls" were plundered and taken away, the fabulous Knights' Hall in the centre of the castle was destroyed; every brick, every block of marble was carried off, every trace of the lovers was to be obliterated. Caroline Mathilde's chamber had resembled a curio cabinet; she was passionately interested in all things Chinese, and that summer she filled her rooms with Chinese vases and dolls which she had the East Asiatic Company bring back for her. Even the beautiful fireplace, which she had procured for the Audience Hall at Hirschholm, the one that "depicted a Chinese woman with parasol", was torn down.

The castle was a disgrace, tainted by the bastard and his mistress; it had to be removed, as when an undesirable face is erased from a photograph, so that history could be freed of something despicable, something that never existed, should never have existed. The island had to be cleansed of its sin.

By 1814, not a trace was left of the castle. Hence its life had been equal to that of a human being from 1746 to 1814; the castle lived to the age of 68. In that sense Hirschholm Castle is the only castle that is completely identified with a summer of love, with love and death and the uttermost boundary of the forbidden, and therefore it was doomed to death and annihilation. Today only a small Empire church, built in the 1800s, stands on the castle island.

Like a prayer. Like a final prayer for forgiveness to Almighty God; a prayer for mercy for the sins which two depraved people had committed.

Otherwise nothing but grass and water.

Although the birds, of course, are still there, the ones she saw on that late evening when she arrived at Hirschholm Castle, saw as a sign that at last she was home, and in safety, among the birds who slept wrapped in their dreams.

Once upon a time a castle stood here. This is where she came. She was with child. And she knew that it was his.

Everyone knew.

"I am with child," she said. "And we know that it's yours."

He kissed her but didn't say a word.

Everything had happened so fast. He had carried out the Danish revolution in eight months; the reforms were signed and would now continue to be signed from that den of iniquity called Hirschholm Castle, which was why it later had to be destroyed, just as one burns the sheets of someone who has died of the plague.

He had issued 564 edicts during the first year alone. In the end there seemed to be no obstacles. It all went so smoothly. The revolution was functioning splendidly, his pen scratched, things were put into effect, and he made love with this extraordinary girl who called herself the Queen of Denmark. He made love, wrote, and signed. The King's signature was no longer necessary. He knew that the chancelleries and civil service departments were roaring with fury, but no-one ventured to approach him. And so he continued on and on.

The desk revolutionary, he sometimes thought. He had always despised that expression. And yet now everything seemed to function from his desk. And it all became reality.

He never left his study, and yet the revolution was put into effect. Perhaps all revolutions ought to happen this way, he thought. No troops are necessary, no violence, no terror, no threats; simply a mad king with absolute power, and a document of proxy.

He realized that he was utterly dependent on this demented boy. Was he just as dependent on her?

When she told him about the child, he was delighted, and he understood at once that the end could be near.

*

They had been incautious in their lovemaking for so long.

He had never met a woman like this young girl; it was incomprehensible. She seemed to lack any fear or shyness, she was inexperienced and had taught herself everything as if in one breath. She seemed to love her body and loved to make use of his. The first night at Hirschholm she sat on him and rode him slowly, with pleasure, as if at every moment she was listening to secret signals inside his body, obeying them and controlling them. No, he didn't understand where this 20-year-old little English girl had learned all this. Finally, as softly as a cat, she had rolled down to his side and said:

"Are you happy?"

He knew that he was happy. And that catastrophe was now very close at hand.

"We must be careful," he replied.

"It's too late for that," she said in the dark. "I am with child. And the child is yours."

"And the Danish revolution? They're going to find out that it's my child."

"I have conceived the revolution's child with you," was her answer.

He got up, went over to the window, and looked out at the water. Dusk fell earlier now, but it was hot and humid and the lake surrounding the castle was full of plants and birds and it smelled of the lake, heavy, full of lust, and sated with death. Everything had happened so quickly.

"We have conceived the future," he heard her say from the dark.

"Or killed it," he said in a low voice.

"What do you mean?"

But he didn't know why he had said that.

He knew that he loved her.

It wasn't just her body, her astounding talent for love, what he thought of as erotic talent. It was also the fact that she was growing at such a pace, that every week he could see that she was someone

194

else, it was the sheer explosiveness of this little innocent English girl. Soon she would catch up with him, and perhaps even pass him, becoming someone that he couldn't imagine. He wouldn't have thought it possible. She truly had many faces, but not a single deranged one, like Christian. She did not have a black torch inside her that would send its fatal darkness over him; no, she was a stranger who seduced him at that very moment when he thought he was seeing her, but suddenly realized that he wasn't.

He recalled her phrase "like a branding iron on an animal".

But was that the way love should be? He didn't want it to be like that.

"I'm just a doctor from Altona," he said.

"Well? So what?"

"Sometimes it feels like a pure-hearted, reluctant, and inadequately educated doctor from Altona has been given a task that is much too big," he said in a low voice.

He was standing with his back to her because this was the first time he dared say this to her, and he was rather ashamed. That was why he was standing with his back turned, not daring to look at her. But he said it, and although it felt right to say it, he felt ashamed.

He didn't want to seem haughty. It was almost a deadly sin to be haughty; that's what he had learned as a child. He was just a doctor from Altona. That was the basic fact. But added to this was the presumptuous idea that he knew he had been given a task, and he didn't think himself too humble, even though that's what he should have thought.

The arrogant people at court would never have hesitated. Those who were not upstarts. They found it quite natural to be presumptuous, since everything they possessed had been inherited and none of it had been acquired through their own efforts. But he wasn't arrogant; he was afraid.

That was what made him ashamed. They called him "The Silent One". Perhaps that frightened them. He was quiet, he was tall in stature, and he knew how to keep silent; that frightened them. But they didn't understand that he was basically just a doctor from Altona who presumed to believe that he had a calling.

The others were never ashamed. That was why he stood with his back to her.

One day, towards the end of the summer, after she had given birth to the child, she came to him and said that Bernstorff, who had been sent away and had returned to his own estate, must be called back.

"He hates us," Struensee told her.

"That makes no difference. We need him. He must be placated and used. Enemy or not."

And then she said:

"We need flank protection."

He merely stared at her. "Flank protection." Where had she found that term? She was unbelievable.

3

It was a magnificent summer.

They abolished all protocol, they read Rousseau, they changed their manner of attire, they lived simply, they lived in nature, they made love, they seemed obsessed with compressing all the elements of happiness so that not a single hour would be wasted. Visitors were shocked by their free behaviour which was, however, as they noted with surprise in their letters, not manifested in indecent language. All regularity was abolished. The servants would often, but not always, serve the food at meals. Responsibility for the cooking was shared. They went on excursions, staying out late into the night. Once the Queen, on a trip to the beach, pulled Struensee into the dunes, unfastened her clothing, and they made love. The attendants noticed the sand in their clothes but were not at all surprised. All titles were abolished. The system of rank disappeared. Everyone was on first-name terms.

It was like a dream. They discovered that everything was much simpler, more peaceful.

That was what they discovered at Hirschholm: that everything was possible, and that it was possible to escape the madhouse.

Christian was happy, too. He seemed to be very far away, and yet quite close. One evening at the dinner table, he said to Struensee with a smile:

"It's late, it's time for the King of Prussia to visit the Queen's bed."

Everyone was startled, and Struensee asked in a light tone of voice:

"The King of Prussia? Who is that?"

"It's you, isn't it?" replied Christian in surprise.

Her pregnancy became more and more visible, but she insisted on riding through the woods and refused to listen to the worried objections of those around her.

She had become a very capable rider. She never fell. She rode swiftly, confidently; he followed apprehensively. One afternoon someone did fall from a horse. It was Struensee who was thrown. His horse threw him, he fell, and he lay on the ground for a long time, with a great deal of pain in one leg. At last he laboriously got to his feet.

She supported him until the summoned assistants arrived.

"My love," she said, "did you think that I was going to fall? But I didn't fall. I don't want to lose this child. That's why you were the one to fall."

He merely replied:

"Perhaps my luck has run out."

He delivered the child himself.

On crutches, at the Queen's bedside and on crutches, Struensee witnessed the birth of his little daughter.

He pulled out the child, that was how he expressed it, he pulled out his child, and at once he was overwhelmed. He had delivered children before, but this one, this one! He leaned on the crutches under his arms, but the crutches fell and he assumed that his injured leg must have hurt terribly, he didn't remember, and he began to sob.

No-one had ever seen him like that before, and they talked about it for a long time; for some people it was clear proof.

But he sobbed. It was the child. It was eternal life that he had pulled out of her; their daughter, who was his eternal life.

After that he got hold of himself and did what he had to do. He went to King Christian VII and informed him that Caroline Mathilde, his Queen, had given him an heir, she had given birth to a girl. The King seemed uninterested and did not want to see the child. Later that evening he again suffered an attack of nervousness, and together with the Negro page Moranti he amused himself by toppling statues in the park.

The little girl was christened Louise Augusta.

4

Within 24 hours the court in Copenhagen knew that the child of Struensee and the Queen had been born. The Dowager Queen summoned Guldberg at once.

She was sitting with her drooling and babbling son to whom, at this perilous moment, she never cast a glance, although she kept a firm grip on his left hand the whole time. She began by saying that the whore's bastard was a disgrace to the country and to the royal house, but that she now wanted to see the whole picture.

She requested an analysis of the situation, and she got it.

Guldberg presented a report.

After the Algerian incident, when a Danish fleet was sent to the Mediterranean and largely decimated, there was a great need to rebuild the navy. The problem was presented to Struensee, and he replied with two communiqués. The first prohibited the production of grain-based liquor and all private home distilling. The second announced that not only was he going to cut the royal household by half, but he would also reduce the military organization of the navy. This meant that the shipyard at Holmen would have to cease its work. The workers, especially the sailors who had been called up from Norway, were now seized with anger. Guldberg had been in contact with them several times. A delegation had also paid him a visit.

They wanted to know whether the rumour was true which claimed that Struensee was holding the King prisoner, with the intention of killing him.

Guldberg had then, by means of "gestures and facial expressions", hinted that this was indeed the case, but that it was necessary to plan and devise actions with great care for the defence of the kingdom and the royal house. He told them that he shared their distress about losing their jobs at the shipyard. As for Struensee's whoremongering, he prayed to God every evening that a bolt of lightning would kill that man, for the sake of Denmark.

They were now planning an insurrection. The workers were going to march on Hirschholm.

"And what then?" asked the Dowager Queen. "Are they going to kill him?"

Guldberg merely replied, without smiling:

"An insurrection by discontented people against a tyrant is never predictable."

And then, as if in passing, he added:

"It can only be initiated, and directed."

The newborn girl was asleep, taking breaths that he could only hear if he put his ear close. He thought she was so beautiful. Now, at last, he had a child after all.

Everything was very quiet that summer.

Oh, how he wished that it might always be that way.

But at nine o'clock at night on September 8, 1771, a coach came driving across the bridge of the lake to Hirschholm Castle; it was Count Rantzau, who wished to speak to Struensee at once. Rantzau was furious, and he said he wanted to "have it out with him".

"You're completely mad," he said. "Copenhagen is full of pamphlets that openly discuss your relationship with the Queen. There's no longer any sense of shame. The ban on distilling has made them furious. Certain sections of the army are trustworthy, but those very sections are now on home leave. Why are you sitting here and not in Copenhagen? I have to know."

"Whose side are you on?" asked Struensee.

"I want to ask you the same question. You know that I have debts. So that's why – that's why! – you institute a law that says: 'legal rights shall be exercised in all debt disputes, without regard to the debtor's status or personal reputation', which sounds splendid except that I think it was done just to ruin me. The ulterior motive! The motive! Whose side are *you* on? I want to know, before ... before ..."

"Before everything falls apart?"

"Answer me first."

"I don't write laws for your sake. And I won't change them for your sake either. The answer is no."

"No?"

"No."

A long silence followed. Then Rantzau said:

"Struensee, you've come a long way since Altona. An inconceivably long way. Where are you thinking of going now?"

"Where are *you* thinking of going?"

Rantzau stood up and said simply:

"To Copenhagen."

Then he left, leaving Struensee alone. He went into his bed-chamber, lay down on the bed, and stared up at the ceiling, trying not to think about anything.

Yet he kept thinking the same thing over and over. And it was: I don't want to die. What am I going to do?

*

"Flank protection," she said.

But how many flanks could not be protected? And then this weariness.

He had not left the royal expedition in Altona. He had chosen to visit reality. How could he go on?

Chapter 12 · The Flute Player

I

Of the group of young enlightened men who once met at Altona, only one remained close to Struensee. Enevold Brandt.

He was Struensee's last friend. He was the flute player.

After being banished, Élie Salomon François Reverdil – "the despicable little Jew," as Rantzau called him – was summoned back from Switzerland. He had kept up correspondences with friends in Denmark during his years of exile in his native country. He felt great sorrow and bewilderment at what had happened, he didn't understand what his beloved boy had meant, he didn't understand anything. But when the offer to return arrived, he didn't hesitate for a second. His task would be to explain the plans, once halted, for the abolition of serfdom.

He would end up with other tasks, however. Nothing would turn out the way he had thought.

The reason why his tasks ended up being different was that a peculiar incident occurred which made it impossible for Enevold Brandt to be Christian's companion. This episode, the index finger incident, would eventually cost Brandt his life.

After the "incident", Reverdil became the King's bodyguard. Before, he had been the King's teacher and friend; now he became his guard. It was a hopeless situation. The wolves had torn to shreds his beloved boy; Christian was now a different person. Nothing was the same as before. Christian had welcomed his old teacher, but not with warmth; he spoke and muttered as if through an icy membrane. The idea that had enticed Reverdil back, the plan to implement the great reform, the plan regarding ascription, faded away.

Reverdil's political influence ceased. Serfdom was not abolished.

During the incident the King was slightly injured.

On the day when the distressing episode occurred - the "index finger incident" as it came to be known – Struensee had sent by courier a decree to Copenhagen regarding the regional Cupping Stations, the financing of the Foundling Institute, a detailed directive for the religious freedom now proclaimed for Reformists and Catholics, laws authorizing Moravian sects to settle freely in Slesvig, and directives for plans to establish a Danish counterpart to the German "Real-Schulen".

The work of an entire week had been sent with a single courier. It had been collecting all week long. Usually a courier was sent every other day.

Little things became interwoven with big things in an entirely natural way. The little things were the reforms. The big thing would turn out to be the index finger.

Brandt was a flute player.

Struensee had known him during his days in Altona, and particularly at Ascheberg. That was the period when people hiked up to Rousseau's hut and read aloud the texts and talked of the time that was to come: when the good people would take command and power, the reactionary hydra would be driven out, and utopia would be achieved. Brandt had enthusiastically adopted all the new ideas, although they seemed to settle on him like butterflies; they glittered and flew off and then came back, and he appeared to be untouched by them. They adorned him. He found, to his joy, that ladies of his acquaintance were enchanted by them, which was perhaps the most significant. He was an artist by nature, it seemed to Struensee, spineless but worth loving.

For him the Enlightenment held a sexual enticement and lent colour to life; it made the nights exciting and varied. But for Brandt the Enlightenment was like it was for the Italian actors, and above all like his flute playing.

It was the flute, Struensee thought during the period at Rousseau's hut, that made him bearable.

There was something about his quiet obsession with the flute that made Struensee end up tolerating his shallowness. His flute playing told of some other side of Brandt. What Struensee remembered from the Altona days and the evenings spent in the hut in Ascheberg Gardens was not so much Brandt's flighty love affairs with "politics" and "art" but rather the solitude that his flute playing created around the young enlightened man.

Which, for whatever reason, could have assumed any countenance at all.

Only the glimmer remained.

Perhaps it was Brandt's flute playing that, in a way, characterized the magnificent summer of 1771. And some of the sounds from Hirschholm spread elsewhere. Sounds of merriment, freedom and flute music simmered like a sensual undercurrent even in Copenhagen during that warm and passionate summer. The great royal parks were opened, by Struensee's decree, to the general public. Entertainments were on the rise, perhaps partly because the authority of the police to restrict bordellos was revoked. A decree was issued making it impossible for the police to continue their custom of "visiting" the bordellos and inns after nine o'clock at night and investigating, through this encroachment, whether any depravity was going on. This visitation principle had regularly been used as a means of black-mailing customers. It had little effect on vice, but it did increase the income of the police. Customers were allowed to pay, on the spot, in order to avoid arrest.

But for the general populace the liberation of the parks was the important thing.

"The desecration of the King's parks" – which referred to engaging in sexual intercourse at night in the royal parks of Copenhagen – had previously been punished with the loss of a finger joint if the person was unable to pay on the spot, which in the end everyone managed to do. Now the parks were opened. Rosenborg Garden, in particular, became a fabulous erotic playground on those warm summer nights in Copenhagen. In the darkness, the lawns and the shrubbery, which both concealed and enticed, became a murmuring, laughing, chirping and playful erotic gathering place, although Rosenborg Garden was soon overtaken by Frederiksberg Garden, which was only partially lit at night.

For three evenings each week this park was specially opened to masked couples. The people's right to a masquerade was proclaimed – in public parks, and at night. In actuality this meant the right, with a certain anonymity (the masks), to copulate freely outdoors.

Masks on their faces, open thighs, and whispering. Before, the royal parks were reserved for the ladies of the court, who would stroll through them at an infinitely slow pace beneath their parasols. But now they were opened to the public, and at night! At night! A wave of passion surged over the previously sacred and closed parks. Overpopulated Copenhagen, where the packed slums meant that all passions of the flesh were relegated to crowded rooms where desires were audible and rubbed up against the desire and shame of others . . . the teeming population of Copenhagen now had access to the new royal preserves of passion.

Parks, night-time, seed, the scent of lust.

It was lewd, offensive, preposterously exciting, and everybody knew that this was the contagion of sin that emanated from the royal whoremongering. Struensee and the Queen were essentially to blame.

So shocking! So enticing! But for how long? It seemed as if a heavy, panting and inflammatory breath were playing over Copenhagen: such days! Over so soon!

It paid to be on guard. No penalties, prohibitions or righteous indignation applied any longer. It was like a race for time. Soon the lechery would be extinguished by a punitive fire.

But until then! These brief weeks! Until then!

It was Brandt's flute playing that set the tone. Gone was the old pietistic regime's prohibition against dances, plays and concerts on Saturdays and Sundays, on fast days or during Advent. When had anything at all been permitted? As if by magic the prohibitions were gone.

And now, in the parks, these shadows, bodies, masks, this lust; and beneath all of it a secretive flute.

2

Brandt arrived at Hirschholm three days after the others, and to his surprise he found that he had been appointed the King's adjutant.

Nursemaid, they called it. He found himself situated in a castle on an island, far from the masked balls and theatre intrigues; his rôle was to pay attention to Christian's games and manic chanting. It was all so pointless and aroused his fury. He was the *maître de plaisir*, after all! The cultural minister! What was cultural about this? This royal kindergarten? He found the excursions into nature to be exhausting. He found the love between the Queen and Struensee to be frustrating and lacking in all interest. He was exiled from the Italian actresses. He found the games that Caroline Mathilde and Struensee played with the little boy, and their adoration of the little girl, to be ridiculous.

He missed the court, Copenhagen, and the theatre. He felt powerless. His task was to entertain the King, whose behaviour was grotesque, as always. He was the guard of a mad monarch.

He had bigger ambitions. And this gave rise to a conflict.

Compared with the consequences, the event itself was a comic trifle.

One day at the Queen's lunch table, the King, who had not participated in the conversation during the meal but true to custom had been muttering to himself, suddenly stood up, and in an oddly artificial tone of voice, as if he were an actor on stage, pointed at Brandt and shouted:

"I will now give you a real thrashing with the rod, give you a beating, because you deserve it! It's you that I'm talking to, Count Brandt, do you hear me?"

There was utter silence. After a moment Struensee and the Queen pulled King Christian aside and spoke to him earnestly, although the others could not hear what was said. Then the King burst into tears. With a gesture, but still shaking with sobs, he called for his old teacher Reverdil; together they went out to the anteroom, where Reverdil spoke soothingly to the King and comforted him. Perhaps he also offered his support and encouragement to Christian, since Reverdil had always despised Brandt, and perhaps he thought that Christian's outburst was in some way appropriate.

In any case, Reverdil did not take Christian to task, and for this he was later criticized.

The others at the table had decided that the King should now be given a lesson to prevent the recurrence of similar offensive behavior. Struensee sternly conveyed to the King that Brandt should be offered an apology and some form of redress, since he had been publicly humiliated.

The King ground his teeth, plucked at his body with his fingers, and refused.

Later, after supper, Brandt went to the King's rooms. He ordered Moranti and the Queen's page Phebe, who were playing with Christian, to withdraw. Then he locked the door and asked the King what weapon he preferred for the duel that must now be fought.

The King, horrified and in mortal terror, just shook his head, whereupon Brandt said that their fists would have to suffice. Christian, who often took pleasure in playful wrestling matches, thought that he would perhaps be able to escape in this jesting manner. But Brandt, who was seized by an inexplicable and astonishing fury, knocked Christian down without the least compassion and bellowed abuse at the sobbing monarch. They ended up wrestling on the floor; and when Christian used his hands in an attempt to defend himself, Brandt bit him on the index finger so that blood began to flow.

Brandt left the King sobbing on the floor, went to find Struensee, and told him that he had now won his redress. The courtiers were hastily summoned to bandage Christian's finger.

Struensee forbade anyone to speak of this incident. If someone asked, the position was to be that the King's life had not been in danger, that Count Brandt had not tried to kill the King, and that the King was accustomed to a playful wrestling match, which was a beneficial exercise for the limbs. But the utmost silence was to be observed about what had taken place.

To the Queen, however, Struensee said anxiously:

"In Copenhagen the rumour is circulating that we wish to kill the King. If this gets out, it won't be good. I don't understand that Brandt."

The next day Brandt was replaced by Reverdil as the head adjutant, and he then had more time for his flute playing. Reverdil, on the other hand, had no time to work on his plan for the abolition of serfdom. More time for flute playing, which had a direct effect on politics.

Brandt quickly forgot all about the episode.

But he would soon have reason to remember it.

3

Autumn came late that year; the afternoons were quiet and everyone took walks, drank tea, and waited.

A year earlier, during the previous late summer at Ascheberg Gardens, everything had been so enchanting and new; now they tried to reconstruct that feeling. It was as if they tried to put a glass bell over the summer and Hirschholm. Out there in the darkness, in the Danish reality, they suspected that their enemies were multiplying. No, they knew it. Their enemies were more numerous than during the late summer at Ascheberg Gardens, when innocence could still be found. Now they felt as if they were on stage, and the spotlight was slowly shrinking around them; the little family in the light, and all around them a darkness that they didn't want to enter.

Of greatest importance was the children. The boy was three years old, and Struensee put into practice all the theoretical principles of childrearing that he had formulated in the past regarding health, natural attire, baths, outdoor life and games. The little girl would soon follow, but she was still too young. She was endearing. The little girl was adorable. The little girl won everyone's devotion. Yet, the little girl had become – and everyone knew this, although no-one spoke of it – the very focus for the Danish hatred of Struensee.

The whore's bastard. They had received reports. Everyone seemed to know.

Struensee and the Queen often sat in the narrow strip of garden along the left flank of the woods, where garden furniture was set up and parasols provided shade. They could see a long way towards the park on the opposite side. One evening they were watching from a distance King Christian, who was always accompanied by Moranti and the dog; Christian was meandering along the opposite shore of the lake, busy toppling statues.

That was the section of the garden where the statues stood. The statues were the constant objects of his anger or humour.

They had tried to anchor the statues better by using ropes so that they couldn't be toppled, but it did no good. It was pointless. They would prop them back up after the King's vandalizing rampage without even trying to repair the damage or broken pieces, disfigurements that occurred whenever the King was struck by melancholy.

Struensee and the Queen sat there for a long time and, without a word, watched his battle with the statues.

It was all very familiar by now.

"We're used to this," Caroline Mathilde said, "but we can't let anyone outside the court see him."

"Everyone knows, anyway."

"Everyone knows, but it shouldn't be mentioned," said Caroline Mathilde. "He's ill. They say in Copenhagen that the Dowager Queen and Guldberg are planning to put him into an asylum. But that would be the end of both of us."

"The end?"

"One day he topples God's chosen statues. The next day he topples us."

"No, he won't," said Struensee. "But I'm nothing without Christian. If it gets out to the Danish people that God's chosen one is nothing but a madman, then he will no longer be able to stretch his hand out to me and point and say: YOU! You will be my arm and my hand, and YOU alone will autocratically sign the decrees and laws. He transfers God's choice to me. If he can't do that, then the only thing left is . . ."

"Death?"

"Or flight."

"Rather death than flight," the Queen said after a moment of silence.

Loud laughter reached them from across the water. Moranti was now chasing the dog.

"Such a beautiful country," she said. "And such ugly people. Do we have any friends left?"

"One or two," replied Struensee. "One or two."

"Is he really a madman?" she asked.

"No," said Struensee. "But he's not a person cast in one piece."

"How ghastly that sounds," she said. "A person cast in one piece. Like a monument."

He didn't answer. But then he said:

"But are *you*?"

She had begun to sit with Struensee while he worked.

At first Struensee thought it was because she wanted to be near him. Later he realized that it was the work that interested her.

He was supposed to explain what he was writing. At first he did so with a smile. Later, when he saw that her attitude was deeply serious, he made a greater effort. One day she came to his room with a list of people she wanted to dismiss; at first he laughed. Then she explained. And he understood. It was not hatred or envy that lay behind the list. She had made an assessment of the power structure.

Her analysis surprised him.

He thought that her extremely lucid, extremely brutal view of the mechanisms of power had been born at the English court. No, she told him, I lived in a cloister. Then where had she learned all this? She was not one of those that Brandt, with some scorn, used to call the "female schemers". Struensee understood that she saw a different kind of pattern to his.

The dream of the good society based on justice and reason was his. Her obsession was the instrument. It was the instrument's handling of what she called "the great game".

Whenever she talked about the great game he would feel uneasy. He knew why that was. It was the tone from the discussions, back then, among the brilliant men of the Enlightenment in Altona, when he realized that he was only a doctor, and kept silent.

He listened, and once again kept silent.

One evening she interrupted him as he was reading aloud from Holberg's *Moral Thoughts* and told him that it was nothing but abstractions.

That all those principles were true, but that he needed to understand the instrument. That he had to see the mechanisms, that he was naïve. That his heart was much too pure. The pure-hearted were doomed to destruction. He hadn't understood how to exploit the nobles. He must divide his enemies. Robbing the city of Copenhagen of its administrative independence was lunacy, and it created unnecessary enemies. He stared at her, surprised and silent. In her opinion the reforms had to be directed both against some things and for others. His decrees flowed from his pen, but they lacked any plan.

He should choose his enemies, she said.

He recognized the phrase. He had heard it before. He gave a start, and asked her whether she had been talking to Rantzau. "I recognize that phrase," he said. "It didn't come out of thin air."

"No," she replied, "but perhaps he saw the same thing I did."

Struensee felt confused. Ambassador Keith from England had told Brandt that he knew quite well that "Her Majesty the Queen is now ruling absolutely through the Confidential Cabinet Minister". Brandt had passed this remark on. Was this a truth that he had suppressed? One day he issued a decree that the church on Amaliegade should be vacated and transformed into a women's hospital, and he had hardly noticed that this was her suggestion. It was her suggestion, and he had formulated it, signed it, and believed it to be his own. But it was her suggestion.

Had he lost control of the situation? He wasn't sure. He had suppressed things. She sat across from him at the desk, listening and commenting.

"I must teach you about the great game," she would say to him now and then, since she knew that he detested that expression. Once, apparently in jest, he reminded her of her motto: "O, keep me innocent, make others great."

"That was back then," she said. "That was in beforetimes. That was so long ago."

"In beforetimes," she used to say quite often, in her odd way of speaking. There were many things that were "in beforetimes".

4

How infinitely quiet the castle had become. As if the silence of the castle, the lake, and the parks had become part of Struensee's inner silence.

He often sat at the little girl's bedside when she slept, looking at her face. So innocent, so lovely. How long would it last?

"What's the matter with you?" Caroline Mathilde asked him one evening. "You've grown so quiet."

"I don't know."

"You don't know?"

He couldn't explain. He had dreamed about all of this, about being able to change everything, about having all power; but now life had abated. Perhaps this was what it was like to die. Just giving up, dozing off.

"What's the matter with you?" she repeated.

"I don't know. Sometimes I have such a longing to sleep. To just fall asleep. To die."

"You're dreaming about dying?" she said in a sharp voice that he didn't recognize. "Well, I'm not. I'm still young."

"Yes, forgive me."

"In fact," she said with a kind of restrained rage, "I'm just starting to live!"

He could find no reply.

"I don't understand you at all," she said.

That day a slight misunderstanding had occurred between them, although it evaporated when they withdrew to the Queen's bedchamber.

They made love.

Whenever they made love during that late summer he was often seized, afterwards, with an inexplicable anxiety. He didn't know what it was. He left her bed, opened the window drapes, and looked out at the water. He heard a flute and knew that it was Brandt. Why did he always want to look outside, and away, after they made love? He didn't know. His nose pressed to the windowpane; was he a bird that wanted out? That was impossible. He had to finish what he had set out to do.

One or two friends left. One or two. Flight or death. Monsieur Voltaire had also been naïve.

"What are you thinking?" she asked.

He didn't reply.

"I know," she told him. "You're proud of yourself. You know you're a fantastic lover. That's what you're thinking."

"Some people are good at it," he said matter-of-factly. "I've always been good at it."

Too late he realized what he had said and regretted it. But she had heard, understood the implication, and at first did not reply. Then she said:

"You're the only one I've ever had. So I have nothing to compare it to. That's the difference."

"I know."

"Apart from the madman. I forgot about that. In a certain sense I do love him. Do you know that?"

She looked at his back to see whether he would be hurt, but she couldn't see anything. She hoped it had hurt him. It would be so amusing if he was hurt.

No answer.

"He's not as perfect as you are. Not as fantastic. But he wasn't as bad a lover as you might think. Are you hurt now? He was like a child that time. It was almost . . . exciting. Are you hurt?"

"I can leave if you like."

"No."

"Yes, I'll leave."

"When I want you to leave," she said in the same, low, friendly voice, "then you may leave. Not before. Not a second before."

"What do you want? I can hear in your voice that there's something you want."

"I want you to come here."

He stood there, knowing that he didn't want to move but that he would probably end up doing so anyway.

"I want to know what you're thinking," she said after a long silence.

"I'm thinking," he said, "that before, I thought I was in control. Now I no longer believe that. Where did it go?"

She didn't reply.

"Monsieur Voltaire, with whom I have also corresponded," he began, "Monsieur Voltaire thought that I could be the spark. Which would light the prairie fire. Where did it go?"

"You've lit it in me," she said. "In me. And now we will burn together. Come."

"Do you know," he told her, "do you know that you are strong? And sometimes I'm afraid of you."

5

At the best of times Christian was allowed to play undisturbed.

The ones who were allowed to play undisturbed were Christian, the Negro page Moranti, little Phebe, and the dog. They played in the King's bedchamber. The bed was quite wide, with room for all four of them. Christian had wrapped a sheet around Moranti, entirely covering him, and they were playing court.

Moranti was the King. He was supposed to sit enshrouded at the head of the bed, and his face had to be completely hidden; he was supposed to be wrapped up in a cocoon, and at the foot of the bed sat Christian and Phebe and the dog. They were pretending to be members of the court and the King was to address and command them.

Moranti issued orders and commands. The members of the court bowed.

It was so amusing. They had tossed off their wigs and clothes and sat there wearing only their lace-trimmed underwear.

From the one wrapped in the sheet came muffled words and commands. The members of the court bowed in such a ridiculous manner. Everything was so funny.

That's how things were at the best of times.

On September 17, when Christian and his companions were playing their game of King and the ridiculous court, a courier arrived at Hirschholm from Copenhagen, bringing a communiqué from Paris.

It contained a celebratory poem from Monsieur Voltaire to King Christian VII. It would later be published as Epistle 109, become very famous, and be translated into many languages. But on this occasion the poem was handwritten, it had 137 verses, and it was titled "On Freedom of the Press".

But it was directed at Christian, and it was written in homage to him. The occasion for the poem was that Voltaire had received word that the Danish King had introduced freedom of speech in Denmark. He could not have known that Christian had slipped into a different sort of great dream which had nothing to do with freedom but with flight, that the boy who played with his little, living dolls was barely conscious of the reform that Struensee had implemented, and that in fact this newly won freedom of speech had resulted only in an abundance of pamphlets, guided and initiated by the reactionaries, who were now methodically working to smear Struensee. In this new free climate, the pamphlets attacked Struensee's lechery and gave fuel to the rumours of his immoral nights with the Queen.

It was not what this freedom was intended for. But Struensee refused to retract it. And thus this flood of filth was directed at him personally. But since Monsieur Voltaire didn't know about all this, Monsieur Voltaire had written a poem, about Christian. Which dealt with the principles that Voltaire hailed, that were correct, and that cast honour on the Danish King.

It was a splendid evening at Hirschholm.

They saw to it that Christian stopped his playing and was dressed. And then they gathered for an evening of readings. First Struensee read the poem aloud, for all of them. And afterwards everyone applauded and looked with warmth upon Christian, who was embarrassed, but happy. Then Christian was exhorted to read the poem himself. At first he refused. But then he gave in and read Voltaire's poem in his marvellously exquisite French, slowly, and with his special emphasis.

> *Excellent prince, though a despot born,*
> *Will you govern me from your Baltic throne?*
> *Am I subject to you, so you treat me like yours,*
> *making happy my days, comforting my cares?*

It was so splendidly written; Voltaire had expressed his joy that now it was permitted in the North to write freely, and humanity was now speaking its gratitude through his voice.

> *From the wilds of the Jura my tranquil old age*
> *lets itself learn of your wise young sway;*
> *and bold with respect, daring yet not vain,*
> *I fall down at your feet in the name of all men.*
> *They speak through my voice.*

And then the magnificent poem continued on, about the absurdity of censorship and the importance of literature, and how it could strike fear into those in power and, on the other hand, about the helplessness of censorship, since it could never have any original ideas. And how impossible it was to kill a victorious idea. *Est-il bon, tous les rois ne peuvent l'écraser!* (If the book is good, not even all the kings can crush it!) If an idea is suppressed in one place, it will appear somewhere else the victor. If it is scorned in one country, it is admired in another.

Who, drawing Truth from the depth of his well,
could make from rude mob a public soul?
Books have done all.

Christian's voice quavered as he came to the end. And then they all applauded again, for a very long time.

And Christian sat down among them, and he was so happy, and they looked upon him with warmth, almost with love, and he was so pleased.

On almost every evening that summer, the sound of a flute came from the balcony of the castle.

It was Brandt, the flute player.

It was the sound of freedom and happiness. The flute at Hirschholm Castle, that fabulous summer palace that lived for only one summer. Something was perhaps going to happen, but not yet. Everything was waiting. The flute player, the last of the friends, played for all of them, but without seeing them.

The King played. The Queen leaned over her child, in a loving pose. Struensee, silent and remote, a bird with his wingtips pressed to the window, a bird that had almost given up.

Chapter 13 · The Sailors' Revolt

I

No, there was nothing comical about Voltaire's celebratory poem. It was one of the most beautiful homages to free speech ever written.

But to Christian? People were searching everywhere for the spark that would light the fire. Back in 1767 Voltaire had written to him that "From now on people will have to travel north to find exemplary ideas; and if only my infirmity and weakness did not hinder me, I would follow my heart's desire to come to you and throw myself at Your Majesty's feet."

Voltaire at Christian's feet. But that was the situation. Those were the circumstances. The young monarchs in the north offered puzzling but enticing possibilities. The encyclopedists also kept in contact with the Swedish Crown Prince, the future King Gustav III. Gustav was admired by Diderot, he read all of Voltaire; the small kingdoms of the north were strange little hotbeds of Enlightenment. Or rather, they could be.

What could the philosophers of the Enlightenment hope for in their exiles in Switzerland or St. Petersburg? With their books burned and their works constantly censored. Freedom of speech and freedom of the press were the keys.

And then there were these peculiar, inquisitive young monarchs in those backward little societies in the north. Freedom of speech was suddenly implemented in Denmark. Why shouldn't the forever targeted and persecuted Monsieur Voltaire write a desperate and hopeful celebratory poem?

He couldn't have known what the true situation was.

2

In the fall of 1771 the reaction came. It came in waves.

The first wave was the revolt of the Norwegian sailors.

It started when the gaunt, stooped Swiss tutor Reverdil gave Struensee some advice concerning the resolution of the Algerian problem. Reverdil was, after all, a sensible person, Struensee used to think. But how to make use of those who were sensible in a madhouse? As guards for the madmen?

It was a mistake to make Reverdil Christian's chief guard. But the King now hated Brandt. And someone had to keep watch over him. What was to be done?

It ended up being Reverdil.

But Reverdil had knowledge about the madhouse that at times could be put to use, even during the late summer of 1771 at Hirschholm. He was given the task of reporting "clearly and plainly" on the problem of the Algerian episode and presenting possible solutions to it. But the problems surrounding "the Algerian episode" grew during those months like an avalanche; there was no clarity other than that of the madhouse.

Struensee had inherited the catastrophe. Long before his time a heavily armed Danish fleet was sent to Algeria. War was declared. The years passed. Then the catastrophe became apparent to everyone. When the royal physician came to visit, the catastrophe already existed, and he inherited it. The clear glow of reason had been dimmed by madness. And Struensee felt powerless.

Logically, in the madhouse, it was thought that Denmark had declared war on Algeria and sent a fleet to the Mediterranean. The logic had long ago been forgotten, but it had something to do with the great struggle for power, Turkey versus Russia. It was also logical that this insane attempt had failed.

Reverdil's reports on the matter – he remembered it of old, and he was glad to be free of Christian's company for a few days – were gloomy. What to do? In addition to the sunken vessels, the loss of men and the tremendous costs that threatened to drive up the national debt and subvert all reforms, in addition to all this there was a bitter feeling that the inherited madness would undermine everything.

Reverdil's lucid analyses were unbearable.

The situation was now such that a small Danish squadron remained in the Mediterranean, under the command of Admiral Hooglandt. It was all that was left of the proud fleet that had set sail. This squadron now had orders to pursue the Algerian corsairs and to wait for reinforcements. These reinforcements, which would save the honour of the Danish navy, were supposed to leave from Copenhagen, but first they had to be built. The shipbuilding was to take place at Holmen's

Shipyard. The newly built squadron would consist of large ships of the line, as well as galliots with powerful cannons and artillery that could be used to bombard Algeria. The squadrons, according to the naval commanders, would total at least nine ships of the line, in addition to frigates, xebecs and galliots.

To build the necessary vessels, 600 sailors had been conscripted from Norway. For quite a while now they had gone idle in Copenhagen, waiting for the starting shot. They had gradually become discontented. Their wages were on hold. The whores were demanding to be paid, and with no wages, no whores. Free liquor had not assuaged them but had instead prompted heavy damage in the Copenhagen taverns.

The Norwegian sailors were also very loyal to the Crown and according to tradition called the Danish monarch "Little Father". In Norway they had learned to use the term in an almost mythological sense, to threaten local Norwegian authorities with intervention by the central power.

The Norwegian sailors were outraged by reports that Little Father Christian had been imprisoned by the German Struensee. The new, freely released and copiously distributed pamphlets had done their job. Little Father's sacred bed had been desecrated. Everything was a disaster. No work. Unwilling whores. Finally starvation began to set in. No whores, no wages, no work, Little Father threatened; their fury grew.

Reverdil was unequivocal and recommended that the Algerian episode be written off. Struensee listened. No ships of the line would be built. But the sailors remained and refused to be transported back to Norway.

They were the ones Guldberg had been in touch with. In October they decided to march on Hirschholm.

There was no doubt about the matter: the news was ominous, the end seemed near.

The reports of the rebellious sailors' march quickly reached

Hirschholm. Struensee listened in silence and then went to the Queen.

"They'll be here in four hours," he told her. "They're coming to kill us. We have 15 soldiers to combat them, handsome uniforms but not much else. Presumably they've already fled. No-one is going to prevent the sailors from killing us."

"What should we do?" she asked.

"We can flee to Sweden."

"That's cowardly," she said. "I'm not afraid to die, but I'm not going to die."

She looked at him with an expression that heightened the tension between them.

"I'm not afraid to die either," he told her.

"Then what *are* you afraid of?" she said.

He knew the answer but kept silent.

He had noticed that the word "terror" or "fear" was appearing in their conversations on a regular basis. There was something about "fear" that belonged to his childhood, long ago, "in beforetimes", as she used to say in her peculiar Danish.

Why was the word "fear" cropping up so often right now? Was it the memory of the story he had read as a child, about the boy who set out into the world to learn to know fear?

It was a fairy tale, that much he remembered. It was about a clever, intelligent, humanistic person who was paralysed by fear. But this intelligent boy had a brother. What was it about the brother? The brother was stupid and energetic. But he could not feel fear. He lacked the capacity to feel fear. He was the hero of the story. He set out to learn to know fear, but nothing could strike terror into his heart.

He was invulnerable.

What was "fear"? Was it the ability to see what was possible, and impossible? Was it a feeler, was it a warning signal inside him, or was it the paralysing terror that he knew could destroy everything?

He said that he was not afraid to die. And he saw at once that this infuriated her. She didn't believe him, and her distrust held a measure of contempt.

"In fact, you long for it," she then told Struensee, which surprised him. "But I don't want to die. I'm too young to die. I don't long for it. And I haven't given up."

He found this unjust. And he knew that she was touching on a sore spot.

"We have to decide quickly," he said, since he didn't want to respond.

It was only people who were cast in one piece who couldn't feel fear. The stupid brother, who could not feel terror, conquered the world.

The pure-hearted were doomed to destruction.

She made a swift decision for both of them.

"We're staying here," she said curtly. "I'm staying here. The children are staying here. You do as you like. Flee to Sweden if you want to. You've actually wanted to flee for quite a long time now."

"That's not true."

"Then stay."

"They're going to murder us."

"No, they're not."

Then she left the room to plan the reception for the rebellious sailors.

3

Afterwards Struensee thought that this was the most humiliating moment he had ever experienced. Nothing that happened later was as dreadful.

Yet everything went so splendidly.

Queen Caroline Mathilde, accompanied by her retinue, walked across the bridge and at the abutment to the bridge, she greeted the rebellious sailors. She spoke to them. She made an overwhelming, charming and enchanting impression. She thanked the sailors warmly for calling on them, and she pointed to King Christian, who stood three paces behind her, shaking with terror but silent and without a trace of his usual spasms or behaviour. On his behalf she asked forgiveness for the sore throat and fever which prevented him from speaking to them.

She didn't mention Struensee at all, but was extremely charming.

She assured them of the King's favour and goodwill, and vigorously refuted the malicious rumours saying that the ships would not be built. Three days earlier the King had already decided that two new ships of the line would be built at Holmen's Shipyard, in order to strengthen the fleet against the country's enemies; everything else was a lie. She apologized for the delay in paying their wages, commiserated with them regarding their hunger and thirst after such a long journey, and explained that in the storehouse refreshments had been arranged, consisting of whole roasted boar and beer. She hoped they would enjoy the repast and assured them that her greatest wish was to visit beautiful Norway with its valleys and mountains, rumoured to be so "enchanting", and about which she had heard so much in the past.

Or "in beforetimes", as she expressed it.

The sailors gave a great cheer for the royal couple and went off to the refreshments.

"Are you crazy?" he said to her. "Two new ships of the line? There's no money for that, hardly any for their wages. It's all an empty promise, it's impossible. You're crazy."

"No, I'm smart," she replied. "And I'm going to be even smarter."

He sat with his face hidden in his hands.

"I've never felt so humiliated," he said. "Must you humiliate me?"

"I'm not humiliating you," she told him.

"Yes, you are," he said.

From across the lake they could hear the wild roars from the rebellious Norwegian sailors who were getting drunker and drunker, who were no longer rebellious, but instead loyal to the Crown. Struensee they had not seen. Perhaps he didn't exist. It was going to be a long night. There was plenty of beer, and tomorrow they would leave; the revolt was defeated.

Then she sat down next to him and slowly stroked his hair.

"I love you," she whispered. "I love you so incredibly much. But I don't plan to give up. Or die. Or give us up. That's the thing. The only thing. Only that. I don't plan to give us up."

4

Guldberg conveyed the information about the outcome of the revolt to the Dowager Queen, who listened with a stony face, and to the Crown Prince, who drooled as usual.

"You have failed," she said to Guldberg. "And we may have miscalculated. The little English whore is harder than we thought."

There wasn't much to say. Guldberg replied evasively that God was on their side and would surely assist them.

They sat in silence for a long time. Guldberg looked at the Dowager Queen, and once again was shaken by the inexplicable love she had for her son, whose hand she was always holding, as if she didn't want to let him go. It was incomprehensible, but she loved him. And she actually believed, with a cold desperation that frightened Guldberg, that this backward son would become God's chosen one, that he would be given all power over the land, that it was possible to disregard his lowly appearance, his deformed head, his tremors, his ridiculously memorized chants, his pirouettes; it was as if she completely disregarded his appearance and saw an inner light that so far had been prevented from emerging.

She saw that God's light shone in this lowly shell, that he was chosen by God, and that their sole task was now to prepare the way. So the light could burst forth. And as if she heard and understood his thoughts, she touched her hand to the Crown Prince's cheek, found it sticky, took out a lace handkerchief, wiped the drool from his chin, and said:

"Yes. God will assist us. And I see God's light in his lowly form."

Guldberg took a breath, a deep breath. God's light in this lowly form. She was speaking of her son. But he knew that the same applied to himself. The lowliest, the least significant, they carried God's light within. He took another deep breath; it sounded like a sob, but it couldn't be.

He pulled himself together. And then he began explaining the two plans he had devised, which would be tried one after the other if the sailors' revolt failed. Unfortunately, this had already happened; but then the lowliest and least significant, who nevertheless bore God's inner light, would continue the fight for purity.

5

Rantzau was sent to Hirschholm that very evening to put into practice the little plan, the one that would follow the revolt of the Norwegian sailors.

It was very simple. Guldberg believed that simple plans could sometimes succeed, those that required few people, no huge concentrations of troops, no crowds, just a few select individuals.

This simple plan included Struensee's two friends, Rantzau and Brandt.

They had met in secret at the inn a mile from Hirschholm. Rantzau explained that the situation was critical and that action was a necessity. The prohibition of home distilling may have been wise, but it was also foolish. People were now demonstrating in the streets. It was only a matter of time before Struensee would be overthrown. Chaos reigned, pamphlets were everywhere containing satires, taunts directed at Struensee and the Queen. Things were boiling over.

"He thinks he's the man of the people," Brandt said with bitterness, "and they hate him. He has done everything for their sake, and they hate him. The people will devour their benefactor. And yet he deserves it. He had to do everything at once."

"The impatience of good people," replied Rantzau, "is worse than the patience of evil people. I taught him everything, everything! But not that."

Rantzau then explained the plan. Brandt was supposed to tell the King that Struensee and the Queen were planning to kill him. Therefore he had to be rescued. The King was the key. Once he was safely in Copenhagen, beyond Struensee's control, the rest would be easy.

"And then?"

"Then Struensee must die."

The following day the plan failed; what happened was so absurdly comical that no-one could have predicted this development.

This is what took place.

The King, at five in the afternoon, was struck by an inexplicable fit of rage; he raced onto the bridge leading to the mainland, shouting that he was going to drown himself. When Struensee came running after him, he suddenly fell to his knees, grabbed hold of Struensee's legs and, weeping, asked him whether it was true that he had to die. Struensee tried to calm him by stroking his hair and forehead, but Christian became even more agitated and asked him whether it was true.

"What does Your Majesty mean?" asked Struensee.

"Is it true that you want to kill me?" the King said in a quavering voice. "Aren't you one of The Seven? Answer me, aren't you one of The Seven?"

That was how it started: the two of them standing on the bridge. And the King called him by name, over and over again.

"Struensee?" he whispered, "Struensee, Struensee, Struensee?"

"What is it, my friend?" said Struensee.

"Is it true what Brandt confided to me?"

"What did he confide to you?"

"He wanted to take me to Copenhagen in secret. After nightfall. Tonight! To prevent you from killing me. Then they were going to kill you. Is it true that you want to kill me?"

That was how the little, very simple plan failed. They didn't understand that Struensee was one of The Seven. Nor did they understand another connection; that's why they failed, that's how they revealed their stupidity, that's why the King wanted to thwart their machinations.

Only Struensee understood, but not until he asked a question:

"Why are you telling me if you think I want to kill you?"

Christian simply replied:

"Brandt was Bottine Caterine's enemy. He maligned her. And she is the Sovereign of the Universe. That's why I hate him."

And that is how the second plan failed.

He summoned Brandt for questioning, and the man confessed at once.

Without being commanded to do so, Brandt fell to his knees.

This was the situation in the state hall to the left of Struensee's study at Hirschholm Castle. It was a late November day, Brandt was on his knees with his head bowed, and Struensee stood with his back to him, as if he couldn't stand to see his friend's predicament.

"I ought to have you killed," he said.

"Yes."

"The revolution is devouring its children. But if it devours you too, then I won't have a single friend left."

"No."

"I won't kill you."

A long silence followed; Brandt was still on his knees, waiting.

"The Queen," said Struensee, "wants to return to Copenhagen as soon as possible. None of us has much hope, but she wants to return. That is the Queen's wish. I have no other wishes. Will you come with us?"

Brandt did not reply.

"How quiet it has grown all around us," said Struensee. "You may leave us if you like. You can go to Guldberg ... and Rantzau. And I wouldn't blame you."

Brandt didn't answer, but began to sob loudly.

"This is a crossroads," said Struensee. "A crossroads, as they say. What are you going to do?"

A very long silence ensued; then Brandt slowly got to his feet.

"I will go with you," said Brandt.

"Thank you. Bring your flute along. And play for us in the calash."

The following evening, before they departed in the coaches, they gathered for a brief conversation, over tea, in the inner salon.

A fire had been lit in the hearth, but there was no other light. They were ready to set off. Present were King Christian VII, Queen Caroline Mathilde, Enevold Brandt, and Struensee.

The only light came from the hearth.

"If we were allowed to live a different life," Struensee finally asked, "if we were given a new life, a new opportunity, what would we be?"

"A stained-glass painter," said the Queen. "In a cathedral in England."

"An actor," replied Brandt.

"Someone who sows the fields," said the King.

Then there was silence.

"And you?" said the Queen to Struensee. "What would you be?"

But he merely gave his friends a long look on that last evening at Hirschholm, stood up, and said:

"A doctor."

And then:

"The coach is here."

That very night they left for Copenhagen.

All four of them sat in the same calash: the King, the Queen, Brandt, and Struensee.

The others would follow later.

The coach was like a silhouette in the night.

Brandt played his flute very softly, like a requiem or a dirge or, as it seemed to one of them, like a hymn to the Sovereign of the Universe.

PART V

MASQUERADE

Chapter 14 · The Last Supper

I

Now Guldberg saw it all much more clearly. The maelstroms of the river were decipherable.

He took advantage of the experience he gained from his analysis of Milton's *Paradise Lost*. It had made him accustomed to interpreting images and at the same time keeping a critical distance from them. The image of a torch that casts great darkness, Struensee's image of Christian's illness, this image could, *primo*: be discarded because it was a breach of logic, but *secundo*: be accepted as an image of the Enlightenment.

He writes that this view of the metaphor shows the difference between the poet and the politician. The poet creates a false image, out of naïveté. But the politician sees through it and creates a field of application, which, to the poet, is surprising.

In this way the politician becomes the poet's assistant, and benefactor.

The black light from the torch could thus be viewed as an image of the Enemies of Purity, those who spoke of enlightenment, those who spoke of light but created darkness.

From a breach of logic was thus created a criticism of the breach of logic. The filth of life from a dream of light. That was how he interpreted the image.

He could give examples from his own experience.

He was aware that the contagion of sin might strike even him. It was the contagion of desire. His conclusion: perhaps the little English whore was the black torch.

At Sorø Academy, Guldberg had taught the history of the Nordic countries. He did so with great joy. He regarded the foreign influence at court as a disease, he despised the French language, which he had mastered to perfection, and he dreamed of some day becoming the subject of a memoir. It would be entitled *Guldberg's Era*, and it would begin with a standard phrase taken from the Icelandic sagas.

"There was once a man named Guldberg." That was what the first line would be.

The reason for this was that the introductory words would set the tone. They would tell of a man who won his own honour, as in the Icelandic sagas. Not by defending the honour of the heroes, the great ones. Those chosen by God would view him as a hero, one of the great ones. Even though his stature was slight.

The King's honour had to be defended. That was his mission. Guldberg had served at Sorø Academy until the time when the pietistic contagion had won a foothold. When the stench of the Moravians and Pietists became too intolerable, he left his teaching position, since his dissertation on Milton had paved the way for his political career. He also left behind his rôle as a writer of history, although he had published a series of historical studies. Most noteworthy was his translation of Pliny's "Eulogy for Trajan", which he supplied with an introductory explication of the Roman form of government.

He started with the origins of history and stopped at Pliny. Pliny was the one who created Trajan's glory, and defended it.

There once was a man named Pliny.

But Guldberg was a passionate person. He hated the little English whore with an intensity that was perhaps a passion of the flesh. When the news of her depravity reached him, he was seized with a furious excitement, the likes of which he had never before experienced. The body which the King, who was God's chosen, should be enjoying was now being penetrated by filthy German genitals. The greatest innocence and purity united with the greatest vice. Her body, which was sacred, was now the source of the greatest sin. It excited him, and he hated his excitement. He felt he was losing control. Hatred and passion were united in him; he had never before felt like this.

On the outside, however, there was no change. He always spoke in a calm, low voice. It puzzled everyone when, during the planning of the final coup, he suddenly spoke in a very loud and almost shrill voice.

As in the Icelandic sagas, he had to defend the King's honour. But when had the torch begun to cast its darkness on his own soul? That, for him, was the turning point of the saga. Perhaps it was when the little English whore had leaned towards him and whispered her shameless question about desire and torment. As if he had been cut off from desire and torment! But ever since, he had thought of her skin, which seemed so white and seductive, and her breasts.

One night he had thought about her so intently, about her betrayal of the King and his own hatred of her, that he had touched his member, and he was then filled with such an overwhelming desire that it was impossible to stop; his shame was almost unbearable. Sobbing, he fell to his knees next to his bed and prayed for a long time to Almighty God for mercy.

At that time he realized that there was only one path. The contagion of sin had struck him too. Now it had to be eradicated.

Struensee was not the one at the core of the contagion. It was the little English whore, Queen Caroline Mathilde.

The little plan had failed. The big plan, meaning the third one, would not fail.

The royal couple's coach reached Frederiksberg Palace around mid-night, and since their arrival had not been announced, they aroused little notice. Then the rumour spread quickly, and it caused a stir.

After the commotion had died down, a vast and unpleasant calm set in.

The Dowager Queen summoned Rantzau and Guldberg.

First she meticulously inquired about what proof there was; not just the rumour of the Queen's depravity, but proof.

Guldberg then reported on his findings.

Two of the chambermaids, those who each day attended to the cleaning of the Queen's rooms, had begun their spying well before the sojourn at Hirschholm. They put wax in the keyhole and some-times wads of paper in the door hinges. In the morning they would find the wax gone and the wads of paper fallen down. Late at night they would sprinkle flour near the door and on the stairway leading to the Queen's bedchamber. The next morning they inspected the foot-prints they found, and were able to conclude without a doubt that the tracks had come from Struensee. They examined the Queen's bed and found it in great disarray, with rumpled sheets; more than one person had slept in it. Christian could not have been that other person. They found stains on the bed, which their feminine modesty forbade them to name. On handkerchiefs and napkins they had found the same type of stains, from dried fluids. And one morning they found the Queen naked in her bed, still half asleep, with her clothing tossed on the floor.

There was abundant proof.

What happened then was, in a sense, surprising. One of these ladies-in-waiting had been gripped by remorse or misplaced sympathy and had told the Queen what she knew, and why, and what she had done. The Queen was seized with fury, threatened her with immedi-ate dismissal, and burst into tears, but – and this is the astonishing thing – basically admitted to the sinful goings-on and then begged her to keep silent. The Queen was then overcome by strong emotions and opened her heart to her chambermaids. Her Majesty asked them whether they had ever felt love or affection for anyone, "because if you have such feelings, you must follow that person in everything, whether it means to the post and wheel, or to hell itself".

All the same, the debauchery continued as if nothing had happened, or as if the Queen, in her arrogance, quite ignored the danger she must have known existed. It was astonishing.

Yet she continued. Ignoring the danger. It was, in a sense, incomprehensible.

Guldberg assumed that she had not reported this to her German lover. What was that cunning little English whore thinking? It was difficult to understand. The greatest naïveté and the greatest willpower.

She should have realized what would happen. After a week the servant girl quite rightly reported everything to Guldberg, although in tears.

So there was proof. And there was a witness who was prepared to step forward in court.

"This means," said the Dowager Queen thoughtfully, "that he can be sentenced under lawful charges."

"And the Queen?" asked Guldberg.

She did not reply, as if this matter was not her concern, which surprised Guldberg.

"Under lawful charges he shall be sentenced to death," she continued pensively, as if she were tasting the words. "Under lawful charges we shall chop off his hand and head, cut him into pieces, slice off the member that has besmirched Denmark, crush his body, and put it on the post and wheel. And I shall personally . . ."

Rantzau and Guldberg stared at her in astonishment, and Rantzau finally interjected the query:

"Witness everything?"

"Witness everything."

"And the Queen?" Guldberg asked the question once more, since he was surprised that the Dowager Queen should be so preoccupied with Struensee's fate but neglect the little English whore, from whom everything had sprung. But the Dowager Queen turned instead to Rantzau, and with a strange smile she said:

"With the Queen we will proceed thus: you, Count Rantzau, since you were Struensee's special friend from Altona and there shared his opinions, and you were also the Queen's friend and fawning confidant, but have now reversed yourself and confessed your sins against the honour of God and Denmark, you will have the delicate task of arresting the Queen. And you will look deep into her beautiful, sinful eyes, like one old friend to another, and tell her that it's over. That's what you will say. It's over."

Rantzau didn't utter a word.

"And," she added, "you won't like it. But that will be your only punishment. The rewards, however, will be plentiful. But that you know."

3

Christian came to see Struensee less and less often.

In practice the King's signature was no longer necessary. Struensee's was sufficient. But one time during this period Christian sought out Struensee to bring him, as he said, an important message.

Struensee invited the King to sit down and took time to listen.

"This morning," said Christian, "I received a message from the Sovereign of the Universe."

Struensee looked at him with a reassuring smile and asked:

"Where did this message come from?"

"From Kiel."

"From Kiel! And what did it say?"

"It said that she is my benefactress," replied Christian, "and that I am under her protection."

He was quite calm; no fidgeting fingers, no babbling, no tics.

"My friend," said Struensee, "I have a great deal to do right now and I would like to discuss this, but we will have to postpone it. And we are all under the protection of Almighty God."

"Almighty God," replied the King, "doesn't have time for me. But my benefactress the Sovereign of the Universe told me, in her message, that when no-one else has time, or when God is too busy with His work, she always has time for me."

"How nice," said Struensee. "And who is this Sovereign of the Universe?"

"She's the one who has time," replied the King.

4

The final plan, the one that would not fail, also required the legitimation of law.

To crush Struensee's "bloody and lecherous regime", Guldberg had persuaded the Dowager Queen that it was necessary to uncover the shameless plan of a coup d'état, which Struensee and the little English whore had devised together. Struensee's plan included the murder of Denmark's King Christian VII.

This plan did not actually exist, but it could be theoretically reconstructed and brought to life.

Thus Guldberg became the author of Struensee's plan. Next he made a certified transcript of it and destroyed the original; this document would be used to convince the sceptics. It was a matter of preventing a shameless coup d'état.

This plan, which was authored by Guldberg and then ascribed to Struensee, presented a clear and plausible logic. It stated that January 28, 1772 was the day on which Struensee was planning to carry out his overthrow of the government. On that day King Christian VII would be forced to abdicate his crown, Queen Caroline Mathilde would be named sovereign, and Struensee would become regent.

That was the basic outline.

To this plan, which bore an air of authenticity, Guldberg had added a comment that would explain to the sceptics the necessity for a swift counterattack.

"No time should be wasted," wrote Guldberg, "for the one who does not hesitate to secure the regency will not hesitate to commit an even worse crime. If the King is killed, Struensee will secure for himself Queen Caroline Mathilde's bed, and the Crown Prince will then either be shoved aside or succumb to a harsh upbringing and thus make way for his sister, the one who is all too obviously the fruit of their shameless love. Because what other reason could there be for Struensee to abolish the law that forbade a divorced woman from entering into marriage with her accomplice in adultery?"

Time was short. It was important to act quickly, and the plan had to be kept secret.

On January 15 they gathered in the rooms of the Dowager Queen; by then Guldberg had written out a series of arrest warrants, which the King would be forced to sign.

On the morning of January 16, the plans were reviewed again, several insignificant changes were added, and the decision was made to execute the coup the following night.

It would be a long night. First dinner. Then tea. After that the masked ball. Then the coup d'état.

5

Reverdil, the Swiss tutor, the little Jew who had concealed his first name, the man who was once so beloved by Christian, who was banished from court but then brought back, the memoirist, the very cautious man of the Enlightenment, the respectable reformer, Reverdil sat at his desk for a few hours each morning to complete his great plan for the emancipation of the Danish peasants from serfdom.

He had been given this task by Struensee. It was to be the culmination of the reform work.

Many of Struensee's laws and directives, 632 of them so far, were important. The 633rd would be the most important of all. Reverdil would be the one to guide Struensee's pen; it would not be in the history books, but he would know. That was enough.

On this morning, the last one of Struensee's era, Reverdil was again sitting and working on the great text about the emancipation. He did not finish. He would never finish. He writes that on that morning he felt quite calm, and had no suspicions. He does not write that he was happy. In his memoirs he doesn't use the word "happy", or at least not in reference to himself.

He is an anonymous author whose great text, the one concerning emancipation, would never be completed.

Nevertheless, before he realizes this, on the last day before the collapse, he is happy. The project is so important, the idea so right. It's so right to be working on this project, even on the morning before the collapse. While he was working he was happy.

No doubt he feels timid.

He is still critical of Struensee, who "moved too swiftly". He sees a cautious emancipation as possible. He is timid and cautious; no darkness from an inner black torch obscures his dreams. He believes he knows, in retrospect, how things should have gone.

They should have observed greater moderation.

6

On that morning "he has no suspicions". Rarely does he seem to have had any suspicions, although he was uneasy about those who moved forward too fast.

At four o'clock on that day he eats dinner with the inner circle, to which he belongs, in spite of everything. "Never had the Queen made a more merry impression or participated with greater charm in the conversation."

It was the last supper.

Documentation of this meal is overwhelming. Eleven people participated: the royal couple, the wife of General Gähler, the Countesses Holstein and Fabritius, Struensee and Brandt, Lord Chamberlain Bjelke, Stablemaster Bülow, Colonel Falkenskjold, and Reverdil. They dined in the Queen's "white apartment". The room had been so named because of its white panels, although some of the walls were draped in red velvet. The carved decorations were gilded. The tabletop was of Norwegian granite. Above the fireplace hung the twelve-foot-high painting *Scipio's Perseverance* by the French historical painter Pierre. Twenty-two candles provided the light in the room. Contrary to previous protocol, which required the gentlemen to be seated to the right of the monarch and ladies to his left, men and women were seated alternately. This was radical. They had drawn lots for their seats. The serving staff had been adjusted according to a directive issued by Struensee, the "new arrangement" from April 1, 1771, which meant that the number of servants had been cut in half. Despite this, the servants numbered 24. The banquet was *en retraite*, however, which meant that the serving staff was in a neighbouring room or in the kitchen, and only one servant at a time was allowed in with a platter. The dinner consisted of nine courses, four salads, and two *relèves* – alternate main courses.

The Queen, as Reverdil notes, was charming. For a moment the conversation moved onto the topic of the "verbose" Princess of Prussia, who had divorced her husband and was now being held prisoner in Stettin. The Queen briefly stated that this princess in her imprisonment, "by creating her own inner freedom", could still hold her head high.

That was all. When they sat down at the table, darkness had already fallen. The candlelight only partly lit the room. It was noticeable that Brandt and Struensee were quiet. Reverdil remarks that perhaps they had some suspicion or had received a message.

But no conclusions can be drawn from this. No actions, only waiting, and a delightful banquet. In fact, everything was just as usual. A small circle, which was growing smaller. Light and surrounding darkness. And the Queen very charming, or desperate.

At seven o'clock that same evening, but after the banquet, Reverdil, strangely enough, paid a visit to the Dowager Queen.

They conversed for an hour. He noticed nothing disquieting about the Dowager Queen, who several hours earlier had given the order for the coup to be carried out that very night, a coup that would also include the imprisonment of Reverdil. They sat and had a very friendly conversation, drinking tea.

Outside it was cold, and stormy. In silence they had watched the gulls being driven back by the storm, past the window. The Dowager Queen said that she felt sympathy for them because they didn't realize it was hopeless to struggle against the storm. Afterwards Reverdil interpreted this metaphorically. He believed that she wanted to give him a warning: the storm would sweep him up as well, if he didn't give up in time and fly along with the inevitable.

Not against it.

He didn't understand. He merely said that he admired the gulls in their situation. They didn't give up but kept on going in spite of the storm driving them back.

Perhaps afterwards, in his memoirs, he gave his reply a figurative touch. He was timid, after all. He was not the type to contradict. He was the quiet man, bent over his papers, now banished, now called back, the one who in silent sorrow watched the wolves rip his beloved boy to pieces, and the one who thought that the Enlightenment should be like a very slow and cautious dawn.

At dinner Struensee and the Queen sat next to each other and held each other's hand without embarrassment. The King did not object. The King seemed paralysed by his thoughts.

Reverdil, who was seated across from the King, had plenty of time to observe him during dinner. It provoked in him "a great sorrow". He remembered when he had first met him, and been confided in: the sensitive and extremely intelligent young boy he had once known. The person he now saw was a grey, apathetic shadow, a very old man paralysed, it seemed, by terror, the cause of which no-one knew.

Christian was only 22 years old.

Afterwards they left the banquet to prepare for the masked ball. Reverdil was the last to leave the room. Preceding him was Brandt, who turned to Reverdil and, with an odd little smile, said:

"I think that we are now very close to the end of our time. It can't last much longer now."

Reverdil did not ask for an explanation. They parted.

7

The plan was very simple.

Guldberg had always held the view that the very simplicity of complicated plans made them successful. They would take bodily possession of the King. They would also take bodily possession of Struensee. It was presumed that these two would not offer resistance or cause any difficulties.

The third step was to take bodily possession of the Queen.

As to this, however, there was some uneasiness, which was more difficult to explain. Overpowering her should not present any problems. But under no circumstances was she to be allowed to contact the King. The King must not be subjected to any influences. He must be forced to understand that he was now the focus of a horrible threat, that Struensee and the Queen wanted to kill him. But if the little English whore looked at Christian with her beautiful eyes, he might hesitate.

The little English whore was the greatest risk. Everything began and ended with that young woman. Guldberg was the only one who understood this. That was why he would destroy her; and never again would the contagion of desire strike him so that in the dark of night, weeping and with the seed of lust sticking to his body, he was brought to his knees.

Bitterly cold that night.

The storm, which during the day had swept in from the east, had died down by nightfall. The moisture had frozen solid, and Copenhagen was clad in an icy membrane.

All memoirs and diaries speak of a great calm that night.

No storm. Not a sound from the troops that were posted. No birds being driven back by the storm.

Still extant are lists of the food that was ordered for the last supper. Six geese, 34 eels, 350 snails, 14 rabbits, ten chickens; the day before, an order was also placed for cod, turbot, and squab.

In a completely natural way these hours consumed, in abundance, the last supper of the Danish revolution, with only 24 servants present.

They went back to their rooms in the castle. They changed into masquerade costumes.

Christian, Struensee and the Queen rode to the masked ball in the same coach. Struensee was very quiet, and the Queen took note of this.

"You're not talking much," she said.

"I'm searching for a solution. I can't find one."

"Then I suggest," she said, "that tomorrow we compose a letter from me to the Russian Tsarina. Unlike all the other regents, she is enlightened. She wants progress. She is a possible friend. She knows what has been done in Denmark during the last year. She is impressed. I can write to her as one enlightened woman to another. Perhaps we can create an alliance. We need great alliances. We have to think big. Here we have only enemies. Catherine could be a friend to me."

Struensee looked at her.

"You are taking the long view," he said. "The question is whether we have time to take the long view."

"We must lift our eyes," she said curtly. "Otherwise we are lost."

When Their Majesties, escorted by Struensee, arrived at the Royal Theatre, the dance had already begun.

Chapter 15 · The Dance of Death

I

Suddenly Struensee was reminded of the performance of *Zaïre* with Christian playing the rôle of the Sultan.

That too was at the Royal Theatre. Wasn't it just after his arrival in Copenhagen, following the long European journey? Perhaps a month later; he couldn't remember. But suddenly he was reminded of Christian in that rôle. That thin, fragile child's figure with such clear diction, such odd and vivid pauses and mysterious phrasing, who had moved about in the stylized decor among the French actors, as if in a slow ritual dance, with his peculiar gestures that seemed entirely natural on that stage and in that play, although they otherwise seemed contrived in Christian's awful real life.

He had been quite brilliant. In truth, the best of all the actors. Remarkably calm and believable, as if the stage, the play, and the acting profession were all that was natural and possible for him.

In fact he had never been able to distinguish between reality and illusion. Not because of any lack of intelligence but because of all his directors.

Had Struensee also become a director for Christian? He had come to visit and had acquired a rôle and delegated a different one to Christian. It may have been a better rôle for the poor, terrified boy. Perhaps back then Struensee should have listened more closely; perhaps Christian, like the actors, had a message that he had wanted to convey through the theatre.

It was so infinitely long ago. Almost three years.

Now, on January 16, 1772, Christian was dancing a minuet. He had always been a good dancer. His body was as light as a child's; in the dance he could move with the established replies of the dance, and yet with freedom. Why hadn't he been allowed to become a dancer? Why hadn't anyone seen that he was an actor or a dancer or anything else? Anything but the absolute ruler chosen by God.

In the end they all danced. They had their costumes and their disguises; even the Queen was dancing. It was here, at the Royal Theatre, during a masked ball, that she had given Struensee the first signal.

It must have been springtime. They were dancing and she had been looking at him the whole time with such an intense expression on her face, as if she were about to say something. Perhaps this was because Struensee had spoken to her as if she were a human being, and she was grateful. Perhaps it was something more. Yes, it was. Afterwards she drew him away with her; into one of the corridors. She gave a swift glance around and then she kissed him.

Not a word. Simply kissed him. And then that mysterious little smile, which he first thought was an expression of enchanting childish innocence, but which he then all of a sudden realized was a grown woman's smile, and that it said: I love you. And you shouldn't underestimate me.

They were all there except for the Dowager Queen, and Rantzau.

Everything was quite normal. After a while the King stopped dancing; he sat down to play *loup* with General Gähler and a few others. The King, after leaving the dance which for a time had made him seem lively, suddenly appeared distracted and sunk in melancholy. He played without thinking and as usual had no money; he lost 332 riksdaler, which the General had to pay and which, after the catastrophe, was never refunded.

In another loge sat Colonel Köller, who was going to command the military part of the coup set for that night. He was playing tarot with the court quartermaster, Berger. Köller's face was composed. It was impossible to read any agitation in it.

Everyone was in place. Except the Dowager Queen, and Rantzau.

The masks were the typical ones. Struensee's was a half-mask of a weeping jester. Afterwards it was said that he wore a mask depicting a skull.

That was not true. He was dressed as a weeping jester.

The masked ball ended at around two.

Everyone agreed afterwards to regard it as uneventful. That was the strange thing, considering that this masked ball would be so discussed and so important, but everyone agreed that nothing had happened. Nothing. Everyone seemed normal and danced and waited for nothing.

Struensee and the Queen danced three dances. Everyone noticed their calm, smiling faces and their carefree conversation.

What did they talk about? Afterwards they couldn't remember.

All night long Struensee had a strange feeling of distance, or of a waking dream, as if he had experienced this before but was now dreaming about it all over again, in short sequences that were repeated. Everything in the dream moved infinitely slowly, with mouths opening and closing, but without a sound, like slow movements under water perhaps. As if they were floating in water, and the only thing that came back over and over was the memory of the King in the rôle of the Sultan in *Zaïre* and his movements and strange, entreating gestures, which almost resembled an actor's, but more genuine, like someone who was drowning, and the way his mouth opened and closed, as if he wanted to utter a message but couldn't get it out. And then the other part of this waking dream: the Queen, whose face came close to his own, and who kissed him without a sound and then took a step back, and the little smile which said that she loved him and that he shouldn't underestimate her and that this was only the beginning of something magnificent, that they were very close to a boundary, and that at the boundary could be found both the greatest desire and the most enticing death, and that he never ever would regret it if they crossed that boundary.

And it was as if these two, Christian the actor and Caroline Mathilde who promised desire and death, flowed together in that dance of death at the Royal Theatre.

He escorted her back.

They were accompanied by two ladies-in-waiting. In the corridor outside the Queen's bedchamber he kissed her hand without a word.

"Are we sleeping tonight?" the Queen asked.

"Yes, my love. Tonight sleep. Tonight sleep."

"When will I see you?"

"Always," he said. "In the eternities of Eternity."

They looked at each other, and she raised her hand to his cheek and touched it with a little smile.

That was the last time. After that he never saw her again.

2

At 2:30, half an hour after the music stopped playing, blank cartridges were issued to the Second Grenadier Company from the Falster regiment, and the soldiers were deployed to their assigned posts.

All of the castle exits were put under guard.

The operational head of the coup, Colonel Köller, who an hour earlier had ended his tarot game with the court quartermaster Berger, informed two of his lieutenants of a handwritten command from the Dowager Queen which ordered the arrest of a number of named individuals. It stated, among other things, that "since His Majesty the

King wishes to ensure his own safety and that of the country and to punish certain persons who are close to him, he has entrusted this undertaking to us. We hereby command you, Colonel Köller, on this night and in the King's name, to implement the will of the King. Furthermore, it is the King's wish that defensive guards be stationed at all exits from the ruling Queen's apartment." The letter was signed by the Dowager Queen and the Crown Prince, and it had been written by Guldberg.

The key to the operation was to seize swiftly the King and the Queen, and to keep them apart. Rantzau was to play a decisive rôle in this. But he had disappeared.

Count Rantzau had been struck by an attack of nerves.

Rantzau lived in the royal residence that was separated by a canal from Christiansborg Palace, and which today is called the Prince's Palace; all day long he had kept out of sight. But while the masked ball was still going on, a messenger was stopped at the entrance to the Royal Theatre. He had made a strange impression, seemed very nervous, and said that he had an important message from Count Rantzau to Struensee.

The messenger was detained by the conspirators' guards, and Guldberg was summoned.

Guldberg, without asking permission and in spite of the messenger's protests, had grabbed the letter and opened it. He read it. The letter said that Rantzau wished to speak with Struensee before midnight, "and keep in mind that if you fail to arrange for this meeting, you will bitterly regret it".

That was all. On the other hand, it was quite clear. Count Rantzau wished to find a solution to his dilemma, another way out of the lion's den.

Guldberg read it and smiled one of his rare smiles.

"A little Judas who no doubt expects to become a country squire in Lolland as a reward. But he won't."

He stuffed the letter into his pocket and ordered the messenger to be taken away and put under guard.

Three hours later all the conspirators were in place and the troops ready, but Rantzau was missing. Then Guldberg, along with six soldiers, headed over to Rantzau's residence at a pace and found him fully dressed, sitting in his armchair and smoking his pipe, with a cup of tea in front of him.

"We've been looking for you," Guldberg said.

Rantzau propped his leg up on a footstool, and with a nervous and glum face pointed at his foot. He had come down with an attack of gout, he stammered, his toe was very swollen, he could barely stand on that foot; he regretted it deeply, and was inconsolable, but because of this he would not be able to complete his task.

"You cowardly wretch," Guldberg said in a calm voice, without trying to soften the rudeness with which he addressed the Count. "You're trying to weasel your way out of it."

Guldberg deliberately used the informal means of address.

"No, no!" Rantzau protested in desperation. "I'm sticking by the agreement, but my gout, I am in despair . . ."

Guldberg then ordered the others to leave the room. After they did so, he pulled out the letter, held it between his thumb and index finger as if it were foul smelling, and said:

"I've read your letter, you rat. For the last time: are you with us or against us?"

Pale as a corpse, Rantzau stared at the letter and realized that there were few alternatives.

"Of course I'm with you," said Rantzau. "Perhaps I could be carried to my assignment . . . in a portechaise . . ."

"Fine," said Guldberg. "And I'm going to save this letter. No-one but me needs to see it. But on one condition. That after this purifying act is completed and Denmark is saved, you do not annoy me. But from now on you're not going to annoy me, are you? So that I'm forced to show this letter to anyone else?"

A moment of silence followed, and then Rantzau said in a very low voice:

"Of course not. Of course not."

"Never ever?"

"Never ever."

"Fine," said Guldberg. "Now we know where we stand in the future. It's good to have reliable allies."

Guldberg then summoned the soldiers and ordered two of them to carry Count Rantzau to his post at the exit in the north arch. They carried him across the bridge, but then Rantzau assured them that he was willing to try to walk on his own, despite the unbearable pain, and he limped to his command post.

3

At 4:30 in the morning on January 17, 1772, they went into action.

Two groups of grenadiers, one led by Köller, the other by Beringskjold, broke into Struensee's and Brandt's apartments at the same time. Struensee was found sleeping peacefully. He sat up in bed, looked in surprise at the soldiers, and when Colonel Köller explained that he was under arrest, he asked to see the arrest warrant.

This he was denied, since no such warrant existed.

He then stared at them with apathy, slowly dressed in the barest essentials, and followed without another word. He was put into a hired coach and driven to the guardhouse at the Citadel.

Brandt didn't even inquire about an arrest warrant. He merely asked whether he could take along his flute.

He too was put into a coach.

The commandant at the Citadel, who had not been forewarned, was roused out of bed, but was said to have received them both with joy. Everyone seemed surprised that Struensee had given up without a fuss. He just sat in the coach and stared at his hands.

He seemed to be prepared.

Of the many sketches that were later done depicting the arrest of Struensee, one shows an act of much greater violence.

A courtier is illuminating the room with a three-armed candelabrum. Through the splintered door the soldiers are pouring in with their rifles raised and their bayonets fixed, pointing them threateningly at Struensee. Colonel Köller is standing next to the bed, holding out the arrest warrant in his left hand. Lying on the floor is the death mask from the masked ball, the mask of a skull. Clothing is scattered all around. The clock shows four o'clock. Crowded bookshelves. Writing materials on a desk. And Struensee in bed, sitting up, wearing only a night-shirt, and with both hands raised, as if in capitulation or in prayer to Almighty God, Whom he had always renounced, to show mercy in this grave hour to a poor sinner in dire need.

But the picture does not speak the truth. He allowed himself to be led away, like a docile lamb to the slaughter.

The King, of course, was not to be arrested.

On the contrary, King Christian VII was to be rescued from a murderous assault, and thus he only had to sign the documents that would authorize the other arrests.

It is easy to forget that he was one of the absolute rulers chosen by God.

Those who poured into his dark bedchamber were numerous. They included the Dowager Queen, her son Frederik, Rantzau, Eichstedt, Köller and Guldberg, as well as seven grenadiers from the Life Guards, who, however, were ordered to leave and wait outside the door because of the King's hysterical reaction and his uncontrolled terror of soldiers and their weapons.

Christian thought he was going to be murdered and began crying and screaming shrilly, like a child. At the same time the dog, his schnauzer, who was sleeping as usual in Christian's bed, began to bark furiously. They finally took the dog out. The Negro page Moranti, who had been sleeping curled up at the foot of the bed, hid in a corner, terrified.

They managed at last to calm the monarch. His life was not in danger. They were not going to kill him.

But what they then told him brought on a renewed fit of weeping. The reason for this night-time visit, they explained, was a conspiracy against the King. Struensee and the Queen were after his life. He had to be rescued. That was why he must sign a number of documents.

Guldberg had composed the wording of them. He led Christian, clad in his dressing gown, over to the desk. There the King signed 17 documents.

He sobbed the entire time, his hands and body shaking. Only at the sight of one document did he seem to brighten. It was the arrest warrant for Brandt.

"This is the punishment," he muttered, "for trying to violate the Sovereign of the Universe. The punishment."

No-one, except perhaps Guldberg, could have understood what he meant.

4

Rantzau was the one who was supposed to arrest the Queen.

He took along five soldiers and a sub-lieutenant; and with one of the arrest warrants signed by the King in hand, he went to the Queen's bedchamber. A lady-in-waiting was sent in to wake the Queen because, as he writes in his report, "respect forbade me from approaching the Queen's bed"; but sub-lieutenant Beck gives a livelier description of what happened. The Queen was awakened by her lady-in-waiting. She came rushing out, wearing only a shift, and furiously asked Rantzau what was going on. Rantzau held out the King's order.

It said: "I have found it necessary to send you to Kronborg Castle, since your behaviour has forced me to do this. I sincerely regret this action, for which I am not to blame, and hope that you will show genuine repentance."

Signed: Christian.

She then crumpled up the warrant and shrieked that Rantzau would come to regret this; she asked who else had been arrested. She was given no answer. Then she rushed into her bedchamber, followed by Rantzau and sub-lieutenant Beck along with a couple of the soldiers. As she berated Rantzau in a rage, she tore off her shift and ran naked around the room looking for her clothes. Bowing, Rantzau then said with an elegance that was characteristic of him:

"Her Majesty must have mercy and not subject me to the magic powers of her voluptuousness."

"Don't just stand there and stare, you damned wheedling toad," exclaimed the Queen, this time in her native language of English. But at that moment lady's maid Arensbach came dashing in with a petticoat, a gown, and a pair of shoes, and in all haste the Queen threw on these garments.

The whole time she kept up her steady and furious attack on Rantzau, who at one point was forced to defend himself with his cane, which he held up to fend off the Queen's blows, but only to defend himself; he had brought along the cane to help him better support his weight on his foot, which on that particular night was aching with gout – something that the Queen, in her wrath, had not taken into consideration.

In his report Rantzau claims that for reasons of discretion, and so as not to sully Her Royal Highness with his gaze, he held his hat in front of his face the entire time, until the Queen was dressed. Sub-lieutenant Beck states, however, that he, Rantzau, and four soldiers carefully and without pause scrutinized the Queen in her bewildered and furious nakedness, and watched her as she dressed. He also describes what garments the Queen put on.

She did not weep but instead railed at Rantzau and, as he emphasizes in his report to the members of the Board of Inquisition, he was incensed in particular by "the contemptuous manner in which she spoke of the King".

As soon as she was dressed – she stuck her bare feet into her shoes, without stockings, which shocked everyone – she raced out of the room and could not be stopped. She ran down the stairs and tried to force her way into Struensee's room. But outside stood a guard who informed her that Count Struensee had been taken prisoner and transported to the Citadel. She then continued her search for help and set off running towards the King's suite.

Rantzau and the soldiers did nothing to stop her.

It seemed to them that she possessed enormous strength, and her breach of modesty, her naked body, and her infuriated attack had also scared them.

But she understood at once what had happened. They had frightened Christian out of his wits. Yet Christian was her only hope.

She tore open the door to his bedchamber, saw at once the small figure huddled at the head of the bed and she understood. He had wrapped the sheet around himself, covering him completely, covering his face and body and legs, and if it hadn't been for the hesitant rocking motion, one might have thought a wrapped-up statue had been placed there, white and swathed in a wrinkled sheet.

Like a white mummy, rocking nervously, concealed and yet at her mercy.

Rantzau stopped in the doorway and signalled to the soldiers to remain outside.

She went over to the small, trembling, white-clad mummy on the bed.

"Christian," she shouted. "I want to talk to you! Now!"

No answer, just those hesitant twitches under the white sheet.

She sat down on the edge of the bed and tried to speak calmly, although she was breathing hard and found it difficult to control her voice.

"Christian," she said in soft tones so that Rantzau wouldn't be able to hear her from the doorway. "I don't like what you've been signing, but it doesn't matter, they tricked you, but you must save the child! Damn it, you must save the child; what were you thinking? I know that you can hear me, you have to listen to what I'm saying, I forgive you for signing the documents, but *you must save the child! Otherwise they're going to take the child away from us and you know what will happen then, you know what will happen, you must save the child!*"

Suddenly she turned to Rantzau in the doorway and roared, "GET OUT OF HERE, YOU DAMNED RAT, THE QUEEN IS SPEAKING TO YOU!" but then in an entreating whisper she went back to talking to Christian. "Ohhh . . . Christian," she whispered, "you think I hate you, but that's not true, I've actually always liked you, yes it's true, *it's true, listen to me, I know you're listening!* I could have loved you if we'd been given a chance, but it wasn't possible in this damn madhouse, IN THIS CRAZY MADHOUSE!" she screamed at Rantzau, and then went back to whispering. "Things could have been so splendid for us, somewhere else, if only we, it would have been splendid, Christian, if only they hadn't forced you to service me like a sow, it wasn't your fault, it wasn't your fault but you must think of the child, Christian, and don't just hide there, I know you're listening! DON'T JUST HIDE THERE, but I'm a human being and not a sow, and you must save the girl, they want to put her to death, I know it, just because she's Struensee's child and you know that too, YOU KNOW IT and you never objected, you wanted it, too, you wanted it yourself, I just wanted to hurt you a little so you would notice I existed, so you would see, just a little bit, then we could have, Christian, we could have, but you have to save the child, I've always liked you, things could have been so wonderful for us, Christian, do you hear what I'm saying, Christian, ANSWER ME, CHRISTIAN you have to answer CHRISTIAN you've always tried to hide, you can't hide from me SO ANSWER ME, CHRISTIAN!"

And then she tore the sheet off his body.

But it wasn't Christian. It was the little black page Moranti, who stared at her with big eyes wide with terror.

She stared back at him, as if paralysed.

"Bring her," Rantzau told the soldiers.

As she passed Rantzau in the doorway, she stopped, gave him a long look and said quite calmly:

"In the very bottom circle of hell, where traitors are banished, you will be tormented for all eternity. And I'm glad. That's the only thing that truly, truly pleases me right now."

And to this he could find no reply.

She was allowed to take the little girl along in the coach to Kronborg Castle. It was nine in the morning when they drove out of the city through Nørreport. They drove along Kongevejen past Hirschholm, but past it.

In the coach they had sent along the lady-in-waiting who was her least favourite.

Caroline Mathilde put the little girl to her breast to nurse. Only then did she begin to cry.

The rumour spread rapidly, and to make the rumour official that the King had been rescued from Struensee's murderous attack, Guldberg ordered the King to make an appearance.

A glass carriage was ordered, pulled by six white horses, with twelve courtiers on horseback to escort it. They rode for two and a half hours through the streets of Copenhagen. In the carriage sat only Christian and Crown Prince Frederik.

The Crown Prince was radiantly happy, drooling and gaping as always, and waving to the cheering masses. Christian sat huddled in a corner of the carriage, pale as a corpse, terror stricken, staring at his hands.

Tremendous rejoicing.

5

That night Copenhagen exploded.

It was the triumphant procession with the six white horses and the terrified, rescued and utterly humiliated King that unleashed it all. All of a sudden it was so clear: a revolution had taken place and had been defeated, the royal physician's brief visit in the vacuum of power was at an end, the Danish revolution was over, the German was imprisoned, the German was in chains, the old regime – or was it the new one? – had been overthrown, and everyone knew that they were at a real turning point in history; and insanity broke loose.

It started with a few mob riots; the Norwegian sailors, who several months earlier had so peacefully marched back from Hirschholm after meeting the charming little queen, these Norwegian sailors found that no rules or laws existed anymore. The police and the military seemed to have vanished from the streets, and the path to the whorehouses and taverns lay open. They started with the whorehouses. The reason for this, they said, was that the Evil People under Struensee's leadership, who so nearly robbed Little Father of his life, had been the Protectors of the Whorehouses.

The whorehouse regime was over. The hour for revenge had arrived.

Because it was Little Father, the King, the Good Ruler, the one they always referred to as their foremost protector up north in Norway, it was he who had been saved. Now Little Father was saved. Little Father's eyes had been opened and he had denounced his evil friends. Now the whorehouses would be cleansed. These 600 Norwegian sailors led the way, and no-one stopped them. Then the spark was ignited everywhere, and the masses poured out: the poor, those who had never dreamed of a revolution but were now offered the comfort of violence, without punishment, without meaning. They revolted, but with no purpose other than the excuse of purity. Sin would be assaulted, and purity would thus be reinstated. The bordello windows were broken and the doors smashed open, the furniture was tossed out, the nymphs were raped free of charge and ran screaming and half-dressed through the streets. Within 24 hours 60 bordellos were crushed, destroyed, burned down; in the sheer momentum several thoroughly respectable houses were also ravaged in error, along with respectable women, as part of the flood of collective insanity that swept through Copenhagen that day.

It was as if pietistic decency had been given a collective release and spread its vengeful seed over the decadence of Struensee's Copenhagen. They began, which surprised no-one, with Gabel the German, who was in charge of serving liquor in Rosenborg Garden, opened to the public by Struensee's decree and which, during the long summer and warm fall of 1771, had been the centre of debauchery for the Copenhagen populace. Gabel's house was thought to be the centre of this lechery, from which the contagion of sin emanated; Struensee and his cohorts had without doubt fornicated there; it had to be cleansed. Gabel himself escaped with his life, but the temple was indeed cleansed of the hawkers. The palace itself was sacred and would not be touched or stormed, but other places associated with the palace and the court were attacked. The house belonging to the Italian actors became the next target; it was cleansed, but at least a few of the actors were not assaulted because it was said that Little Father had made use of them, and thus they were to some extent sacred objects. Others, however, were assaulted as a tribute to Little Father; but the reason for all the violence was no longer clear, nothing was. It was as if the hatred for the court and the respect for the court unleashed a great furious confused rape of Copenhagen. Something had happened up there among the rulers, something scandalous and obscene, and now a cleansing was permitted, and the cleansing was being done; they were permitted to desecrate and purify, and the liquor was free and was consumed, and revenge was demanded – for something, perhaps for a thousand-year-old injustice, or for Struensee's injustice, which came to be the symbol for all injustice. Schimmelman's palace was cleansed, for reasons that were unclear although they had something to do with Struensee and sin. And suddenly all of Copenhagen became a drunken, destroying, raping hell; fires burned all over, the streets were full of glass, not one of the hundreds of taverns remained untouched. No police anywhere. No military called out. It was as if those behind the coup, the Dowager Queen and the victors, wanted to say: With this great, dissolute, and vengeful celebration, sin in the Danish capital would now be burned away.

God would allow it. God would use this great unleashed savagery of the people as a tool for cleansing the whorehouses, the taverns, and all the havens of fornication that were used by those who had brought down morality and decency.

It lasted for two days and two nights. Then little by little the riots collapsed, as if from exhaustion, or sorrow. Something was over. The people had taken vengeance on what had existed. The era of the Enlightenment criminals was over. But their exhaustion also contained a great sorrow; there would no longer be any open and illuminated parks, and the theatre and entertainments would be banned, and purity would reign, along with piety, and that was as it should be. Things would no longer be as amusing. But this was necessary.

A kind of sorrow. That was it. A kind of righteous, wrathful sorrow. And the new regime, which was decent, would not punish the people for this vengeful but strangely desperate sorrow.

On the third day the police began to appear in the streets, and it was over.

The Queen, under heavy guard, with eight dragoons on horseback, was taken to Kronborg Castle. Inside the coach were only the Queen, the little child, and one lady-in-waiting, now her entire retinue.

An officer sat on the seat beside the coachman, with his sabre drawn.

Commandant von Hauch, in all haste, had lit fires to warm up several rooms in Hamlet's old castle. It had been a bitterly cold winter, with many storms sweeping in from Øresund, and he was unprepared. The Queen said nothing but held the child pressed close to her body and pulled tight her fur coat, which she never took off.

In the evening she stood for a long time at the window facing south and looked towards Copenhagen. Only once did she say anything to her lady-in-waiting. She asked her what the strange, faintly flickering light in the sky due south was emanating from.

"It's Copenhagen lit up," her lady-in-waiting told her. "The people are celebrating their release from the oppressor Struensee and his cohorts."

The Queen spun around and gave her lady-in-waiting a box on the ear. Then she burst into tears and begged her forgiveness, but she went back to the window and, with the sleeping child held close, she stared for a long time into the darkness and at the faint glow of illuminated Copenhagen.

Chapter 16 · The Cloister

I

If he bent his legs at an angle and slowly lowered them, he could hardly feel the shackles, and the chains were about three yards long so that he could move. In truth, they weren't actually necessary, because how could he flee? *Where shall we flee from Your visage and where shall I seek my refuge Lord God in this hour of need* – the old passages from the Bible lessons with his gloomy father, Adam Struensee, had cropped up, absurdly enough; how could he be remembering that? Wasn't it all so very long ago? But the torment of the chains had a greater effect on his mind; it had taken him little time to become accustomed to the physical pain. He had made an effort to be courteous. It was important to remain calm and not show despair or criticism. They had been respectful and businesslike; he was quite firm about this and repeated it often, and they had treated him well, he would like to emphasize this. But at night when the cold came seeping in, as if it were his terror that had frozen solid inside him like a block of ice, at night he didn't have the strength to be positive and good-natured. Then he could no longer pretend. Occasionally it would also occur in the daytime, when he looked up at the meaningless ceiling and saw the drops of moisture gathering for an onslaught, finally letting go and attacking; then his hands would shake so badly he couldn't control them, then came a torture that was worse than not knowing what had happened to Caroline Mathilde and the child, or whether she would be able to save him. *O God, you who do not exist, who do not exist, I ask you whether they will subject me to an intense examination and whether the nails will puncture my testicles and whether I will be able to endure it,* but otherwise everything was quite satisfactory, the food was good and full of flavour, the servants of the guardhouse were kind, and he found no reason whatsoever to criticize or complain about the way he had been treated, in fact he had expressed to the commandant his surprise at the humane treatment, at the way he was treated *but to think the journey never took place that would have taken me to the distant East Indies, where doctors are sorely needed, and if only I had left them in Altona,* and this constant harping, and the same thing at night, and then the nightmares about Sergeant Mörl started appearing, the way they had for Christian; he began to understand what Christian had dreamed about, the nightmares about Mörl, the nightmares, *it was not like resting in the wounds of the Lamb, instead they stuck nails into him and he screamed in wild desperation, Christian had said,* but he was quite calm and obliging, and now and then he even managed to tell the guards little jests, which he believed were generally appreciated.

On the third day Guldberg came to visit.

Guldberg asked him whether everything was satisfactory, to which he answered in the affirmative. Guldberg had brought along a list of possessions that had been confiscated and asked him to verify that it was correct. It was the list that began with "35 Danish ducats", continued with "a jar of toothpaste" (in Danish!), and ended with "one comb", with the odd comment that "Struensee almost always wears his hair pinned up with a comb fastened to it in back like a woman". He pretended not to see the comment, but instead verified the list and nodded his approval.

He hadn't brought much with him at the time of his arrest. They had suddenly stood there in the flickering light and he had simply thought: This is inescapable. It's inevitable. He didn't even remember how it all happened. He was just stunned with fear.

Guldberg asked Struensee how he had received the wounds on his head. He didn't reply. Guldberg then repeated the question. Guldberg said that according to the guards' report, Struensee had tried to take his own life by throwing himself headfirst against the stone wall.

"I know a way to increase your will to live," said Guldberg, "in this new situation."

He then handed Struensee a book. It was *The Life Story of a Converted Freethinker*, written by Ove Guldberg, published in 1760.

Struensee thanked him.

"But why?" he asked after a long silence.

And then he added:

"I'm going to die anyway. We both know that."

"Yes, we know that," said Guldberg.

"Then why are you here?"

It was such a strange meeting.

Guldberg seemed concerned about Struensee's welfare, he was worried about the apathy shown by the prisoner. He wandered about the prison cell, nosing around like a dog, restless, worried; yes, it was as if a much-beloved dog had been given a new doghouse and the dog's master was now inspecting it with displeasure. Guldberg ordered a chair to be brought in and sat down. They looked at each other.

Without shame, thought Struensee, he is looking at me "without shame".

"A modest text," said Guldberg in a friendly voice, "written during my days at Sorø Academy. But it contains an interesting conversion story."

"I'm not afraid to die," said Struensee. "And I'm very difficult to convert."

"Don't say that," replied Guldberg.

Just before he left, Guldberg handed a picture to Struensee. It was a copper engraving depicting Caroline Mathilde and Struensee's little daughter, the princess, when she was about four months old.

"What do you want?" asked Struensee.

"Think the matter over," said Guldberg.

"What do you want?" Struensee repeated.

Two days later Guldberg came back.

"The days are short and the light is poor," said Struensee. "I haven't been able to read the book. I haven't even started."

"I understand," said Guldberg. "Are you thinking of starting?"

"I repeat that I'm difficult to convert," said Struensee.

That was in the afternoon, the cell was very cold, they could both see their breath.

"I want you to take a good long look at the picture of the little girl," said Guldberg. "A bastard child. But very sweet and charming."

Then he left.

What was his intention?

Those brief, often repeated visits. Otherwise nothing but silence. The guards told him nothing, the windows of the cell were high up, the book he had been given was the only thing to read, aside from the Bible. Finally, almost in anger, he began reading Guldberg's tract. It was a touching story, excruciating in its grey plainness, the language like a sermon, the story without drama. It described a thoroughly good person, intelligent, forthright, with many friends and loved by all, and how this man was lured into freethinking. Afterwards he realized the error of his ways.

That was all.

With some effort and great willpower he made his way through the 186 pages written in Danish, and he understood nothing.

What did Guldberg want?

Four days later he returned, had the little chair brought in, sat down, and looked at the prisoner sitting on the bed.

"I've read it," Struensee told him.

Guldberg did not reply. He merely sat quite still and then, after a long silence and in a very soft but clear voice said:

"Your sin is great. Your member has besmirched the country's throne, you ought to cut it off and throw it away in disgust, but you also have other sins on your conscience. The country was thrown into upheaval, and only God and His Almighty Mercy could save us. Denmark has now been saved. All of your decrees have been revoked. A solid government is ruling the land. You will now, in writing, admit to the abominable and sinful intimacy that you have had with the Queen, confess your guilt. Then, under the guidance of Pastor Balthasar Münter who, like yourself, is German, you will draft a written statement in which you describe your conversion, how you have now given up all heretical ideas of the Enlightenment, and confess your love for the Saviour, Jesus Christ."

"Is that all?" asked Struensee with what he thought was restrained irony.

"That's all."

"And if I refuse?"

Guldberg sat there, small and grey, and stared at him, as usual without blinking.

"You won't refuse. And therefore, since you will agree to this conversion and thereby set a pious example such as I described in my unassuming book, I will personally see to it that your little bastard child is not harmed. Is not killed. That the many, many people who wish to prevent her from pretending to the throne of Denmark do not have their way."

And at last Struensee understood.

"Your daughter," Guldberg added in a friendly tone of voice, "is your belief in eternity. Isn't that what freethinkers believe about eternal life? That it exists only through children? That your eternal life rests in that child alone?"

"They wouldn't dare kill an innocent child."

"They are not lacking in courage."

They sat in silence for a long time. Then Struensee, with a vehemence that surprised even him, exclaimed:

"And what do *you* believe? That God chose Christian! Or the drooling Crown Prince?"

Then Guldberg, in a very calm and quiet voice, said:

"Since you're going to die . . . I'll have you know that I don't share your view that these 'royal wretches' – that's the essence behind your words! The essence! – are not embraced by the grace of God. I believe that these small individuals also have a task that may have been given to them alone. Not to the arrogant, lecherous, admired, and handsome creatures like yourself. Who regard them as wretches."

"I do not!" Struensee fiercely interjected.

"And! And that God has given me the task to defend them against the representatives of evil, one of which is you. And that my, *my* historic mission is to save Denmark."

At the door he said:

"Think the matter over. Tomorrow we'll show you the machines."

They took him into the room where the machines, those used at the "intense interrogations", were kept.

A captain of the guards was the guide, meticulously detailing the use of the various instruments. He also remarked on several cases when the criminal, after only a few minutes' treatment, was willing to co-operate, but the rules required that the intense interrogation should continue for the full time allotted. Those were the rules, and it was important that both parties acknowledged this; otherwise there was always a risk that the person under interrogation might think that he could instantly halt the torture if he so wished. But it was not the person being interrogated who decided on the duration of the intense interrogation. It could not be cut short once it had begun, even with a complete confession, unless this had been agreed to by the interrogation commission and it was done in advance.

After the tour of the instruments, Struensee was escorted back to his cell.

That night he lay awake, at times sobbing violently.

The length of his chains prevented him from throwing himself headfirst against the wall.

He was utterly imprisoned, and he knew it.

The next day he was asked whether a certain Pastor Münter might visit him, a clergyman who had declared himself willing to guide him and to record his story of conversion.

Struensee said yes.

2

Brandt, in his cell, was assigned Dean Hee, and he immediately declared himself willing to co-operate fully with a report and to describe to the public his complete conversion, his guilt, and how he had now cast himself at the feet of the Saviour, Jesus Christ.

Without being asked, he also declared himself eager to repudiate all ideas of the Enlightenment, and in particular those that were championed by a Monsieur Voltaire. As to this individual, he could speak of him with even greater expertise because he had once, and this was before the King's European tour, visited Voltaire and stayed with him for four whole days. At the time it was not a question of discussing ideas of the Enlightenment but instead matters of theatre aesthetics, which interested Brandt more than politics. Dean Hee did not want to hear anything more about these conversations on the theatre, saying that he was more interested in Brandt's soul.

Brandt assumed, in fact, that it was unlikely he would be convicted.

In a letter to his mother he assured her that "no-one could be angry with me for long. I have forgiven everyone, just as God has forgiven me."

During the first weeks he spent his time whistling and singing opera arias, which he regarded as in keeping with his title as *maitre de plaisir*, or with the later title of cultural minister. After March 7 he was given his transverse flute and entertained everyone with his skilful playing.

He assumed it was only a matter of time before he would be released, and in a letter written in prison to King Christian VII, he requested for himself a government position, "no matter how lowly".

Only when his attorney informed him that the foremost and perhaps only charge against him would be that he had physically abused the King, and thus offended royal authority, did he grow alarmed.

It was the story of the finger.

It was such an odd incident that Brandt himself had almost forgotten about it; but it was true that he had bitten Christian on his index finger and had drawn blood. Now the story came out. For this reason he devoted even greater effort, together with Dean Hee, to shaping his defection from freethinking and his loathing for the French philosophers, and this conversion document was also very quickly published in Germany.

In a German newspaper this confession by Brandt was reviewed by a young Frankfurt student by the name of Wolfgang Goethe, then 22 years old, who indignantly described the whole thing as religious hypocrisy and assumed that the conversion was a result of torture or some other form of pressure. In Brandt's case, this was not true; but the young Goethe, who later on was also incensed by Struensee's fate, had done a pen and ink drawing for the article, depicting the shackled Brandt in his prison cell, with Dean Hee standing before him, who with sweeping gestures was instructing him on the necessity of conversion.

As a caption to the illustration there was a short satiric poem or dramatic sketch, perhaps the very first Goethe ever had published, which said in its entirety:

> *Dean Hee:*
> *"Soon, O Count, you will bask in joyful angelic glow."*
> *Count Brandt:*
> *"Alas, my dear Pastor, to my woe."*

And yet everything was under control.

The physical control of the prisoners was most effective, their left foot shackled to their right arm with a chain a yard and a half long; this chain, in turn, was fastened to the wall with very heavy links. The legal control was also quickly devised. A court of inquisition was established on January 20, followed by the final body of the Board of Inquisition, which came to include 42 members.

There was only one problem. It was quite clear that Struensee had to be and would be condemned to death. But the constitutional dilemma overshadowed everything.

The dilemma was the little English whore.

She was locked up at Kronborg; her four-year-old son, the Crown Prince, had been taken from her, although she was allowed to keep the little girl, "since she was still nursing". But the Queen was made of different and harder stuff than the other prisoners. She admitted to nothing. And she was, after all, the sister of the English King.

Certain preparatory interrogations had been made. They were not encouraging.

The Queen was the real problem.

They sent Guldberg and a supporting delegation of three commission members up to Hamlet's castle to see what could be done.

The first meeting was very brief and formal. She categorically denied that she and Struensee had had an intimate relationship and that the child was his. She was furious but quite formal, and demanded to speak to the British Ambassador in Copenhagen.

At the door Guldberg turned around and said:

"I'm asking you one more time: Is the child Struensee's?"

"No," she replied, curt as the crack of a whip.

But all at once terror filled her eyes. Guldberg saw it.

Thus ended their first meeting.

Chapter 17 · The Wine Treader

I

The first interrogation of Struensee began on February 20, lasted from ten o'clock until two, and produced nothing.

On February 21 the interrogation continued, and Struensee was presented with further proof that he had had an immoral and intimate relationship with the Queen. The evidence, it was claimed, was indisputable. Even the most loyal of his servants had testified; if he had believed himself to be surrounded by an inner circle of protective individuals who would defend him, he must now realize that this inner circle did not exist. Towards the end of the long interrogation on the third day, when Struensee asked whether the Queen wouldn't soon give orders to put an end to this shameless farce, they told him that the Queen had been arrested and was being held at Kronborg, that the King wished to initiate divorce proceedings, and that Struensee, at any rate, couldn't count on support from her, if that was what he was thinking.

Struensee stared at them as if stunned, and then understood.

Suddenly he burst into wild and uncontrolled weeping and asked to be taken back to his cell to think over his situation.

The Board of Inquisition naturally denied his request since it was judged that Struensee was now unbalanced and that a confession was near, and it was decided to extend that day's interrogation. Struensee's weeping did not stop, he was in utter despair and at once acknowledged, "with great despondency and resignation", that he had indeed had an intimate relationship with the Queen, and that intercourse ("*Beiwohnung*") had taken place.

On February 25 he signed a complete confession.

The news spread quickly through all of Europe.

Indignation and contempt characterized the comments. Struensee's actions were condemned; not his intimate relationship with the Queen but the fact that he had confessed. A French observer, upon hearing the news, wrote that "a Frenchman would have told everything in the world, but he would never have confessed".

It was also clear that Struensee had now signed his own death sentence.

A commission of four men was dispatched to Kronborg to present the Queen with Struensee's written confession. According to the directive, the Queen was to be allowed to read only an authorized copy. The original would be taken along, and she would be given the opportunity to compare the copy to verify its authenticity, but under no circumstances was she to be given physical access to the original; it would be held up for the Queen to look at, but it would not be put in the Queen's hand.

They were aware of her determination and feared her rage.

2

She always sat at the window and looked out across Øresund, which for the first time in all the years she had lived in Denmark was frozen solid and covered with snow.

The snow often drifted in thin streaks across the ice, and it was quite beautiful. She had decided that snow drifting over ice was beautiful.

She didn't think many things in this country were beautiful anymore. Everything was actually ugly and icy-grey and hostile, but she held onto whatever might be beautiful. Snow drifting across the ice was beautiful. At least sometimes, especially one afternoon when the sun broke through and for several minutes made everything . . . well, beautiful.

But she missed the birds. She had learned to love them during the time before Struensee, when she would stand on the beach and see how they "wrapped themselves in their dreams" – that was the expression she used later on when she told Struensee about them – or occasionally rose up and disappeared into the low, hovering mist. The idea that birds could dream had become so important: that they had secrets and dreamed and could love, just as trees could love, and that the birds could "have expectations" and harbour hopes, and would then all of a sudden rise up and beat the tips of their wings against the quicksilver-grey surface and disappear towards something. Towards something, a different life. It had seemed so splendid.

But there were no birds now.

This was Hamlet's castle, and she had seen a performance of *Hamlet* in London. A mad king who forced his beloved to commit suicide; she had wept as she watched the play, and the first time she visited Kronborg the castle had seemed so impressive in some way. Now it was not impressive. It was just a horrible story in which she was imprisoned. She hated *Hamlet*. She didn't want her life to be written by a play. She imagined that she would write her own life. "Imprisoned by love", Ophelia had died; what was *she* now imprisoned by? Was it the same as Ophelia, by love? Yes, it was love. But she had no intention of going mad and dying. She was determined that, under no circumstances, none whatsoever, would she become Ophelia.

She refused to become a play.

She hated Ophelia and the flowers in her hair and her martyr's death, and her demented song that was merely ridiculous. I am only 20 years old, she would constantly repeat to herself; she was 20 years old and not imprisoned in a Danish play written by an Englishman, and not imprisoned in anyone else's madness, and she was still young.

O, keep me innocent, make others great. That was the tone of Hamlet's Ophelia. How ridiculous.

But the birds had forsaken her. Was that a sign?

She also hated everything that was a cloister.

The court was a cloister, her mother was a cloister, the Dowager Queen was a cloister, Kronborg was a cloister. In a cloister a person lacked any talents. Holberg was not a cloister, the birds were not a cloister, riding in men's attire was not a cloister, and Struensee was not a cloister. For 15 years she had lived in her mother's cloister and lacked any talents; now she was sitting once again in a kind of cloister; and in between was the Struensee era. She sat at the window and stared out across the snowdrifts and tried to understand what Struensee's era had been.

It meant growing up, from being a child who thought herself to be 15, to becoming 100 years old, and having learned.

In four years everything had changed.

First the horrible scene with the mad little King who serviced her, then the court, which was insane, like the King, whom she nevertheless occasionally had loved; no, the wrong word. Not loved. She brushed that aside. First the cloister, then those four years. It had all happened so quickly; she realized that she was not without talents and, this was the most astonishing of all, she had taught them – them! – that she was not without talents, and thus taught them to feel fear.

The girl who set out to teach them to feel fear.

Struensee had once told her an old German folk tale. It was about a boy who could not feel fear; he had set off into the world "to learn to know fear". How very German that phrase was, and mysterious. She thought it was a strange story, and she almost never thought about it.

But she remembered the title: "The boy who set out to learn to know fear."

He had recounted it in German. The boy who set out to learn to know fear. Yet, in his voice, and in German, the expression had sounded beautiful, almost magical. Why had he told it to her? Was it a story that he wanted to tell about himself? A secret sign? Afterwards she thought that he had been talking about himself. There was, of course, another boy in the story. He was clever, gifted, good and beloved; but he was paralysed by fear. Of everything, of everything. Everything terrified him. He was full of admirable talents, but fear had paralysed them. The gifted boy was paralysed by fear.

But the Stupid Brother didn't know what fear was.

The Stupid One was the victor.

What did it mean, this story that Struensee had chosen to tell her? Was it about himself? Or was he talking about her? Or about their enemies, and how it was to live? The condition, or conditions, that existed but to which they refused to adapt? Why that ridiculous goodness in service of the good? Why hadn't he purged his enemies, banished them, bribed them, adapted to the great game?

Was it because he was afraid of evil, so afraid that didn't want to sully his hands with it, and hence all was now lost?

A delegation of four men came to tell her that Struensee had been thrown into prison, that he had confessed.

She assumed they had tortured him. She was almost certain of this. And then of course he had confessed to everything. Struensee didn't have to set off into the world to learn to know fear. Deep inside he had always been afraid. She had seen it. He didn't even like wielding power. She didn't understand this. She had felt a unique pleasure when she understood for the first time that she could instil terror.

But he did not. There was something fundamentally wrong with him. Why was it always the wrong people who were chosen to do good? God couldn't be the one who did this. It must be the Devil who chose the instruments of good. So he picked the noble ones who could feel fear. But if the good people could not kill or destroy, then goodness was powerless.

How horrifying. Did things truly have to be this way? Was it true that she herself, who lacked all fear and enjoyed wielding power and felt happy when she saw that they were afraid of her, that it was people like her who should have carried out the Danish revolution?

No birds outside. Why were there no birds now that she needed them?

He had told her a story about a young boy who had everything but who knew fear. But it was the other boy in the story who was the hero. The one who was evil, wicked, foolish, who lacked all fear; he was the victor.

How could someone conquer the world if he was only good, and lacked the courage to be evil? How was it then possible to put a lever under the house of the world?

Endless winter. Snow drifting across Øresund.

When would it be over?

Four years she had lived. Actually less. It began at the Royal Theatre, when she decided to kiss him. Wasn't that in the spring of 1770? That meant that she had lived only two years.

How little time it took to grow up. How little time it took to die.

Why was it Johann Friedrich Struensee that she had to love so terribly when the good were doomed to fall and those who could not feel fear would triumph?

"O, keep me innocent, make others great."

It was so infinitely long ago.

3

The delegation of four accomplished nothing.

Four days later Guldberg arrived.

Guldberg came alone, signalled to the guards to wait outside, and sat down on a chair. He looked her in the eye, his gaze unwavering. No, this little man was no Rantzau, no cowardly traitor, he shouldn't be underestimated, he was not someone to be toyed with. Before, she had thought of him as almost grotesque in his grey smallness; but he seemed to have changed; what was it that had changed? He was not insignificant. He was a deadly adversary, and she had underestimated him; now he sat in his chair and stared at her without blinking. What was it about his eyes? People said that he never blinked, but wasn't there something else? He talked to her calmly and in a cold voice, stating that Struensee had now confessed, as she had recently been told, that the King now wished for a divorce, and a confession from her was necessary.

"No," she said to him in an equally calm voice.

"In that case," he said, "Struensee has slandered Denmark's queen. And he must be punished more severely. We will be forced to condemn him to a slow death by crushing under the wheel."

He looked at her, quite calm.

"You swine," she said. "And what about the child?"

"A price must always be paid," he said. "Paid!"

"And that means?"

"That the bastard and spawn of a whore must be taken from you."

She knew she had to maintain her composure. The child's life depended on it, and she had to stay calm and think.

"There's just one thing I don't understand," she said in her most controlled tone of voice, although it sounded to her shrill and quavering, "I don't understand this desire for revenge. How was someone like you created? By God? Or by the Devil?"

He gave her a long look.

"Lechery has its price. And my task is to persuade you to sign a confession."

"But you didn't answer me," she said.

"Do you truly want an answer?"

"Yes. I truly do."

Then, without a sound, he pulled a book out of his pocket, looked through it thoughtfully, turning the pages, and began to read. It was the Bible. He had a beautiful voice, she suddenly thought, but there was something horrible about his tranquillity, his composure, and the text that he read aloud. "This," he said, "is Isaiah, Chapter 34; shall I read part of it?" And he read: *"For the Lord is enraged against all the nations, and furious against all their host, he has doomed them, has given them over for slaughter. Their slain shall be cast out, and the stench of their corpses shall rise; the mountains shall flow with their blood. All the host of heaven shall rot away, and the skies roll up like a scroll. All their host shall fall, as leaves fall from the vine, like leaves falling from the fig tree."* And he turned the page very slowly and meditatively, as if he were listening to the music of the words. Oh God, she thought, how could I ever have thought this man was insignificant? *"For my sword has drunk its fill in the heavens; behold, it descends for judgement upon Edom, upon the people I have doomed. The Lord has a sword; it is sated with blood, it is gorged with fat, with the blood of lambs and goats, with the fat of the kidneys of rams, yes"*, and his voice grew in strength and she couldn't help staring at him with something like fascination, or terror, or both. *"Their land shall be soaked with blood, and their soil made rich with fat. For the Lord has a day of vengeance, a year of recompense for the cause of Zion. And the streams of Edom shall be turned into pitch, and her soil into brimstone; her land shall become burning pitch. Night and day it shall not be quenched; its smoke shall go up for ever. From generation to generation it shall lie waste; none shall pass through it for ever and ever . . . They shall name it No Kingdom There, and all its princes shall be nothing. Thorns shall grow over its strongholds, nettles and thistles in its fortresses. It shall be the haunt of jackals, an abode for ostriches. And wild beasts shall meet with hyenas, the satyr will cry to his fellow; yea, there shall the night hag alight and find for herself a resting place,* yes", he continued in the same calm, intense voice, "these are the words of the prophet. I read them only to give a background for the Lord's words about the punishment that will strike those who seek impurity and corruption, impurity and corruption," he repeated, all the while staring at her, and suddenly she saw his eyes, no, it wasn't that they didn't blink, but they were light-coloured, almost ice-blue, like a wolf's. They were very pale and dangerous, and that was what had frightened everyone, not the fact that he didn't blink, but that his eyes were as unbearably ice-blue as a wolf's, and he continued in the same calm voice: "Now we come to the passage which the Dowager Queen, upon my advice, recommended be read in all the churches of the realm next Sunday, as an expression of thanksgiving that this country was not forced to share Edom's fate, and I will read now from the Prophet Isaiah, Chapter 63." And he cleared his throat, fixed his gaze on the open Bible, and read the text which the Danish people would hear on the following Sunday. *"Who is this that comes from Edom, in crimsoned garments from Bozrah, he that is glorious in his apparel, marching in the greatness of his strength? 'It is I, announcing vindication, mighty to save.' Why is thy apparel red, and thy garments like his that treads in the wine press? 'I have trodden the wine press alone, and from the peoples no-one was with me; I trod them in my anger and trampled them in my wrath; their lifeblood is sprinkled upon my garments, and I have stained all my raiment. For the day of vengeance was in my heart, and my year of redemption has come. I looked, but there was no-one to help; I was appalled, but there was no-one to uphold; so my own arm brought me victory, and my wrath upheld me. I trod down the peoples in my anger, I made them drunk in my wrath, and I poured out their lifeblood on the earth.'"*

Then he stopped reading and looked up at her.

"The wine treader," she said, as if to herself.

"I was asked a question," said Guldberg. "And didn't want to shun giving the answer. Now I have done it."

"Yes?" she whispered.

"That's why."

For a moment she thought, as she watched the wine treader reading slowly and methodically, that perhaps it was a wine treader that Struensee had needed at his side.

Calm, quiet, with ice-blue wolf eyes, bloodstained garments, and with a temperament for the great game.

She felt almost sick when this thought occurred to her. Struensee would never have been tempted by the idea. It was the fact that she herself was tempted that made her ill. Was she "the night hag"?

Did she have a wine treader inside her?

Never, she persuaded herself. Where would it all end? Where would it end?

In the end she signed.

Nothing about the little girl's birth. But about the adultery, and she wrote with a steady hand, with fury, though giving no details; she confessed in this matter, "to the same as Count Struensee has confessed".

She wrote with a steady hand, and so that he wouldn't be tortured to a slow death because he had accused her of lying, and thus offended royal authority, and because she knew that his terror of this would be so great; but the only thing she could think of was: *but the children, the children, and the boy is so big, but the little girl, whom I must nurse, and they'll take her, and they will be surrounded by wolves, and what will happen, and little Louise, they'll take them both from me, who will nurse her then, who will enfold her with love among these wine treaders?*

She signed. And she knew that she was no longer the bold girl who knew no fear. Fear had finally sought her out, fear had found her, and at last she knew what fear was.

4

Keith, the British Ambassador, was finally allowed to visit the imprisoned queen.

The problem had been elevated to a higher level. The great game had been initiated, although the great game did not concern the two imprisoned counts, or the minor sinners who had been arrested at the same time. They were later released and banished and fell into disfavour or received small fiefs and were pardoned and provided with pensions.

The minor sinners quietly disappeared.

Reverdil, the cautious tutor, Christian's tutor, nursemaid, and the boy's beloved advisor for as long as advice could be given, was also banished. He was given a week's house arrest but sat calmly and waited; conflicting dispatches arrived; eventually came an effusive and courteous expulsion order instructing him to seek his home country as soon as possible, and there find peace.

He understood. At a slow pace he travelled back from the centre of the storm because, as he writes, he didn't want to give the impression that he was fleeing. In this manner he disappeared from history, stage by stage, restrained in his flight, once more banished, gaunt and stooped, sorrowful and clear-sighted, with his once stubborn hopes still alive; he disappeared like a very slow sunset. This is a poor image, and yet it suits Élie Salomon François Reverdil. Perhaps he would have described it thus if he still availed himself of one of the images he loved to use, of slowness as virtue: the images of the cautious revolution, the slow retreats, of the dawn and dusk of the Enlightenment.

The great game did not concern the minor characters.

The great game concerned the little English whore, the little Princess, Denmark's crowned Queen, the sister of George III, the enlightened woman on Denmark's throne who was so esteemed by

Tsarina Catherine of Russia; meaning the little, imprisoned, weeping, totally confused and furious Caroline Mathilde.

This night hag. This demonic angel. Nevertheless she was the mother of two royal children, which gave her power.

Guldberg's analysis was crystal clear. They had won her confession of adultery. A divorce was necessary to prevent her, and her child, from claiming power. The ruling group surrounding Guldberg was now, he admitted, just as Struensee had been, wholly dependent on the legitimacy of the mad King. God had given power. But Christian was still the finger of God that granted life, grace, and the spark of power to the one who possessed the strength to conquer the black void of power created by the King's illness.

The royal physician had visited this vacuum, and filled it. Now he was gone. Others would now visit the void.

The situation was essentially unchanged, although reversed.

The great game now concerned the Queen.

Christian had acknowledged the little Princess as his own. To declare her a bastard child was an affront against him and would diminish his power to legitimize the new government. If the girl was a bastard, the mother might be permitted to keep her, and there would be no reason to keep the girl in Denmark. That must not happen. Neither would Christian be declared insane, for the same reason; then all power would revert to his legitimate son, and indirectly to Caroline Mathilde.

Ergo the adultery had to be established. The divorce had to take place.

The question was how the English monarch would react to this insult to his sister.

There was a period of confusion: war or not? George III ordered a great naval squadron to be outfitted for an attack on Denmark if Caroline Mathilde's rights were denied. Yet at the same time the British newspapers and pamphlets were publishing sections of Struensee's confession. The freedom of the press in England was both admirable and notorious, and the amazing story of the German doctor and the little English queen was irresistible.

But war – over that?

It appeared, as the weeks passed, more and more difficult to enter into a major war because of an insult to national pride. Caroline Mathilde's sexual infidelity made public support uncertain. Many wars had been started for lesser and more peculiar reasons, but England was now hesitating.

They settled on a compromise. The Queen would escape the planned life imprisonment at Aalborghus. The divorce would be accepted. The children would be taken from her. She would be exiled for life from Denmark and would be forced to take up voluntary but supervised residence at one of the British King's palaces in his German possessions, in Celle, Hanover.

She would retain the title of Queen.

In Helsingør harbour on May 27, 1772, a small British squadron arrived, consisting of two frigates and a shallop, a royal yacht.

That same day the little girl was taken from her.

They had told her the day before that she would have to give up the child on the following day; she had known about this for a long time, it was only the exact time that had been so horribly uncertain. She wouldn't leave the little girl in peace but all the time carried her around in her arms; the girl was now ten months old and could walk if someone held her hand. The girl was always good-natured, and the Queen refused to allow any of the ladies-in-waiting to tend to her during those last days. When the child grew tired of the rather simple games that the Queen devised to preoccupy her daughter, and thus herself, the task of getting dressed came to play an important rôle. It took on an almost manic quality, *I have confessed everything that I did wrong if only I could keep the girl and God are you a wine treader I see how they're coming with their bloody garments and these wolves will now take charge*, but often her way of dressing and undressing the child, sometimes of necessity but often quite unnecessarily, was a form of ritual or invocation, in order to win forever the little girl's favour. On the morning of May 27, when the Queen saw the three vessels lying at anchor in the harbour, she had already changed the little girl's clothes ten times, for no reason whatsoever, and the protests of her ladies-in-waiting were met only with vehemence and outbursts of anger and tears.

When the delegation from the new Danish government arrived, the Queen lost all control. She shouted without restraint, refused to let go of the child, and only the firm exhortations of the delegation not to frighten the innocent little girl but display dignity and resolve made her stop her steady weeping, *but this humiliation oh if only I were a wine treader at this moment but the girl.*

At last they succeeded in tearing the child away from her without harming either the girl or the Queen.

Afterwards she stood at the window, as usual, and seemed quite calm, staring south with an expressionless face, towards Copenhagen.

Everything empty. No thoughts. Little Louise had been turned over to the pack of Danish wolves.

5

On May 30, at six in the evening, the handover was carried out. Then the British officers came ashore, escorted by a bodyguard of armed British sailors, 50 men strong, to take Caroline Mathilde away.

The encounter with the Danish military guard troops at Kronborg was quite extraordinary. The British officers did not greet the Danish guards in the customary fashion, they did not exchange a single word with the Danish courtiers or officers; instead, they met them with coldness and the utmost contempt. They formed a guard of honour around the Queen, greeting her with military courtesy, and a salvo of salutes was fired from the vessels.

Down at the harbour she walked between rows of British soldiers standing in formation and presenting arms.

Then she was escorted on board the British sloop and conveyed out to the frigate.

The Queen was very calm and resolute. She conversed in a friendly manner with her countrymen, who with their contempt for the Danish guard troops wished to show their repudiation of the way in which she had been treated. They closed ranks around her with something that could not be described in military terms, but was perhaps love.

No doubt they had decided that she was still their little girl. More or less. All descriptions of their behaviour indicate this.

She had been badly treated. They wanted to show the Danes their contempt.

Composed, she walked between the rows of British sailors as they presented arms. No smiles, but no tears either. In this sense her departure from Denmark was unlike her arrival. Then she had wept, without knowing why. Now she did not weep, although she had reason to do so; but she had made up her mind.

They escorted her away, with military honours, with contempt for those she was leaving, and with love. That was how the little English girl was taken home from her visit to Denmark.

Chapter 18 · The River

3

The day of Vengeance and the Wine Treader would come.

But there was something about this very enticing idea that seemed wrong. Guldberg didn't understand what it was. They had read the sermon text in the churches, with each interpretation more shocking than the last; Guldberg thought it proper that this had occurred; he had chosen the passage himself, and it was the right one, the Dowager Queen had agreed, the day of judgement and vengeance had come, *I trod down the peoples in my anger, I made them drunk in my wrath, and I poured out their lifeblood on the earth.* These were the right words, and justice would be done. Yet when he read the text to the little English whore it had been so appalling. Why had she looked at him in that way? She had brought the contagion of sin into the Danish kingdom, he was certain of that, she was the night hag; *It shall be the haunt of jackals, an abode for ostriches. And wild beasts shall meet with hyenas, the satyr will cry to his fellow; yea, there shall the night hag alight and find for herself a resting place.* She deserved this, she knew that she was the night hag, and she had forced him to his knees at his bedside and her power was great, and Lord, *how shall we protect ourselves from the contagion of sin?*

But he had seen her face. When he raised his eyes from the righteous and true Scripture, he saw only her face, and afterwards it had obscured all else, and he did not see the night hag but a child.

That sudden, utterly naked innocence. And then the child.

Two weeks after the second meeting with Caroline Mathilde, but before a verdict was pronounced, Guldberg was all of a sudden struck by doubt. This was the first time in his life, but he would characterize it as despair. He could find no other word for it.

What happened was as follows.

The interrogations of Struensee and Brandt were now very near completion; Struensee's guilt was clear, the sentence could only be death. Guldberg then paid a visit to the Dowager Queen.

He spoke to her about what would be the wisest course.

"The wisest course," he began, "the wisest course from a political perspective would not be a death sentence but something less severe . . ."

"The Russian Tsarina," the Dowager Queen interrupted him, "wishes for a reprieve, I don't have to be told about that. As does the King of England. As do certain other monarchs who have been struck by the contagion of the Enlightenment. I have only one response to that."

"Which is?"

"No."

She was intractable. She suddenly started talking about the great prairie fire of purity that would sweep across the world and annihilate everything, everything that was part of Struensee's era. And then there would be no room for compassion. And she continued on in this way, and he listened; everything seemed to be an echo of what he had said himself *but oh God, is there truly no place for love or is there only filth and lechery* and he could do nothing but agree. Although afterwards he did start to speak again of what would be wise, and sensible, and of the Russian Tsarina and the King of England, and the risks of serious complications, but perhaps that wasn't what he meant but rather *why must we cut ourselves off from what is called love and is it only wrathful like the wine treader's love* and the Dowager Queen did not listen.

He felt something akin to weakness rising up in him, and he became confused. This was the basis for his despair.

At night he lay awake for a long time, staring up at the darkness, where the avenging God could be found, and mercy, and love, and justice. It was then that he was seized with despair. There was nothing there in the dark, there was nothing, only emptiness, and a great despair.

What kind of life is this, he thought, when justice and vengeance triumph, and I can't see God's love in the darkness, but only despair and emptiness?

By the next day he had pulled himself together.

Then he paid a visit to the King.

As far as Christian was concerned, he seemed to have given up completely. He was terrified of everything and sat quaking in his rooms, with reluctance eating the food that was now always brought to him, and he spoke only to his dog.

The Negro page Moranti had disappeared. Perhaps on that vengeful night when he had tried to hide under the sheet as Christian had taught him but was unable to flee, perhaps on that night he had given up, or wanted to return to something that no-one knew anything about. Or he was killed on that night when Copenhagen exploded and the incomprehensible rage gripped everyone and they all knew that something was over and that their wrath had to be directed at something, though for reasons that no-one understood, but the anger existed and revenge had to be taken; no-one ever saw him after that night. He vanished from history. Christian had ordered a search for him, but it had proved fruitless.

Now he had only the dog left.

Guldberg was troubled by reports of the King's condition, and he wanted to determine for himself what was going on with the monarch. He went to see Christian and spoke to him soothingly, assuring him that all threats against the King's life had now been averted and that he could feel safe.

After a moment the King, in a whisper, began "confiding" to Guldberg certain secrets.

In the past, he told Guldberg, he had suffered certain delusions, such as that his mother, Queen Louise, had had an English lover who was his father. And sometimes he had believed that Catherine the Great of Russia was his mother. He was convinced, however, that in some way he had been "exchanged". He might be the changeling child of a peasant. He constantly used the word "exchanged", which seemed to mean that an exchange had occurred or that he had been consciously traded away.

Now, however, he was absolutely certain. The Queen, Caroline Mathilde, was his mother. The fact that she was imprisoned in Kronborg Castle was for him the most terrifying news. But that she was his mother was quite clear.

Guldberg listened with increasing alarm and bewilderment.

Christian, in his present state of "certainty", or rather with his now quite certain demented image of himself, seemed to be blending in elements from Saxo's portrayal of Amleth. Christian could not have seen the Englishman Shakespeare's *Hamlet*, which Guldberg knew quite well (it was, of course, not performed during the King's stay in London), and there had not yet been any Danish performance.

Christian's confusion, as well as his strange delusion about his birth, was nothing new. Since the spring of 1771 it had become more and more evident. The fact that he experienced reality as theatre was well known to everyone by now. But if it was true that he now thought he was taking part in a play in which Caroline Mathilde was his mother, then Guldberg had to ask himself with some anxiety what rôle he had assigned to Struensee.

And how would Christian himself act in this real play? What script would he follow, and what interpretation would occur? What rôle did he intend to give himself? The fact that a deranged person might think he was acting in a dramatic performance was not at all unusual. But this actor did not see reality symbolically, or figuratively, nor was he without power. If he thought he was part of a performance, he had the power to make that performance real. It was still the case that an order and a directive from the King's hand had to be obeyed. He held all formal power.

If he was given the opportunity to visit his beloved "mother", he could be used by her, and anything might happen. The murder of a Rosencrantz, Guildenstern, or Guldberg was far too easy.

"I wish," said Guldberg, "that I might give Your Majesty advice in this most intricate matter."

Christian stared at his bare feet – he had taken off his shoes – and murmured:

"If only the Sovereign of the Universe were here. If only she were here, and could. And could."

"What?" asked Guldberg. "Could what?"

"Could give me her time," whispered Christian.

Guldberg then left. He also ordered that a tighter watch be kept on the King, and said that under no circumstances was he to have contact with anyone without Guldberg's written permission.

And he sensed with relief that his momentary weakness had receded, that his despair was gone, and that he once again could act in a thoroughly sensible manner.

2

The pastor for the German congregation of Saint Peter's, theologian Doctor Balthasar Münter, had at the request of the government visited Struensee in his prison cell for the first time on March 1, 1772.

Six weeks had passed since the night Struensee was imprisoned. And bit by bit he had fallen apart. There were two breakdowns. First the small one, in front of the Board of Inquisition, when he confessed and sacrificed the Queen. Then the big one, the internal one.

At first, after his breakdown before the Court of Inquisition, he felt nothing at all, only despair and emptiness, but later came the shame. It was guilt and shame that took possession of him like a cancer and ate at him from the inside. He had confessed and had exposed her to the greatest humiliation; what would happen to her now? And to the child. He was at his wits' end and couldn't talk to anyone; he had only the Bible, and he hated the thought of resorting to that. He had already read Guldberg's book about the now happily converted freethinker three times, and each time it had seemed to him more naïve and more conceited. But he had no-one to talk to, and at night it was bitterly cold and the chains rubbed oozing sores into his ankles and wrists; but that was not it.

It was the silence.

Once upon a time they called him the "The Silent One", because he listened, but now he understood what silence was. It was a hostile beast that waited. The sounds had ceased.

That was when the pastor arrived.

For every night that passed, he seemed to be carried farther back into memory.

He was carried a long way. Back to Altona, and even farther: back to his childhood, which he had almost never wanted to think about, but now it came to him. He was carried back to what was unpleasant, to the pious home. Also to his mother, who was not strict but rather filled with love. During one of their first meetings the pastor had brought a letter from Struensee's father, and his father had given voice to his despair: "Your promotion, which we read about in the newspapers, did not please us," and now, he wrote, their despair knew no bounds.

His mother had added a few words of sorrow and sympathy; but the essence of the letter was that a complete conversion and submission to the Saviour Jesus Christ and His mercy would be able to save him.

It was unbearable.

The pastor sat on his chair and looked at him, and in his discreet voice he dissected Struensee's problems into logical structures. It was not done without sensitivity. The pastor had seen his wounds and lamented at the cruel treatment, and let him cry. But when Pastor Münter spoke, Struensee suddenly experienced that strange feeling of inferiority, the feeling that he was not a thinker or a theoretician, that he was simply a doctor from Altona and had always wanted to sit in silence.

And that he was inadequate.

But the best thing was that the little pastor with his sharp, gaunt face and calm eyes formulated one problem that pushed aside the worst of it. The worst was not death or the pain or the fact that he might be tortured to death. The worst was another question that was grinding inside him, night and day.

What did I do wrong? That was the worst question.

*

One day the pastor, almost in passing, had stumbled onto this. He said:

"Count Struensee, how could you from your study, in such isolation, know what was right? Why did you believe you possessed the truth when you knew nothing of reality?"

"I worked for many years in Altona," Struensee told him, "and I knew reality."

"Yes," said Pastor Münter after a pause. "As a doctor in Altona. But what about those 632 decrees?"

And after a moment of silence he added, with a certain curiosity: "Who did the research?"

And Struensee replied, with the hint of a smile:

"A dutiful government official always does the proper research, even if it's to plan his own dismemberment."

The pastor nodded, as if he found the explanation both true and self-evident.

He had not done anything wrong.

From his study he had directed the Danish revolution quite calmly, without murder or imprisonment or coercion or banishment, without becoming corrupt or rewarding his friends or procuring personal benefits or coveting this power for some obscure egotistical reason. And yet he must have done something wrong after all. And in his nightmares he returned again and again to the oppressed Danish peasants and to the episode with the dying boy on the wooden horse.

That was it. There was something about this episode that would not let go.

It was not that he had been afraid of the mob when it came rushing towards him. Rather, it was because this was the only time he had ever been near them. But he had turned on his heel and run after the coach in the dark and the mud.

In truth, he had betrayed himself. He often wished that he had concluded his European tour in Altona. But he actually *had* ended it back in Altona.

He had sketched people's faces in the margin of his doctoral dissertation. There was something important about this that he seemed to have forgotten. To see the mechanism, and the great game, and not to forget the people's faces. Was that it?

It was essential to push this away. And so the logical little pastor formulated a different problem for him. It was the problem of eternity, whether it existed, and in all gratefulness he stretched out his hand to the little pastor and accepted this gift.

And thus he could let go of the other question, which was the worst of all. And he was grateful.

Twenty-seven times Pastor Münter would visit Struensee in his prison cell.

During the second visit he said that he had learned with certainty that Struensee was to be executed. The following intellectual problem thus arose. If death meant complete annihilation – well, that was it. Then there would be no eternity, no God, no heaven or eternal punishment. Then Struensee's meditations during these last few weeks would mean nothing. Therefore! *primo*: Struensee ought to focus on the only other possibility, which was that a life after death did exist; and *secundo*: investigate what opportunities existed for getting as much as possible out of this remaining possibility.

Humbly he asked Struensee whether he agreed with this analysis, and Struensee sat in silence for a long time. Then Struensee asked:

"If the latter is true, will Pastor Münter come back often so that together we can analyse this second possibility?"

"Yes," said Münter. "Every day. And for many hours each day."

Thus their conversations began. And Struensee's conversion story was initiated.

The more than 200 pages in the conversion document take the form of questions and answers. Struensee diligently reads his Bible, discovers problems, wants answers, and receives them. *"But tell me,*

Count Struensee, what is it about this passage that you find objectionable?"
"Here, where Christ says to his Mother: 'Woman, what have I to do with you?' it seems hardhearted and, if I dare use the word, indecent." And then follows the pastor's exhaustive analysis, although whether it was delivered directly to Struensee or was composed later is unclear. But there are many pages of exhaustive theological answers. Then a brief question and a detailed answer, and at the end of the journal's notes for the day, an affirmation that Count Struensee now understands, has a full grasp of the matter.

Brief questions, long answers, and ultimately mutual understanding. About Struensee's political activities there was nothing.

His conversion confession was later published, and in many languages.

No-one knows what was actually said. Pastor Münter sat there, day after day, bent over his notebook. Everything would be published and become quite famous: as the apology of the infamous freethinker and man of the Enlightenment.

It was Münter who wrote it all down. The Dowager Queen later perused the text, before it was published, and made certain deletions and censored some passages.

Then it was printed.

The young Goethe was indignant when he read it. Many others were indignant. Not at his conversion, but at the fact that it was extracted under torture. Although this wasn't true, and he never renounced his enlightened ideas; but he seemed to have cast himself with joy into the arms of the Saviour, to hide himself in His wounds. Although those who spoke of apostasy and hypocrisy extracted under torture could hardly have imagined how it was: with that calm, analytical, soft-spoken, sympathetic Pastor Münter who, in his gentle, melodic German – he spoke in German! At long last in German! – talked to him and steered clear of the most difficult question – why he had failed in this world – and talked about eternity, which was the easy, merciful question. And all of this, in

German, seemed sometimes to carry Struensee back to a starting point that was warm and secure: which included the University of Halle and his mother and her admonishments and piety and his father's letter and the fact that they would hear that he now was resting in the wounds of Christ, and their joy, and Altona and the cupping and his friends in Halle and everything, everything that seemed to have been lost.

But now was found, and during these days and hours, was reawakened by Pastor Münter, sitting on his chair in front of him, in this appalling, ice-cold Copenhagen, which he never should have visited, and where only the logical, intellectual, theological conversations for a few hours could free "The Silent One", the doctor from Altona, from the fear that was his weakness and perhaps, in the end, his strength.

3

Struensee's sentence was signed by the Board of Inquisition on Saturday, April 25.

The reasoning behind it was not that he had committed adultery with the Queen but that he had consciously worked to satisfy his own hunger for power and had abolished the Council, and that it was his fault that His Majesty, who loved his people so dearly, had lost faith in the Council and that Struensee had then caused a series of violent acts; and because of his self-interest, and his contempt for religion, decency, and proper morals.

Nothing about infidelity, only a vague reference to "an additional misdeed, due to which he is guilty of lese-majesty to the highest degree". Nothing about Christian's madness.

Nothing about the little girl. And yet "lese-majesty" and "to the highest degree". The sentence was formulated in accordance with Danish law, the first paragraph of Book 6, Chapter 4:

"That Count Johann Friedrich Struensee shall, deserving as he is of punishment and as an example and admonition to others like him, hereby forfeit his honour, life, and possessions and be stripped of the rank of count and all other honours bestowed upon him; and the seal of his rank shall be broken by the executioner; the right hand of Johann Friedrich Struensee shall also be cut off while he lives, and thereafter his head; his body shall be dismembered and placed on the post and wheel, but his head and hand shall thereafter be placed on a pole."

Brandt's sentence was the same. Hand, head, dismemberment, display of his body parts.

The findings of the court were, however, significantly different; it was the strange incident of the index finger that was the reason for his death sentence and the form of execution.

He had violated the King's person.

Twenty-four hours later, on the afternoon of April 27, the sentences were to be sanctioned by King Christian VII. His signature was necessary. There was great uneasiness about this; the risk of a reprieve was great. For this reason, Christian was kept very busy, as if they wanted to exhaust him, to benumb him with ceremonies, or ritually escort him into a theatre world where nothing, in particular a death sentence, was real.

On the night of April 23, a grand masked ball was given at which the King and Dowager Queen graciously received all the invited guests in person. On the 24th, a concert was given at the Danish Theatre, attended by the royal family. On the 25th, the sentences were handed down against Struensee and Brandt, and that evening the King attended the opera *Hadrian in Syria*. On the 27th King Christian, now (according to witnesses) extremely exhausted and quite confused, was escorted along with members of his court to a dinner at Charlottenlund, from which he returned at seven that evening, signed the sentences and was at once led off to the Opera House where, largely dozing or sleeping, he listened to an Italian opera.

There had been great fear that the King would grant a reprieve. Everyone suspected a counter-coup, and then many heads would roll. The anxiety that other powers might intervene was quelled, however, when a courier arrived from St. Petersburg on April 26 with a letter to the Danish King.

It was carefully studied.

Catherine the Great was worried but not threatening. She appealed to the King, saying that "the compassion which is natural to every honourable and sensitive heart" must allow him to "prefer the counsel of leniency rather than severity and harshness" towards those "unfortunates" who had now drawn his wrath, "however justified it may be".

Christian, of course, was not allowed to read the letter. The tone was mild. Russia would not intervene. Neither would the King of England. They could safely purge themselves of the lecherous ones.

The final problem was Christian.

If only Christian, in his confusion, would not cause any problems now, but just sign! Without his signature there was no legal legitimacy.

Yet it had all gone very smoothly. Christian sat at the Council table and muttered, rocking back and forth, confused; only for a moment did he seem to wake up and then he complained about the peculiar and complicated language of the exceedingly long document; all of a sudden he exclaimed that whoever wrote such peculiar language "deserved 100 lashes of the whip".

Then he continued his helpless muttering, and without objection he signed.

Afterwards, on his way out to the carriage that would take him to the Opera House, he stopped Guldberg, drew him aside, and in a whisper "confided" something to him.

He confided to Guldberg that he wasn't certain that Struensee had wanted to kill him. But, he said, if it were true that he himself, Christian, was not a human being but one of God's chosen, then his *actual* presence would not be required at the place of execution in order to pardon the condemned man! Wasn't it sufficient if he asked God, as his mandator, to pardon him? Did he have to appear in person? And, he further confided to Guldberg, since he had long been uncertain as to whether or not he was a human being, if he indeed was a flesh-and-blood person, perhaps a changeling whose real parents were peasants from Jutland, wouldn't this execution supply proof for him? Proof! So that if, if he, through his thoughts alone, and whether he was present or not present at the execution, could command a pardon, it would then be proof – yes proof! – that he was not a human being. But, if this was not successful, then he would have also, also proven that he was, in truth, a *human being*. In this way the execution would be the sign that he had so long wished for, a sign from God of what his origins were, and an answer to the question about whether he was human.

Whispering and insistent, he told this to Guldberg and finally simply uttered:

"A sign! At last a sign!"

Guldberg listened to this confused outpouring without revealing even a hint of his emotions. He noted that the King did not mention a word about Caroline Mathilde being his mother.

"An accurate and brilliant analysis," was Guldberg's only reply.

Whereupon Christian was carried off to the Opera House. Guldberg gazed after him for a long time, deep in thought, and then began to take precautionary measures with regard to the execution, which he now realized were absolutely necessary.

4

They constructed the execution site like a stage set.

Immediately after the sentence was signed by the King, they began to build the scaffold at Østre Fælled. It was a rectangular structure made of wood, about 15 feet high; on its roof an extra section was built, a platform that would make both the executioner and the victim quite visible; elevated even higher was the block, on which the head and hand would be severed.

They built it quickly, and a small orchestra was ordered to lend a ceremonial air to this theatre of death. The news spread fast; the executions were to take place on the morning of April 28 at nine o'clock, and a few hours beforehand the great migration began. Nearly 30,000 people left Copenhagen in those morning hours to walk, ride, or be driven to Østre Fælled, a field that lay just north of the city ramparts.

All the military forces in Copenhagen were called out on the occasion of the executions. It was calculated that almost 5,000 men were posted around Østre Fælled, some of them guarding the execution site itself, some of them grouped around the field in order to intervene should there be any disturbances.

The two pastors, Münter and Hee, arrived in the early morning hours to be with the condemned men. The prisoners were to leave the Citadel at 8:30, accompanied by a procession of coaches guarded by 200 foot soldiers, their bayonets fixed, and 234 dragoons on horseback.

The prisoners rode in separate hired coaches.

During the last hours of his life, Brandt played his flute.

He seemed cheerful and unafraid. He had read the sentence and the findings of the court with a smile. He said he was well acquainted with the ceremony surrounding this comedy; he would of course be pardoned since the charges were so absurd and the punishment so out of proportion with the charges. When they took his flute away before departure, he simply said:

"I will continue my sonatina tonight, when this comedy is over and I am pardoned and free."

When they told him that he would be executed before Struensee, he seemed perplexed for a moment, perhaps even alarmed; he thought it would be natural in the pardoning process for the more serious offender, meaning Struensee, to be executed first, whereupon the innocent man, meaning himself, could then be pardoned as a matter of course.

But he now assumed that they would both be pardoned.

He would have preferred, he said as he stepped into the coach, to see the pardon granted on the way to the scaffold so that he wouldn't risk being subjected to the violence of the mob. He felt that his position as *maître de plaisir*, responsible for the cultural entertainment of the court and the capital, in other words, the cultural minister, had aroused the animosity of many in the populace. Among commoners there was a strong hostility towards culture, and if he were to be pardoned on the scaffold, he might risk the reactions of the people: "I risk having the crowds flay me alive."

He was reassured, however, by the news that 5,000 soldiers had been called out to protect him from the people. He was dressed in a green frock coat with gold braiding, and over this he wore a white fur coat.

The coaches drove very slowly.

Over by the scaffold, at the foot of the stairs, stood Brandt's latest lover and mistress; Brandt greeted her with a cheerful and jaunty expression and asked the guards whether it was truly necessary for him to go up on the scaffold before the pardoning, but then agreed to do so.

Dean Hee escorted him up the stairs.

Upon reaching the top, he gave Brandt absolution for his sins. The sentence was then read, and the executioner, Gottschalk Mühlhausen, stepped forward, displayed the coat of arms belonging to Brandt's rank of count, broke it in half, and uttered the customary and prescribed words: "This is not done without cause, but as is deserved." Dean Hee then asked Brandt whether he regretted his lese-majesty, and Brandt replied affirmatively; this was of course the prerequisite for the pardon, which would now follow. Before it came, he was ordered to remove his fur coat, hat, the green frock coat, and his waistcoat; this he also did, although with annoyance, since he considered it unnecessary. He was then forced to kneel and place his head on the block, with his right hand stretched out on another block nearby. He had now turned pale but was still jaunty, since this was the moment when the word "Pardon" would be proclaimed.

At that very moment the executioner chopped off his right hand with the axe.

Only then did Brandt understand that this was serious. As if in convulsions he turned his head and stared at his truncated arm from which blood was now gushing, and then he began screaming in terror; but they held him fast, pressed his head to the block, and with the next blow, his head was severed from his body. The head was then lifted up for all to see.

There was complete silence among the spectators, which surprised many.

The body was then stripped, the genitals cut off and tossed into the cart that stood under the 15-foot-high scaffold. The abdomen was sliced open, the intestines pulled out and discarded, and the body cut into four parts, which were then thrown into the cart.

Brandt was mistaken. No pardon had been planned, or at least no pardon for him, and not by anyone who now held power.

Perhaps there would have been a chance. But this chance was forestalled.

The night before, King Christian VII had commanded that he be woken early; at eight o'clock in the morning he had gone out alone and, without saying a word about what he intended to do, walked across the palace courtyard to the coach stables.

There he ordered a coach and driver.

He seemed nervous, his whole body was shaking as if he were frightened by what he was about to do, but in no respect was he contradicted or refused; a coach was, in fact, standing ready, the horses were saddled, and a troop of six soldiers under the command of an officer from the Life Guards closed ranks around the coach.

The King showed no suspicion of any kind about this, but commanded the driver to take him to the execution site at Østre Fælled.

No-one contradicted him, and the coach with its escort set off.

During the drive the King sat huddled in a corner with his gaze fixed on his feet as usual; he was pale and seemed confused, but he didn't look up until almost half an hour later when the coach stopped. Then he peeked out and realized where he was. He was on the island of Amager. He threw himself at both doors, which he found to be locked; he opened a window and shouted to his escorts that he had been taken to the wrong place.

They did not reply, but he understood. They had driven him out onto the island of Amager. He had been betrayed. The coach now stood motionless 100 yards from the shore, and the horses were being unharnessed. He asked what the meaning of this was; the officer in command rode up to the coach and informed the King that they were forced to change horses since these were exhausted, but that they would continue on their way as soon as fresh horses arrived.

Then he quickly rode off.

The doors of the coach were locked. The horses were unharnessed. The dragoons, on their horses, had positioned themselves 100 yards away and were lined up, waiting.

The King sat alone in his coach without horses. He stopped shouting and sank onto the seat of the coach in bewilderment. He looked out at the shore, which at this spot was not covered with trees, and across the water, which was very still. He realized that it was now time to pardon the condemned men. He would not be able to get out of the coach. His shouts would not reach anyone. The dragoons saw him at the open window making odd pointing gestures with his arms and hands towards something overhead; as if he were stretching his hands up towards the sky, towards a God who might have chosen him as His son, who might exist, who might have power, who might possess the power to pardon; but after a while his arms seemed to tire or he was struck by despondency; his arms dropped.

He was still sitting in the corner of the coach. From the east came rain clouds rolling in over Amager. The dragoons waited in silence. No horses arrived. No God manifested Himself.

Perhaps by now he understood. Perhaps he had been given his sign. He was only a human being, nothing more. The rain began to fall, harder and harder, and soon the horses might come and perhaps they would then head back, perhaps to the palace; perhaps a benevolent God did exist *but why then have You never shown me Your face or given me any guidance or advice or given me any of Your time, Your time, given me time*, and now the rain was ice-cold and coming down hard.

No-one heard his shouts. No horses. No God. Only human beings.

5

The Swedish King, Gustav III, was crowned in the year 1771, in the midst of the Struensee era which he had observed with such mixed feelings and with such great interest, and from this coronation there is a famous painting done by Carl Gustaf Pilo.

It is called *The Coronation of Gustav III*. Pilo had been the young Christian's drawing teacher, and he lived at the Danish court during the Struensee era, but in 1772 he was banished and returned to Stockholm. There he began his great painting of the coronation of Gustav III, though he never managed to complete it, and the painting was to be his last work.

Perhaps he was trying to portray something that was much too painful.

In the centre of the painting is the Swedish King, still young; he emanates the appropriate dignity and breeding, but he is also, as we know, filled with the ideas of the Enlightenment. It is still many years before he will be changed, and before he is murdered at a masked ball. Around him are grouped the members of his equally illustrious court.

It is the background that is perplexing.

The King and his court do not appear to be portrayed in a throne room; they have been placed in the midst of a very dark wood, with mighty, dark trunks, as if this coronation scene were being played out in a centuries-old primeval forest in the wilderness of northern Europe.

No, there are no pillars, no columns of a church. Darkness, inscrutable tree trunks, a primeval forest in ominous darkness, and in the middle the dazzling assembly.

Is it the darkness that is light, or the luminous that is dark? A choice must be made. The same is true of history, people choose what to see, what is light and what is darkness.

6

Struensee had slept peacefully that night, and when he awoke he was quite calm.

He knew what was going to happen. He had lain with open eyes and stared for a long time up at the grey stone ceiling of his cell, concentrating on a single thought. It had to do with Caroline Mathilde. He focused on what had been so splendid and on the fact that he loved her and that he had received a message from her that she forgave him for confessing; then he thought about how he felt that time when she told him she was with child, and that it was his. He had actually realized even then that all was lost, but it didn't matter. He had a child, and the child would live, and the child would give him eternal life, and the child would live and give birth to children and therein lay eternity and nothing else mattered.

That was what he thought about.

When Pastor Münter entered his cell, the clergyman's voice quavered as he read a passage from the Bible, and he was not as logical as usual, but surrendered to a storm of emotions, which was surprising and which seemed to indicate that he did not regard Struensee with animosity but, on the contrary, was quite fond of him.

But Struensee told him with kindness that on this morning, his last, he wished to be surrounded with silence and to concentrate purely on the meaning of eternal life, and he was glad that the pastor could understand this.

And the pastor nodded vigorously and understood. And so they spent those morning hours in silence and tranquillity.

Then the departure.

Münter did not accompany Struensee in his coach but stepped inside only at the scaffold; the coach had stopped quite close to it, and from their position they could see Brandt climb the stairs, and from the open window they heard Dean Hee's words and those of the executioner, and then Brandt's screams when his hand was, to his surprise, chopped off, and next the heavy, dull thuds as the dismembering took place and the pieces were tossed into the cart at the foot of the scaffold.

Münter was not of much help. He started to read his Bible, but began to tremble and sob without being able to control himself; Struensee spoke to him and tried to soothe him, but it did no good. The pastor's whole body was shaking as he wept; sobbing, he tried to stammer consoling words from his Bible, but Struensee offered him a handkerchief and after half an hour the dismemberment of Brandt was finished, the thudding of the body parts had ceased, and it was time.

He stood on the scaffold and looked out at the sea of people. So many had come! The sea of people was endless: it was these people he had come to visit, and it was them he had supposedly helped. Why hadn't they thanked him? But this was the first time he saw them.

Now he saw them, *I saw, O God, who perhaps exists, an aperture there, it was my task to force my way in, was it for their sake and is everything now in vain, should I have asked them, O God, I see them and they see me but it is too late and perhaps I should have talked to them and not isolated myself and perhaps they should have talked to me but I sat there in my room and why should we meet for the first time in this way now that it is too late* and they broke his coat of arms and spoke the words. And undressed him. The block was heavily smeared with Brandt and he thought, *this is Brandt this piece of flesh and this blood and this slime, what is a human being when the sacred disappears, is it only flesh, sludge and blood and this is Brandt, what then is a human being.* They gripped him by the arms and, as docile as a sacrificial lamb, his head was placed on the block and his hand on the other block and he stared straight ahead, at the endless host of faces which, pale and grey and with open mouths, were staring up at him, and then the executioner chopped off his hand with the axe.

His body was then gripped with convulsions so strong that the executioner, when he was about to cut off his head, completely missed his mark; Struensee rose up on one knee, opened his mouth as if he wanted to speak to all of the thousands he now saw for the first time, *only one picture do I have Lord Jesus and it is the picture of the little girl but if I could also speak to all of these who have not understood and before whom I have sinned because I did not* and then he was forced down on the block again, and when the executioner raised his axe for the second time, the last words he had said to her came flickering back *in the eternities of Eternity* and the axe at last found its mark and severed the head of the German royal physician; and his Danish visit was over.

From the east heavy rain clouds came rolling in, and as the dismemberment of Struensee's body was begun, the rain began to fall; but that was not what made the crowds leave the site.

They left the scene as if they had had enough, as if they wanted to say: no, this we do not wish to see, something is wrong, this was not the way we wanted it.

Have we been deceived?

No, they didn't flee, they simply began to move away, first a few hundred, then a few thousand, and then they all left. As if this was enough, they took no joy in what they had seen, no malicious delight and no revenge, everything had simply become unbearable. At first they were an endless mass staring up in silence at what was happening – why so silent? – and then they began to move back, slowly at first, then ever more swiftly, as if in sorrow. They walked and ran towards town, the rain fell harder and harder, but the rain they were used to; at last it seemed to have occurred to them what this drama was all about, and they no longer wanted any part of it.

Was it the cruelty they couldn't stand? Or did they feel betrayed?

Guldberg had ordered his coach to stop 100 paces from the scaffold; he did not get out of the coach but commanded 20 soldiers to stand by, as guards. What were they supposed to guard against? Everything proceeded according to plan. But all at once something felt ominous and out of control; what was it about those crowds? Why did they leave the scene, what was there in those tired, sorrowful, worn faces that made him feel uneasy? They moved past him like a grey, embittered mass, a river, a plaintive funeral procession that had no words and no emotions but seemed to express only . . . yes, sorrow. It was a sorrow that was deathly silent and at the same time out of control. They had witnessed the definitive end of the Struensee era, but at the same time Guldberg had a feeling that the danger was not past. That the contagion of sin had also spread to them. That the black glow from the torches of the Enlightenment had not been extinguished. That these ideas in some strange way had infected them, even though it was unlikely they could read, and in any case could not understand, and would never come to understand, and that therefore they must be kept under control and be led; but perhaps the contagion was still there. Perhaps the Struensee era was not over; he knew that now it was important to be extremely vigilant.

The head had been severed but the ideas were still there, and the people had not wanted to stay and watch; why did they leave?

It was a warning sign. Had he done something wrong? What could he read in those worn, sorrowful faces? Was it resignation? Yes, perhaps. Then so be it. He sat there in his coach and the mighty procession of people surrounded him like a river, not on the bank of the river, but in its midst! In its midst! And he did not know how this should be interpreted.

Extreme vigilance was now essential. The Struensee era was over. But the contagion.

The 30,000 had not greeted the severed head with cheers. They had fled, at a run, stumbling, dragging away the little children who had been brought along, away from the scaffold that was now shrouded in rain falling harder and harder. They didn't want to look anymore. Something was wrong. Guldberg sat motionless in his coach, well guarded. But what he would always remember was how this endless crowd moved, though in silence; how the crowd was like a river that divided around his coach, and he sat there, not on the bank as an interpreter but in the middle of the river. And for the first time he knew that he could not interpret the maelstroms of the river.

What had filled their hearts? Had the Struensee era not ended after all?

Quite recently, only three months before, the sense of unity had been so great. He recalled the joyous riots in January. The wrath of the people was so great. But now they fell silent and left, stunned and showing no joy, in a gigantic funeral procession filled with a silence which for the first time made Guldberg feel fear.

Was there something left that could not be chopped off?

The cart stood under the scaffold.

When the cart that was to carry the body parts to Vestre Fælled, where the heads and hands would be raised on poles and the genitals and intestines be put on the wheel, when the cart was at last loaded and about to set off, the field was deserted: except for the 5,000 soldiers who silently, without moving, and in the heavy rain, stood guard over the void remaining after the 30,000 had long since left the site where it was thought that the Struensee era had been decapitated and brought to an end.

Epilogue

She learned of the execution the day after.

Then, on May 30, the three English ships came for Caroline Mathilde and took her to Celle, in Hanover. The castle, which stood in the centre of town, had been built in the 1600s and had been unoccupied, but it now became her residence. She was said to have retained her lively manner, to have shown great interest for the welfare of Celle's poor, and to have demanded respect for Struensee's memory. She often spoke of him, calling him "the blessed count", and she soon became much loved in Celle, where they embraced the idea that she had been unjustly treated.

Many people were interested in her political rôle for the future. Christian, who was now wholly submerged in his illness, was still King, and the son that Caroline Mathilde had given him was the heir to the throne. The King's illness created, as it had in the past, a vacuum at the centre, which had been filled by others than Struensee.

The true holder of power was Guldberg. In reality he became the absolute ruler, with the title of Prime Minister; and yet discontent was brewing in certain circles in Denmark, and plans were being forged to reinstate Caroline Mathilde and her child by means of a coup, and to overthrow Guldberg and his party.

On May 10, 1775, these quite advanced plots were suspended when Caroline Mathilde very suddenly and inexplicably died from a "contagious fever". Rumours that she had been poisoned on orders from the Danish government could never be confirmed.

She was only 23 years old. She never saw her children again.

The revolution that Struensee had initiated was quickly stopped; it took only a few weeks for everything to revert to the way it was before, or to even earlier times. It was as if his 632 decrees, issued during the two years known as the "Struensee era", were paper swallows, some of which landed, while others were still hovering low over the surface of the field and hadn't yet managed to alight on the Danish landscape.

Guldberg's era followed, and it lasted until 1784, when he was overthrown. It was quite obvious that everything would revert back during his era. It was just as obvious that of Guldberg's era nothing would remain.

Struensee's astonishing political productivity was remarkable. Yet how much of it became reality?

The image of him as merely a desk intellectual endowed with extraordinary power is hardly accurate. Denmark was never the same after Struensee's era. Guldberg's apprehensions proved to be right; the contagion of the Enlightenment had taken hold, words and thoughts could not be decapitated. And one of the reforms that Struensee never managed to carry out, the abolition of "ascription" and serfdom, had already become a reality by 1788, the year before the French Revolution.

Struensee would also live on in another way.

Louise Augusta, the daughter of Struensee and Caroline Mathilde, was brought up in Denmark; her brother, Christian's only child, took an active part in the coup of 1784 which overthrew Guldberg, and in the year 1808 he would succeed his demented father to the throne.

The girl, on the other hand, met a different fate. She was described as very beautiful, with a "disquieting" vitality. She seemed to share her father's fundamental political views, took a keen interest in the events of the French Revolution, sympathized with Robespierre, and of her father she said that his only fault was that he possessed "more spirit than cunning".

Perhaps this was indeed a correct analysis. Her beauty and vitality made her attractive, although not always the most tranquil or serene of partners in a relationship. She married Duke Frederik Christian av Augustenborg, who was not her equal in any way. Yet she had three children by him, one of which, a daughter named Caroline Amalie, married in 1815 Prince Christian Frederik, Denmark's heir to the throne and future monarch; and thus everything came full circle at the court in Copenhagen. In this way many of Struensee's descendants slipped into the peculiar and mysterious European royal houses that were soon to disintegrate, where he had been such a brief and unwelcome guest. His great-great-grandchild Augusta Victoria married the German Kaiser Wilhelm II and had eight children. Today there is hardly any European royal house, including the Swedish, that cannot trace its lineage back to Johann Friedrich Struensee, his English princess, and their little girl.

Perhaps this has little significance. If occasionally, in prison, Struensee had a dream of eternity that was biological, that eternal life meant living on through one's children, then his wish was granted. His dream of eternity and his view of human beings were both something that he was never done with – something that he, with his characteristic theoretical vagueness, attempted to describe as "the human machine". But what in truth was a human being, who could be dissected or dismembered and hung up on the post and wheel, and yet in some way continued to live on? What was it that was sacred? "The sacred is what the one who is sacred does," he had thought: the human being as the sum of his existential choices and actions. But in the end it was something else altogether, something more important, that remained of Struensee's era. Not biology, not just actions, but a dream of humanity's possibilities, that which was the most sacred of all and the most difficult to capture, that which existed as the simple, persistent note of a flute from Struensee's era and which refused to be cut off.

One evening at the Royal Theatre in September 1782, Ambassador Keith from England reported to the British government about an incident.

It was his encounter with King Christian VII and Prime Minister

Guldberg. Christian hinted that Struensee was still alive, and Keith noticed the rage, no matter how controlled, which this provoked in Guldberg.

Everyone talked about the Struensee era. It wasn't fair. It wasn't fair! Later that evening Christian disappeared.

Where he went that evening, we have no idea. But it was known where he usually disappeared to, and that he did so often. And to whom. And thus it is possible to imagine what happened on that particular evening as well: that he walked the short distance from the Royal Theatre to a house in central Copenhagen, on Studiestræde. And that he also, after the incident which Keith describes, entered the house on Studiestræde and met the woman he so stubbornly called the Sovereign of the Universe, who had now returned, who had always been the only one he could trust, the only one he loved with his peculiar way of loving, the only benefactor left for this royal child who was now 33 years old, and whom life had so severely mistreated.

It was Bottine Caterine who, many years earlier, after her stay in Hamburg and Kiel, had returned to Copenhagen. Now, according to contemporary descriptions, she was grey-haired, plumper, and perhaps also wiser.

It must be assumed that on that evening as well, the same rituals were played out as before, the love ceremonies which had made it possible for Christian to survive for so many years in that madhouse. He sat down at her feet on the little stool he always used, and then he took off his wig, moistened a soft piece of cloth in a bowl of water and wiped all the powder and make-up from his face; and then she combed his hair as he sat there, quite calm, his eyes closed, seated on the stool at her feet, with his head resting on her knee.

And he knew that she was the Sovereign of the Universe, that she was his benefactress, that she had time for him, that she had all time, and that she *was* time.